"It is quite extraordinarily funny, and it never stops, the whole point of the affliction being that it *cannot* stop . . . There is nothing ashen about LAUGHIN' BOY, which is one of the funniest novels of the past decade."
—John Clute, SCIFI WEEKLY (SCIFI.COM)

"Denton has a splendidly savage time dissecting the American national psyche . . . He skewers bloggers, TV journalists, politicians, psychologists, and entertainers, among many other factions. His satisfyingly grim plot drags Clayton ever downward, until a final redemption. . . . [T]his funny, scathing assault on the current booboisie has few peers."
—Paul Di Filippo, THE WASHINGTON POST BOOK WORLD

"Denton's ear for the cacophony of talk radio, chatrooms, and political interviews is flawless. He also has a good eye for the painful absurdities of a world bloated with information but starved for understanding."
—PUBLISHERS WEEKLY

"A past winner of the World Fantasy Award, Denton is a veteran satirist whose works often straddle the line between fantasy and mainstream fiction. Here, Denton deftly surveys the landscape of contemporary media and its current obsession with terrorism in a finely nuanced and entertaining black comedy."
—Carl Hays, BOOKLIST

"Innovative, uncompromising, and uncomfortably thought-provoking, LAUGHIN' BOY is a 21st Century novel demonstrating Denton's sharp eye for media trends and standards, tempered with the wit of an accurate satirist who knows just where to point the finger and the right buttons to push."
—Russell B. Farr, TICONDEROGA ONLINE

"With "Laughin' Boy" (aka Danny Clayton), Denton creates one of his most accomplished characters, a sad, unlucky weirdo who typically finds himself in the wrong place at the wrong moment. . . . [T]he interviews with politicians and psychologists and the comments offered by talk show participants about the Wichita tragedy are real masterpieces of humor and realism. Which, once again, makes it hard to properly label Denton's fiction (fantastic realism, anyone?). . . . But great writers defy classification, don't they?"
—Mario Guslandi, SF SITE

"LAUGHIN' BOY may just be a speculative fiction landmark, a cut-and-paste, post-cable, post-Internet novel that assimilates the forms and the chaos of the media-scape and spits them out in a frenzied satire of American lethargy and overload. Denton has updated the entire literary toolkit, popped out the old-style analog tapes and dropped in pixilated digital edits to create a hyped-up look at crime, punishment, and very good people subjected to very bad people. . . . Expect to have your mind blown and sewn back together by a world on crystal methamphetamine."
—Rick Kleffel, AGONY COLUMN

"[This] is Denton at his best, throwing satirical barbs at conservatives, liberals, religion, the media, foreign policy, the political climate, and anyone who takes himself too seriously. . . . Readers will find themselves laughing out loud and cringing in horror, frequently at the same time, as they become more and more involved in Danny Clayton's bizarre life."
—Mark Graham, THE ROCKY MOUNTAIN NEWS

Laughin' Boy

Laughin' Boy

Bradley Denton

Wheatland Press

Library of Congress Cataloging-in-Publication data is available upon request.
ISBN 978-0-9794054-4-0
Printed in the United States of America
Interior design by Deborah Layne.
Cover art and design by Darin Bradley.

http://www.wheatlandpress.com

Author's Note

Although the first edition of *Laughin' Boy* appeared in 2005, and this edition is appearing in 2008, its text (except for minor revisions) was completed prior to September 11, 2001.

Channel Guide

2000 A.D.

Spring

The
United
States
of
America

Video Clip (1)
Laughin' Boy Appears in Your Living Room

IT WAS ON TV, OF COURSE. Everything here at the turn of the century is on TV. Celebrity murder trials, fat-free enchiladas, trailer-trash trollops, animated ducks, bobsled wrecks, Bryant Gumbel—and the bloody convulsion that was the birth of Laughin' Boy.

According to the print media, it happened in Wichita, Kansas on Saturday, May 20, 2000 A.D. at 4:17 P.M. Central Daylight Time. But in virtual and video truth, it happened everywhere and at every time, because everyone everywhere watched it happen on CNN, ABC, MTV, ACTIONNEWS.COM, and ten thousand other electronic outlets over and over again. And then they bought, rented, borrowed, stole, and/or downloaded it so they could watch it some more.

But no matter how many times they've seen it, everyone remembers where they were and what they were doing as they saw their first replay. They remember that initial viewing with a glassy digital clarity that makes it seem as if it's happening still.

And somewhere, on somebody's monitor, it is:

Smoke from the incendiary grenades blots the blue-sky background. Shredded carnival-game and food-vending booths burn orange and black, as does the abandoned bandstand. Torsos and limbs twitch like dissected frogs alongside the green riverbank of the Little Arkansas. Here and there the jerking camera finds a face ripped or obliterated from bullets or shrapnel. The shrieks of sirens begin to mingle with the cries of the injured and dying. A dog yipes incessantly.

Among the dying is the man operating the camcorder. He is a retired dentist named Arnold Steck. TV news crews will soon record the surrounding horror from more professional angles -- but this video is the one we'll all remember.

The view is upward from the spattered grass of South Riverside Park, so everything looks towering and immense. It's an amazing job, especially considering that Arnold Steck has been hit in the chest and will drown in blood before the tape runs out. The picture quality actually improves as he approaches death. The jerking stops, and the focus sharpens. It is as if Dr. Steck becomes determined, at the end, to leave a good piece of tape as his legacy. Or perhaps it's that the camcorder's autofocus programming takes over as Dr. Steck fades away.

The camera pans over the carnage, then stops and focuses on a kneeling figure who looms like a giant in the center of the frame, perhaps ten feet away. The figure is a shuddering man.

The frame shrinks around this man as the camera zooms in. And then, paradoxically, we see him not as a giant, but as a slender Caucasian. His brown hair is mussed, and it gleams wetly. His age is difficult to guess because his hands are pressed to his face.

And although we can't be sure just yet, he appears unharmed. Given all else that we've just seen, it's difficult to imagine how he could have avoided injury . . . unless he was one of the perpetrators of the crime.

But we've had a glimpse of them as they fled the scene, and they all wore camouflage fatigues and black hoods. This man is wearing blue jeans and a plain white shirt.

He is not one of the perpetrators. He came to the park to hear the blues bands, as did all the other innocent victims. We see now that his shirt is speckled with red, and so are his hands. The gleam in his hair is blood, too.

He kneels there with his hands pressed to his face, and his body shakes. Perhaps shrapnel has caught him in the eyes.

But there doesn't seem to be enough blood for that. So perhaps, instead, he is weeping at the tragedy. He may even be in hysterics. This would only make sense, because he's seen the same horrible things that we have. And he's had to see them without the twin buffers of television and time.

Then his hands fly away from his face, and he begins rocking back and forth and slapping the ground. And his face, an ordinary adult-male, Midwestern face, is unharmed. His eyes are fine. He is near the center of the field of fire, but has miraculously escaped the sprays of flame and metal that killed or maimed all the others.

His features are streaked with blood, but none of it is his. Men, women, and children have blown apart around him like water balloons, and this is the result. Even seeing the red speckles on his shirt and hands hasn't prepared us for what this foreign blood looks like on his face. It is unnatural and hideous. It would look better if any of it had come from a wound of his own.

That isn't what shocks and enrages us, though.

What shocks and enrages us are the happy bleats coming from his open mouth. What shocks and enrages us are the curves of his cheek muscles and the light flashing from his white teeth and aqua eyes.

What shocks and enrages us is the sudden sure knowledge that he is neither weeping nor in hysterics. There is no grief, horror, or insanity in what he does.

He is, purely and simply, laughing his ass off.

Sound Bites (1)

Thank you, John.

Here at what can now only be described as the killing field of South Riverside Park in Wichita, Kansas, all remains in chaos almost an hour after a baffling attack on festival-goers by masked, camouflaged gunmen.

All around me I see police, firefighters, and paramedics, as well as frantic parents and others still searching for their loved ones among the living . . . and the dead.

We don't yet know the number of casualties, and we may not have an accurate number any time soon. But I can tell you that, given the things I've seen since arriving on the scene a few minutes ago, the number of victims is almost certainly over a hundred. The horror here is almost beyond belief.

(Blip)

Ma'am, do you have a moment? I see there's blood on your blouse. Are you injured?

I don't think so. I just can't find my boyfriend.

Were you separated from him when the shooting began?

Yeah, he had to go to the bathroom.

And he hasn't returned yet?

I don't know. I can't find him. Excuse me, please.

Of course. Good luck to you. (Pause.) Sadly, it seems unlikely that the young woman I just spoke with will, in fact, have any good luck at all. From what I could see as I entered the park, it looked as if all of the porta-johns had been riddled with bullets.

What did you say? WHAT DID YOU SAY? GOD, NO! LARRY! LARRY, OH GOD NO!

(Blip)

We're here with Captain Arnold Frank of the Wichita Police Department. Captain Frank, based on your preliminary assessment of the scene here at South Riverside Park, is there any clue as to what the terrorists wanted?

Yeah. They wanted to kill people.

(Blip)

These brave paramedics are—

Get the hell out of the way!

(Blip)

Mr. Lyman Carlton, wounded in the shoulder, is waiting here in the designated triage area for an ambulance to become available. In the meantime, paramedics have stopped his bleeding, bandaged his wound, and given him something for the pain. Mr. Carlton, can you tell us, from your perspective, what happened here today?

They killed my wife.

Who did, Mr. Carlton?

They were dressed like soldiers. They had machine guns and grenades.

Did you get a good look at them, Mr. Carlton?

It was too crowded. But I heard something go pop-pop-pop, and I looked through the people and saw the camouflage uniforms. And then people started screaming, and my wife fell backwards in her lawn chair and landed on the ground. I got down beside her and saw she was gone. (Sobs.)

Is there anything you would like to say to the people who did this, Mr. Carlton?

Yes. (Sobs.) *I want to say you better whoop it up while you can, Laughin' Boy, because your time will come. Your time will for damn sure come.* (Sobs.)

Thank you, Mr. Carlton. (Pause.) Mr. Carlton was no doubt referring, just now, to the man who was reportedly laughing in the aftermath of the attack. Some eyewitnesses are saying that this laughing man was one of the terrorists, and others insist he was not.

But it is difficult to imagine an innocent bystander behaving as if the things we have seen here today are funny.

We are told that a videotape of the attack has been discovered in a camcorder belonging to one of the victims, and that this "Laughin' Boy," as Mr. Carlton calls him, appears on it. Perhaps, then, the authorities will begin their investigation of this tragedy with him.

And perhaps then "Laughin' Boy" won't be quite so amused by the pain and suffering of others.

We'll return with more from South Riverside Park in Wichita, Kansas, in just a moment. But for now—

Back to you, John.

Therapy Transcript (1)

(Laughter deleted)

Before the mob burned my house, I had a TV that I loved.

I loved it even though it had only a nineteen-inch screen. I had a 27-inch before Karen divorced me. She and Lindy still have it. At least, I think they do.

But when it's just you, and you're on a junior-college salary, and you have to budget for child support and Chuck E. Cheese . . . you buy a smaller TV to go with your smaller house. I was only renting the house, though. Karen and Lindy stayed in the bigger house, the one we bought. They're still there. At least, I hope they are.

My new TV sat on a cart so I could roll it back and forth between my bedroom and living room. It was a short trip. But although the house was tiny, it had two bedrooms. That was important because I wanted Lindy to have her own room when she stayed with me. And I wanted it to be in a house, not an apartment. So it would feel like home.

She only stayed two weekends. She had bad dreams because of the traffic noise. And the house smelled different, and the bathroom wasn't where it ought to be—and even though her daddy was right across the hall, she still wanted her mommy.

So I decided to let her spend every night with Karen in our old house, even if it was my weekend. I couldn't stand knowing she was having nightmares. Besides, I still had the daylight hours with her. When it was my weekend.

Anyway, the TV. You want to know about the TV. I shouldn't have used the word "love." I just *liked* it, okay?

What I liked most was the timer.

See, one of the things I dreaded after the divorce was waking up alone. I dreaded hearing the alarm clock beep, and then sitting up to find that there was no warm wife next to me, and no little girl clambering up to snuggle between us. I didn't want to wake up in a place like that.

But the TV timer helped. With it, the first things I heard every morning were friendly voices, and the first thing I saw was a cheerful glow. And when I sat up, there were familiar faces atop the cart, telling me what was new out in that bright TV world of theirs. Matt Lauer and Katie Couric, or Diane Sawyer, or Bryant Gumbel. Remember when Letterman painted Bryant's ankles orange? That was great.

On weekends, I woke up to cartoons. But that wasn't always comforting, because today's cartoons aren't like the ones I watched when I was a kid. Back then we had Daffy Duck and Yogi Bear, but Lindy's generation has Pokemon and the Powerpuff girls. They just aren't the same. Not that I'm criticizing. To everything, turn, turn, turn.

Sometimes, though, it doesn't matter what's on the screen. Sometimes, all that matters is that *something*'s there. Because whatever it is, it's better than the world outside the glass. It's brighter. Happier. Safer.

Funnier.

This knowledge came back to me after the divorce. I had forgotten it for a while, but once I was alone it became clear again: TV would keep me safe.

That was the first thing I ever learned. In fact, my earliest memory is of the happy light from the TV in my parents' house.

My second-earliest memory is of toddling away from that light into the backyard twilight, all alone in nothing but training pants, and being attacked by the neighbors' bull terrier. It tore open my fat little thigh while I screamed.

I don't remember my mother or father coming to rescue me. So it might have been the neighbor. It might have been a cop. I couldn't say.

What I do remember, though, is being in the hospital, sitting up in bed, and watching a TV that sat on a platform near the ceiling. The Three Stooges were on, and I was laughing. I was just old enough to understand that if something with lots of running, yelling, and falling down was on TV, you were supposed to laugh.

Besides, I was happy to be safe again. When I'd stopped watching TV, a monster had gotten me . . . but now I was watching again, and everything was fine.

So as long as I was watching TV, I couldn't be hurt.

I knew that last Saturday, too. I knew it when Karen called and told me I couldn't take Lindy to the River Festival. Grandma had come to town, and Grandma hardly ever got to see her granddaughter. So I could give up this one weekend, couldn't I? I understood, didn't I? I could go to the Festival by myself and listen to the blues band, couldn't I? I would enjoy that more than taking Lindy to the kiddie rides anyway, wouldn't I?

Karen has always had the power to talk me into anything. So I should have stopped listening once I agreed to give up my weekend. I should have stayed home and watched my wonderful TV.

But Karen said I should go out, and I believed her.

So I left my tiny house and went to the Festival alone. I went to the meadow in South Riverside Park where the blues band was playing. They were good. Good enough to be on TV.

And when people started running, yelling, and falling down, I realized that I had imagined leaving the house. I had imagined getting on the bus and riding to the park. I had imagined walking past the concession booths and kiddie rides toward the music.

Because I was fine. Nothing bad was happening to me. So what I saw in the bright light before me couldn't be taking place in a real park in Wichita, Kansas. It couldn't be taking place where I was standing.

It could only be on TV.

And if it was on TV, there was only one thing to do.

Whether it was funny or not.

Newsgroup Posts (1)

Subject: Wichita Attack
From: johndoe99@bullmoose.net (Nathan Lawrence)
Date: 2000/05/20
Message-ID: <johndoe99-4971800FE3.228LB9@bullmoose.net>
Newsgroups: soc.us.violence.terror

Ladies and germs, the s*** has hit the fan once again, and once again the fan it's hitting is in the heart of the nation. This time the slaughter has occurred in the buckle of the Bible Belt, the Breadbasket of the World, the Sunflower State, Dorothy's Gateway to Oz, and the bane of any motorist trying to get from St. Louis to Denver. So even though the first reports are just coming in—apparently, a crowd at some sort of circus or state fair has been machine-gunned by three or more unknown persons wearing military-style garb—I'll go out on a limb and predict that if the terrorists in question are caught, they'll turn out to be home-grown white boys. See, your basic International Ragheads tend to go for big symbols recognized all over the planet, like the World Trade Center in NYC. But only your basic dumbass inbred Amurrican Crackers think they can make their point by attacking a place the rest of the world couldn't give a damn about.

As for the guy at the scene who supposedly found the whole thing funny: Who the f*** knows?

Episode One
Mom and Dad Disapprove

DANNY LAY FACE-DOWN ON his old bed in his parents' house for the first time in years. He had a musty pillow stuffed into his mouth as far as it would go, and another clamped over his head. He was breathing through his nose, and it made a whistling sound. He wasn't getting much air. He felt dizzy and sick, and the whistling sound wove through the thunk-*thunk*, thunk-*thunk* of the pulse in his skull.

But even through the pillows, the whistling, and the thunk-*thunk*, even through the closed door, he could hear his father and the TV out in the living room.

"Good God," his father was saying. "God almighty. What in God's name? God in Heaven." As far back as Danny could remember, his father had called on God like this, no matter what the situation. When Danny had fouled out in Little League. When his mother had miscarried what would have been Danny's little sister. When the refrigerator had leaked all its Freon, and the cottage cheese had gone bad. It was as if Dad thought God had an equal interest in everything.

The words from the TV were less distinct. But that was just as well, because Danny knew what would happen if he heard them. It was all he could do to control himself as it was. He couldn't decide whether the pillow jammed into his mouth was helping, or whether it was tickling his uvula and making things worse.

"For the love of God," his father said. "Louise, they're calling him 'Laughin' Boy.' God have mercy." This was said as if Dad knew that God would do no such thing.

It wasn't funny. It wasn't funny at all, so Danny couldn't stop himself. The pillow blew out of his mouth as he roared, and he scrambled to stuff it back in.

"God help us," his father said.

The pillow blew out again. Danny slapped the mattress, howled, and rolled off onto the floor. The walls shook as he landed. Then the door opened and whacked him in the head. It hurt like hell, so Danny laughed even harder.

"Oh honey, I'm sorry," his mother said as she came into the room. "What are you doing on the floor?"

Danny flopped onto his back and clamped a hand over his mouth as he looked up at Mom. She was wearing her church clothes and peering at him upside-down. Her face was framed by the star chart he had thumbtacked to the ceiling twenty years ago, and her octagonal-lensed eyeglasses had slid so far down her nose that she looked as if she had little Stop signs on her cheeks.

Now the laughter subsided, so Danny sat up and gulped air. His head was ringing, but he couldn't tell how much of that was from laughing and how much was from being whacked by the door.

"Thanks, Mom," he said. "That was a bad one." He tried to stand up, but he was still dizzy, so he sat on the edge of the bed instead.

Mom pushed her glasses up from the end of her nose. They slid right back down again.

"You have to see a doctor, dear," she said. Her voice had the same strained tone as when he'd wrecked the family Dodge on his eighteenth birthday. "It's obvious that something has gone off kilter in your noodle. One of your cannons is rolling around on your poopdeck." She hesitated. "It probably has something to do with how badly that Karen has treated you. You do have health insurance, don't you? Or don't they do that at community colleges? I still think you should have applied for that job at Wichita State."

Danny's dizziness began to fade. "Karen hasn't treated me badly," he said. It was mostly true. She had kept their house and insisted on custody of their five-year-old daughter, but she had also taken over the mortgage payments and hadn't asked Danny for anything except child support. And she let him see Lindy almost any time he wanted. "Besides, we split up over a year ago. Whatever's wrong with me now doesn't have anything to do with her."

His voice was hoarse, his throat hurt, and he was exhausted. He hadn't slept more than an hour in the past twenty-four.

"I don't understand why you always stick up for her," Mom said. "Unless that's a symptom of whatever illness she's inflicted on you."

Danny knew that arguing was pointless. His mother had the gift of looking past the obvious in order to focus on the irrelevant, and that ability overwhelmed any argument. It was also what had gotten her through Dad's layoffs, her miscarriages, and her parents' deaths from carbon monoxide poisoning. Among other things.

But skirting the reality of the current situation might not work out so well. "Mom, I think my 'illness' is more likely the result of what happened yesterday. Don't you?"

He had to suppress a chuckle as he spoke. Just mentioning yesterday's events made him visualize them all over again, and that in turn provoked the urge to laugh.

Mom frowned. "Daniel, the Lord saw fit to spare you, so you should thank Him and let Him take the burden in your stead." She put her hand on the doorknob. "Now you'd better get cleaned up if you're coming to church. Just because your father's decided to lie around instead of giving an hour to Jesus is no reason for you to do the same. Especially if you're staying in my house. I'm leaving in fifteen minutes, so hurry up."

Danny stared at her. She was amazing. Her dark blue dress had a flower pinned to its left shoulder. Her graying hair was shellacked and gleaming. Her face was powdered to luminescence, and her lips were as red as a Jolly Rancher cinnamon square. She was ready to go out and face God and everybody. She was ready to sing "Bringing in the Sheaves," chant the Lord's Prayer, and recite a Psalm or two.

Either she was incredibly strong in her faith, or she didn't have a clue. But she had always been like this, and Danny had never been able to figure out which it was. Or whether there was a difference.

He started giggling again.

"Stop it, Daniel," Mom said. She sounded peeved now. "If you can't, maybe you shouldn't come to church after all."

Danny tried to keep it down to a giggle, and he succeeded long enough to say, "I think that would be best."

Mom made a noise in her throat, turned, and left the room. She closed the door behind her so hard that the rush of air made the star chart billow and rattle. The sound reminded Danny of his youth, and of the fact that Mom had always seemed disappointed in him. For one thing, she had always wanted him to go to church. And although he had gone, he had never been able to pretend that he'd liked it.

But the thought of attending services today, of all days, was more than merely unappealing. It was appalling.

Danny had seen fathers, mothers, brothers, daughters, and babies ripped apart like pink tissue paper yesterday, and by now every TV viewer on earth had watched him laugh about it. This was no time for him to be showing his face in public.

He already had proof of what a bad idea that would be. Yesterday evening, after the police had taken him to his car at the impound lot and then released him, he hadn't been able to get to his small rental house on Dougherty Street because of a cluster of news vans and a mob of angry citizens clogging the street. The police had told him to expect the news vans, but the mob had come as a shock.

In less time than it would have taken him to drive to Topeka, he had become the most hated man in America. Maybe the world. And to top it off, his mother was annoyed with him for his reluctance to accompany her to church as if nothing had happened.

Meanwhile, a large number of Wichita families had funerals to plan.

Laughin' Boy

It was tragic, so Danny laughed. He didn't know why he kept doing that, but he knew he couldn't help it. Once those people at the River Festival had started dying, laughing had been the only thing he could do.

Yesterday evening, after fleeing Dougherty Street before the news cameras and enraged citizens could spot him, he had driven to his parents' home on 53rd Street still wearing his blood-spattered clothing. He had borrowed sweatpants and a T-shirt from Dad, and then Mom had taken his shirt and jeans, shaken her head, and said that she didn't think any of it would come out in the wash. Danny had waited too long, she'd said. He should have soaked his clothes in cold water and detergent right away. But he hadn't, so the stains had set.

Danny had known Mom was only lecturing him about the stains so she wouldn't have to think about what they meant. So he hadn't replied. But what he'd wanted to say was that he had seen the top of a little girl's head fly off like a golden-curled Frisbee, and that he had sort of forgotten about the basics of stain removal after that.

In fact, he had sort of forgotten about everything except how that little girl could have been Lindy . . . if he had insisted on his usual Saturday afternoon with her instead of letting Karen take her to a Disney movie with his ex-mother-in-law instead.

Now Mom thought he should go to church and thank God for sparing him.

"Hoo boy," he said, gasping. His chest ached.

The golden-haired little girl's death wasn't recorded on the videotape the networks were showing, but her body was visible near the spot where Danny could be seen whooping it up. So he was pretty sure that if he went to church today, the Methodists would nail him to a pew, drink gallons of grape juice, and take turns pissing on him. At least, that was what he would do if he were them.

At that thought, it occurred to him that the Methodists might not treat his mother too well, either. After all, she had given birth to a man who laughed when little girls were killed. And there was no telling what the non-Methodists out there might do. They might decided to treat the mother of Laughin' Boy the way the men in camouflage fatigues had treated the people at the Festival.

Even as he guffawed, Danny managed to lurch up from the bed. He got the door open after three tries, and then he staggered down the hall to the living room.

Mom wasn't there, but Dad was sitting in the La-Z-Boy, watching the tube. A grim news anchor was announcing that the death toll from the Festival attack had reached 87.

"And that," the anchor said, his jaw tense with fury, "is no laughing matter."

Danny almost fell over.

Dad, wearing an orange jumpsuit, his cheeks aglow with razor burn and Aqua Velva, turned and glared. The old man's eyes were enormous.

"What in God's name has gotten into you, Daniel?" Dad asked. He sounded disgusted, frightened, and grouchy all at once. Disgusted and grouchy were normal, but Danny had never heard Dad sound frightened before.

Danny struggled to get himself under control enough to speak. "I guess I'm—*yeeeawhawhawuh*—sick."

Dad looked back at the television. "The news people seem to think you're crazy. My God, you're not crazy, are you, son?"

Danny didn't answer, because he was afraid that maybe he was.

Out in the driveway, a car engine started. Danny had assumed that Mom was in the bathroom—but no, she had decided not to wait the fifteen minutes she had promised. Danny had chosen not to thank God, so neither God nor Mom was going to cut him any slack.

Mom was going to face the wrath of the Methodists alone.

Danny turned away from his father, yanked open the front door, and ran outside. Mom's Chevy Lumina was backing out to the street as Danny's feet hit the porch—and at that moment, a blue-and-white police car began pulling in. And Mom wasn't looking backward. She was looking at Danny. So Danny tried to yell for her to stop, but she had her windows up.

The Lumina's rear bumper crunched into the police car's grille, and both cars stopped dead with a *whump*.

Then a black sedan pulled in and hit the police car from behind.

There was a sound like a siren and then another like an explosion, but those sounds didn't come from the police car or the black sedan. They came from the other side of the high wooden fence that separated Danny's parents' tiny plot of land from the rest of the world.

Danny fell off the porch laughing as the first firebomb came sailing into the yard.

Sound Bites (2)

Governor, what was your reaction when you heard the news from Wichita yesterday?

Well, of course the first thing I did was pray, which was what I did when I heard about the church shooting in my own state last year. Faith and prayer are the only things that help in situations like this. And of course my heart goes out to all the victims and their families. I, for one, have not been laughing about this tragedy.

You're referring to the blood-spattered man at the site of the rampage who seemed to find the scene hilarious. So tell us, Governor, what is your take on this so-called "Laughin' Boy?"

I am appalled. And I don't know if Kansas has any Good Samaritan laws on the books, but if they do, I would hope they would make use of those laws to indict that man for failure to render aid.

What should he have done, Governor?

He should have rendered aid. Wasn't I clear on that?

Do you have such "Good Samaritan" laws in your state, Governor?

Listen, I'm getting awfully tired of these kinds of questions when there are larger issues at stake. I won't play "Gotcha." For one thing, the fact that a man like that would laugh under those circumstances indicates the extent to which the moral fiber of the nation has deteriorated. And if you ask me, the lack of moral leadership and character at the top, in Washington, is the biggest part of the problem.

Which brings us to your bid for the Presidency. Governor, if you win your party's nomination and then become President, what action will you take to prevent incidents such as this?

Aside from providing moral leadership, all the Executive branch can do—in fact, all that the Federal government should do—is see to it that states and cities remain free of interference from Washington and are thus able to support their law enforcement officers in the pursuit and punishment of those responsible.

Governor, are you saying that crimes involving automatic weapons and interstate or international conspiracies should be handled on a local level without the involvement of the FBI or ATF?

I suppose it depends.

On what, Governor?

What is this, twenty questions?

Governor, if elected, will you support tougher legislation against assault weapons and the terrorists who use them?

Now, we've been down this road before. I don't know how many times I have to make this point, but I'll do it again: We already have plenty of laws, and they obviously don't work. So more laws aren't the answer. After all, what are we going to do, ban fertilizer? How would our farmers feel about that?

You seem to be making a reference to the 1995 bombing of the Murrah Federal Building in Oklahoma City. But with all due respect, Governor, yesterday's attack in Wichita wasn't committed with a fertilizer bomb, but with assault weapons—with guns.

Look, the problem isn't with guns, or with people who own guns. The problem, again, is with character and moral leadership. It's not with law-abiding, patriotic citizens exercising their rights, but with people who break laws that aren't working in the first place. And it's with people in Washington placing limits on freedom, which is not what our Founding Fathers intended. And frankly, when you get right down to it, it's with people not praying enough. Which is exactly why we have to have prayer in our schools again.

So in order to prevent another tragedy like yesterday's, Governor, you're saying that further anti-gun legislation wouldn't help—but more prayer would?

It would certainly be a good start.

Governor, are you suggesting that if yesterday's victims had only prayed enough, they might still be alive?

Okay, you're putting words in my mouth now. Who lives and who dies, or who goes to heaven or who goes to hell, is up to God, not me. But I will say to the good folks of Wichita that I'm sure the born-again Christians who died in Wichita yesterday are in heaven beside our Lord Jesus Christ right now.

According to early information, Governor, at least nine of those who died yesterday were Jewish, two were Muslim, and one was of the Bahai faith. And still others seem to have been Catholic, Unitarian, Mormon, and various other Christian denominations that do not define themselves as "born-again." Did they all go to hell?

I already told you, that's up to God. But I'm praying for all of the victims, of course. Are we about through here?

Governor, did you attend church services this morning?

As you know, I'm campaigning away from my home state and my home church, and I don't want to barge into some strange sanctuary with a cluster of security people and reporters and whatnot and disrupt services in somebody else's congregation. But I did spend the morning praying in my hotel room.

All morning?

9:15 to 9:45. That was all the time I had before you people started asking for interviews. Jim here can show you the schedule if you like.

That won't be necessary, Governor.

(Blip)

Mr. Vice President, would you tell us your reaction to yesterday's events in Wichita, Kansas?

Like all Americans, I grieve for the victims and families of the horrible terrorist attack in Wichita, and my thoughts and prayers are with them. Furthermore, I abhor the behavior of anyone who would treat such a tragedy as if it were funny.

Mr. Vice President, what needs to be done to prevent attacks like this?

Sadly, this latest assault on innocent Americans might have been avoided had Congress seen fit to pass our administration's legislation to establish a nationwide gun buy-back program similar to those which have been so successful in some of our larger cities.

Sir, are you suggesting that the terrorists who committed yesterday's atrocity might have turned in their weapons for cash instead of turning them on innocent people?

Well, since they didn't have the option, we'll never know, will we?

How much money per gun would the administration's proposal have provided for such a program?

We would have been careful not to touch Social Security or Medicare, and would have used only a small part of the projected budgetary surplus. So, assuming that we could have bought back three to four million guns, our legislation would have provided up to sixty-five dollars per weapon.

Would that have been for a pistol or an assault rifle?

Yes, it would.

Mr. Vice President, indications are that the terrorists in Wichita also made use of hand grenades.

That's a good point. When we resubmit the legislation we'll have to see whether funds might be available for hand-grenade buybacks as well.

(Blip)

Senator, do you have a comment?

Yes, thank you. As you know, the Vice President and I disagree on many issues, but I do agree with him that something must be done about the growing cancer of gun violence. If yesterday's events aren't a wake-up call, I don't know what is.

So you support the administration's national buy-back proposal?

No, I do not support that proposal for the simple reason that it is unworkable—and even if it did work to some degree, a large number of weapons would still be left on the streets.

In that case, Senator, if you were to win your party's nomination and go on to become President, what would you do instead?

I would propose a far-reaching, long-term Federal crackdown on gun violence. In my plan, any crime anywhere in the nation that involved the use of a firearm would be considered a Federal offense, punishable by imprisonment in a Federal penitentiary.

You are also on record, Senator, as saying that you would support a ban on handguns altogether.

I remain steadfast on that issue. Despite what the pro-gun lobby would have you believe, the Second Amendment does not guarantee the right to carry a weapon you can hide in your pants. Our Founding Fathers didn't do that, and neither should we.

But Senator, it seems that no handguns were used in yesterday's assault. All of yesterday's deaths and injuries appear to be from automatic rifle fire and hand-grenade shrapnel.

I would insist on a ban on automatic rifles and hand grenades as well. That's only common sense. In fact, I'm pretty sure hand grenades are off-limits already.

What weapons would not be included in your proposed ban, Senator?

Hunting rifles and most shotguns would still be legal, although I'd want stricter regulation of ammunition, and a limit of two weapons per household. In addition, I would offer a modest tax break to those sportsmen who voluntarily limit themselves to muzzle-loaders.

Senator, we have to ask if you're joking.

Not at all. Unlike that bizarre individual who was seen laughing at the bloodshed yesterday, I don't find any aspect of this topic the least bit laughable. For one thing, muzzle-loaders were good enough for our Founding Fathers, so they ought to be good enough for us. For another, just think how many more innocent people would have survived yesterday had the terrorists been forced to rely on black powder, wadding, musket balls, and tamping rods instead of multi-round clips.

But Senator, it's not as if we can uninvent—

I'm speaking speculatively, of course.

Any final thoughts, Senator?

Yes. I want the victims and families of yesterday's tragedy to know that my heart goes out to them. I, along with all Americans, share in their grief over this senseless act of violence.

Thank you, Sen—

They are in my prayers.

(Blip)

Congressman, could you give us your reaction to what's now being called the "Wichita Massacre?"

It's terrible, of course, but I have to say that it's exactly the sort of thing that will happen over and over so long as the anti-freedom forces in this country continue to prevent our citizens from arming themselves. Why, if yesterday's victims had only been carrying weapons of their own, they could have returned fire and won the day.

But Congressman, the assault took place at an outdoor concert with two thousand people in attendance. If members of the audience had begun shooting as well, wouldn't even more people have died in the crossfire?

Being hit by friendly fire is always a possibility. But at least some of the additional people killed would have been terrorists.

Congressman, do you think that would that have been any comfort to the additional victims or their families?

I think they would have understood that sacrifice is sometimes necessary. And I think they would have been proud, as Americans, to offer that sacrifice.

What is your reaction, Congressman, to the man being called "Laughin' Boy"?

Had decent persons in the crowd been properly armed, they could have shot him as well.

In closing, Congressman, is there any message you would like to send to the Wichita survivors and to the families of the victims?

Don't make the same mistake twice. Arm yourselves. And, of course, my thoughts and prayers are with you.

(Blip)

Ladies and gentlemen, the President of the United States:

My fellow Americans.

Once again, our nation is in mourning as the result of a senseless act of gun violence. That yesterday's tragedy in Wichita seems to have been the result of careful planning on the part of evil and cowardly individuals, and that it seems to have been a source of sickening amusement for others, only adds to the magnitude of our grief and outrage.

I come to you tonight with a threefold purpose. First, I want to assure the survivors of the Wichita Massacre—and, indeed, all Americans—that such a willful, evil act of terrorism shall not go unpunished. I have directed the Attorney General, the Federal Bureau of Investigation, and other appropriate agencies to pursue all appropriate avenues of investigation and to lend all appropriate support to the relevant authorities in Kansas. Whether foreign or domestic in origin, the perpetrators of this atrocity will be brought to justice.

Second, I want to urge every parent, teacher, and guidance counselor throughout the nation to see to it that our children do not become confused by the things they have seen on television and the Internet as a result of this tragedy. It is imperative that we make our children understand why such an awful event is a matter not for laughter, but for tears.

And finally, I want to tell the good citizens of Wichita—especially the families and loved ones of yesterday's victims, as well as the hospitalized survivors still bravely fighting for life—that they are not alone. My friends, you have the support of all Americans, and you have my promise as your Commander in Chief that we will not abandon you, nor forget what has happened.

You are in our thoughts and prayers.

Therapy Transcripts (2)

(Laughter deleted)

No, I'm not surprised that everybody's latched onto me as a symbol of the Massacre. How could they do otherwise? After all, it's my image they see every time the story gets an update.

I'm not blaming the media, though. They have to show something, and my image is what they have on tape. They don't seem to have much else.

You'd think that somebody besides that poor dentist would have been videotaping that afternoon, but apparently not. Or maybe they were, and the FBI got hold of the tapes before the media did. Maybe the Feds are keeping them secret so they can use them to help identify the murderers. The terrorists. Whatever you want to call them.

Is that what's going on?

Not that I'd expect you to say so even if you knew. I know you're trying to help me, but I also know who signs your checks. No, it's okay. I don't blame you either.

That image of me on my knees laughing, though . . . that's not me. I've never in my life felt the way I look there. I don't even know what I felt at that moment, but it sure wasn't what was showing on my face. Or in my body.

All I know is that I couldn't stop laughing. And that was all I knew then, too. It wasn't anything that came from inside, but a force from outside that took me over. It was as if an alien laugh ray caught me in its hot rosy glow, and the aliens turned the knob all the way up to twenty.

And I'd be laughing just as hard right now if you didn't have me doped up on whatever crap you have me doped up on. Loramoralawaddatadine. Good crap like that.

So I wasn't myself there in the park, and I'm not myself here in your study. Between the laughter and the good crap, I don't know who I am.

I do know that I'm not a husband anymore. But that was true before I started laughing. Karen erased that part before I even went to the Festival. There was already a blank spot for the laughter to fill up.

Now, though, I guess I'm not a teacher anymore, either. You think they've hired a replacement yet?

Not that it matters. Only two or three of my writing students ever really learned anything, and they could have done that without me. Community colleges aren't for learning, anyway. They're for passing through on your way to somewhere else. Unless you're one of the instructors. And maybe even then. Heck, look at me.

Where did you say we were?

Never mind, I already know: I'm everywhere. I'm a million sick pixels being replicated on a billion TV screens from Hong Kong to Hamburg, bouncing from satellite to satellite in between.

That's me now. I'm not anybody's son anymore. I'm not anybody's daddy anymore.

It seems like a year since I've seen Lindy. And what's it been, really, a week? Eight days, nine days? What day is this?

I don't even know where or when I am. Much less who.

But I did. I did know where my feet touched the ground, and what day it was. And I knew who I was, too.

I knew all of that right up until those people beside me started bursting open red and yellow and red. They started bursting open and crying and falling. And ever since then, all I can see of myself is the same thing everyone else sees.

That happy laughing motherfucker right there.

Turn it off.

Turn it off right now.

Web Surfing [Graphics Disabled] (1)

<click> *Connecting to HTTP Server . . .*

Welcome to the Wack Report, Dedicated to All That Which Is Wack. All video captures and other wizardry performed exclusively by the Wackmeister. [<Click Here> to send email to wackmeister@acidnet.net.]

[For the Best in Anime, <Click Here>.]

Be sure to click on our advertisers, or risk Wackdom. We couldn't maintain the Wack Report without them.

[<Click Here> for the Hottest Young Teens on the Net.]

Today is Sunday, May 21, 2000 A.D. On this date in history, nothing too terribly Wack occurred.

Yesterday's date, however, will be a different matter from now on.

On May 20, 2000, a number of gunmen (current estimates are between 8 and 15) dressed in camouflage uniforms and black hoods, and armed with automatic weapons and explosives, attacked an outdoor festival-concert crowd in Wichita, Kansas, and then escaped by means unknown.

According to the most recent CNN updates, the death toll stands at 84, with 22 wounded persons remaining hospitalized with injuries ranging from trample-contusions to bullets-in-the-head. [<Click Here> for the current casualty list according to CNN.]

This incident will go down as one of the most Wack events in recent American history for various reasons, the most striking of which include:

—The fact that roughly a dozen douchebags wearing paramilitary uniforms and carrying heavy firepower just waltzed into a park, slaughtered people willy-nilly, and then waltzed right back out again with no difficulty whatsoever. Where was security? Where were the cops?

—Well, there were cops, but they were overwhelmed and outgunned. CNN says that two uniformed officers were killed along with all the civilians. [<Click Here> for CNN vidcap JPEG of the dead cops.]

—All of the "professional" news organizations, almost twenty-four hours after the event, are still saying that no one has claimed responsibility and that they have no idea who did it. Christ on a crutch, haven't they been paying attention? Dudes, yesterday was ARMED FORCES DAY. Now, no one outside the military pays any attention to Armed Forces Day . . . but that's your answer right there. These guys were pissed-off U.S. veterans who chose this particular day in order to make their point, whatever it was.

—Ironically, the Wichita festival would have included a nighttime orchestra performance of the "1812 Overture," complete with howitzers and fireworks, in honor of Armed Forces Day. But the commando-veterans chose to attack a small pop concert in the afternoon, which resulted in the cancellation of all subsequent events. Thus, they screwed themselves out of being honored. Wack to the max.

—A mental case being called "Laughin' Boy" [<Click Here> for JPEG photo] has so far been getting more press than the gunmen and victims combined. Why? Why aren't we concentrating on the crime and its aftermath instead of on this nimrod? Why is the world (as reflected in the media) outraged at Laughin' Boy's behavior, but matter-of-fact about the carnage that preceded it? (Maybe it's because we're used to seeing people shot to smithereens [<Click Here> for links to 112 examples], but not so used to seeing someone yuck it up in the midst of the gore.)

Yes, my friends, such an incident is the essence of Wack. However, the Wackmeister is horrified to realize that he actually feels some gratitude toward those responsible, and toward

Laughin' Boy as well. Because thanks to them, we'll all know what Wackosity to expect in the days ahead.

In other words, for a week or so we'll be able to turn on our TVs with some confidence that we'll finally be seeing something OTHER than the repetitive Wackitude of:

—Cindy Crawford discussing the remarkable development of her genetically perfect Uberchild as if she were the first woman in history to give birth.

—Ditto Kathie Lee Gifford.

—Tom Brokaw making snide cracks about the homeless while copping a 'tude as if he were responsible for the Allied Victory in World War II.

—Tom Hanks accepting yet another award.

—Matt Damon doing anything.

—Johnnie Cochran, period (although if the perpetrators of the Wichita Massacre turn out to be former football players or foul-tempered rap moguls, we might be seeing even more of the Cochsman than we are now).

—The increasingly lame Presidential Candidates engaging in yet another bullshitting contest about how they'll Cut Taxes, Save Social Security, Get Tough on Crime, Strengthen the Economy, and Keep Their Dicks In Their Pants. (Forgive me, Lord, but I'm at the point where I'll take Laughin' Boy's bizarre chortles over G.W. Bush's bizarre smirk any day of the week. It's the smirk of a man wearing something that vibrates.)

—Yet another heartwarming story of a white Midwestern couple who desperately wanted children (well, more children; they already had one or two), took drugs (not BAD drugs, mind you, but GOOD drugs), and then dropped a litter of chipmunk-sized homunculi, praise be to Jaysuss (who must work for a pharmaceutical company) for this miraculous gift. (Yeah, that's all we need . . . seven or eight more mewling, spoiled Caucasian brats who'll receive many thousands of dollars in donated goods and services, not to mention various forms of governmental support, while a little girl in Houston's Fifth Ward goes hungry because her mommy not only isn't white, but didn't take the right kind of drugs).

—David Letterman threatening, once again, to show us his scar. [He already did. <Click Here>].

—Rudy Giuliani ratcheting his queasily effeminate snottiness toward Hillary Clinton up yet another notch.

—Regis Philbin and/or Jesse Ventura. (These two might be the same guy; I can't tell.)

—Al Gore.

—Al Roker.

—Al D'Amato.

—Al Sharpton.

—Al Michaels.

—Al Franken.

—Anyone else named Al.

—The latest sighting of the Virgin Mary (or her boy) in a potato skin, blob of ice cream, warped window, corn tortilla, patch of soot, hubcap ding, water-blood-sweat-mustard-olive-oil-axle-grease-or-ketchup stain, etc.

—Anyone who uses a little Cuban kid as a club against Castro while getting rich from investments in companies that do business in China. (Apparently, Communist governments that treat their people like serfs are only evil if Americans can't make buttloads of money off the serfs, too.)

—Anything having to do with Monica Lewinsky, Lucianne Goldberg, Linda Tripp, Vernon Jordan, Kenneth Starr, Bettie Currie, Kathleen Willey, Paula Jones, Gloria Allred, that creepy ponytailed guy in Oregon, or any of the other cast members of the most pervasive and popular musical comedy of 1998-99, "The Blowjob that Ate Sheboygan." (I'd include Bill, but you *know* we're gonna see him again.)

—Any footage of Tipper Gore playing drums. Please, God, NOOOOOOOO!

[<Click Here> for MPEG of Tipper Gore playing drums, but be prepared to claw out your eyes and begin screaming "Give me some light!" And before turning on the sound as well, ask yourself if you really want to be this generation's Helen Keller.]

But seriously, folks. I predict that we'll soon be begging for any of the above Wackiliciousness again, because we're about to be inundated with image after sickening image and interview after ludicrous interview of any and all persons connected to the Wichita Massacre . . . but *especially* of the Wack-beyond-all-measure "Laughin' Boy."

[<Click Here> for MPEG of Laughin' Boy whoopin' it up amongst the dead.]

Wait and see.

And that's the Wack Report for May 21, 2000 . . . but check back tomorrow, gang, because it's all bound to get Wack-ier still!

Until then—Wack . . . Off!

All content Copyright (c) 2000 Wackmeister Enterprises.

You are Visitor 63549 since January 1, 2000.

[<Click Here> for the Archives of Wack.]

[<Click Here> for Horny European Sluts.]

<click> *Connecting to HTTP server . . .*

WELCOME TO HOES. ENTER OVER21 VERIFICATION PASSWORD and VISA or MASTERCARD ACCT NO.:

<click> *Logging Off.*

Therapy Transcripts (3)

(Laughter deleted)

You want to know about my wife.

I don't have one. She divorced me.

Technically, we divorced each other. It was mutual and friendly and all that, because we still loved each other. And we both still wanted to be Lindy's mommy and daddy.

That last part is true. As for the rest . . .

Karen never wants to hurt anyone's feelings. She was raised to be polite. So she said she still loved me, but that she had to leave me anyway. And that was the worst possible thing she could have done, because it left me with hope. It was like spinning down a slow drain.

This is why people who don't want to hurt other people's feelings should just go ahead and do it. Yank that Band-Aid. Sudden death is always better than slow torture.

Sorry. I just reminded myself of something. No, please. No more drugs. I can stop laughing on my own. Bathroom grout. Pine mulch.

All right. Where were we?

Karen.

Yes, I still love her.

You want my definition of love? Now, that's funny. That'll keep the giggles at bay for a while.

Why? Because I'm the guy who busted a gut when men, women, and children were machine-gunned in front of me—and now you're asking me to tell you what love is. As if a monster would know.

All right, fine: Love is what I felt when Karen quivered around my cock.

That was supposed to disgust you. But I see it didn't. Wish I could say the same for myself.

I'm not disgusted because I felt that way. I'm disgusted because I said it out loud to you. Despite the fact that I was raised by television, and despite the fact that television has led us to expect everyone to expose everything about themselves, I still think some parts of our lives should stay private.

And not just private, but secret. Otherwise, they're on the same level as everything else, and they lose their power to move us.

The TV people won't leave my wife and daughter out of this, will they?

I have the feeling that you envy me. And if that's true, then who's really sick here? While I'd do anything for less publicity, you'd probably do anything for more. Sometimes I think you only took me on so you can play yourselves when they make the movie.

I'm sorry. That wasn't fair. I don't know anything about you, your marriage, or your motives. And none of it's any of my business.

But I, my marriage, and my motives are *your* business, aren't they? And everybody else's. Fall prey to fame, or to infamy, and the world is your proctologist.

All right. I'll tell you about her.

I met Karen at the University of Kansas. We were both sophomores, and we were living in two big dormitories next door to each other. We met at a party at my dorm—although she didn't remember that until I reminded her on our wedding night.

She was there with a date, but he must have been in the bathroom when I came down from my room to grab some of the free snacks. I was studying that night, even though it was Saturday, because my physics course was giving me fits. I had no time for parties, and I was no good at them anyway. I had discovered that my freshman year. But there were snacks, and those were as much mine as anyone else's. So I came down for some chips.

And there she was in front of the Doritos talking to another girl. She was really pretty, although I confess that I didn't make more than passing note of that at the time. After all, the girl she was talking to was pretty too. So were most of the girls there. So were most of the girls in the world. And I didn't know how to deal with any of them.

At the moment, these two were blocking me from the Doritos. So I asked them if I could get around them, and Karen looked at me and said, "Excuse me, but we're talking. There are more Doritos over *there*." And she pointed to the next table where, sure enough, there were more Doritos. So I went over and got some. And when I turned back around, the other girl with Karen had been replaced by the guy who'd been in the bathroom or something. He had a thick neck.

As I walked by them, Karen looked at me and said, "Enjoy your Doritos."

She was being sarcastic, but in a sweet way. It's hard to explain, and I certainly can't imitate it. But she can do that. She can use nothing more than the inflection of a word or two to gut you in such a way that you smile at the sight of your own steaming entrails.

And that would have been the whole encounter, except that Thick Neck gave me a look, and then gave her a look, and I heard him ask her, "What was *that* about?"

At which point she apparently took offense at his tone, and walked away from him. Walked past me, brushing my shoulder without looking at me, and left.

I watched her go, but that only took a second or two. When she was gone, I went on my way.

But Thick Neck came after me, caught me on the stairs, and knocked the Doritos out of my hands.

"Stay the fuck away from Karen," he said. He was drunk, although I couldn't smell it on his breath. But he was one of these big, handsome guys, and I was pretty scrawny and pimply at the time. The only way he could have perceived me as a threat, Karen-wise, was if he was drunk.

"You got me, asshole?" he said.

I didn't say anything. Saying anything, even if it's mollifying, to a big drunk guy who's pissed off at you is never a good idea.

But I didn't want to just turn and run, either, because there were people down at the bottom of the stairs watching us. I was too big a coward to bear having people *think* I was a coward.

So I said nothing, and I did nothing. This was what I was used to, actually. This was one hundred percent me.

But the key to doing nothing is to create the illusion of doing *something*, so the non-thing I did was bend down to pick up the small paper bowl that had held my Doritos. It had landed on the step between my feet, right-side up, and there were still a few chips in it. I hoped that Thick Neck would think I was cringing, and that the people at the bottom of the stairs would think I was being cool by retrieving my snack instead of responding to the big drunk guy. In fact, of course, I was scared shitless. But I had been threatened by big drunk guys before, and I knew they usually just went away after making their threats, just so long as you didn't make eye contact.

So I was leaning down to get the bowl, and I guess Thick Neck leaned in toward me at the same moment. He was probably going to punctuate his threat by getting right in my face and snarling.

What happened, though, was that the top of my skull caught him in the nose, and he lost his balance and fell backwards down the stairs. Fortunately, we were only six or seven steps up from the floor, so he didn't crack open his skull. He just wound up sprawled on his back with his head on the bottom step and his feet two steps down from my Doritos bowl.

He lay there staring up at me, and he had a bit of a bloody nose. But because of the way he was lying, and because he tried to wipe it away with one of his big drunk hands, the blood got all over his face. And then he looked like he'd been hit by a bus.

No, I didn't laugh. The situation wasn't really comparable to—

Give me another minute.

All right. Thick Neck was lying there all bloody, but I didn't think he was really hurt. So I went ahead and picked up my bowl and then stood there on the stairs for another fifteen seconds until some of the onlookers helped him to his feet. He was clearly okay. Or would be when he sobered up.

It seemed to me that it was time for me to leave. But as I started to turn away, Thick Neck broke free of the people holding him, and he made a move as if he was coming back up the stairs at me. I had a moment where I thought I might really have to do something after all. Like flee.

But then Thick Neck stopped, braced himself on the handrail, and threw up all over himself.

At that point I went up to my room, where I examined my head in the mirror. It was fine. Didn't hurt at all. The collision had been perfect.

By morning it was all over the dorm that Thick Neck had taken a swing at me, and that I had retaliated by head-butting him until he puked. It wasn't quite the truth, but I neither confirmed nor contradicted it. And since Thick Neck turned out to be a frat rat, my status went up. Plus, I don't recall ever seeing him again.

But even though Karen lived in the dorm next door to mine, I didn't see her again until the next semester, when I spotted her going into a classroom where I knew a Calculus II session was being taught. As it happened, I was going to another Calculus II session being taught in another room in the same building at the same time. And right after class, I went to the Math Department office and switched my enrollment to Karen's section.

It was the most aggressive thing I had ever done. And four weeks later, after I encountered her on a sidewalk near the dorms, she spoke to me. She said, "Hey, aren't you in my Calculus class?"

We studied for the midterm together in her dorm's common room. And while we were talking during a break, I realized that she didn't recognize me from the Doritos incident. I also realized that she was having an affair with her English professor.

Because she told me, that's why.

How did that make me feel? How the fuck do you think it made me feel?

It was horrible. It was the worst thing I'd ever felt, up to then.

In her eyes, I was so utterly neutral that she could tell me the most intimate secret without fear that it would have any consequences whatsoever. I would neither condemn nor champion her, but stay safely in that demilitarized gray zone of male-friend-you-can-talk-to.

She had sensed that I was perfect for that. She had sensed that as far as real life was concerned, I was strictly a TV kid. I would watch and listen, but never participate.

And she was right. Up until the moment that I realized that was how she saw me, that was precisely what I was.

But I wasn't home anymore. There wasn't a TV on all the time. I had to do some things for myself now. After all, hadn't I managed to change my Calculus II section for no good reason other than that I wanted to be near Karen? Wasn't that proof that I was capable of not just watching, but doing?

For about a month, though, I remained in the demilitarized zone. I just listened. I just watched. I did think about sending the English professor an anonymous threatening letter, but decided against it. Because if Karen and I wound up together, as we did in my imagination, I would eventually have to tell her about such a letter. And I didn't think she would appreciate it.

What I eventually did, at a study session during finals, was say one short sentence after her latest lament about how the professor ignored her except when they were alone.

"That's because he thinks you're a toy," I said without looking up from my double integrals.

She didn't speak again for fifteen minutes, and when she did, it was strictly calculus. So I was sure I had lost her, and when I went back to my dorm that night I began composing the letter to the English professor.

But I never sent it. Two days later, we had our Calculus final, and Karen invited me back to her room afterward for a celebratory beer. Of course I went. And when she invited me to bed, I asked if she was sure.

She smiled and assured me that one beer wasn't enough to make her stupid.

Then she told me what she wanted me to do, and everything was fine.

Karen and I married the summer after our junior year, moved into married-student housing for our senior year, and started trying to make a baby right after graduation.

We lost three in ten years before finally having Lindy.

I didn't laugh any of those times, either.

Video Clip (2)
The Ex-Bride of Frankenstein

(airs on late local news in Wichita on Sunday, May 21; on national morning news shows Monday, May 22)

The picture jerks as the cameraman runs up a suburban sidewalk. The grass bordering the concrete is a lush green, but well-edged and cropped. The view moves upward, and we see the arm of the Talent moving in and out of frame. The Talent has a microphone in his hand. (We know the Talent is a man. We see a pale blue shirtsleeve; we see big masculine knuckles.) He is clutching the microphone as if it were a billy club.

A red-brick housefront comes into frame as the camera stabilizes. A delicate-featured brunette woman of about thirty is standing on a cement porch before a white front door. A tangle of keys hangs from her right hand. Her left hand is holding the hand of a tiny blonde girl in a crisp puppy-dog-print dress. Two brown paper sacks of groceries are at their feet. One of the sacks has fallen over and spilled blue boxes of macaroni and cheese onto the porch.

The camera comes to a stop, and the Talent appears on the porch with the woman and child. The Talent is ever-so-slightly disheveled. He has been burning the midnight oil since yesterday's tragedy. He has been tracking down eyewitness sources, profiling suspected militants, cadging cop interviews, and telephoning the FBI. He has been working his Stairmastered butt to a frazzle. (Some of us who are watching suspect that he is looking to get out of Wichita, that he is angling for New York or L.A.) His hair is the color and consistency of bathroom porcelain.

The brunette woman stares at him as if he were a paid assassin. She places herself between him and her child without ever taking her eyes off him.

He thrusts the microphone toward her, a matador with a sword.

"Karen Clayton!" the Talent cries. "Former wife of the so-called Laughin' Boy, Daniel Clayton, who seemed so gleeful in the midst of the horror at the River Festival yesterday! Your reaction to what's happened?"

The former Mrs. Clayton is silent for a few moments, staring at the fuzzy black ball at the end of the microphone. That fuzzy black ball might be an animal. It might be a rat about to spring up and bite her face.

Then we hear a child's squeal, and the camera swivels downward to show us the tiny face smiling from behind her mother's legs. This face is the innocence of childhood personified. This little blonde girl knows nothing of yesterday's horror. She knows nothing of the children who were ripped to shreds without warning or cause. How we wish we could be like her again.

The camera swings back upward, and when Karen Clayton's face is centered in our screens again, she is weeping. She is weeping like a parent who knows that it could have been her own child killed at the river. If they hadn't spent yesterday afternoon at grandma's or in the back yard or watching *The Lion King* or *Pokemon: The Movie* for the thirty-fifth time instead, she too might be planning a funeral today. If she herself had survived.

She is weeping a mother's tears, weeping for all who lost their lives or their loved ones in those awful moments.

Everyone there, after all, was someone's child.

"I think it's terrible," she says. She can barely get the words out.

The Talent's own voice quavers as he asks his next question.

"Do you think," he asks, and we can hear how he hates to even suggest such a thing to this sweet woman, "do you think that, given his reaction, your ex-husband could have had anything to do with the attack?"

The picture zooms in tight on Karen's face. All we can see are her lips, nose, eyes, and tears. She is looking right at us.

Hers is the face of all our mothers as we would want them to be.

"No," she whispers. Her voice is scarcely audible. But the movement of her lips has us mesmerized. We can read every syllable. "No, Danny could never do anything like that."

There is no question of whether we believe her or not. She would never lie to us.

But she might not be able to accept the truth, either. For she is now our mother . . . and we know that our mother could never accept or admit that our father might do us harm.

We cannot fault her for this. We never have.

The Talent reaches out with his free hand as if to place it on Karen's shoulder in a comforting gesture, but then hesitates and withdraws. And this too we understand.

We know we can never make our mother happy. Only one man on earth can do that, and he has failed. That's why they're divorced.

So as much as Karen's tears have made us love her, they have made us hate the man who caused them.

They have made us hate him all the more.

Newsgroup Posts (2)

Subject: Re: Wichita Attack
From: olddon8@freesearch.com (Don Oldenberg)
Date: 2000/05/21
Message-ID: <olddon8-52998LP.2700JBK2@freesearch.com>
Newsgroups: soc.us.violence.terror

In article <4971800FE3.228LB9@bullmoose.net>, Nathan Lawrence <johndoe99@bullmoose.net> wrote:

> the bane of any motorist trying to get from St. Louis to Denver.

Not funny, Nate. A bunch of innocent people are murdered, and you make fun of where they live(d). Well, IMHO, they don't need you laughing at them. They already got that treatment right after they were shot.

As for your comments concerning "Ragheads" and "dumbass inbred Crackers," I can only point out that ethnic or cultural groups who resort to violence often do so because they're tired of being called things like "Ragheads" or "Crackers," not to mention "Niggers," "Wops," "Kikes," "Fairies," "Micks," "Aggies," "Okies," "Redskins," "Spics," "Wetbacks," "Coons," "Puerto Potties," "Haggis Heads," "Lime Suckers," "Japs," "Krauts," "Chinks," "Hebes," "Bohunks," "Polacks," "Cheesers," "Dykes," "Beaners," "Greasers," "Mackerel Snappers," "Wogs," "Frogs," or "Swiss."

Next time, please think before you post.

Radio Talk (1)

All right, next caller. Dave in Irving, you're on the air.

Yeah, I wanted to talk about that SQUEEEEEALLL talk about that thing in SQUEEEEEALLLLLL about that thing up in Kansas SQUEEEEEEAAALLLLLL that thing up in

Dave, please turn down your radio.

Kansas because it's gonna give all them SQUEEEALL gonna give all them liberal anti-freedom SQUEEEEALLLLLLLLLLL

So much for Dave. Why can't these morons figure out we're on a freakin' delay here, Miss Candi?

You got me, Jimmy Joe Bob.

I do keep trying to get you, Miss Candi. And speaking of delays, I don't think I can hold out much longer. The time has come for you to let me into your pants.

I keep telling you, Jimmy Joe Bob, I'm a good girl.

Yeah, I'll bet. June Anne in Plano, you're on the air.

Jimmy Joe Bob? Is that really you?

Yes, June Anne. You're on the air with Jimmy Joe Bob and Miss Candi.

Oh, my God! I can't believe it! This is like the millionth time I've called, and you've never put me on the air before.

Okay, then, it's your lucky day. What's on your sweet little mind?

Well, you know, it's just that awful shooting up in Wichita. It seems like something like that happens every other day anymore. If it's not a post office, it's a school. If it's not a school, it's a McDonald's. If it's not a McDonald's, it's—it's whatever that thing in Wichita was.

I think it was a festival of some kind, June Anne. They were having a concert or something like that.

Yes, that's what it was, you're right. Well, I just think it's terrible.

Yeah? And?

Well, it's terrible, that's all.

All right, then, June Anne. It's terrible. We can all agree on that. But what are we going to do about it?

Well, my God, what CAN we do about it? I guess we can pray, but that's about all.

There have been some shootings like this at churches, too, June Anne. Don't you think those people prayed?

Well, I guess they probably did. But they probably didn't pray about this specifically.

About what specifically?

Not getting shot.

All right, then, June Anne. Anything else?

I guess maybe we need more police.

I'm with you on that, June Anne. By the way, how old are you?

Twenty-seven.

Well, that's a little old for me, June Anne, although there's something to be said for experience. I guess you've seen a gun or two by now yourself, eh?

Well, my Daddy had one.

Your Daddy, you say? Oh my, June Anne! Was it a BIG gun?

I guess so. He never shot nobody with it, though. Not a person, I mean. He shot a dog came and crapped on our driveway once.

Fascinating, June Anne. How much do you weigh?

I don't know. About a hundred and twenty, I guess.

Ooh. That could be good or bad. How tall are you?

Five foot six in spike heels.

Hmm, jury's still out. You got a big chest, June Anne?

Oh my, yes. I got me a beautiful big chest, Jimmy Joe Bob.

Oh yeah? Well what's your face like? Never mind, I don't care. Can you come down to the station?

I don't know. I'm supposed to go to work.

Where do you work, June Anne?

At a compact disc store. Can I say which one?

I don't care which one, June Anne. But I'll tell you what, you'd better NOT go in to work today. You know why? Because those guys who shot up that concert in Wichita hated music.

They did?

They sure did. Why else would they shoot up a concert? So they way I figure it, they'll be hitting compact disc stores next. You go in to work today, you might get shot right in your beautiful big chest.

Oh, now you're just trying to scare me.

I am not, June Anne. I'm telling you the truth. You go to work today, you're in danger. The only safe place for you is here at the radio station with me.

I dunno, Jimmy Joe Bob. That don't sound like it'd be all that safe.

I promise you, June Anne, there's no place safer. I guarantee that if you come down to the station right now, I'll do everything in my power to protect your beautiful big chest.

Oh really, Jimmy Joe Bob? What'll you do?

Well, first I'll have to perform a manual examination to determine the extent of the protection required. And then, if any masked gunmen break into the studio, I'll shield you with my body. In fact, what the hell, I'll do that with or without the gunmen.

Ooh, I'll be right there.

Not so fast, June Anne. E-mail me a naked picture of yourself first.

I don't have a naked picture of myself.

Really? Want to buy one?

You're terrible, Jimmy Joe Bob.

How would you know, Miss Candi? You rotten little tease. Next caller. Elijah from Palestine, you're on the air with Jimmy Joe Bob and Miss Candi.

Hello.

Well, hello yourself. And I must say, you have quite a manly voice for someone with such a fruity name.

Elijah isn't my real name. I can't tell you my real name.

Oh yeah? Why's that, Elijah? You gay or something? You afraid I'll OUT you?

No. I'm not a homosexual. The homosexuals will all be purged.

No kidding? You sent by God or something like that, Elijah?

Something exactly like that, Jimmy Joe Bob. And I want you to tell your listeners that what happened Saturday in Wichita was a wake-up call.

Wait a minute, boys. I have to jump in here. Saturday was a wake-up call, Elijah? For what? For people to keep laughing and partying no matter what happens?

Stay out of this, Miss Candi. This is man stuff. You wouldn't understand.

Well, excuse me for not having a penis.

I can't do that unless you take off your pants and prove it.

Not in this lifetime, Jimmy Joe Bob.

"Not in this lifetime," eh? So all we have to do is die first, is that it, Miss Candi? In that case, are you aware that an orgasm is also known as a "small death"?

No doubt very small, in your case.

Ouch! Miss Candi! I want you more than ever!

Excuse me.

Shut up for a second, Ezekiel. I'm busy coming on to Miss Candi.

Elijah.

Huh?

He's saying that he's not Ezekiel, he's Elijah.

Like I care. As far as I'm concerned, he's Liberace, because he's obviously a fairy.

The laughing man was not part of the wake-up call.

Excuse me, Liberace? What's that?

The laughing man was not a member of the Army of the Lord. I have been in contact with some of the soldiers who took part in Saturday's action, and they assure me that the laughing man was not one of theirs.

All right, then, listeners, you heard it here first direct from Liberace himself. The laughing idiot at Saturday's bloodbath—Now, can I call it a bloodbath, Miss Candi? Is that politically correct?

I don't know why it wouldn't be, Jimmy Joe Bob.

Oh, good. I was afraid you might think I was making a crack about your time of the month.

You suck, Jimmy Joe Bob.

Of course, Miss Candi, but do YOU?

Am I still on the air?

For crying out loud, Liberace, what's your problem? Does it make you gay guys shrivel to the size of a peanut to hear a real man angling for a woman?

No.

So you admit you're gay.

No, I'm not. And my name's not Liberace.

Miss Candi, didn't Liberace here just admit to being gay?

That's what it sounded like to me, Jimmy Joe Bob.

You hear that, Liberace? Miss Candi thinks you're gay.

I'm not gay.

Of course you are. You're just a big, prancing, tushy-touching, namby-pamby, paisley-wearing, interior-decorating, Liza-Minnelli-worshipping, man-loving fruit loop. Why else would you call yourself Liberace?

I don't call myself Liberace. I call myself—

Miss Candi, did he just answer to the name Liberace?

I think he did, Jimmy Joe Bob.

Case closed, Liberace. Next caller. Steve from Dallas, you're on the air with Jimmy Joe Bob and Miss Candi.

Hey, Jimmy Joe Bob. First-time caller, long-time listener, dude!

Gosh, I've never heard that one before, Steve. So what's on your mind this fine morning?

Yeah, well, first of all, I just wanna say that you totally fEEEEEEEEEEEP.

Okay, now, Steve, I just had to bleep you. You can't use the F word on the air, all right? You can say nigger, kike, wop, greaser, chink, or dyke if you want, and you can also say bang, boff, boink, or bouncy-bouncy, but not the F word, the S word, the D word, the P word, or either of the C words. This is a family show, isn't it, Miss Candi?

I suppose so, if the family's incestuous.

Whoa there, Miss Candi! This is Texas, not Arkansas! Although I confess that I do think of you as my sister—every time I spy on you going to the bathroom.

I hate you, Jimmy Joe Bob.

Oh, please, you want me and you know it. I can hear your chair cushion making squishing noises all the way over here. Now then, Steve, you were saying?

I was saying that you effing rule, Jimmy Joe Bob.

I certainly do, and I have the twelve-inch ruler to prove it. Don't I, Miss Candi?

I'm not touching that one, Jimmy Joe Bob.

I can dream, can't I? So, Steve, was there anything else on your mind?

Yes, Jimmy Joe Bob. I just wanted to point out that if all those poor dumb s.o.b.'s in Wichita had been carrying firearms of their own, that whole damn situation would have gone different. They could have taken out those effing sand coons or whatever, and then they could have wasted that effing bastard who was laughing at them, too. But because of all the goddamn anti-gun propaganda and laws

that have been forced on us, a whole lot more innocent but stupid people just got their asses shot off.

Well, I have to say, Steve, you make a good point.

Wait a minute, Jimmy Joe Bob. He just called the victims stupid. Why were THEY stupid?

Because they should have been carrying weapons to defend themselves.

Steve, they were attacked by terrorists with automatic weapons and grenades at a blues concert. Are you saying that they should have taken automatic weapons and grenades to the concert themselves, just in case? Are you saying that they should have EXPECTED to be attacked as if they were in a war zone, and that it's their fault they're dead because they DIDN'T expect it?

Pretty much, yeah.

Well, then, what if they'd been attacked by some maniac who had stolen a tank? Or a howitzer? Should they have taken a few tanks and howitzers to the concert too?

Now you're just being silly.

Cut Miss Candi some slack, Steve. It's not her fault. See, chicks just don't understand the basic concepts of self-defense and freedom. As Joseph Conrad wrote, "It's queer how out of touch with truth women are. They live in a world of their own, and there has never been anything like it, and never can be. It is too beautiful altogether, and if they were to set it up it would go to pieces before the first sunset. Some confounded fact we men have been living contentedly with ever since the day of creation would start up and knock the whole thing over."

Huh?

Jimmy Joe Bob, I believe those were the words of a man in one of Conrad's stories, not of Conrad himself. You can't ascribe the beliefs of a fictional character to the character's author. Not unless you're an idiot.

Miss Candi, you sweet, beautiful piece of ass, it just so happens that those were the words of the narrator Charlie Marlow in "Heart of

Darkness," and many scholars believe that he probably WAS speaking for Conrad himself.

Charlie who?

Jimmy Joe Bob, even if Conrad DID voice his own opinions through Marlow, I doubt very much that he meant people ought to carry machine guns and hand grenades to outdoor concerts in Wichita, Kansas or anywhere else!

Perhaps not, Miss Candi, but the world has changed for the worse since Conrad's day. Wichita, Kansas, or anywhere else in America in the year 2000 might as well be the heart of the effing Congo in 1895, or Omaha Beach in 1944. We DO live in a war zone, Miss Candi, and the forewarned had sure as hell better get themselves forearmed.

What are you guys talking about?

Well, I don't know about Miss Candi, Steve, but I'm talking about the right to defend oneself against the slavering craphounds and murderous hyenas who would just as soon kill you where you stand, even if where you stand is a school cafeteria, a fast-food restaurant, or a grassy park where a blues band is playing. Are you with me, Steve?

Uh, I guess so. I mean, if you're saying that we all ought to have our own guns so we can kill anybody who messes with us, then yeah. I'm with you there. I didn't get some of the rest of what you said, though.

That's because you're an uneducated moron, Steve, but by God you're a good American and I can get behind that like Tommy Lee can get behind his lovely wife Pamela. So I'm sending you two tickets to Wrestlemania this coming Friday night, how about that?

Wow! Really? Holy shEEEEEEEEEEEEEEEP.

Okay, I just had to bleep Steve again, so I'm keeping those Wrestlemania tickets for my NEXT caller. In the meantime, Miss Candi, let's go over to you for this hour's news update.

Thank you, Jimmy Joe Bob. Our top story remains Saturday's military-style terrorist attack at an outdoor blues concert in Wichita, Kansas, and the nation's reaction to it. The latest wire updates now list the death toll at eighty-three, which makes this the worst incident of terrorism on U.S. soil since the 1995 bombing of the Murrah Federal building in Oklahoma City, in which one hundred sixty-eight people died. No group has yet claimed responsibility for the Wichita attack, but several of the hooded attackers can be seen on a videotape recovered from one of the victims. Also seen on this tape is a man who seems to find the whole incident rather funny, so authorities have reportedly been questioning him as to—

Excuse me, Miss Candi. I have to interrupt because we have a distraught listener on the line. Erica, are you there?

Y-y-yes, J-J-Jimmy Joe B-Bob. I'm here.

Okay, Erica, calm down. I can help you. Just tell me what's wrong.

It's all s-s-so s-sad. Every time I turn on my T-T-TV, it's so awful . . .

I understand, Erica. Now listen to me. The first thing you have to do is stop watching TV for a while. I want you to turn off your TV and leave it off for at least twenty-four hours. Can you do that for me, Erica?

I-- I-- I guess so.

Is it off right now?

I have it on with the s-sound off.

Turn the picture off too, Erica. Turn it off right now. Tell me when you've done it.

Okuh-kuh-kay, Jimmy Joe Bob. It's all the way off.

All right, then, Erica. Good. The pictures were upsetting you, weren't they?

Well, of c-course. All those people, sh-shot and bleeding . . .

But there are plenty of channels without those pictures, Erica. Couldn't you have watched Starz or Comedy Central?

N-no. We don't have c-cable, and my boyfriend says satellite dishes are too expensive.

Boyfriend, huh, Erica? Are you telling me that you're living with your boyfriend?

Uh-huh.

Is he home right now?

N-no.

Jimmy Joe Bob, I think there might be something more going on here than just what Erica has seen on TV. Maybe this boyfriend of hers has been abusive, or—

Hush, Miss Candi. I'm busy helping this poor woman, and I don't have time to run out and get you some Midol. Erica, how old are you?

N-nineteen.

Ah. Nineteen and already living with a boyfriend. I'm not too sure I approve, but we'll talk about that later. At the moment, though, your boyfriend is off at work and you're home alone with all the awful things on TV, aren't you?

He's not at work. He doesn't have a job. I don't know where he is.

That's beside the point, Erica.

What IS the point, Jimmy Joe Bob?

The point, Miss Candi, is that I can help this girl. Erica, how tall are you?

I-- I'm five-three.

Five three, eh? How much do you weigh? What's your cup size? And while we're at it, do you have any facial scars or deformities hideous enough that your head might require a bag?

Uh . . . I weigh about a hundred. Sometimes I'm a B cup, or sometimes a C. And my face is okay, I guess. My boyfriend says I look sort of like Drew Barrymore with darker hair and less baby fat.

Pardon me for a moment, I have to loosen something. Oh, yeah, that's much better. Erica, I have to ask you something very important now: Can you come down to the station?

I -- I guess I could, if I take the bus.

You do that, Erica. You take the bus down here. Put on a pretty bra that unhooks in the front and take the bus down here right now.

Oh, I would, Jimmy Joe Bob, but I don't think my boyfriend would like it.

Yeah? Well, how would your boyfriend like a couple of tickets to Wrestlemania?

Ohmigod! He'd LOVE that!

I thought so. You coming down?

Umm . . . okay. I can be there in, like, an hour.

Make it forty minutes, Erica. Otherwise, I'm giving these tickets to someone else, and I'll call your boyfriend and tell him how you screwed up. Understand?

I'm on my way!

All right, then. Back to you, Miss Candi.

Up yours, Jimmy Joe Bob.

Now, now, Miss Candi. You had your chance. So, what's in the news?

Episode Two
The Walter Cronkite Voice

THE FBI DETAINED DANNY for twenty-four hours—sixteen hours longer than the Wichita police had kept him on Saturday evening—and made sure that he had a Legal Aid lawyer present for every minute of it. They had learned their lesson in recent years: Don't violate any Amendments if there's a video or TV camera in the vicinity.

And in the case of Laughin' Boy, there were a lot of all kinds of cameras in the vicinity.

As Danny came out of the Federal Building in Wichita on Monday afternoon, minus the lawyer but surrounded by a knot of G-men and cops, the Media surged toward him like a pack of dogs toward a roadkill. Simultaneously, the G-men and cops closed in tight, crushing the air from his lungs. They hustled him toward a black Chrysler at the curb while various on-air Talents tried to use their microphones as cattle prods to penetrate the law-enforcement cluster.

In the crush, a female FBI agent was pressed against Danny's ribcage, and he found himself liking it. This was the first woman who had touched him since Karen. But the agent seemed oblivious to the fact that one of her breasts was in Danny's armpit. She had her left hand on his belt and her right hand inside her jacket, ready to produce a government-issue Glock and pop anyone who tried to pull a Hinckley.

"Mr. Clayton! Mr. Clayton!" the Talents cried.

"Shitheel!" someone outside the ring of cameras yelled.

"Fucking child-killer!" another cried.

"Murderer!" someone else shouted. Then that voice was joined by another, and another.

The cries of "Murderer!" would be heard on the news shows that evening. But "Shitheel" and the "Fucking" in "Fucking child-killer" would not, even though all the shouting was going on simultaneously. Danny would marvel at the skillful editing.

Right now, though, he was in a stupor. The sensation of the female FBI agent pressed against him was the only thing keeping him awake. He hadn't slept in he didn't even remember how long. Nor had he bathed. But bathing was far down his list of priorities. At the moment, all he wanted to do was lie down right here and close his eyes. He didn't care that right here was a concrete sidewalk. It would be comfortable enough. The female FBI agent could stay with him if she liked. That would be all right. She didn't have a wedding band. He had noticed that in the interrogation room. He couldn't quite remember her name, though. Special Agent Wurble. Yarkle. Barbell. Something like that.

He didn't have a wedding band either. But there was still a pale circle around his finger. It was three inches from his eyes. One of the male agents, a tall African-American man in sunglasses, was grasping Danny's left arm so that his hand was pulled up in front of his face.

On the videotape, it would look as if Danny were trying to hide from the cameras. But it would still be clear that he was giggling.

"Mr. Clayton! Mr. Clayton!"

"Cocksucking coward!"

"Mr. Clayton!"

The Talents were shouting questions, too, but the only things Danny could understand were his name and the curses. Everyone was yelling at once, and the combined sound was a pulsing cacophony.

"Baby-butcher!"

That one would make the news, too.

Why weren't the FBI people saying anything? Danny wondered. They had questioned him almost nonstop since picking him up at his parents' house, and now they knew—they *knew*—that he hadn't been involved in the attack except as a bystander. Yet they were letting the crowd shout at him as if he were one of the terrorists.

He guessed it was because he still couldn't stop laughing, and they were angry at him for it. But the laughter wasn't his fault, and they ought to have figured that out by now. Especially since he had told them so.

Someone put a hand on Danny's head and pushed him into the Chrysler's back seat. The tall African-American agent slid in beside him, and another agent slid in on the other side. The female agent and a driver sat up front.

Danny was disappointed. He had hoped that the woman would stay beside him. She smelled like Karen, and he thought she was nice. She had brought him water three times during his interrogation. Once, she had brought him a Coke. But most of it had sprayed from his nose when he had laughed at a photo of a man who had been decapitated during the attack.

He looked at the female agent's face in the rearview mirror. It was plain and stoic, but Danny thought it might appear that way only because of her professional demeanor. She looked about thirty-five, and she was in great shape. An FBI agent would have to stay in great shape. She could probably break a baseball bat over her knee.

She could probably break Danny's legs that way, too. And she might want to.

The agents began to close the car doors, but one of the Talents managed to jam his microphone arm inside the door beside the African-American agent before it had closed all the way.

The Talent let out a yelp.

"Remove yourself and step away," the African-American agent said.

But the Talent, his forehead sweating, his face contorted, jabbed his microphone past the agent so that it bopped Danny on the nose. "Mr. Clayton!" the Talent squealed. "Are you a member of any militia or white-supremacist group? Or were you simply in the wrong place at the wrong time? If so, why did you remain unharmed while everyone around you died, and why did you find that so amusing?"

The African-American agent opened the door a little, then slammed it on the Talent's arm. Even through the crown noise, Danny heard the crunch. He began to laugh.

The Talent fell away from the car, and the African-American agent closed the door.

"Drive," he said.

The driver shook his head. "I can't pull out without running over some of these people"

"They'll move," the African-American agent said.

The female agent looked over her shoulder. She had a Mona Lisa smile on her face now. "What if they don't?"

The African-American agent shrugged. "Then we'll book them for destruction of government property and assault on Federal agents. Broken bones can heal in Leavenworth as well as anyplace else"

The driver grinned into the rearview mirror. "Okay, Special Agent Armstrong. You're the boss"

"Thank you for noticing," Armstrong said. "And don't pull out slowly, either. The crowd will pile on if you do. Just plow through"

So the Chrysler plowed through, and as Armstrong had predicted, most of the crowd got out of the way. But the same eager Talent who had jammed his arm into the car now seemed to think his microphone was a magic wand that could stop an automobile. He wound up on the hood of the car with his face pressed against the windshield.

To Danny, the man looked like Popeye. And since that was funny, Danny was able to stop laughing and catch his breath.

"Take a left at this corner," Armstrong said. "A sharp left"

The driver took the left, the Chrysler's tires squealed, and the Talent rolled off the hood into the intersection. Meanwhile, Danny was pressed against Armstrong on his right, and the other back-seat Fed was pressed against Danny's left. Danny howled again.

He was so overcome with laughter that he couldn't sit up again after the Chrysler's trajectory straightened. The agent on his left sat up and scooted away, but Danny remained collapsed against the big shoulder of Special Agent Armstrong. He looked up at Armstrong's face and tried to say that he couldn't help himself. But Armstrong looked so stern with his sunglasses and granite jaw that all Danny could do was laugh harder.

After a moment, Armstrong took off his sunglasses and stared down at Danny. His eyes were dark and unblinking.

"Sit up," he said in a monotone. "If you're unable to do so, I'll assist you"

Almost instantly, Danny was able to stop laughing and sit up straight. He was puzzled by this for a few seconds, but then realized that the utter lack of any emotion in Armstrong's eyes and voice had done the trick.

"Thank you," Armstrong said. "Now, where do you want us to take you?"

Danny hadn't been expecting that. "You're turning me loose?" he asked.

"You've already been released, Mr. Clayton. In fact, you were never in custody. The Bureau's position is that you volunteered to come in and tell us what you could about Saturday's tragedy. And now that you've done so, we're driving you to the destination of your choice as a courtesy." Armstrong's eyes flickered. "But I should inform you that your rental house and everything in it has burned to the ground as the result of multiple acts of arson. Firefighters were unable to get close enough to save anything because of the crowd surrounding it."

Armstrong sounded so matter-of-fact that Danny wasn't sure he'd heard him right. So he glanced around at the other agents, but they were all staring straight ahead now, expressionless.

"Mr. Clayton?" Armstrong asked. "Your destination?"

Danny looked at him again. "My house has burned down?"

"That's correct. I hope you have renter's insurance."

Danny felt a giggle coming on, but managed to suppress it. "No. It was that or child support. I couldn't afford both."

"I'm sorry." It was a polite response with no sincerity behind it. "So. Would you like us to return you to where you were picked up? The Molotovs that were thrown into the yard there did no damage to the domicile. Just to the grass."

Now Danny couldn't hold back a short bark. "That's my parents' house. I think they'll be safer if I stay away."

Armstrong gave a curt nod. "I agree. The Wichita police are keeping a car parked out front, but that might not be enough if you return. Also, they've agreed not to prosecute your mother for backing into their cruiser, but only if there's no further difficulty at that address." He paused and looked toward the driver. "We talked them into that one by pointing out that we ran into them too. Rammed them from behind. Didn't we, Agent Tompkins?"

The driver frowned. "They were in our way."

"They're local cops," Armstrong said. "Of course they were in our way. But you still could've hit the damn brakes." He turned back to Danny. "Is there anyplace else you can go?"

Danny tried to think of someplace and couldn't. "No. My ex-wife sure isn't an option. Even if she'd let me stay, I couldn't put her or my daughter at risk. So you can just take me to a motel, I guess. A cheap one."

Armstrong put on his sunglasses and faced forward. "We could do that," he said. "Or we could take you to a hotel room that has already been reserved for you. Your stay there will be paid for by the Bureau, in the event that you choose to cooperate in our investigation."

Danny was puzzled. "I've already been cooperating, haven't I?"

"To an extent. You've answered our questions, and we're convinced you had nothing to do with the incident in question. But the cooperation we're hoping for now is of another sort."

Armstrong sounded grim now, so Danny couldn't hold it in anymore. He doubled over and howled.

"I'll take that as a yes," Armstrong said.

The hotel room turned out to be a tower suite in the downtown Holiday Inn. Armstrong and the other Feds brought Danny into the building through the loading dock and took him up to the suite in a service elevator. They didn't encounter anyone on the way, but there were two men and a woman waiting for them in the suite. All were Caucasian.

Armstrong closed the door, took off his sunglasses, and looked across at the three people on the couch as if gauging the distance of a target. For the first time, Danny saw the hint of an emotion in his eyes. Armstrong wasn't happy. And the other Feds seemed nervous.

It made Danny chortle.

Armstrong's eyes flicked toward Danny for an instant, then back at the people on the couch. So Danny looked at them too.

The woman and one of the men had familiar faces, but Danny couldn't place them. They were chubby and florid, and the man was balding. They wore identical gray suits, except that the woman's had a skirt.

The other man was movie-star handsome, and he had the same lean, muscular frame and wore the same plain suit as the FBI agents. His eyes were ice-blue, and his chestnut hair was thick and wavy. He was exactly the sort of man, Danny thought, that Karen would have drooled over.

It was a bitter thought, so Danny had to giggle.

Armstrong exhaled. "Rob Royce," he said. "I didn't think they'd send *you*"

The handsome man stood. "Lawsy, Allan, honey," he said. "Is dat ennyway to say howdy to de fren whut done save yo' mis'ble life?"

Danny was startled. He looked sidelong at Armstrong and wondered if he was about to witness more violence.

Armstrong closed his eyes and squeezed the bridge of his nose between his thumb and forefinger. At this gesture, the other agents moved away from him. Danny tried to go with them, but the female agent shook her head to make him stay put.

"Do me a favor, Rob," Armstrong said. "Just don't speak, all right?"

"Dat's gwyne to be mos' pow'ful diff'cult, dad fetch it," Royce said. "I's been assigned to yo' detail, en I'se s'posed to consult wid you on de sp'sifik stattegee to ketch dem whut done blowed up de carnival down by de river sho'"

Armstrong took his hand away from his face and reached into his jacket.

"Rob," he said, "shut up or I'm going to shoot you." Then he looked at Danny. "Mr. Clayton, your giggling is getting on my nerves. Please go into the bedroom and stuff a blanket into your mouth"

Danny hurried across to the doorway Armstrong had indicated. The female agent followed him, but she stayed outside the room and closed the door after him.

The drapes in the bedroom were drawn, and the room was dim. But there was enough daylight seeping in for Danny to see. The first thing he did was go to the bed and cram the corner of the coverlet into his mouth. Then he let out the laughter in long, muffled screams until he collapsed on the mattress.

He could hear a siren shrieking somewhere on the streets of Wichita. It sounded just like the ones he had heard on Saturday. It sounded just like his life ending.

Maybe he should have realized that was what it had meant when all those people had started dying. But he hadn't been able to think straight then. Nobody could have thought straight then. Even if they hadn't been racked with laughter.

But now, after two days of convulsions and interrogations, he had a moment alone. He had tried for such a moment in his old room at his parents' house, but now he knew that he couldn't have been alone with the ghost of his child-self in there with him. He couldn't have been alone with the sounds of his mother ignoring reality and his father barking at God.

Here in the Holiday Inn, though, there was just him. The Feds in the next room didn't count. Not even the female one. They were like the wind. Or bullets. Or gravity. Or television cameras. They were forces of nature, and he had no control over them or anything they might do to him. They had nothing to do with anything in his soul.

And what was in Danny Clayton's soul now was the certainty that he was just as dead as all those who had died around him.

He had no home. It was ashes. And if he went to his parents' home again, it would turn to ashes as well. He couldn't even visit his daughter. Not for a long time, anyway. Maybe months. Maybe years. And by then Lindy might not remember him as anything but a laughing man surrounded by corpses.

As for Karen—

Before this past weekend, he had been able to imagine that she might still love him. But that fantasy had crumbled during his interrogation when one of the FBI agents had shown him a clip of Karen and Lindy being cornered by a reporter. And he had seen in Karen's eyes that she'd put several more light years between them, and that the gulf could never be crossed again.

Well, who could blame her? Who would want to be anywhere near the monster called Laughin' Boy?

Danny was also pretty sure that his teaching job was gone along with everything else. In the corner of his eye he could see the glowing red numerals of a clock radio, and they said it was 2:35 P.M. Right now he was supposed to be forty miles away at Butler County Community College, teaching his spring-semester Technical Writing class.

What the hell. If you didn't have a life, you didn't need to make a living.

So maybe being dead wouldn't be all that bad. He would miss Lindy, but the rest of it . . .

The rest of it was smoke from burning carnival tents. The rest of it was blood on sunbaked grass.

Yes, Danny Clayton had died with all the others at the River Festival. The terrorists had gotten him after all. But he'd never been much fun anyway. No wonder he'd been replaced by Laughin' Boy.

"You can still call yourself Danny," he mumbled into the coverlet. "But the TV people know better"

The siren outside was getting louder, and it was joined by others. Something was on fire, or someone had died. Or both.

Danny's body tried to laugh, but it was worn out. So the urge just hung there like a tickle in his chest. The only way to get rid of it would be to tear himself open and rip out whatever he found there.

"The TV people know best," he said.

Then he dozed in fits and starts, grinning all the while, to the sound of the sirens.

When Danny awoke he was lying on his back, his head propped up by pillows against the headboard. His neck hurt. The lamp on the nightstand was on, but that was the only light in the room. There was no sun-glow around the drapes now.

Four people were in the room with him. Special Agent Armstrong and the handsome man named Rob Royce stood at the foot of the bed. Sitting in chairs on either side of the bed were the man and woman in gray suits.

Danny blinked, sucked in a deep breath, and winced at his own odor. Then he pushed himself up to a semi-sitting position that wasn't so hard on his neck. "Where's everybody else?" he asked. He was thinking of the female agent.

"They've been reassigned," Armstrong said.

Danny was disappointed. "Oh," he said. Then he giggled.

The chubby man in the gray suit leaned forward. "You were attracted to the woman who was here earlier, weren't you, Daniel?"

Danny stared at him. "Excuse me?" he asked, still giggling.

The chubby man smiled. "It's quite all right. You have slept, and have awakened with an erection. This is normal, even in times of stress. There is no need for guilt"

Danny stopped giggling. This guy was goofy.

The woman in gray leaned forward as well. "He's right, Danny. You really are blameless. And we understand. I am Dr. Carla DeWitt, and this is my husband, Dr. Ralph DeWitt. If you wish, you may call us Dr. Carla and Dr. Ralph. Perhaps you've seen us being interviewed on television, or listened to our radio program"

Now Danny recognized them. "Well, no," he said. "But I've seen your pictures in *People* magazine"

Dr. Carla smiled and patted Danny's hand. "That's all right, Danny. We're not in the business we're in to be famous. We're in it to help people"

"And we want to help *you*," Dr. Ralph said. "We understand that what has happened to you is not your fault. Given all that you've been through in the past two days, you may think you're the only person who knows that. But we do too"

Danny looked from one DeWitt to the other, then at the two

men at the foot of the bed. The DeWitts were smiling at him, but Armstrong and Royce were not.

He looked back at Dr. Ralph. "You mean the way I've been laughing. You know that I don't want to?"

Dr. Ralph nodded. "Of course. Many people have hysterical reactions to traumatic events, but that's not quite what we believe has happened to you. If you would, please, tell me your reaction to what my wife is holding."

Danny turned toward Dr. Carla, who showed him a large color photograph of a man, woman, and little boy who had all been disemboweled. Their eyes were open, and their faces were frozen in expressions of pain and horror.

So Danny's aching belly convulsed, and he twisted onto his side. It was a bad attack, and the more he tried to stop it, the worse it got. He curled up into a fetal ball. Exacerbating the situation was the fact that he'd woken up with not only an erection, but a full bladder as well. He was in serious discomfort.

Dr. Ralph appeared before him with a syringe. "Daniel," he said, "I'd like to inject you with a mild sedative and muscle relaxant. I'll understand if you decide against it. But I'm a physician, and I do recommend it"

Danny managed to nod. So Dr. Ralph pulled up Danny's shirt and tugged his jeans down far enough to stick the needle into his hip.

It hurt so much that Danny was convinced the needle had broken off. And that made him laugh even harder.

But a few moments later, after Dr. Ralph had removed the needle, the air in the room began to ripple like water. So Danny rolled onto his back again and giggled. His life was over. He was dead. And he had to pee.

"Help," he said. "Bathroom"

Dr. Carla gave him a sympathetic smile. "We understand," she said.

Armstrong and Royce stepped forward and grasped Danny under his armpits. They hauled him to the bathroom with his toes dragging on the carpet, then supported him at the toilet as he struggled to unzip and relieve himself. He managed, but it was messy. That was a little funny, though, so the giggling subsided.

When he'd finished, they lugged him back to the bed and had him sit on the edge of the mattress. Dr. Ralph and Dr. Carla were sitting with their chairs beside each other now, facing Danny. Their smiling faces stretched in his vision like Silly Putty.

"How are you feeling now?" Dr. Carla asked.

Danny thought about it. "Doped," he said.

"Do you feel like laughing?" Dr. Ralph asked.

Dr. Ralph's and Dr. Carla's heads swam toward each other until they were joined at the ears.

"Nope," Danny said.

"All right, then," one of the DeWitts said. Danny couldn't tell which one, because now their mouths were joined as well. And they had a new voice that sounded like Walter Cronkite in an echo chamber. "We have an offer we hope you'll consider. As you may have read, we now specialize in treating persons with unclassifiable behavioral disorders. Sometimes these disorders are purely psychological in nature, and sometimes there is a physiological component as well. But in all cases, the subjects are unable to function in society. That's where we come in. We treat as many symptoms as possible, and we do our best to discover the root causes of the individual disorders. In addition, we publicize our work in order to explain to the world that the behaviors such disorders induce are not voluntary"

Royce made a throat-clearing noise.

"You heah dat, Allan honey?" he asked. "De doctah heah say dis way I been talkin' ain't ol' Rob's fault, en dat's de Gospel trut'"

Royce, unlike the DeWitts, did not sound at all like Walter Cronkite.

Danny looked at Special Agent Armstrong. Armstrong's face was stretching and swimming too, but Danny could tell that it wasn't smiling.

"Exactly," one or both of the DeWitts said. "Special Agent Royce does indeed suffer from a disorder of the sort we're talking about. But thanks to the understanding of his superiors at the Federal Bureau of Investigation, he's now under our care. We'd like you to be under our care as well, Daniel. In fact, you'd be living with us for the duration of your treatment. We understand that you value your independence—but without our help, you may never enjoy that independence again"

The DeWitts' compound face shimmied back into view, one big smile splitting both halves.

These people were beginning to give Danny the creeps. So he felt like laughing again, but his chest was so slack that he could hardly breathe.

"I don't think my HMO will pay for you guys," he said.

"They won't have to," the DeWitts said. "The FBI has agreed to compensate us for your care for at least a month"

Danny thought the drugs must be making the Walter Cronkite voice say weird, surreal things. But he decided to roll with it.

"Why would the FBI do that?" he asked.

Armstrong's face swam into view again, and it attached itself to the already conjoined DeWitts. His right cheekbone melded with the DeWitts' single long eyebrow.

"Mr. Clayton," Armstrong said, "do you know how we caught the Unabomber?" His voice sounded like Tom Brokaw.

Danny thought this must be a trick question. "With solid detective work?" he asked.

Even with Armstrong's face melded to the DeWitts', it was clear that he still wasn't smiling. "We caught the Unabomber," he said, "because he became envious. A bigger bomb set off by an even sicker bastard in Oklahoma City got a lot of media attention, and the

Unabomber was annoyed that this attack and this bastard were getting so much more publicity than he ever did. So he sent manifestos to major newspapers and made more bombs. As a result, his brother recognized his rhetoric in the manifestos and alerted us, and the new bombs in his shack provided evidence. His need for attention did him in." Armstrong paused, and when he spoke again his voice was low. "You see, Mr. Clayton, a terrorist doesn't just want to do the crime. A terrorist wants the media to give him airtime for having done it. He wants his cause publicized and his exploits splattered all over the TV, the newspapers, and the World Wide Web."

Danny really wanted to lie back down, but couldn't seem to move. "What does that have to do with the FBI paying for my health care?" he asked. Now even his own voice sounded like a TV personality. He sounded just like Barbara Walters.

The DeWitts leaned closer to him, sucking part of Special Agent Armstrong's face along with them. They were three-eyed now, because the two eyes closest to each other had merged.

"You see, Daniel," the DeWitts said, "we've worked with the FBI before. We've helped them profile abnormal psychologies and predict the behavior patterns of serial killers. But we've also helped them publicize such things when publicity would be useful. And this is just such a case. You had nothing to do with the dreadful attack on Saturday, yet much of the media's attention has been focused on you because of your unusual reaction to the event. So if we can keep you in the public eye, while at the same time providing treatment—"

"The media will keep their cameras on you instead of on the terrorists and whatever their cause might be," Armstrong said. "And that will improve the odds that the bad guys will expose themselves."

Danny squeezed his eyes shut, but he could still see the DeWitt-Armstrong compound face undulating before him.

"You mean they'll be envious of me," Danny said. "Like the

Unabomber was of that other bastard . . . "

He felt himself floating downward, and he opened his eyes to find that Rob Royce was lowering him to the pillows. Strangely, Royce's face wasn't distorted at all. It was chiseled, blue-eyed, and photogenic. Danny hated it a lot.

"Dat's right, Danny honey," Rob Royce said.

He let Danny sink into the pillows, then stepped back and gave him a grim smile.

"We is settin' out a trot line in de muddy wawtah," he said. "En you is gwyne to be de bait."

Sound Bites (3)

Our top story on today's edition of *U.S. Morning* is, once again, "Massacre at Mid-Continent: The Killings in Kansas."

Almost three days after the assault, the death toll has reached eighty-six, and authorities are no closer to discovering the identities of those responsible. FBI spokespersons now say that Daniel Clayton, better known as "Laughin' Boy," was not involved in the attack—but as yet they have no comment regarding who *was* involved.

However, various experts on violent crime and terrorism have proposed their own theories, and we have two of those experts with us this morning. Dr. Emil Jameson is a senior analyst specializing in international terrorism at the Liberty Bell Institute, and Dr. Stanley Milstead is a Professor of Political Science at the University of California at Berkeley. Dr. Jameson joins us via satellite from Langley, Virginia, and Dr. Milstead joins us from San Francisco, California. Gentlemen, good morning.

Good morning, Kathy.

"Good morning, Kathy."

Dr. Jameson, we'll begin with you. Yesterday you said that you believe the Wichita attack was carried out by foreign extremists. What evidence do you have for that?

Kathy, terrorists from or sponsored by Algeria, Libya, Saudi Arabia, Iran, Iraq, Syria, Lebanon, Yemen, Afghanistan, and elsewhere have been plotting to launch such attacks on American soil for years. And now they've managed to pull one off.

Professor Milstead, you're shaking your head. I take it you disagree.

"I certainly do. You may have noticed, in fact, that Dr. Jameson didn't answer your question about evidence. That's because he has none. His assertion is based solely on the kind of prejudice that should have been eradicated from public discourse in this country thirty years ago."

No, my assertion is based on the statements of the terrorists I mentioned—Osama bin Laden, among others—as well as intelligence gathered by sources I'm not at liberty to reveal . . . sources with whom Professor Milstead, with his history of anti-American activities, would not be familiar.

Professor, your response?

"Kathy, I'll ignore Dr. Jameson's reactionary jab at my patriotism, and will instead remind you that he made similar statements regarding "foreign terrorists" in 1995 after the Oklahoma City bombing. He even accused a group of Middle Eastern students at the University of Oklahoma of having committed that atrocity. But when the actual perpetrator of the bombing was discovered, lo and behold, he turned out to be a blond-haired, blue-eyed American."

The only reason those so-called "students" didn't commit the Oklahoma City bombing was because someone beat them to it.

Gentlemen, if we could get back to—

And I'd like to point out that the supposedly "American" terrorist who did commit that bombing had previously spent time in Saudi Arabia, Kuwait, and Iraq.

"That's because he was a U.S. soldier taking part in Operation Desert Storm."

During which time he was brainwashed by Islamic fundamentalists.

"That's ridiculous. However, it does seem that it was during his time in combat that he discovered he enjoyed killing people."

I think you're referring to the fact that he eliminated some Iraqi troops in the course of his duty. After that, however, he was brainwashed into becoming an anti-American assassin—much like the cultists who murdered Sharon Tate in 1969.

That's quite an allegation, Doctor. But what does it have to do with—

It's only the tip of the iceberg, Kathy. With the Wichita Massacre, Islamic terrorists have started an all-out war, and it's only going to get worse for us if we don't strike back now and strike hard. And despite what the FBI says, I believe we'll eventually find that this "Laughin' Boy" person is involved—since, clearly, he too has been brainwashed. And for that, either Arabs or—no offense, Kathy—the U.S. news media are to blame.

Do you have a response, Professor Milstead?

"Well, I used to think that Dr. Jameson was misguided, but now I'm afraid he may be deranged. For one thing, it seems obvious that Laughin' Boy, rather than being a victim of Arab-induced mind control, is simply an unwell man who was in the wrong place at the wrong time. Furthermore, the Wichita Massacre bears all the earmarks of having been perpetrated not by Islamic fundamentalists, but by a Christian militia group based right here in the United States and consisting of American citizens."

I doubt that's the case, but if it is, I guarantee that those American citizens will have been indoctrinated and trained by hostile foreigners dedicated to the destruction of the United States—much like the hippies who killed Dr. Jeffrey MacDonald's wife and children in 1970. And they certainly won't be Christians.

Gentlemen, I'm afraid we're out of time, but—

"Kathy, I can't let this end without defending myself. Dr. Jameson knows that I once had long hair and that I demonstrated against the Vietnam War, so he's insinuating that I and people like me are murderous, anti-American— "

"Acid is groovy," Professor." Sound familiar?"

"This is so ludicrous, I'm about to start laughing myself."

And now I'm afraid we really are out of time, gentlemen, and I thank you both. This is *U.S. Morning,* and we'll be back right after these words.

You and your comrades tend to laugh and giggle quite a lot, don't you, Milstead?

"Jameson, any time you want a piece of— "

(Blip)

This morning on *Hello, America!* we're examining one of the more troubling questions to arise from the Wichita Massacre: Did the pervasive influence of violent films, video games, television shows, and other media cause a group of teenage boys to obtain firearms, dress up in camouflage fatigues, and go on a killing spree? And was the shocking spectacle of Laughin' Boy indicative of the callousness that results from repeated exposure to such violent media?

Our guests for this segment are Dr. Felicia Yankow, a nationally renowned expert on teen violence; Mr. Irving Metz, an attorney representing the National Free Speech Coalition; and Mr. Butch Schlammer, president of Ozone Army Software and creator of the popular computer games *Giblet Frenzy, Giblet Frenzy II,* and *Ultimate Giblet Frenzy: Maximum Guttage.* They join us via satellite from Washington, St. Louis, and Chicago, respectively.

First of all, Dr. Yankow, why do you contend that the perpetrators of the Wichita Massacre were teenagers?

Not just teenagers, Debra, but either teenaged males or males in their early twenties. I've come to this conclusion because the Massacre echoes the misogynistic murder fantasies that are continually marketed to boys in the guises of movies and video games. I would add that Mr. Schlammer's games are especially vile offenders. All three of the games you mentioned involve armed men opening fire on crowds of innocent people, predominantly women. Furthermore, the bloody results of these virtual attacks are often made out to be funny. Victims twitch, gibber, and flop while virtual spectators laugh at them—and the real-world results are events like the Wichita Massacre and people like Laughin' Boy.

Mr. Schlammer, how do you respond to that?

"I guess I respond by pointing out that the ratio of female to male targets in my games is almost precisely one to one, that watching bad guys flop and twitch is funny, and that I drive a Ferrari thanks to millions of satisfied, law-abiding customers. So I must be doing something right."

My counter-response, Debra, is that the female "targets" in Ozone Army products are deliberately made more colorful and provocative in order to draw fire, and that forty-five of the eighty-six victims in the Wichita Massacre were women and girls. And none of the victims were "bad guys," yet Laughin' Boy laughed anyway, just like a character in an Ozone Army game. As for Mr. Schlammer's Ferrari, well, I've observed that arms merchants and drug dealers make a lot of money, too.

Dr. Yankow, are you comparing computer games to illegal weapons and drugs?

Wherever effects are similar, comparisons of causes are inevitable.

Debra, may I interject?

Certainly, Mr. Metz.

Thank you. I have to jump in because Dr. Yankow is failing to recognize a key difference between the items she's mentioned. Computer games, unlike guns and drugs, are media for creative expression. They therefore constitute free speech, and are protected under the Constitution.

Mr. Metz, is it free speech when someone threatens to shoot another person in the head? No, it's a terroristic threat. So why should we consider it free speech when a piece of technology actually teaches its user what weapons and behaviors to employ in order to carry out such a threat?

Because we're not talking about terrorist training camps, Ms. Yankow. We're talking about games made for entertainment purposes. They are neither realistic nor meant to be so.

"Whoa, I have to disagree with that. I can't speak for other companies, but Ozone Army goes to great lengths to ensure that our games are ultra-realistic, right down to the make and caliber of the shotguns and assault rifles. And the same goes for their specific effects on, for example, a bus full of Catholic schoolgirls."

You see, Debra? He's gotten wealthy from promoting misogynistic atrocities, and he's proud of it!

"What's wrong with being proud? Do you have any idea how brilliant your code has to be to make a virtual head explode just like a real one? Just consider the San Diego Zoo sequence in *Giblet Frenzy II*: The player has to shoot a lion, a zebra, a hippo, a dingo, a cotton-candy vendor, a rhesus monkey, an ocelot, and a kid in a stroller all in a time span of about thirty seconds. That's eight different kinds of blood, bone, and tissue right there!"

Which leads us to a related issue, Mr. Schlammer. How do you feel about placing warning labels and age ratings on your games? And what about the idea of coloring the blood green or blue so that it's obvious the targets aren't meant to represent real living things?

"I love the ratings, Debra, because telling a kid that he isn't old enough for something only makes him want it more. In fact, *Giblet Frenzy* sales have tripled since we added the rating stickers. As for pretending that the targets are zombies with green blood or something, man, that's just wussing out. And we don't wuss out at Ozone Army. You don't have to be a zombie to be a bad guy, and our games acknowledge that."

What about "kids in strollers"?

"Okay, I should have clarified that. The kid in the stroller is actually a midget who works for the Russian Mafia. You have to kill him, or he wastes you with an Uzi hidden inside his snuggle bunny."

You have a comment, Mr. Metz?

Yes, Debra, I'd like to note that I personally don't like Mr. Schlammer's games. However, they are protected speech, so I'll continue to defend them as such.

How can you defend something that teaches young men that violence and murder are just fine and dandy?

Dr. Yankow, no computer game has ever killed anyone. Furthermore, a certain percentage of young people managed to commit violent acts long before computer games, comic books, gangsta rap, or movies existed. Besides, if we start banning things like Giblet Frenzy, we'll wind up banning things like Romeo and Juliet—which, after all, presents teenage role models who rebel against their parents, engage in violence, have sex, and commit suicide.

That comparison is so bizarre as to be unworthy of comment. As if any of these hideous simulations of carnage deserved to be compared to Shakespeare!

"Actually, that's my next project."

What do you mean, Mr. Schlammer?

"I mean Ozone Army's next release will be *Butch Schlammer Presents William Shakespeare's Blood, Bones, and Babes*. See, since Shakespeare's been so popular in the movies these past few years, we figured his stuff was a natural for gaming. And hey, it's all in the public domain, so we can do whatever we want with it!"

This is sickening.

"No, it's gonna be amazing! There are thirty-seven levels, see, and each level's based on a different play in the canon, right? So on one level, you'll have to waste Hotspur! On another, you'll cast spells with the Weird Sisters! On another, you'll have to hold Ophelia underwater so she can't change her mind! You'll seduce Cleopatra! You'll chop up Tamora's boys and cook 'em in a humongous pie! You'll wipe out the entire French army!"

Unbelievable.

"But the coolest thing is that you won't be limited to the weapons available in Shakespeare's time. As you gather talismans—Yorick's skull, for example—you'll be able to update your arsenal. So you might wind up taking out the French with a Gatling gun. Or hand grenades."

And then, Mr. Schlammer, you'll have succeeded in recreating the Wichita Massacre at Agincourt. What an accomplishment.

"Thanks. I might buy a Lamborghini."

We're almost out of time. Any final comment, Dr. Yankow?

Yes. I believe that when the perpetrators of the Wichita Massacre are apprehended, they will be found to be teenaged boys who play violent computer games. And after listening to Mr. Schlammer, I feel confident that they'll be big fans of his . . . as will Laughin' Boy, who also seemed to find human carnage a matter for amusement.

Mr. Metz?

All I can say is that the Bill of Rights extends to every form of expression, whether we like it or not. Or the person who made it.

Mr. Schlammer, you'll have the last word.

"Hey, I'd just like to let Laughin' Boy know that I'll hire him as a play-tester. But other than that, Debra, all I want to say is that I've really enjoyed being your guest this morning. And if you're ever in Chicago, give me a call. I'll let you play the Shakespeare demo—and then I'll give you a glimpse of what we'll do after that: *Butch Schlammer's Battles of the Cyber-Bible*. Then you can be the first, virtually speaking, to slaughter Philistines with the jawbone of a robotic ass, to napalm the Sodomites, to nuke Jericho, or to slice off John the Baptist's head with a laser. You might even get to nano-crucify a troublemaker or two, if you make it to the top level."

Thank you, but—

"And then I'll take you out to dinner. Ever ridden in a Lotus?"

Newsgroup Posts (3)

Subject: Animals Killed in Massacre?
From: meatfree@veggie.com (M.T. Free)
Date: 2000/05/23
Message-ID:
<meatfree76TRMBN9300.BGPR22@veggie.com>
Newsgroups: talk.usnews.gun-violence

I have watched various videos of the Witchita Massacre several times over and am concerned that while animals were almost certainly killed in this event we have seen no such mention on any news reports. Only people are shown and talked about, as if animals' lives weren't as precious to them as ours are to us. This was a park setting and many people take their dogs or ferrets to parks, and it is clear in the videos that some of the dead people are holding things that look like leashes, except there is no dog or ferret at the end that we can see because the end is offscreen or the scene cuts away too fast to tell. Has anyone out there heard if any such animals were killed or wounded in this Witchita event, and if so, if any of the wounded animals or animals whose people were killed or wounded might need adoption? Also, I just want to say that a friend of mine says she has read an article in Time or Newsweek where it says that this Laughin' Boy person was known to torture animals, specifically shooting sparrows and mice with bb guns, as a child. She also says she heard that this Laughin' Boy eats alot of red meat like cow steak and likes it raw and bloody because he finds it amusing. So once again the fact that animal torture & meat-eating go hand-in-hand with other sick behavior is made clear. But anyway, what about the hurt animals in Witchita?

Subject: Re: Animals Killed in Massacre?
From: vichitjr@camelot.org (Vic H. Jr.)
Date: 2000/05/23
Message-ID: <vichitjr-8375309.BR549@camelot.org
Newsgroups: talk.usnews.gun-violence

In article <76TRMBN9300.BGPR22@veggie.com>, M.T. Free <meatfree@veggie.com> wrote:
>Witchita

It's Wichita, not Witchita. As for whether any animals were killed in the Wichita (not Witchita) Massacre, I have no idea. But since the best theory I've heard about who the shooters were says that they were PETA activists angry about all the hot dogs and barbecue being consumed at the River Fest, it's probable that if any animals were killed, it was animal lovers who did it.

Also, I lived in Wichita (not Witchita) for years, and I doubt that anyone there would TOUCH a ferret, much less take one for a walk. (A weasel by any other name . . .)

Finally, a rare steak isn't amusing. It's DELICIOUS.

Web Surfing [Graphics Disabled] (2)

<click> *Connecting to HTTP server . . .*

Today is Wednesday, May 24, 2000. The time is 8:43:27 GMT. You are Visitor Number 167742 since Monday, May 22, 2000 at 22:36:18 GMT when this site went online.

You have reached the unofficial Wichita Massacre Web Site. This site has been created and is being maintained anonymously. It is compiled from various sources, all of which are checked for accuracy. To point out errors or report dead links, send e-mail to anon016@wantodanet.net.

Some of the following links lead to sites out of this Webmaster's control, so please be sure of your location before reporting errors to this site.

Current Contents:

Editorial: Are the WM and "Laughin' Boy" Evidence That We Are in the Last Days?

Sequence of Events on May 20

Upcoming TIME Magazine article

Quotes from Other News Sources, plus Links (CNN, Washington Post, ABC, Wichita Eagle, AOL, etc.)

Map of Massacre Site

Wichita and other Kansas Links

Terrorist Theories

Teenager Theories

Militia Theories

U.S. Military Theories

Disgruntled Employee Theories

"Fifteen Lone Gunmen" Theory

Laughin'-Boy-as-Assassin Theory

Comparisons of WM to Littleton and Waco

Interviews with Survivors

Interviews with Family Members of Victims

Interviews with Reporters Regarding How Reporters Have Been Reporting the Story

Interviews with Parents and Ex-Wife of Laughin' Boy

Other Laughin' Boy-related Links (more all the time)

Current Victim Roster <click>

The death toll in the Wichita Massacre Stands at 86. Victims are listed in their apparent order of death, and victims with known Web links are highlighted. (Information about additional such links would be welcome.)

1. Elizabeth Engel, 43
2. Edward Engel, 46
3. **Carlos Braun**, 23
4. Emma Geis, 55
5. **Julia Wells**, 48 <click>

Julia Wells, Journalist and Novelist:

After studying Journalism at the University of Kansas, I embarked on a career as a newspaper reporter—first in Fort Scott, Kansas, and then in Joplin, Missouri. Now, having wound up in Wichita, Kansas through circumstances I'd rather forget, I've shifted my career track from full-time journalism to freelance writing. Currently, I'm a stringer for the *Kansas City Star*, and I also contribute book reviews to the *Star* and other publications.

Primarily, though, I've been writing mysteries and thrillers. I've completed five novels, but so far have had no luck finding a literary agent who isn't too booked up (!) to take me on. (Note: This is one of the drawbacks of living in Wichita instead of New York. Don't get me started.)

So, in the hope of attracting an agent or editor, I've uploaded the texts of my first two novels to this site. And who knows—even if you aren't an agent or editor, you might want to take a look anyway!

To read my first novel, a murder mystery entitled *The Siamese Paw-Print Conundrum*, <Click Here>.

For my second novel, a techno-thriller about genetic engineering and international intrigue entitled *The Deadly Feline Sequence*, <Click Here>.

For pictures of my cats, Clarissa and Matisse, <Click Here>.

<Back>

6. Bettina Haskel, 22

7. David R. Jones, 24

8. Richard Jenkins, 39

9. Carol Middleton, 36

10. Peggy Johnson, 27

11. **Catherine Collins**, 17

<click>

Hi! This is the home page of **Cathy Collins**.

I am a senior at Valley Center High in Valley Center, Kansas, and am planning to go to Kansas State University in the Fall of 2000. I don't know what I'll major in yet, but I think I would like to wind up in banking or finance. Or I might go in a completely opposite direction and be a photographer—either news, fashion, or sports.

Some of my photos are in the 2000 VCHS Yearbook. For samples from the yearbook, <Click Here>. For other pictures (family stuff, party stuff, a picnic, etc.), <Click Here>.

The cute guy with the dark hair and glasses in the party pictures is my boyfriend, James. He's going to K-State in the fall, too, majoring in Business. (He'll be a millionaire by the time he's 23—I'm no fool!!!)

<Back>

12. James Byron, 18

13. **Ronald Pierce**, 26

14. Angela Braun, 23
15. Sally Mason, 28
16. Jameel Farouk, 26
17. Alice Foster, 8
18. **Roy Schuur**, 54

<click>

Professor Schuur's Office Hours are 8:30-10:00 AM MWF and 2:00-4:00 PM TTh, or by appointment.

Required Texts for Professor Schuur's section of ENGL 443 for Spring 2000 are as follows: Twain, *Letters from the Earth*; Lewis, *The Screwtape Letters*; Novello, *The Lazlo Letters*; Cheever, *Collected Letters*;

<Back>

19. Diane Johnson, 17
20. Karen Webb, 14
21. Brenda Driver, 14
22. Frances Smythe, 53
23. **Raymond Crandall**, 24

<click>

Here are DEL MAYNOR and the WALKIN' BLUES, the hottest lickin' and loudest honkin' BLUES BAND in WICHITA, not to mention the WHOLE DAMN MIDWEST (yeah, that's right, including Chicago and Kansas City)! To hear a few bars of "Down and Out on Douglas Avenue," the title cut from their very first CD, <Click Here>.

For upcoming gigs and booking info, <Click Here>. You'll be glad you did! Reasonable Rates, Satisfaction Guaranteed!

DEL MAYNOR and the WALKIN' BLUES are: Del "Da Lips" Maynor, vocals and harmonica—Carlos "Killer" Braun, guitar—Ray "Say Hey" Crandall, guitar and backing vocals—Bobby "Too Blue" Benson, bass and backing vocals—and Ronnie "Punchin'" Pierce, drums.

Playing smokin' originals and rockin' faves, Del and the boys

<Back>
24. Curtis Burrell, 34
25. John Sanderson, 33
26. William Wayne, 7 months
27. **Sarah Wayne**, 29 <click>

I write this simple song
For my **husband** and my **son**
Who give me hope and joy
Through the night and through the dawn
May **Jesus** bless this family
In our travels or at home
And may our humble prayers
Please the **Lord** upon His throne

<Back>
28. Daniel Wayne, 34
29. **William Patterson**, 4

<click>

An Online Album for Grandparents, Aunts, Uncles, and Admirers of William L. Patterson (Child Genius).

<Click Here> for the William L. Patterson Milestone Timeline (featuring the fastest toilet training since Mozart); <Click Here> for Chronological Photo Gallery (including a dramatic re-creation of the moment of WLP's First Step); <Click Here> for Preschool Highlights (including Cookie Day and Graduation); and <Click Here> for a video (with sound) of William L. Patterson telling his very first Knock Knock Joke (said joke having been authored by WLP himself, and involving monkeys).

<Back>
30. Phyllis Islington, 62
31. Norma Engles, 50
32. Henry Patterson, 31
33. **Robert Benson**, 25
34. Desiree Wood, 41

35. Allen Hall, 43

36. **David Meyers**, 34 <click>

This site, created and maintained by Dave Meyers, is a tribute to the goddess *JENNIFER*ANISTON*, whose beauty and style know no

<Back>

37. Diana Webb, 33

38. **Jeanne Morrison**, 56

<click>

Hello, fellow soccer grand-moms! I've enjoyed "surfing" through your web-circle so much that I've decided to join it myself—and thanks to my granddaughter Karen, who is as skilled at all of this high-tech folderol as she as at kicking goals, I actually have some photos here for your enjoyment. The first one is of me, my daughter Diana, and Karen just before a game. The second is of Karen as she breaks free of the pack and

<Back>

39. Arthur Jefferson, 54

40. Christine Kaminsky, 18

41. Mohammed Hallabin, 42

42. Thomas Woods, 34

43. Patricia Jones, 63

44. Stephen Owens, 58

45. **Dana Irwin**, 21

<click>

Online Resume for DANA J. IRWIN—4722 N. Rock Road, Wichita, Kansas -- (316) 299-0043 -- danajirwin@netlink.net.

Objective: Seeking a position in Internet software consulting, Web page design, or related fields.

Education: Wichita State University, B.S. with Honors, December 1999—Computer Science. Highland Park High School, Topeka, Kansas—Diploma, May 1995. Salutatorian.

Experience: Student Union Computer Lab, WSU, January 1999-December 1999. Assistant Manager.

Freelance Web Page Consultant, February 1996-present.

Shoney's Restaurant, Wichita, June 1995-February 1996. Waitress, Cashier, and Hostess.

Honors, Activities, and Achievements: <Click Here>

<Back>

46. Rose Thompson, 72

47. Jean Morton, 37

48. Hugh Cregg, 48

49. Jane Peters, 33

50. Joseph Ryan, 12

51. **Barry Bickel**, 12

<click>

My best friend Joe and I are in Tae Kwon Do together, and Master Lee says we are at exactly the same skill level. Joe says I am better and that Master Lee is feeding us BS, but I don't know, Joe is pretty good. Here is a picture of me and Joe sparring. Joe has black gloves. Mine are red.

<Back>

52. Lawrence Bickel, 42

53. Virginia Nelson, 6

54. Vera Palmer, 61

55. **Frederick Adair**, 15

<click>

Eight Short Films by F. Jason Adair: 1. Fat Cop Eats Ice Cream <Click Here> 2. Dog Takes a Dump on Church Lawn <Click Here> 3. An Old Man Kisses an Old Woman at the Library <Click Here> 4. My Dad "Rocks Out" to Jimi Hendrix <Click Here> 5. Erica Freaks Because I'm in Her Closet <Click Here> 6. Mom Finds a Decomposing Squirrel in the Laundry Hamper <Click Here> 7. Junior Varsity Cheerleader Pyramid Collapses <Click Here> 8. Zits <Click Here>

<Back>

56. Martin Adair, 49
57. Norma Mortenson, 54
58. Roberta Andrews, 28
59. Ronald Baker, 30
60. Thomas Bethel, 34
61. **Dawn Garrison**, 39

<click>

Dawn's Kansas Gallery: Six years ago, after my divorce, I began taking weekend drives around the Sunflower State with no goal in mind other than getting away for some alone time. In the process, though, I found there's a lot of beauty here—a fact I never realized while growing up.

So here are some of my favorite photographs from six years of weekend drives. The more famous sites are here, of course—the Statehouse, the courthouse in Cottonwood Falls, the Keeper of the Plains statue in Wichita—but my personal favorites are of rock fences, windmills, the Flint Hills, old stock barns and grist mills, river-bottom glades, cottonwood seeds in the air, and

<Back>

62. Anne Fowler, 40
63. Donald Fowler, 37
64. Martha Fowler, 11
65. Mary Fowler, 11
66. Paula Smith, 36
67. **Leonard Alvin**, 66

<click>

This is my father, Leonard Alvin, who was among the dozens killed on Saturday, May 20 at South Riverside Park in Wichita, Kansas.

He had just retired from Raytheon (formerly Beechcraft) as an assembly-line sheet-metal specialist five months ago. He was an avid skeet shooter and fisherman, and he had planned to spend a lot of time engaged in those activities in his retirement years. He had hoped that his friend Louis Lindley would accompany him on many of his adventures. Mr. Lindley was with him at the park on Saturday, and also died.

Since the death of my mother seven years ago, the thought of retirement and the freedom it would bring became foremost in my father's mind. It was the only way he could cope with the loss. And now that his moment had finally come, it was taken away from him.

A double funeral for my father and Louis will be held on Wednesday, May 24, at 2:00 PM at Grace Baptist Church in Augusta. Anyone who knew these fine men is encouraged to attend to share your reminiscences.

After the funeral, I intend to dedicate my life to the punishment of those responsible for the events of May 20. I include both the gunmen and "Laughin' Boy" in this promise. My father's death was not funny. Nor was his life, which was composed of equal parts hard work and dignity.

I am offering a personal reward of $5000 for information revealing the identities of any or all of the gunmen.

As for Laughin' Boy, I am pledging another $5000 toward any lawsuit that I and/or others may be able to bring against him. What he did may not be prosecutable in a criminal court, but it for damn sure ought to be worth a civil suit. I would appreciate advice regarding this possibility.

Interested attorneys or potential co-plaintiffs may contact me at dougealvin@stefcorp.com.

I have lost my father, and my children have lost their grandfather . . . all because he went to the park to enjoy his retirement.

I swear this crime will not go unpunished.

<Back>

68. Louis Lindley, 68

69. Margaret Reed, 25
70. Donna Petersen, 23
71. Michelle Prince, 17
72. **Susanne Rivers**, 16

<click>

Susanne's Journal:

Friday, May 19, 2000. School will be out in a few weeks, and then my final summer of "freedom" will begin. By that I mean that I won't have to get a job unless I want to, and I won't have to worry about heading off to college in the fall. I have one more year of high school, and it's always been easy and fun. So no pressure, right?

Except that I feel different than I used to. I feel like I should be doing something, but I don't know what. My mother says that I should use this summer just to have fun, since it may be the last time in my life that there's nothing else I have to do. But when I think of all the things I might do to have fun, either by myself or even with friends like Jen and Kelli, it all sounds kind of pointless. Not horrible, you understand. Just more of the same. And I feel different, so I want something different too.

Maybe what I want is to go somewhere. Europe or something. Travel around. Ride the trains. Sleep in hostels. Go up the Eiffel Tower. See the Crown Jewels and the exact spot where Anne Boleyn was beheaded. Flirt with guys in Luxembourg (to name but one of many countries that may contain flirtable guys).

But my mother says no way for this year. She makes enough money that she says I don't have to work, but not enough to send me to Europe.

So here comes another summer in Wichita. Maybe I should get a job just for the fun of it, if I can find one that's fun. I could work at the Gap, and sooner or later I'd see everyone I know. But I don't know if you can work at the Gap when you're 16. I'll be 17 in July, though.

Or maybe I should do volunteer work. My mother used to be a candy-striper at St. Francis when she wasn't much older than I am. If they still have that, or some similar program, maybe I should try it. That might also help me decide whether I really want to be a doctor—or if, as my mother claims, I only got interested in medicine because of George Clooney.

I don't know. I just feel like something has to happen.

I don't think it has to do with guys.

But I do have a date tomorrow with an "older" guy. My mother was dubious, but then I pointed out that it's not like he's 25. He's 19. But he's in college. He goes to Friends University. He told me, however, that he's not a Quaker—as if I really thought you had to be Quaker to go to Friends.

Actually, it was kind of funny the way he said it. He didn't make it sound like he thought I was stupid.

It'll be an okay date, I'm sure, but I don't think I'll go out with him again. That might sound awful before we've gone out even once, but that's what I'm thinking. There's nothing wrong with him. He's a nice guy. (He really is. I don't want him to find my Web site, read this, and think I hate him or something.) It's just a feeling I have that nothing right now is going to be very permanent.

I'm getting a lot of those kinds of feelings lately. I wouldn't mind too much if I knew what to do about them.

<Back>

73. Charles Young, 18

74. **Delbert Maynor**, 27

75. Jennifer Tracy, 19

76. Edith Atkins, 35

77. **Jonathan McGrath**, 44

<click>

My attempt to trace my family history prior to its Kansas period has not been too fruitful, despite all of the help now available on the Internet.

The problem in my case is that the name "McGrath" has been the legal name of my family only since 1878, when my great-great-grandfather Moses McGrath gathered up his wife, children, and orphaned nephews and left the plantation-turned-sharecropping farm in Mississippi that had been his family's "home" since the early part of the century.

"McGrath" was not the name of the original plantation owners, however, nor of the profiteering carpetbaggers who purchased it after the war. As a result, I cannot even be sure just where in Mississippi the plantation was located. But my elders, and their elders, have always said that it was definitely in Mississippi.

According to family legend, "McGrath" was the surname of an elderly white widow-woman who gave Moses and his family food and shelter during six days of hard weather in the course of their trek. But that is as far as the story of the widow-woman goes. I cannot even venture a guess as to whether her home was located in Mississippi, Louisiana, Arkansas, or Missouri. It is unlikely, in fact, that Moses himself could have said just where it was—for he was an "Exoduster" walking to the Promised Land of Kansas, and everything between his journey's beginning and its end was still the hateful Old South. And that was a place he was determined to leave behind forever . . . along with slavery, sharecropping, and even the name of his former master.

The widow McGrath may have been a white Southerner, but she also must have been a kind and generous person indeed for Moses to honor her by taking her name and giving it to his family. I carry it to this day, as I carry the admonition my grandfather gave me during my justifiably angry youth: "Now Jonny, we know for a fact there are a *few* good white folks. If there weren't, Moses might not have made it to Nicodemus, and you might not be here at all."

Moses McGrath and his wife Mary, along with their four children and three nephews, arrived in the African-American settlement of Nicodemus in Graham County, Kansas, in April 1878. They found a town composed of dugout houses on a forbidding plain that

<Back>

78. Joyce Stevens, 54

79. Ruby Franklin, 74

80. Tina Gaines, 5

81. Gordon Gaines, 39

82. **Arnold Steck**, 69

<click>

Following are stills from the video of the Wichita Massacre shot by victim Arnold Steck and featuring Massacre survivor Daniel Clayton, aka "Laughin' Boy." For an MPEG file containing the most graphic and damning 4.2 minutes of the video, <Click Here>.

<Back>

83. Harold Robinson, 72

84. Natalie Jenkins, 22

85. Michael Spears, 55

86. Randall Franklin, 8

The final four victims on this list lived through the attack, but have since died in the hospital from their wounds. Eighteen others remain hospitalized, but as of May 24, all are expected to survive. Three, however, may spend the rest of their lives as para- or quadriplegics.

<Click Here> for details.

<click> *Logging Off.*

Therapy Transcript (4)

(Laughter deleted)

No more injections. Please. I'll take the pills if I have to, but the shots are too much. They keep the laughing down, all right, but the side effects knock me on my ass. The last one made everyone look like fish. You were a carp, Dr. Carla. Dr. Ralph was an eel. A moray, with all those sharp teeth.

I have a problem with drugs anyway. In my family, medicine of any kind was seen as a last resort. And going to the doctor was an outright sign of weakness. I don't remember my father ever being sick, and my mother made it a point of pride to suffer through her endless head colds without complaint. Well, not without complaint. But without treatment.

She went to a doctor just once that I remember, and that was because of the miscarriage she had when I was eight. I didn't know that was what had happened, of course. I hadn't even known she was pregnant. I only heard about it months later, when one of my aunts opened her big mouth at a Christmas potluck and asked Mom if she and Dad were still "trying for another" after losing "the little girl."

I don't know whether there was any real certainty that the baby would have been a girl. But the fact that my aunt referred to it that way gave me the idea that Mom had wanted a girl in the first place, but got stuck with me instead.

No wonder we couldn't connect.

As for Dad . . . well, I don't think Dad ever connected with anyone, much less me. He was an alien. Something funny or sad would happen on TV, so I'd laugh or cry—and he'd look at me as if I had farted in church. Or, more to the point, as if I had farted in church and he had never heard a fart before. And whenever he'd give me that look, he'd shake his head and mutter "God have mercy," or something like that. God and my father have kept up a dialogue based on mutual bewilderment for four or five decades now.

Considering his roots, though, Dad was a model parent. I mean, if he was from Mars, then Grandpa was from Neptune. On one rare visit, I listened to that old man brag about shooting a stray cat and her kittens, and then I watched him drink Red Man spittle from a Folgers coffee can. So I think it was probably a miracle that Dad turned out well enough to live a decent life among other human beings. To expect him to also laugh or cry at the same things as other human beings, or to react to his own son with anything other than confusion, would be asking too much.

Mom, on the other hand, did laugh or cry at the same things on TV that I did. But then she'd stop all at once, and instead of giving me a look like the one I'd get from Dad, she wouldn't look at me at all. This sort of thing happened most often on Saturday evenings, and she'd be extra fervent about getting to church the next morning.

Church was always important to Mom, but she wasn't on a first-name basis with God the way Dad was. Her relationship with the Almighty was more that of an airplane pilot's relationship with the control tower. She had a checklist, and she was determined to verify each dutiful-Christian item before requesting permission to take off. But she never seemed to get through the list. She was never satisfied that everything was perfect.

Meanwhile, I was the ill-behaved little boy that someone had let up into the cockpit.

Now stop right there, Dr. Carla. I was using an airplane as a metaphor for my mother's spiritual life. I don't care if flying usually symbolizes sex. It doesn't in this case. Trust me.

Okay, so Mom and Dad did it at least twice that I know of. But if Dad said "God" at any point, it was because he was puzzled. And if Mom said it, it was because she was thinking of asking for permission for something . . . but could never quite get to the actual request.

No, sex was never central to anything in my family.

That role was filled by television.

More often than not, TV didn't just bring us the world. Instead, it *was* the world.

Books were sound baffles in the school library. Newspapers and magazines were for stacking up and giving to paper drives. Even radio was nothing more than something to fiddle with on boring car trips to Christmas potlucks. What mattered, what was real, was Arnold's Drive-In. Morley Safer and Mike Wallace. A girl who could turn the world on with her smile. Jacques Cousteau. The bluest skies you've ever seen, in Seattle. Couldn't get that in the "real" world, now, could you? Or on radio, either.

No offense. I know that you and Dr. Ralph have made your name in radio. But even the two of you are branching out into television now, aren't you? In fact, sometimes I think that's why you've taken me on. Because I can be your ticket to the tube.

I'm sorry. That wasn't fair. If not for you, I'd be out on the street. Where I'd last less time than the opening shot in a music video.

And we're back to TV. It only makes sense, I suppose, that my televised fit turned me into Laughin' Boy. In many ways, TV made me everything I was before that moment. So if I was going to become anything else, it was up to TV to take care of that too.

Boy howdy, didn't it, though?

Okay, so we'll talk about that later. You want to stay on the childhood stuff for now, huh?

Jesus Christ, I'm sorry I used the airplane thing. Maybe a better image for my mother's life would be a train unable to leave the station . . . but no, that's even worse.

Stuck with a son, Mom tried for a while to bond with me the way that she had probably hoped she would bond with a girl. But her attempts in this area didn't get too far.

An example. Of course, you want an example. Well, I don't want to give one.

No, it has nothing to do with sex!

Okay, then.

It was a Saturday in July, a bright Wichita summer morning, and I was nine. I was sitting on the floor in the living room watching cartoons, same as I always did on Saturday mornings. But I don't remember precisely what I was watching at the moment Mom came into the room. Could have been *Huckleberry Hound. Rocky and Bullwinkle.* Or *The Amazing Spider-Man.* Remember the song? "Spider-Man, Spider-Man, does what-ever a spider can . . . Something something, something something . . . Action is his re-ward . . . Look Out! Here comes the Spider-Man . . ."

Mom came in and said she wanted to go for a walk, and that she wanted me to go with her. She stood there looking down at me and said it was too nice a day to start it off by sitting in the house, and that I watched too much TV anyway.

I must have looked up at her with the same I-can't-believe-you-farted-in-church expression that Dad always gave me. And then she reached over my head and turned off the TV. There was a snap and a crackle, like breakfast cereal, and then the screen went black except for a shiny dot in the middle that lasted for a few seconds before fading.

It was confusing. The TV was hardly ever off. But since it was, I got up off the floor and went for the walk with Mom. I didn't know what else to do.

When we stepped outside, our dog, Buster, came bounding up and then went on the walk with us.

Didn't I mention that we had a dog back then? Well, we did. He was a big black and tan shepherd mix with floppy ears and a tongue the size of Florida.

You see, I didn't really spend all day every day watching TV. I did play outside some. When there was nothing on. And when I wanted to spend time with Buster.

This was back in the days when, in the suburbs, almost nobody kept their dogs in a fenced yard. A few people used chains, but that made their dogs go nuts and bark all night. So most of the mutts in our suburb ran free. It was a bad system, but that was what everybody did.

Buster was known for blocks around. He played with everybody's kids, and hung around at a polite distance waiting for scraps whenever anyone had a barbecue. But he was our dog, and he came back to our house every night.

He probably would have stayed closer to home the rest of the time if I hadn't been inside watching TV so much. So what happened on that morning in July was really my fault. Not Mom's. All Mom wanted was to go for a walk.

So we went for a walk, and Buster came along. He was happy beyond happy that Mom and I were both outside at the same time and doing something that he could do with us. He bounced along beside us as if on springs.

Block after block, Mom would point out the houses of the people we knew from church and tell me what was going on in their lives. And Buster would run up into their yards and back again, then take off ahead of us until he was almost out of sight before coming back again. Mom laughed at his goofiness, and I laughed too. We were beginning to have fun. Even without TV. Just me, Mom, and Buster walking past the neighbors' houses on a sunny morning, dodging sprinkler spray and speculating on what some of the people in the houses might be if they weren't Methodists.

Then we came to the edge of the neighborhood, to U.S. Highway 81, and Buster ran out onto it before we could turn around and head back.

I saw the car hit him. It was green. It hit him hard and carried him on its grille for I don't even know how far before he fell underneath.

The next thing I remember is Mom pinning me down in the ditch. I guess I'd started to run up onto the highway, so she'd tackled me. Twenty seconds before we'd been laughing. But now she was crying, and I was screaming.

That was the last time my mother ever tried to take me away from the TV so we could go do something else together.

And all of that reminds me: The last time I saw Lindy, she asked when she could have a puppy.

I was going to do things better with her, you know. But it's too late for that now. What happened in South Riverside Park has taken my daughter away from me for good. And me from her.

Believe me, I know how selfish I am to be saying that, and I feel ashamed. Because I know that at least Lindy and I are both still here. After all, there were parents and children who lost even more than we did that day.

I know. I saw them. I saw what happened to them.

But that doesn't make my loss any easier to bear. It makes it worse.

It makes it worse because I know that because of what those parents and children lost, and because my reaction was put on TV for all the world to see, my own daughter will never be able to think of me as anything more than Laughin' Boy. Not as long as she lives.

I should have stayed home and watched cartoons.

Sound Bites (4)

. . . so it looks like that's one mama gorilla who gives the phrase "You're grounded!" a whole new meaning.

Over to you, Mark.

Thank you, Lisa.

In the five days since the Wichita Massacre, the mystery posed by Daniel Clayton, the man known as Laughin' Boy, has only deepened—and the clamor from angry citizens has intensified. Who is this callous man, they ask, and what were his motives for behaving so atrociously in the midst of such tragedy?

Our efforts to answer these questions have been frustrated by the fact that Laughin' Boy vanished from public view just one day after the Massacre. But now, at last, we may be able to shed some light on this dark puzzle. For the first time, Laughin' Boy's parents, Donald and Louise Clayton, have consented to be interviewed. They join us this morning from their home in Wichita, Kansas.

Mr. Clayton, let's begin with you. First of all, sir, your son seems to have disappeared. Do you know where he is, and have you been in contact with him?

"God help me, I wouldn't tell you if I did know where he was, which I don't. But he's called once or twice and spoke to Louise."

What did he tell you, Mrs. Clayton?

Not very much. We couldn't talk long because he was having trouble with his voice.

Do you mean he was laughing?

I'd rather not say.

Mr. and Mrs. Clayton, I know this may be a painful topic, but do either of you believe it's possible that your son had anything to do with the terrorist attack itself?

Certainly not.

"God in heaven, no. Danny can't even shoot. I tried to teach him once, and he was awful."

Mr. Clayton, no one has suggested that your son fired any shots. The question is whether he was involved with those who did. After all, almost everyone around him was killed or wounded, yet he remained unhurt. How could that happen?

"God Almighty, how should I know? You tell me."

The speculation, sir, is that the assailants spared your son because they knew him. And if they knew him, then it's possible he knew the attack would take place. Why else would he be at South Riverside Park at the time of the attack, emerge unscathed, and find the deaths so amusing? Why else would he seem so pleased?

"Good God, you people have no room to talk about seeming pleased. You've made a lot of hay out of this 'Laughin' Boy' thing, so you keep yammering about that instead of telling us who really did it. God knows you must have some idea. Don't people like that send you letters and tapes and whatnot to claim responsibility?"

Yes, Mr. Clayton. This network alone has received over six hundred such items since last Saturday, and we've turned them all over to the proper authorities.

"My God, why haven't you been reporting that instead of harping on my son?"

We *have* reported the fact that we've received such items, but the FBI has asked us not to discuss their contents. Besides, how could we determine whether any of the items really came from the terrorists, or whether they were all hoaxes?

"God have mercy, I thought that was your job."

We aren't investigators, Mr. Clayton. We're journalists. Now, *Mrs.* Clayton, are you as angry at the media as your husband seems to be?

Oh, I'm not angry, and neither is Donald. We're just concerned because so much of the attention this week has been on Danny, and Danny didn't do anything.

With all due respect, Mrs. Clayton, how can you be so sure of that?

Because I know him. And my husband is right about Danny never liking guns. Also, he has a little girl, our granddaughter Linda, and he loves her so much. Anyone who ever saw him with her wouldn't be able to think anything awful about him.

On that note, Mrs. Clayton, we'd like you to listen to a few comments from relatives of Massacre victims, and then give us your reactions. Please keep in mind, as you listen, that these people are your fellow Wichitans.

I'm sorry, but I don't—

(Blip)

That was my niece there, dead on the ground and all bloody and mutilated, just a sweet little girl who hadn't done a thing to anybody, and he looked right at her and he laughed, he looked right at her like he was looking at something on television and he just laughed and laughed, and I want to know how a person like that can be allowed to walk around in this world, how a person like that can be allowed to live among decent human beings who love their children and don't think it's funny when monsters come along and kill them. That's what I want to know.

(Blip)

My daughter Sarah was a Christian, so I know she's in Heaven along with my son-in-law Dan and their baby William. But I also know that's why they killed her. A friend of mine who knows someone who was wounded in the Massacre told me that this wounded man said the terrorists walked through the crowd asking people if they were Christians, and when they said they were, they shot them. They were there to kill Christians for sport. And when they came to that Laughin' Boy, they asked him, and he said no, so they killed all the Christians around him so he could laugh for the pleasure of Satan. And I think we ought to send him to be with his infernal master.

(Blip)

The terrorists wore hoods and gloves, but in the clips you can see skin at the wrists and neck and around the eyes. They were white. And I believe that's why they killed my father—because he was black. I know they killed white people too, but while black people were only about ten percent of the crowd, they were almost twenty percent of those killed. What does that tell you about why my father died? What does that tell you about why a white man thought it was the most hilarious goddamn thing he'd ever seen?

(Blip)

I can't talk about my sister. I can't talk about Donna. We had a big fight Saturday morning because she said I used her computer without asking, so I yelled back and said I wouldn't go to the Festival with her because I didn't want to be anywhere near her. But I wish I had. I wish I had gone with her so when that man started laughing, I could have made him stop. I don't know what I would have done, but I would have made him stop.

(Blip)

My son is dead, and someone else's son laughed when he died. I don't know why, but I'll tell you this: If it had been the other way around, my son wouldn't have been amused. My son wouldn't have laughed.

(Blip)

Now, Mrs. Clayton, how do you answer all those grieving families?

All I can say is that Danny must have laughed because it was so awful that he didn't know what else to do, and he lost his mind. And those poor people are only angry with him because they don't know who else to be angry with. They don't know who did it—because you news people won't tell them.

I've already explained that, Mrs. Clayton. As for your suggestion that people are only angry with your son because he's a convenient scapegoat, well, it's not quite that simple, is it? After all, the video shot by the mortally wounded Dr. Arnold Steck seems pretty conclusive about your son's behavior during the Massacre. So, knowing him as you do, what explanation can you give for it?

I just told you, he must have been out of his head, as anyone would be in a situation like that.

Unfortunately, Mrs. Clayton, your son didn't seem "out of his head" to the general public or to the various psychologists and psychiatrists we've interviewed over the past week. To them, he seemed to be having a fine time.

Well, he wasn't. Different people go out of their heads in different ways, and there are some famous psychiatrists right here in my living room who say so.

Pardon me?

You heard me. I have famous psychiatrists right here. So I'm just going to unclip this microphone and give it to Dr. Carla DeWitt. She's on the radio, and millions of people listen to her every week.

Mrs. Clayton, you agreed to an exclusive interview with us, and there was no mention of—

>>Hello, Mark, this is Dr. Carla DeWitt. It's a pleasure to be on your show this morning. But if you'll excuse me for a moment . . . Mr. Clayton, would you mind giving your microphone to my husband, Dr. Ralph DeWitt?<<

"God, yes. I mean, no. I mean, for the love of God, here, take it."

Mr. Clayton, please keep your microphone. I have more questions for you.

I'm sorry, Mark, but this is Dr. Ralph DeWitt, and Mr. Clayton has just handed his microphone to me. He and Mrs. Clayton have authorized Dr. Carla and me to answer for them from this point on.

All right, then. This is against my better judgment, but since my director is telling me to continue, I'll do so. However, I must point out that you've just staged an unconscionable publicity stunt.

>>Do you have any questions for us, Mark?<<

Yes, of course. Dr. Ralph and Dr. Carla, as well-known radio personalities with an equally well-known penchant for publicity, why have you inserted yourselves into this interview today?

Mark, we're here because we wanted to assure Mr. and Mrs. Clayton that their son is not the demon the media have made him out to be. On the contrary, he's a decent man and loving father who is deeply traumatized as the result of the horrors he witnessed at South Riverside Park last Saturday.

And you know this because . . . ?

>>We know this because Mr. Daniel Clayton, aka Laughin' Boy, is now under our care. And we have determined that he suffers from a syndrome that causes involuntary laughter, although it goes much deeper than that.<<

Can you explain?

Indeed we can, Mark, and we'll do so tomorrow in a number of interviews. I believe we're appearing on both the Today show and Howard Stern's radio program in New York, then flying to Chicago for a special live edition of Stan Symmons and Friends! That Chicago show will be especially important because the entire hour will be devoted to three extraordinary patients of ours, including Laughin' Boy.

Dr. Ralph, I must point out that thanks to the tabloids, the Internet, and your own radio show, America is already quite familiar with the bizarre nature of your "extraordinary patients." So aren't you afraid that—

>>Mark, I have to interrupt to point out that in addition to the New York-based programs Dr. Ralph already mentioned, we'll also be stopping by **Regis and Kathie Lee**. Oh, and although our interview in Chicago will be broadcast live at 4:00 PM Central Daylight Time, I'd like to remind viewers to check their local listings. A number of markets shift the Symmons show to a later time slot.<<

Well, I'd like to remind *you*, Doctors, that at the moment you're still on *this* show. So, if I may continue: You've said that Laughin' Boy suffers from a mental disorder, but—

I didn't call it a "mental disorder," Mark. That term has connotations that Dr. Carla and I prefer to avoid.

I'm sure you do. However, Dr. Ralph, the question remains—

>>Mark, all of America's questions about Laughin' Boy will be answered tomorrow. So until then, thank you, and good day.<<

Dr. Carla, we still have a minute or two, and—

Thank you, Mark!

Dr. Ralph? Dr. Carla? Mr. and Mrs. Clayton?

Uh, Phil?

(Blip)

Ladies and gentlemen, we seem to have lost our satellite feed from Wichita, and we apologize for that.

However, despite the fact that our interview with Mr. and Mrs. Clayton was cut short, I believe we can say that two things have become clear:

One, the tragic fallout from the Wichita Massacre will continue for a long time to come.

And two, the strange story of Laughin' Boy is about to become . . . even stranger.

We'll be back right after this.

Newsgroup Posts (4)

Subject: Re: Whodunnit?
From: bigload64@cutnshoot.com (Bill Raynes)
Date: 2000/05/25
Message-ID:
<bigload64-4369WKRP.WOLD82@cutnshoot.com>
Newsgroups: alt.weirdusa.wichita-massacre

Without quoting everything already posted, let me try to summarize our theories so far in the following "bullet points." (Thank you, thank you, I'm here all week.)

With the exception of body-snatcher, space-alien, and other X-Fileish notions, the theories so far seem to be falling into these categories:

1. RELIGIOUS NUTS. The Wichita gunmen were Muslims, Jews, Buddhists, or Christians (various varieties), all of whom are oppressed SOMEWHERE in the world and who often take out their frustration anywhere they can get away with it. [And although I can't imagine any true Buddhist taking up arms, I also can't rule it out. After all, there was a time in history (when Romans were Romans and lions were lions) when no one could imagine any true Christian taking up arms, either. But these days, even Quakers have NRA memberships.]

2. ETHNIC OR FOREIGN NUTS. This has plenty of overlap with Category 1, but also contains folks who don't justify their hatred with the Word of God, but with skin color or dotted lines. We gotcher white folks who hate

nigras an' Jews; we gotcher black folks who hate Whitey an' Jews an' Koreans; we gotcher Native Americans who hate white folks an' black folks (remember the Buffalo Soldiers?); we gotcher A-rabs who hate all of the above; and we gotcher Irish, yer Basques, yer Serbs, yer Croats, and yer Cubans. (A few comments in this thread have also noted that French Canadians have been spotted in Nebraska, just one state up from Kansas.)

3. PATRIOTIC OR ANTI-GOVERNMENT NUTS. The fellers in this slot overlap with both Category 1 and Category 2, but have a charm all their own. Who can forget the wacky shenanigans of the "Freemen," "The Order," the "Posse Comitatus," the "Montana Militia," the "Republic of Texas," or "The Gun, the Sword, and the Arm of the Lord"? In fact, my own money is on some bunch from this category being responsible for Wichita. They tend to be small in number, but they also tend to have weapons, rage, and a fanatical devotion to the Pope. (Or was that the Spanish Inquisition? I always get them and the Posse Comitatus confused.)

4. GOVERNMENT NUTS. The variations on this theory suggest that the ATF, FBI, CIA, DEA, or some other set of Federal initials set up the Wichita Massacre either A. as a way to kill one or two of their enemies (the 80-plus other victims being "collateral damage"); B. as a way to make the public cry out for more Federal cops to protect them from such attacks; or C. as a smokescreen to draw our attention away from what they were REALLY up to. (My own opinion: The Wichita Massacre, although ugly and bloody, was WAY too efficient to have been perpetrated by any Federal agency.)

5. TEENAGE NUTS. Some of you are adamant about this one, but I doubt it. Ever since Columbine, a lot more parents have been keeping an eye out for gun-barrels-on-

dressers, bomb-kits-in-the-garage, and big red X's accompanied by the words "Today We Strike!" on Rammstein wall calendars. I sure hope so, anyway.

6. LAUGHIN' BOY, THE NUT. This theory suggests that Daniel Clayton, "Laughin' Boy," is not some pathetic loser but an evil genius. In other words, he arranged the Massacre—hired mercenaries, provided guns, sewed the outfits, etc.—just so he could appear on TV doing something so wildly unacceptable (and yet not illegal) that he would become just as famous as he's become. But I dunno. It seems to me that if he were smart enough to pull it off, he'd be smart enough to realize that his fame would be INfamy . . . and that a lot of people would therefore want to shoot him just as dead as the Massacre's victims.

Besides, a report today says pop-psychiatrists Ralph and Carla DeWitt claim that Laughin' Boy is neither evil nor a genius. He's just very, very sick . . . and a bit dim.

So if we accept that assertion (and I do), that leaves us with Theory Categories 1 through 5 for discussion.

Or, if you'd rather, we can talk about just what the hell kind of sickness could make someone behave like Laughin' Boy.

Video Clip (3)
Sic Semper Television

Selected segments from the syndicated daytime talk show *Stan Symmons and Friends!*, broadcast live from Chicago on the afternoon of Friday, May 26, 2000:

THEME MUSIC

FADE IN TO:

The silver-haired HOST (down at first-row-AUDIENCE level, looking stern): Good afternoon, ladies and gentlemen, and welcome to this special live edition of *Stan Symmons and Friends!* I'm your host, Stan Symmons.

AUDIENCE: [Cheers, applause, and whistles.]

FADE THEME MUSIC

HOST (adjusting necktie): Thank you. Thank you. Now, we've all seen the videotape shot by that poor dying dentist in Wichita, Kansas last Saturday. We've all seen the nightmare scene that surrounded him—

Cut to AUDIENCE. They are men and women, black and white, yellow and brown, old and young. Their expressions match that of the HOST. Some are nodding as he speaks.

HOST: —and we've all seen the man who was laughing at the carnage.

The AUDIENCE tenses, and their expressions become angrier. Some snarl. Some hiss. Some boo. Some mutter words we can't hear. But we can read their lips.

Cut back to HOST, who steps up onto the stage, where a platform holds five chairs arranged in a curving row. The infamous dying-dentist video of Laughin' Boy begins playing on a giant screen behind the chairs.

HOST: That man doesn't look ill or hysterical, does he? He looks as if he has his wits about him and is *enjoying* what's happening, doesn't he?

AUDIENCE: Yeahhh! [Plus assorted disparaging remarks.]

The video running on the giant screen zooms in and freezes on Laughin' Boy's face. This image will provide a backdrop of blood-streaked hilarity for most of the show.

HOST: Well, our first guests today claim that this so-called "Laughin' Boy" does in fact have a previously unknown mental disorder, and that his behavior is therefore not at all his fault!

AUDIENCE: Booooooo!

HOST: They also claim that two of their other clients suffer from similar disorders, and that these people also bear no moral responsibility for their actions. Yet one of them behaves like a sniggering racist at a cross burning, and the other deliberately makes herself vulnerable to sexual assault!

AUDIENCE: [Disbelieving murmurs.]

HOST: It sounds bizarre, but they swear it's true! So ladies and gentlemen, please welcome renowned radio-show advisors and self-proclaimed Shrinks to the Damned, Drs. Ralph and Carla DeWitt!

The DeWitts emerge from backstage to a chorus of applause, cheers, and denunciations, some of which are pre-recorded and pumped into the studio through loudspeakers. The DeWitts are wearing their trademark his-and-hers gray suits, and they smile and wave as they step up onto the interview platform. They sit down in the second and third chairs from the AUDIENCE's left. DR. CARLA crosses her legs.

The HOST waves the AUDIENCE and the loudspeakers to relative silence, then puts one foot on the platform and leans toward the DeWitts, shaking his head.

HOST: I have to say, Doctors, that the story you're telling sure sounds like more of the same blame-the-other-guy syndrome we've heard for so long now. But most Americans are starting to realize that it's high time people took responsibility for their own behavior. Do you feel otherwise?

DR. CARLA: Not at all, Steve. But the people we're talking about aren't shirking their responsibilities. On the contrary, they're doing their very best to overcome their afflictions.

AUDIENCE: [Skeptical mumbles and an isolated Bronx cheer.]

DR. RALPH: Dr. Carla is absolutely right, Stan. In fact, once America hears the true stories of how these people are struggling for normalcy, I believe they will be seen as heroes.

AUDIENCE: Bahhhh! Booooo!

HOST: Heroes? Really? Do you mean to tell me that you see that man (he indicates the frozen blow-up of Laughin' Boy) as a *hero*?

DR. RALPH (without looking at the blow-up): First of all, please remember that Daniel Clayton is not a suspect in that awful incident. He, like those who died, was simply there to enjoy a carnival. He was, as the cliche goes, an innocent bystander. And his reaction to what happened there was the result of a disorder that Dr. Carla and I are now attempting to treat.

HOST (shaking his head again): I dunno, Doc. His reaction just looks cold-blooded to me. Those people around him—men, women, and children—were torn to pieces, and instead of trying to help them, he yukked it up.

AUDIENCE: Yeah! Yeah! [Applause.]

DR. CARLA (loud enough to be heard over the applause): Steve, those people were beyond help, and Danny Clayton himself—

HOST (scowling at DR. CARLA): My name is Stan.

DR. CARLA: I'm sorry. This is the third show we've done today.

DR. RALPH (grinning): But by far the most important!

The HOST and AUDIENCE laugh, and the AUDIENCE applauds.

HOST: With the best audience in the business!

AUDIENCE: [Goes wild.]

The HOST waits twenty seconds, then waves his hand again to

quiet the AUDIENCE.

HOST: All right, then, Doctors, let's bring out your first, um, *patient* so we can make up our own minds. Ladies and gentlemen, please welcome Ms. Amanda Larkin!

A slender, pale woman with short auburn hair steps out from backstage. She is wearing a plain navy blue pantsuit and flat shoes, and she is carrying a large black purse on a shoulder strap. She looks out at the AUDIENCE with obvious apprehension as she crosses the stage, and she stumbles a bit as she steps up onto the interview platform. She takes the fourth chair, which is beside DR. RALPH.

HOST (moving to crouch in front of the newcomer): Well, Ms. Larkin, I understand that some in the media have taken to calling you "Porno Girl," as if your affliction were a super power of some sort.

AUDIENCE: [Nervous chuckles.]

PORNO GIRL (holding her purse against her abdomen): One of the tabloids did that. I don't care for it much. But it seems to have stuck.

DR. CARLA: I'd also like to point out that it's the tabloids that call me and my husband the "Shrinks to the Damned." We've never referred to ourselves as such.

HOST (ignoring DR. CARLA): So just what is it that's earned you that moniker, Ms. Larkin? I must say that you *look* perfectly normal. In fact, you're quite attractive. But there must be something—

PORNO GIRL (matter-of-factly): I have a compulsion to seek out and view graphic and perverse sexual images. I make use of both photos and videos, as well as images from the Internet, so long as they depict real people performing the most extreme and sometimes repugnant acts imaginable. In order to find such material, I often venture into what most people would consider dangerous, or at least unsavory, neighborhoods and businesses. For reasons of personal safety, I would probably use the Internet exclusively—but too many porn sites on the Web are either too expensive, too tame, have pitiful bandwidth, or use altered images. And part of my problem is that I have to see the real thing in quantity, and I go out of my mind waiting on slow downloads.

AUDIENCE: [Mutters and groans. Some are clearly disapproving, but others merely sound disappointed that PORNO GIRL's affliction is so dull.]

HOST: Have you appeared in pornography yourself?

PORNO GIRL (visibly disgusted at the suggestion): No. I'm an attorney, for crying out loud.

HOST: Well, then, do you have sex with the men you meet in the places where you buy such material?

PORNO GIRL: I don't have sex at all.

AUDIENCE: [Gasp.]

HOST (shocked): You mean you're *celibate*?

PORNO GIRL: I mean I'm a virgin.

AUDIENCE: [Louder gasp. Sounds of disbelief.]

HOST (looking baffled): How old are you?

PORNO GIRL: Thirty-two.

HOST: Do you mean to tell me that you're a thirty-two-year old virgin—and you love *pornography*?

PORNO GIRL: I don't love it. I don't even like it. And I certainly don't experience any sexual impulses as a result of looking at it. I'm not even sure what such impulses would feel like. But ever since I was twenty, I've been compelled to seek out perverted sexual images. If I don't, I become physically ill. I can't eat, and I can't sleep. I have to have it, or my health suffers. After a day, I start throwing up. After two days, I lose bowel and bladder control. In fact, I'm convinced that if I had to go three days or more without at least a glimpse of group sex or double penetration, I would lapse into a coma and die.

AUDIENCE: Wauugggh!

DR. CARLA: You see, Steve? This is a perfectly decent woman in every way. Prudish, even, and intelligent. She finished at the top of her class at Baylor University Law School. She takes no pleasure in her behavior. She is, in fact, essentially asexual. Yet her family has disowned her, and the Dallas law firm that went out of its way to recruit her has now fired her—all because of this compulsion. And the only reason she has been condemned instead of treated with compassion is because her disorder is virtually unique.

DR. RALPH: In other words, Stan, if Ms. Larkin had diabetes, for example, and she required insulin injections to maintain her physical health, no one would think any less of her. But because what she needs, through no fault of her own, is regular exposure to extreme sexual images, she has become an outcast in our society.

HOST (ignoring both DR. CARLA and DR. RALPH): Amanda, when you say you're a virgin, do you mean that you've never even had *oral* sex?

PORNO GIRL (making a face): Of course not. That's disgusting.

HOST (turning toward camera, bug-eyed): And on that bizarre note, let's take a break to flush out our brains! We'll be back in a few moments, first with the only man to have ever been burned in effigy at a Rainbow Coalition convention . . . and then with the infamous *Laughin' Boy*!

AUDIENCE (and loudspeakers): [Thunderous applause.]

FADE OUT TO:

Commercials for feminine hygiene spray, taco seasoning, disposable diapers, low-fat yogurt, odor-fighting insoles, food processors, and a psychic hotline. There's also a teaser for a late-night newsmagazine show that will focus on the search for the Wichita terrorists . . . and investigate just how sure we are that Laughin' Boy wasn't in cahoots with them.

FADE IN TO:

HOST: We're back! Now, you might not have been too shocked by the DeWitts's first "damned" patient today—after all, compared to some folks we've had as guests on this show, a thirty-two-year-old virgin who's addicted to violent pornography might as well be Mother Teresa!

AUDIENCE: [Chuckles.]

HOST (facing camera): But our next patient is another story. He once wore a bulletproof vest as part of his job, but now that he's unemployed he still has to don Teflon if he so much as steps outside to buy a quart of milk. You'll understand why when you meet . . . Robert Royce, the Racist Ranger!

A handsome Caucasian man in a dark suit emerges from backstage and strides to the interview platform with the easy grace of an athlete. This is the RACIST RANGER, and the AUDIENCE doesn't know how to react. From the HOST's setup, they were expecting someone they could boo. But this is the sort of man they have been trained to admire. This guy is a cross between Matthew McConaughey and Harrison Ford, with a touch of Arnold Schwarzenegger at the shoulders and biceps. So a few members of the AUDIENCE boo, and a few applaud. But most of them murmur and shift around in uncomfortable confusion.

The RACIST RANGER takes the chair on the far right end of the row, next to PORNO GIRL. He gives the AUDIENCE a dazzling grin. His teeth are impossibly straight and white. The murmurs in the AUDIENCE intensify.

PORNO GIRL gives the newcomer a sidelong glance. There is no hostility in her look, but there's nothing else either. She is unimpressed. The RACIST RANGER's gorgeous presence has no effect on her. There are gasps from the AUDIENCE as they realize this.

HOST: Now, this may be difficult to believe, ladies and gentleman, but the man you see before you, a former Texas Ranger turned FBI agent—

DR. CARLA: That's not quite right, Steve. Mr. Royce was never a Texas Ranger. He grew up in San Antonio, so he's a Texan, and he was indeed an FBI special agent. The rumor that he was once a Texas Ranger was started, again, by the tabloids so that they could dub him the "Racist Ranger."

HOST (visibly annoyed, without looking at DR. CARLA): My

mistake. *Stan* stands corrected.

AUDIENCE: [Nervous titters.]

HOST (turning quickly and thrusting his microphone toward the RACIST RANGER): But you're not an FBI agent anymore, are you, Mr. Royce? You were drummed out of the Bureau because you *are* a racist, aren't you?

The RACIST RANGER's smooth forehead crinkles, and he turns to look at DR. RALPH and DR. CARLA.

DR. RALPH: It's all right, Rob. I understand your reluctance. But go ahead and answer.

HOST (fiercely): Yes, Mr. Royce, let's hear it! Are you or are you not an African-American-hating white supremacist?

RACIST RANGER (looking past the HOST at the camera): Nossuh, Mars Steve, I sho' ain't. Kase dat truck dah is trash, en don' you be jawin' 'bout dat no mo'.

The AUDIENCE explodes, and we see a shot of their reaction. Many of them come to their feet. The camera zooms in on several of their faces in succession. They are angry.

To say the least.

HOST (facing AUDIENCE, holding up both hands in a plea for calm): All right! All right! I don't blame you one bit! But if we can try to keep our feelings in check for just a moment, perhaps the Shrinks to the Damned can tell us what the Sam Hill is going on in the Racist Ranger's head to make him behave this way!

The AUDIENCE simmers down to a low growl and retakes their seats. The HOST turns back to the interview platform.

DR. RALPH: All right. Please listen. You see, although Mr. Royce's speech patterns may seem calculated to be offensive, they are in fact the result of an affliction beyond his control. Like Ms. Larkin, he suffers from a rare disorder—

HOST: You mean he's a racist *and* he's addicted to porn?

DR. CARLA: No, Steve. Mr. Royce's disorder is similar to Ms. Larkin's only in that it is unclassifiable and unique. At first it was thought that he might be suffering from a variation of Tourette's syndrome, but it soon became clear that what was wrong with him was something else entirely.

HOST: Just what would you call it, then?

DR. RALPH: We've been tossing around some suggestions. "River Raft Syndrome" is the one we've come back to most often.

HOST (puzzled): He's afraid of water? Or of drifting?

RACIST RANGER: Not one ner t'other, Mars Steve. Kase ah talks jus' like de character Jim in dat book *Adbentures o' Huckleberry Finn*, we's been a-callin' it Ribber Raf' Sinderome. Dat's on 'count o' ol' Jim, he spen' mos' o' his time in dat nobbel floatin' on de raf' in de ribber.

As the RACIST RANGER speaks, the camera cuts away from him to the HOST, then to the AUDIENCE, and then back to the RACIST RANGER again. The HOST and AUDIENCE are staring, their mouths literally hanging open, as if they cannot believe what they're hearing. The AUDIENCE gives the impression that they are letting their shock and hatred build so that it will be all the more righteous once they let it out again.

As for the RACIST RANGER, his facial expression and hand gestures do not match the grotesque sound of his speech. Visually, he appears no different to the camera than he did when he entered. If any of the viewers at home have their TV sound turned down, they have no indication (other than the reactions of the HOST and AUDIENCE) that the RACIST RANGER is being offensive in any way.

HOST (as if it is all he can do to keep himself from physically attacking the RACIST RANGER): I must say, Doctors, I find it hard to believe that such behavior is the result of a "disorder." Mocking, offensive speech of this nature seems entirely deliberate—and therefore deliberately insulting to African-Americans.

AUDIENCE: [Shouts of "Yeah!" "You tell 'em" and "Burn the racist bastard!"]

DR. CARLA: Both of those assumptions are false, Steve. First of all, Mr. Royce was a nineteen-year veteran of the Federal Bureau of Investigation when his affliction first manifested itself, and it ruined his career. We're talking about a man who received seven commendations, was wounded twice, and who was responsible, among many other things, for infiltrating the Ku Klux Klan in Mississippi and putting four Klansmen behind bars for a series of church-burnings. He had everything going for him in his career, and his service record indicates that he is anything but racist. So why would he deliberately engage in behavior that would ruin both career and reputation? The answer, of course, is that he wouldn't! His behavior, therefore, *must* be the result of an illness.

DR. RALPH: As for your second assumption, Stan—that Mr. Royce's speech patterns are insulting to African-Americans -- I must point out that the character Jim in *Huckleberry Finn* is arguably the bravest and most admirable figure in all of American letters. Now, I'm not a literary critic, but I do know something about human behavior, and Jim's is exemplary. For one thing, he struggles against all odds in order to gain his freedom. For another, he is selfless and tireless in the defense of his friend Huck. The fact that Jim's speech patterns and the novel's use of the "n-word" are offensive to modern sensibilities is irrelevant. That's just the way people *talked* back then. It doesn't change the fact that Jim is the hero of the book. Some critics have argued, in fact, that Huck is merely the narrator of Jim's story.

HOST (looking baffled): Are you saying that the Racist Ranger speaks the way he does because he *admires* a fictional African-American?

DR. CARLA: That's one possible trigger mechanism, yes. The actual process that results in the observed behavior is probably much more complicated than that.

RACIST RANGER: But honey, I'se gwyne to tell you, dey ain't no doubt dat Jim, he 'uz one fine nigger. En pooty smart, too.

The AUDIENCE explodes again.

HOST (turning toward camera, shaking his head, shouting to be heard): And believe it or not, ladies and gentlemen, it only gets worse! When we come back after these messages, you'll meet—the single most despised man in the world!

FADE OUT TO:

Commercials for minivans, weight-loss centers, laundry detergent, instant pudding, gourmet cat food, feminine hygiene spray, geriatric vitamins, and drain opener. There's also a non-profit religious organization's plea for us to adopt a Third-World child for seventeen cents a day, plus another teaser for the late-night newsmagazine.

FADE IN TO:

HOST (grimly): Welcome back to the show. It took us most of the break to calm down our studio audience, but things seem to be under control now. We don't blame them one bit for being upset—but we promised our guests that we'd let them come on the show and have their say, and that we'd give Porno Girl and the Racist Ranger the benefit of the doubt. Right, Audience?

AUDIENCE: [Assorted grudging noises of acquiescence.]

HOST: Our next guest, though, might be another story. It's not easy to be fair to a man when you've seen him laughing at the horrid deaths of innocent children. But that's exactly what the Shrinks to the Damned insist we must do, for they claim that Daniel Clayton was *not* amused by Saturday's tragedy. Rather, they believe that he suffers from a *disease* that was triggered by the horror of that day. So, ladies and gentlemen, please do your best to welcome our final guest for today—the man now known around the world as *Laughin' Boy*!

AUDIENCE: Booooooo! Booooooo!

Daniel Clayton, aka LAUGHIN' BOY, appears onstage and blinks in the glare of the bright lights. He is wearing tan slacks and a plain white shirt. He looks pale, thin, and out of shape . . . especially in comparison to the RACIST RANGER.

AUDIENCE: Booooooooo! BOOOOOOOOOO!

LAUGHIN' BOY makes his way across the stage to the interview platform. To our surprise, he isn't laughing, or even smiling. In fact, he looks slack-jawed and dopey. His stride wobbles. As he reaches the platform, DR. CARLA goes to him and helps him up, then guides him to the chair at the left end of the row.

The HOST waves at the AUDIENCE for quiet, and their boos subside.

HOST (jabbing his microphone at DR. CARLA as she retakes her seat): So what's the deal here, Dr. Carla? The infamous Mr. Clayton appears to be whacked out on drugs! Is that perhaps the reason behind his behavior in the first place?

DR. CARLA: No, Steve. Dr. Ralph and I have put Danny on medication to help him cope with his affliction. We're still adjusting the dosage. We've found, however, that if we administer no medication at all, Danny is unable to function. Sooner or later he succumbs to fits of laughter that are quite incapacitating, as well as painful. I'm sure your audience members have all laughed so hard at one time or another that their chest and abdominal muscles ached. Well, just imagine how difficult it would be to live your life if that ache was constant.

HOST (with a bit of a sneer): I'm sure my audience can imagine all kinds of things. They are, after all, intelligent people. But I *don't* think they can imagine laughing at suffering and death under any circumstances!

AUDIENCE: [Assorted cries of "No!" "No way!" and "You got that right, Stan!"]

DR. RALPH: They can't imagine hysteria?

HOST (rolling his eyes): Come on, Doc. We've all seen the Dying Dentist video, and we've all heard the tapes that were leaked from the Wichita police interrogation. Daniel Clayton wasn't in hysterics that day. He was having a blast!

AUDIENCE: [Assorted cries of "Yeah!" "We heard him!" and "You got that right, Stan!"]

DR. RALPH: I'm not suggesting that Daniel was in hysterics. What I *am* suggesting is that if you can imagine someone suffering from hysteria, then you should also be able to imagine someone suffering from another disorder that could result in inappropriate laughter.

HOST (giving camera a sidelong skeptical glance): By which I assume you mean that Laughin' Boy suffers from such a disorder?

DR. CARLA: That's what we've been saying all along, Steve. Like Ms. Larkin and Special Agent Royce—

RACIST RANGER: Dat's fo'muh Sepeshial Agent, Miz Carla. Dey done took away mah badge en sech.

AUDIENCE: [Threatening rumble.]

LAUGHIN' BOY looks up at the glowering AUDIENCE and giggles.

The HOST now leaps toward LAUGHIN' BOY, brandishing his microphone like a rapier.

HOST (nastily): Did you say something, Mr. Clayton? Did something strike you as *funny*?

LAUGHIN' BOY: I'm sorry, I can't help—heeheeheehee.

DR. CARLA (reaching inside her jacket): Would you like an injection, Daniel? Your medication seems to be wearing off prematurely.

LAUGHIN' BOY: No, I—hawhaw—don't want any more. It makes me sleepy. Whoohoohoo.

RACIST RANGER: Dat med'cine don't seem to do de bwah no good nohow, dad fetch it.

AUDIENCE: [More rumbling.]

HOST: Again, Mr. Clayton, I ask you what's so funny!

LAUGHIN' BOY (covering his mouth): Snarksnark hurp snarksnarksnark.

DR. RALPH: Stan, I suspect that Daniel is experiencing a mild attack of his disorder because of your negative, aggressive demeanor and the similar demeanor of your audience. You see, while our tests indicate that Daniel's internal emotional states are more or less consistent with external stimuli, his outward expressions of those states have gone haywire. In other words, he smiles or laughs when sad, bored, frightened, or horrified—and does *not* smile or laugh when happy, excited, amused, or delighted.

HOST (facing camera, eyes wide in indignation): Oh, so now it's *our* fault, is it?

DR. RALPH: That's not at all what I meant to suggest.

HOST (voice picking up speed and volume): This is precisely what I was talking about earlier, ladies and gentlemen. We live in a society in which deviants and miscreants of all stripes have discovered that they can get away with their sick behavior if only they figure out how to blame someone else!

DR. CARLA: Steve, listen to what you just said. You referred to "sick behavior," and that's exactly right. These clients of ours aren't blaming you or anyone else for their difficulties, but neither are they themselves to blame. They are, rather, sick. They suffer from disorders that they didn't ask for and cannot control. They are people to be helped, not condemned.

HOST (turning on DR. CARLA): Two things, Dr. Carla. First, *my name is Stan!* And second, it's awfully goshdarn hard for normal, caring people to avoid condemning someone who would laugh at something like *this*—

The HOST jabs a finger at the giant screen behind the interview platform, and LAUGHIN' BOY's frozen face dissolves into an overhead shot of the Wichita killing field. The blood is fresh on the grass, and we can see at least a dozen blasted corpses, including several children. Two of these children are lying against their mother's legless torso.

The AUDIENCE gasps and moans in revulsion and horror.

Everyone on the stage begins to turn to look at the screen as well. But DR. RALPH stops suddenly and reaches across DR. CARLA to grab LAUGHIN' BOY's arm.

DR. RALPH: Daniel! Look at me!

But it's too late. LAUGHIN' BOY has turned in his chair, and he sees the awful scene.

LAUGHIN' BOY: Hee hee hee hee hee HAW HAW HAW HAW HAW HAW!

Within seconds, LAUGHIN' BOY has doubled over with the force of his laughter. A moment later, he has fallen out of his chair and is howling on the floor.

The AUDIENCE bellows in disbelief and rage, and the camera cuts to them. They're leaping up from their seats, screaming.

The camera cuts back and forth between the AUDIENCE and LAUGHIN' BOY. LAUGHIN' BOY has rolled to the edge of the interview platform. A boom microphone comes into the picture as it tries to follow him, but the HOST waves it away and places his hand-held microphone next to LAUGHIN' BOY's mouth.

Now LAUGHIN' BOY's laughter roars in the studio like a tidal wave. It almost drowns out the furious screams of the AUDIENCE.

HOST (shouting): This is shameful, ladies and gentlemen! Shameful!

The camera draws back so that we see the entire interview platform again.

DR. CARLA, though still in her chair, is bending down and reaching toward LAUGHIN' BOY.

DR. RALPH is staring up at the AUDIENCE and seems to be petrified in a half-sitting, half-standing position.

PORNO GIRL also stares up at the AUDIENCE, but only for a moment. Wide-eyed and trembling, she looks down, opens her purse, and pulls out a copy of *Ass Masters* magazine.

The RACIST RANGER is shaking his head.

RACIST RANGER (barely audible): Lawd! Lawd!

LAUGHIN' BOY rolls off the interview platform and lands on the HOST's shoes. The HOST drops his microphone and jumps away as if bitten by a snake. He trips and lands sprawled on his back at the RACIST RANGER's feet.

As the HOST falls, LAUGHIN' BOY's laughter subsides a little. He manages to get up to his hands and knees.

And at this moment, a large dark-haired man wearing black jeans and a black turtleneck charges into the picture from the AUDIENCE. He leaps onto the stage, screams something unintelligible, and slashes his arm downward at LAUGHIN' BOY's neck.

It will only be later, as we run our VHS tapes and TiVo hard drives in slo-mo over and over again, that we will see the short, sharp blade in the ATTACKER's hand.

LAUGHIN' BOY raises his left arm, his camera-side arm, to try to ward off the blow. The ATTACKER's hand hits him at the shoulder and slices down to his wrist, splitting the entire length of his shirt sleeve.

The RACIST RANGER leaps up from his chair, but the supine HOST is against his legs. The RACIST RANGER falls forward over the HOST, but manages to turn it into a somersault.

The ATTACKER raises his hand in preparation for another downward slash. LAUGHIN' BOY falls forward onto his face. His white shirt sleeve already has a wet shimmer of red along the gash.

The AUDIENCE's scream goes up an octave.

DR. CARLA and DR. RALPH recoil. It is as if they have each been slapped by an invisible man.

PORNO GIRL covers her face with her open copy of *Ass Masters.*

The ATTACKER begins to bring his arm down again. LAUGHIN' BOY has collapsed. The next blow will bury the knife—we can see it now—in LAUGHIN' BOY's neck.

But the RACIST RANGER has come up from his somersault, and he springs over LAUGHIN' BOY onto the ATTACKER. The RACIST RANGER's left hand closes on the attacker's right wrist, stopping the knife. Then, before the ATTACKER can react, the RACIST RANGER steps behind the ATTACKER and jams his right thumb into the hollow of the ATTACKER's throat. The RACIST RANGER bends the ATTACKER backwards and brings his right knee up into the small of the ATTACKER's back.

ATTACKER: Gaaaaggggkkkk!

We're just able to hear this through the screams of the AUDIENCE. What we don't hear (but have no trouble believing later) are three of the ATTACKER's vertebrae breaking.

The RACIST RANGER rips the knife from the ATTACKER's hand and shoves him off the stage. The ATTACKER rolls under the camera's field of view, and we won't see him again until a tabloid newspaper smuggles photos from his heavily-guarded hospital room.

AUDIENCE: [Goes nuts.]

LAUGHIN' BOY tries to stand, but he collapses again before making it up to his knees. The RACIST RANGER throws down the knife, then leans over to help LAUGHIN' BOY to his feet as the boom microphone swings toward them.

RACIST RANGER: Oh Lawd, Mars Danny, dat arm dah look pow'ful bad!

LAUGHIN' BOY blinks. He is dazed. He's bleeding all along the length of his arm. His shirt sleeve has turned a deep, dark red.

He looks down at his wound for the first time.

And then he grins.

Then chuckles.

And then he's howling as if his bloody arm is the single funniest thing he's ever seen in his life. If not for the RACIST RANGER, LAUGHIN' BOY would crumple to the floor again.

At this moment, we hear a subtle change in the sound coming from the AUDIENCE.

Wait a minute, the sound seems to say. Why is he laughing at his *own* blood?

The disheveled HOST picks himself up and rushes over to stand next to the RACIST RANGER and LAUGHIN' BOY.

HOST (breathlessly): Ladies and gentlemen, I can hardly believe what I've just seen, and what I'm seeing right this minute! A disgraced former FBI agent has proven that he is still a true hero, and a man I would have spat on two minutes ago is laughing in the face of danger, and at his own pain! What does it all mean? And what will happen to these brave men now? We'll try to figure that out—right after these messages!

The AUDIENCE applauds and cheers, and the THEME MUSIC swells.

The HOST's shoulders slump, and he steps away from the RACIST RANGER and LAUGHIN' BOY. He looks down at his feet and shakes his head. He is unaware that we have not yet cut to commercial.

HOST (softly but audibly): Goddamn. Goddamn.

He stops and massages his forehead.

HOST: God*damn*, I'm glad we're in sweeps!

FADE OUT TO:

Commercials for rental cars, frozen pasta entrees, cellular telephones, cocktail wieners, flea collars, exfoliating sponges, tub and tile cleaner, unfinished furniture, a chain of auto-lube centers, and feminine hygiene spray.

Therapy Transcript (5)

(*Laughter deleted*)

What do you mean, what do I think of them? I just met them. I know they're your patients too. What more could I know about them at this point?

Let's stick to talking about my family, if we talk about anybody. Not that talking about my family will make any difference. It hasn't so far. What little success I've had in controlling the laughter has come from the pills and from the list of Dull Things I've started.

I'll be honest, Dr. Ralph. I suspect you've only had me talk about my parents and my marriage so you'll have plenty of material for a tell-all book about Laughin' Boy.

Right there, that was your chance to deny it. Instead you just asked me why I feel that way. But I guess that's what a therapist does. On the other hand, that's also what a prevaricator does.

It occurs to me that you've never mentioned doctor-patient confidentiality. So maybe we don't have any. Maybe since you're doing this in partnership with the federal government, the usual ethical code doesn't apply. Or maybe since you and Dr. Carla have treated so many patients over the radio, "confidentiality" is a foreign concept.

There wasn't much "confidentiality" on the Stan Symmons show either, was there?

You're damn right I'm feeling hostile. If you'd lost your home, your job, and your child, you'd be hostile too. Or if your gut had a constant ache from laughing when nothing was funny. Or if your arm had been sliced open on a talk show. It still hurts like a mother, by the way. Not that you asked.

And why should you? You stand to profit from the fact that those things have happened to *me.* The phone in your study hasn't stopped ringing since we got to New York. Hell, it probably started at the moment the tip of the knife touched my skin. We just couldn't hear it because we were in Chicago.

Or maybe it started when the Racist Ranger broke that poor bastard's back. There's nothing like excessive force to make the ratings spike. And ratings mean phone calls, and phone calls mean money, don't they?

Why did I call my attacker a "poor bastard"? Because I feel sorry for him, that's why. Odds are that he had nothing to do with what happened in Wichita.

Give me a minute.

Okay. I think I can talk again. As I was saying, odds are that the guy who cut me is just an unhappy schmuck who thought he'd be doing the world a favor if he took me out of it. I doubt that he's alone in that, by the way.

And don't tell me I should be grateful to the Racist Ranger. He didn't do what he did for my benefit. He did it either out of sadism or out of reflex, and I don't know which is worse. If he's a sadist, then he used the attack on me as an opportunity to snap someone in two without fear of repercussion. But if he did it out of reflex, then he's nothing but a machine programmed for violence.

I'm speaking hypothetically here, you know. I have no idea whether he fits either of those descriptions. All I know is what I saw him do.

I have to cut him some slack on the Uncle Tom speech patterns, though. If I didn't, then I couldn't cut myself any slack on my laughter—which is also offensive, and which isn't something I can control at all. So I guess I have to take his word for it when he says he can't control the way he talks.

He tried to talk to me on the flight from Chicago, by the way. Just your average chit-chat, except that he had his "yassuh, Mars Dan'l" thing going on. So that made it hard to take. Not that I wasn't giggling anyway. For all I know, that was hard for him to take, too.

I don't think the topics of conversation mattered. I think he just wanted someone to talk to who couldn't come right out and judge him. He told me about his childhood, his college days, his early years in the Bureau . . . all the stuff that no one else wants to hear now that he's the Racist Ranger. And neither did I. But we were on an airplane. What was I going to do, step outside?

He and I are from different planets. For one thing, he told me that he hardly watched TV as a child because he was too busy playing Little League baseball and Pop Warner football. And when he wasn't doing that, he was competing in the Math Olympics. Real Rhodes Scholar material.

Oh he was, was he? Well, goody for him.

I'm sorry. It's just that he's so many of the things I wanted to be and never was. And he did a lot of good before his affliction hit. He protected the weak and punished the wicked. People needed him.

Who ever needed me? Not Karen. Not really. And Lindy just needs me to stay away from her. Not that she'll understand that. All she'll understand for the next few years is that her daddy never comes to see her anymore.

Another minute, please.

The Ranger has never been married and has no children. So there's one more way he beats me out.

Still, here we both are. Both demented sons of bitches. Except that he's bigger, stronger, smarter, and handsomer. I'm almost glad Karen dumped me before all of this happened—because if she hadn't, she might leave me for him. As long as he didn't talk. One of Karen's virtues is that she has no tolerance for racism.

I know, I know. He's not really racist.

But I still don't like him.

As for "Porno Girl" —

If you must know, I think she's wonderful.

I have no idea what I'm basing that on. It's just what I think, all right?

Maybe I fall for any woman I lay eyes on now that I can't lay eyes or anything else on my wife anymore. I sort of liked that woman FBI agent too, remember? Not as much as I like Porno Girl, though.

Maybe she reminds me of my mother.

And that's so far from funny that I probably won't laugh for thirty or forty seconds. But it's making me queasy, so I'll try not to think of it again.

I saw her for the first time at the Symmons show and then looked across at her on the plane while the Racist Ranger was yammering . . . and I could see that she was incredible.

No, I haven't even spoken with her. So you tell me. You're the shrink. You tell me why I feel this way. You tell me why I think Porno Girl is wonderful.

Well, sure, she's pretty. And as you point out, there's also her fascination with pornography. All men are perverts, so we're all going to be attracted to that.

No. It's not that simple, because she isn't obsessed with porn because of any actual desire. She's all about sex, and yet she's *not.*

She doesn't *do* anything. All she does is watch.

She's the antithesis of a guy like the Ranger, or of a woman like my ex-wife. She's not powerful, active, or aggressive. She's not a goddamn Rhodes scholar.

All she does is *watch.*

Of course I understand that she's not well. I understand that her compulsion has destroyed her career and alienated her family and friends . . . not to mention that it's also made her the butt of jokes around the world.

But I also understand that she needs someone who'll accept her anyway. The way her family should, but doesn't. The way a parent accepts a child. The way I wanted . . .

Sorry. That was a bad one. How long did I laugh? I've lost my train of thought.

Oh, yes. I remember now. Porno Girl.

All I'm saying is, I think I understand who she is and what she needs.

So how could I not love her?

Newsgroup Posts (5)

Subject: "Laffin' Boyz" by Ramrod N DJ-DP
From: rushtnme@subnorm.net (NoName 4 U)
Date: 2000/05/28
Message-ID:
<rushtnme-346587321P.LOL23SKI@subnorm.net>
Newsgroups:
rec.music.hiphop.wazzup alt.fan.laughin-boy

Yo, y'all go to <ramrodndjdp.com>.

For those of you who don't know, Ramrod N DJ-DP are a coupla white hip-hop geniuses outta Kansas City, MO, of all places. Don't let that prejudice you, though. They use a black bass player and beat programmer outta NYC, so the sound is dope.

Their new one's on their site. It's called "Laffin' Boyz," and it KICKS. It's already been getting play on 'Net radio stations outta KC and Chicago (KCDOGG.com and KBLOW.com for sure), and maybe more by now.

Here's a partial transcription (I think I got the words n rhymes right):

Put your hands up, Daddy, buy me Kandy KORN
Says da birthday girl on da day she was BORN
So Daddy goes to da booth in da Wi-ch-ita PARK
And when his back is turned, da poppers find their MARK
He turns back around and sees his little girl's DEAD
She's lyin' on da ground and she's missin' her HEAD
Yo, but Daddy got no time to be a grievin' WRECK

'Cause da next camo popper gets him right in da NECK

And da last thing he hears in all da poppin' NOISE

Is da happy dope leader of da LAFFIN' BOYZ

Yeah Boyz (HA-HA) Yeah Boyz (HEE-HEE) Yeah Boyz (HO-HO)

Yeah Boyz (HA-HA) Yeah Boyz (HEE-HEE) Yeah Boyz (HO-HO)

Dan's da happy dope leader of da LAFFIN' BOYZ

When da muzzles started flashin' Dan went to his KNEES

Like a pipe-suckin' HO doin' her usual SLEAZE

Yo, he saw niggaz die, and he saw bitches HURTIN'

Did he laugh 'cause it's funny? Who can say for CERTAIN

But ask DP and Ram, we say it's stankin' RAW

To pop all them motherfuckahs in da pissant TAW

Wastin' round after round on country asses was HEINOUS

Shit y'coulda gone to Detroit, yo, and popped Slim ANUS

And da last thing he'd hear in all da poppin' NOISE

Would be da happy dope leader of da LAFFIN' BOYZ

Yeah Boyz (HA-HA) Yeah Boyz (HEE-HEE) Yeah Boyz (HO-HO)

Yeah Boyz (HA-HA) Yeah Boyz (HEE-HEE) Yeah Boyz (HO-HO)

Dan's da happy dope leader of da LAFFIN' BOYZ

There's more, but you get the idea. Check it out. (It's better with the beat n soundz, of course. I think they're using samples from the Sex Pistols or Who or somebody like that—if you know who those niggaz were.)

Internet Chat

LISAMAXX: Welcome, everyone, to the NetMaxx Featured Forum for Tuesday, May 30, 2000. I'm your host, Lisa—or LisaMaxx :) —and I'm very excited about tonight's special guests. For the first time live on the Net, here are Doctors Ralph and Carla DeWitt along with their newest and most controversial patient, Mr. Danny Clayton, better known around the world as—Laughin' Boy!

DRRALPH: It's a pleasure to be here, Lisa. Especially since "here" for me is my own townhouse in Manhattan!

DRCARLA: And I'd like to add that it's a new experience for me to be interviewed with my husband when we're in the same house but not in the same room. I think I like it. :)

LISAMAXX: LOL. And speaking of LOL, where's Laughin' Boy? Is he in his quarters there in your home?

DRRALPH: He's here in my study with me, but we have a separate terminal set up for him. However, I may have to scoot over and enter some of his responses. For one thing, his left arm aches a bit from the events of last Friday. In addition, sometimes his laughing attacks leave him unable to perform tasks such as typing, although he can usually still speak well enough to be understood.

LISAMAXX: Freaky! How's he doing at the moment?

LAUGHINBOY: I'm all right. The doctors gave me some medication at dinner, so I'm only giggling a little.

LISAMAXX: Wow, I can't believe we're really talking with you! Welcome, Laughin' Boy!

JOHNDOE99: Yes, welcome!

TOEBUNNY: Welcome!

BOGART27: W

VBARBARINO: :-D

MONKEYGOD: Peace be with you.

RUSHTNME: Let the running of the gauntlet begin.

LISAMAXX: I'll start off the questions, and then everyone else should feel free to join in! Laughin' Boy, we all saw how you reacted to the Wichita Massacre. And you certainly caught a lot of flak for it.

RUSHTNME: So to speak.

BOGART27: HH

VBARBARINO: :-7

LISAMAXX: But since then we've been told that your reaction didn't reflect your true feelings. So tell us, Laughin' Boy, what ARE your true feelings about the WM?

LAUGHINBOY: I was horrified. I still am. Anyone would be.

JOHNDOE99: Well, not anyone. The people who did the shooting weren't. Any idea who they were, Laughin' Boy?

LAUGHINBOY: None whatsoever. By the way, I hope nobody minds, but I would rather be called by my name than by "Laughin' Boy."

RUSHTNME: OK, this is typical. Somebody gets famous, then complains about being known for what got them famous. It's like SMG getting all PO'd when people call her Buffy. Get over it, b*tch!

TOEBUNNY: It's not the same thing. SMG chose to be Buffy. Mr. Clayton didn't choose to be Laughin' Boy.

RUSHTNME: I'm not so sure about that.

JOHNDOE99: Mr. Clayton, just change your nick QLAB so we see a different name on our monitors. Then no one'll call you Laughin' Boy.

LAUGHINBOY: I'm sorry, I don't know how to do that. Someone else set up the terminal for me.

BOGART27: RTFM

LISAMAXX: It doesn't matter, Mr. Clayton. We'll remember. Next question, someone?

MONKEYGOD: What meds are the docs giving you, Mr. Clayton?

LAUGHINBOY: I'm not sure about all of them. I know there's Valium, but only on good days because it doesn't really help much. Some of the other medications make me feel a little dopey. But it's better than the laughing attacks.

MONKEYGOD: Have you tried smoking or eating marijuana?

BOGART27: HHOJ?

MONKEYGOD: No, I'm serious as a heart attack. Hemp has amazing calmative properties.

DRRALPH: Daniel's medications vary depending on his symptoms, and depending upon what Dr. Carla and I find has been working best. We're still in the early stages of treatment, though, and we have to "tweak" the medications and dosages day by day. So I'd rather not comment on what we're currently prescribing, because some folks out there with similar problems might try to self-medicate.

RUSHTNME: Who the h*ll else has a "similar problem"?

DRCARLA: However, we can tell you that we would never use anything other than clinically proven, FDA-approved psychotropics.

MONKEYGOD: No weed, then?

DRRALPH: No.

MONKEYGOD: IMHO, I don't think you're doing your duty if you don't at least _try_ marijuana in this case. You're doctors, and it's nature's own mellowing agent.

JOHNDOE99: I dunno, MG. Mr. Clayton's problem is that he laughs too much as it is. So I'm not sure that a big fat doobie is really what he needs.

DRRALPH: I concur with Mr. 99.

BOGART27: BFN

TOEBUNNY: Bye, Bogie!

JOHNDOE99: Shee ya later, shweetheart.

VBARBARINO: :-(

RUSHTNME: Okay, "Mr. Clayton." Here's another question. Were the terrorists of the towelhead variety, or were they homegrown?

LAUGHINBOY: I have no idea.

RUSHTNME: Oh, come on. You didn't hear them shout orders? You didn't see whether their hands were brown or white or yellow or red?

LAUGHINBOY: I'm sorry, but no. I would have told the police and the FBI if I'd heard or seen anything like that. But the terrorists were wearing hoods and gloves, and with all the noise I dint'dfl

DRRALPH: Just a moment, everyone.

LAUGHINBOY: With all the noise from the guns and with all the people around me shouting and screaming, I couldn't tell whether any of the terrorists spoke or not.

DRRALPH: FYI, I turned to Daniel's terminal to type that last comment for him. He's just now had a mild attack, but it seems to be subsiding.

LAUGHINBOY: I'm okay.

BOGART27: RE

TOEBUNNY: Welcome back, Bogie!

JOHNDOE99: Heresh lookin' at you, kid.

VBARBARINO: :-]

LISAMAXX: Clearly, Mr. Clayton, people's initial impression of you right after the Massacre was unfair. But now public opinion seems to have swung the other way, for the most part. In fact, many people see you as a hero both for having survived a terrorist assault and for facing up to your emotional dysfunction. So at least half of the people who admire you want to know—Are you single?

VBARBARINO: :-P

TOEBUNNY: Shut up, V-Bar. Some of us are interested.

VBARBARINO: (*)

TOEBUNNY: Gross!

LAUGHINBOY: I'm divorced.

TOEBUNNY: And your little girl is really cute, BTW, although your ex-wife looks kinda mean. Anyway, I think what LisaMaxx meant was, are you seeing anybody right now?

JOHNDOE99: Like Porno Girl, you mean?

DRCARLA: By the way, Ms. Larkin is here in my study at the moment.

JOHNDOE99: Porno Girl? Porno Girl is watching us chat?

BOGART27: HS!

VBARBARINO: :-B~

RUSHTNME: Now, now, gentlemen, we must all show proper respect, so none of that. And let us refer to the little nympho as "Ms. Larkin."

TOEBUNNY: Ignore Rushtn, everyone.

BOGART27: DTMWTD

TOEBUNNY: Sorry, Bogie; didn't mean to be bossy.

BOGART27: NP

LAUGHINBOY: This is Dr. Ralph typing for Daniel again. No, he's not romantically involved at the moment. He is concentrating on the problems at hand.

RUSHTNME: Hey, if he hasn't hooked up with Porno Girl—oops, "Ms. Larkin"—then I guess all his problems _are_ "at hand"!

JOHNDOE99: LOL, Ru!

VBARBARINO: %-D

BOGART27: G

DRCARLA: This is "Porno Girl" using Dr. Carla's terminal. Call me whatever you like, Rushtnme, if that'll make you feel as if you have an actual penis. I don't care, because I'm going to bed.

VBARBARINO: >;-P~~

TOEBUNNY: Oh, that's _so_ attractive.

RUSHTNME: I guess this wouldn't be Porno Girl's favorite part of the Net, anyway, IYKWIM. No pictures.

BOGART27: HHOS

RUSHTNME: Exactly.

LISAMAXX: Next question for Mr. Clayton?

BOCADUDE: Hey, y'all! I finally got here!

BOGART27: BFD

TOEBUNNY: Hi, Bocadude!

JOHNDOE99: Hey, dude.

BOCADUDE: Christ, I didn't know Borg27 was gonna be here. No offense to the rest of you, but I don't care to be assimilated. TTFN.

BOGART27: FYAH

JOHNDOE99: ROFL, Bogie! Can you do that in a Schwarzenegger accent?

RUSHTNME: Careful, Bogie. LisaMaxx just sent me a private note to the effect that I'm being a big meanie-bully-poophead and that she'll boot me out if I don't play nice.

VBARBARINO: :~{

RUSHTNME: Yeh, boo-f*ckin'-hoo.

LISAMAXX: Listen, everyone—but especially our celebrity guests—I apologize for Rushtnme's rudeness. But we can continue now without him interrupting. I've blocked him.

BOGART27: FWIW WYA

LISAMAXX: Whatever. Now, Mr. Clayton, another question—As the most famous survivor of the WM, are you concerned that the terrorists might try to track you down and assassinate you?

RUSHTNME: Moohoohahahaaaa! I'm baaa-aaaaack . . .

LISAMAXX: Just a moment, everyone. I'll bump him again.

RUSHTNME: Forget it, girlie. My mojo beats your mojo. I am the God Emperor of Hack. I am Wax On, Wax Off. I am Bad Bad Leroy Brown, the baddest man in the whole d*mn town.

BOGART27: TYS LM

DRRALPH: I'll answer your question for Daniel, Lisa. Given what happened on the Stan Symmons television show last Friday, we know that Daniel has to be careful. However, it seems unlikely that he

JOHNDOE99: Yeah, how's his arm? It looked bad.

DRRALPH: has much to fear from the Wichita terrorists, who apparently wanted to kill people at random and then flee. Instead, Daniel has to watch

TOEBUNNY: Katie Couric said yesterday that Laughin' Boy's wound turned out to be superficial.

DRRALPH: out for disturbed individuals who might strike out at him on the spur of the moment simply because he's become

RUSHTNME: Guys, Dannyboy was never knifed at all. The whole thing was staged as a PR stunt. And boy, did it work.

LISAMAXX: RU, please leave. If I can't get you off, you should at least have the courtesy to do it yourself. Don't be rude to your fellow Netizens.

RUSHTNME: Oh pleeaase get me offff. Don't make me do it mysellllf . . .

VBARBARINO: :-9

RUSHTNME: . . . because I'm so tiirrred from virtually kicking your sweet little MAXXASS.

DRRALPH: well-known. Such was the case at the Stan Symmons studio. The man with the knife is still unconscious and hasn't been identified, but it seems probable that he was a mentally unbalanced homeless man. Not a terrorist.

JOHNDOE99: OT, but I've had a hardon for Katie Couric ever since the Gulf War.

RUSHTNME: Please, dude. She's got kids.

TOEBUNNY: What's wrong with kids?

LISAMAXX: Speaking of children, how has your recent change in circumstances affected your daughter, Mr. Clayton?

DRRALPH: So far as we know, Daniel's daughter is doing well. She is, of course, too young to understand what's happened—which will be all to the good in the long run, so long as the news media give her the space that every child needs to grow and thrive.

RUSHTNME: You should run for office, doc.

LADYGWHIZ: Hi, everyone! I finally found you. Dr. Ralph, I just want to say that I love your radio show, and that I've called several times but never made it to the air. Guess my problems aren't all that bad! *g*

DRCARLA: Hello, LadyGWhiz.
LADYGWHIZ: Wow! I didn't know Dr. Carla was here too! Wait a sec while I scroll up and see what I missed.
TOEBUNNY: Hi, LadyG!
JOHNDOE99: Welcome, LadyG!
BOGART27: W
RUSHTNME: Howdy from the cheap seats, LadyG.
LISAMAXX: Glad you could make it, LadyG!
VBARBARINO: >;->
MONKEYGOD: Yo, LadyG!
JOHNDOE99: Say, Doctors, is the Racist Ranger around? If so, is there any chance we can ask him a question or two as well?
RUSHTNME: "Racist Ranger." Now there's a piece of work. Archie Bunker on steroids. David Duke meets Kwai Chang Caine. George Wallace walking.
DRCARLA: Those comments are unfair and inaccurate.
RUSHTNME: Oh, really? Then answer me this—If the dude who waved that pitiful little knife on the Symmons show was mentally ill, why did Royce all but kill the poor guy? What does that say about him?
MONKEYGOD: That he needs to mellow out.
RUSHTNME: It says he not only insults niggers, but beats up retards!
BOGART27: JK?
RUSHTNME: No, man, the guy's dangerous!
BOGART27: IANAL—WOF TPTB
RUSHTNME: Thanks, Bogie, but I'm not worried.
LISAMAXX: You should be. TPTB are working on bumping you out of here for good this time.
VBARBARINO: =):-)>
LISAMAXX: It's not a free speech issue, V-Bar. It's just a matter of being courteous to our guests!

LAUGHINBOY: This is Robert Royce on Daniel Clayton's keyboard. I just want to point out that "Racist Ranger" is a label the media have slapped on me. I am neither.

JOHNDOE99: You're not Royce, either.

RUSHTNME: Nope. We have us a faker on board. 'Cause de real Royce be talkin' like de brothers circa 1840.

LAUGHINBOY: I don't type the way I speak. And I didn't always speak the way I do now.

DRRALPH: I can vouch for the fact that Robert is using Daniel's terminal at the moment. Daniel had to excuse himself from the room temporarily.

JOHNDOE99: He should have said so. It's rude to walk out without letting us know.

BOGART27: HIWTH—PITA

VBARBARINO: >:-(

DRRALPH: I apologize for Daniel. This is his first Internet discussion, and he hasn't learned the etiquette.

VBARBARINO: :-/

DRRALPH: He respects your customs, but doesn't know them all yet.

BOGART27: OIC TNX 1.0E6

LADYGWHIZ: You crack me up, Bogart27!

BOGART27: TYVM LG—CUF2FIRL?

LADYGWHIZ: Boy, you don't waste any time, do you?

CARLOTEX: PMFJI, but is this the Laughin' Boy interview? I've been trying to get in forever, but there's some sorta bottleneck.

LISAMAXX: Yes, you're in the right place. We've limited access tonight to keep the discussion manageable. And Laughin' Boy is currently AFK, but will be back shortly.

CARLOTEX: Oh, good. I wasn't sure.

TOEBUNNY: Hi, C-Tex!

LISAMAXX: Yes, hi, and welcome.

JOHNDOE99: Yo, C-Tex.

BOGART27: W

RUSHTNME: Never seen you online before, C-Tex. You're a guy, right?

LAUGHINBOY: Still Robert Royce here until Mr. Clayton returns. Any questions for me?

RUSHTNME: Yeah, you repugnant bigot. How do you live with yourself?

CARLOTEX: Yes, I'm a guy. Sorry, RUSHTN.

LAUGHINBOY: I live with myself by remembering that I am suffering from a syndrome that isn't my fault,

TOEBUNNY: RU, please try to be nice. Some of us are here because we want to understand rather than condemn.

LAUGHINBOY: that I served my country with honor until I became ill,

VBARBARINO: :-T

LAUGHINBOY: that I don't have a racist bone in my body,

BOGART27: BS IMO—WYSIWYG

CARLOTEX: Hey, Toebunny, are you the same Toebunny who's into Garbage?

JOHNDOE99: Sick, dude!

CARLOTEX: The band, the band! *g*

TOEBUNNY: That's me! And I even look kinda like Shirley Manson, only my eyes are closer together! *eg*

LAUGHINBOY: and that I can snap snotty little geeks like you over my knee.

VBARBARINO: :-@

LAUGHINBOY: That was for Rushtnme, ToeBunny.

LADYGWHIZ: I like Garbage, too, but I prefer Hole. I look like Shirley Manson, too, though. ;)

JOHNDOE99: Thank God, considering the alternative implied by your taste in "music." RFD—"Courtney Love, Evil Skank or Soulless Succubus?"

LISAMAXX: Guys, I hate to do this, but as moderator I have to point out that we've gotten a little OT.
TOEBUNNY: Sorry, LisaM.
LADYGWHIZ: Yes. Sorry.
BOGART27: DYJHIW TPTB TTWA?
LISAMAXX: Just doing my job, Bogie.
LAUGHINBOY: It's Danny Clayton again. My apologies for stepping out. I had another attack, but I'm better now.
RUSHTNME: Why, did the Racist Ranger snap your attack over his knee? Did he put it into the hospital in a coma?
BOGART27: ROTFLOL
LISAMAXX: I don't think that was funny at all.
BOGART27: SOHF
LISAMAXX: Whatever. Mr. Clayton, how's your arm? The one that was slashed?
RUSHTNME: I already told you, that was bogus.
LAUGHINBOY: It'll be okay. Sixteen stitches, but it wasn't deep.
TOEBUNNY: Does it hurt?
LAUGHINBOY: Somewhat. But it only happened four days ago, so that's not surprising. Hurts a little more this evening because of typing.
VBARBARINO: :~*
CARLOTEX: Laughin' Boy, what's the weather like there in Wichita tonight?
LAUGHINBOY: I'm in New York, staying with Dr. Ralph and Dr. Carla. Weather's fine here.
JOHNDOE99: Buy a clue, C-Tex. Even if you don't watch the news, you could have scrolled up and known he's in NYC.
BOGART27: SPAM—RTFM
LADYGWHIZ: Be nice, guys.
CARLOTEX: Excuuse me and FYA. Outtahere.
JOHNDOE99: Jeez, what's his problem?
BOGART27: IDK

LADYGWHIZ: Mr. Clayton, if Mr. Royce is still there, I'd like to ask him if he could take his shirt off the next time he's on TV. <:)

DRRALPH: Robert is here in the room, and he says he'll think about it.

RUSHTNME: Ask Porno Girl to think about it, too.

DRCARLA: If you knew how traumatic Amanda's affliction is for her, you wouldn't make a joke like that.

RUSHTNME: Wasn't a joke. I wanna see her ti**ies.

DRCARLA: What a charming person you are. But your request is in vain.

VBARBARINO: :-<

TOEBUNNY: What about Mr. Clayton? Any chance of some beefcake?

JOHNDOE99: Ha! Good one, ToeBunny!

VBARBARINO: %-D

TOEBUNNY: Shut up, I think he's cute.

BOGART27: YMBJ

LAUGHINBOY: My hope is to never be on television again, with or without a shirt.

DRRALPH: It's understandable that you feel that way, Daniel, but not realistic. You're in high demand as a symbol of hope and courage.

DRCARLA: You're living proof that one can stand up to horror and survive.

DRRALPH: And television and radio are vital tools for communicating that message to the world.

CARLOTEX: Don't believe it, Laughin' Boy! The Internet kicks tv's ass. Two years from now, there won't even _be_ any tv stations as they exist today. Or radio stations, or book publishers, or newspapers, or magazines, or compact discs. Or even off-the-shelf software. Everything—music, literature, video, software, news, sports, games, _everything_—will be on the Web! And every other content-medium will be as dead as the dodo.

JOHNDOE99: I thought you left, C-Tex.

LISAMAXX: And please call Mr. Clayton by his name instead of "Laughin' Boy."

JOHNDOE99: You'd know that if you'd bothered to scroll up, C-Tex. Pull your head out.

BOGART27: SITD?

LADYGWHIZ: LOL, Bogie! You're terrible!

BOGART27: GD&R

LADYGWHIZ: No, you stay right where you are, cutie!

BOGART27: TNX

LISAMAXX: This question is for all three of our special guests. Doctors, and Mr. Clayton, what's the prognosis? How full a recovery is possible from Mr. Clayton's affliction, and how long will it take?

RUSHTNME: That's three questions, dipsh*t.

DRRALPH: At the moment it's impossible to give you a definite answer, Lisa. Our therapy has only begun, and is still in the experimental stage. At present, we're only able to attack the symptoms, not their cause.

MONKEYGOD: I'm telling you, try cannabis.

DRCARLA: Furthermore, it may be that some of Daniel's problem is rooted in the traumas of childhood, while the rest is rooted in the trauma of what he experienced on May 20. It's too soon to say. But it's possible that no cure will present itself until that trauma is resolved.

JOHNDOE99: What does that mean?

BOGART27: TANSTAAFL

DRRALPH: It means that Daniel may need closure beyond what is possible through therapy and medication. It means that the terrorists may actually have to be brought to justice before he can achieve any kind of peace.

DRCARLA: Otherwise, he may only be able to conquer his syndrome to a certain degree, and then be forced to live with it at that level for the rest of his life.

TOEBUNNY: Mr. Clayton, I would like to be your girlfriend.

LAUGHINBOY: That's very kind of you.

TOEBUNNY: I live in Philadelphia, so I'm not that far from NYC. I could come visit some weekend.

DRCARLA: Probably not a good idea for the foreseeable future, ToeBunny.

TOEBUNNY: I'm thinking about you kissing my toes, Mr. Clayton. Does that sound nice to you?

VBARBARINO: :-}~~

TOEBUNNY: I could be a good mommy for your little girl, Mr. Clayton. I would teach her how to paint her toes and sing the piggy song.

MONKEYGOD: Whoa!

TOEBUNNY: I would make her toes pretty like mine.

DRRALPH: LisaMaxx, are you there?

TOEBUNNY: I'll bet you laugh all the time because you're really sad, Mr. Clayton. And I'll bet you're sad because your awful ex-wife wouldn't let you do things with her toes.

LAUGHINBOY: I'm sorry but i jusd donntotn oth9in

RUSHTNME: Looks like somebody just went Chernobyl.

TOEBUNNY: But you can do whatever you want to my toes, Mr. Clayton. All you have to do is tell me where to meet you.

DRRALPH: LisaMaxx?

RUSHTNME: LisaMaxx can't help you, doc. She's not here anymore. Not that I would know how that happened. IAE, although Toebunny has carte blanche, I'm in charge now. Moohoohahahaaa!

VBARBARINO: :-() :-() :-()

RUSHTNME: And the first question of the new regime is—Tell us, Laughin' Boy, if your laughter is an illness triggered by the shock of what happened in Wichita, why didn't you laugh for Oklahoma City, Jonesboro, Columbine, Atlanta, or any of the other violent American tragedies of recent years?

LAUGHINBOY: This is Dr. Ralph at Daniel's terminal once again. I would point out to Mr. Rushtnme that Daniel wasn't present at any of those other events. However, he _was_ present in Wichita ten days ago.

RUSHTNME: BS. ITFP, I don't believe he was "there" at all, at least not in the way that you use the term. And ITSP, I would point out that reality is whatever our senses reveal, and that therefore whatever we experience via whatever medium is real—more real than "reality," in fact, because we can experience it many times over. So good ol' Laughin' Boy shoulda been laughin' for about five years straight by the time of the WM.

DRRALPH: LisaMaxx?

RUSHTNME: This is why the reality of the Web, which grows ever closer to being everywhere and everywhen, will render your old "reality"—and for that matter, doctors, your jobs—obsolete.

CARLOTEX: Ahem, didn't I already say that?

JOHNDOE99: Not nearly as well, newbie.

DRCARLA: Well, I suppose it's time for us to say goodnight.

LISAMAXX: No, wait! I'm here. Just got bumped off for a minute. What did I miss?

DRRALPH: Unfortunately, Lisa, we really do have to log off now. Daniel is having another episode, and I don't think he'll be able to return to the keyboard tonight. But on his behalf, I'd like to thank all of you for your questions, interest, and concern. Together, we can stand tall against our demons—both those within, and those without.

VBARBARINO: <:?

DRCARLA: I'd like to remind you all that there is a one million dollar reward for information leading to the arrest and conviction of those responsible for the Wichita Massacre. If you have such information, or if you would like to contribute to the reward fund, please log on to the FBI's public web site, or visit us at drralphdrcarla.com.

DRRALPH: And with that, we must bid you adieu.

LISAMAXX: Well, if you have to go, you have to go! So on behalf of NetMaxx, thank you Dr. Ralph DeWitt, Dr. Carla DeWitt, and Mr. Daniel Clayton, for being our guests on tonight's NetMaxx Featured Forum. And btw, your words have reached more people than you might think, because we had quite a few silent lurkers this evening.

DRCARLA: Thank you all very much.

LISAMAXX: Plus, this Forum will be posted to a link at netmaxx.com no later than 9:00 AM tomorrow—so even more Netizens will be able to learn more about the real people behind the Laughin' Boy phenomenon!

DRRALPH: That's wonderful. Good night, all. Or, as I'm told is proper under these circumstances—BCNU!

DRCARLA: Yes, good night from myself and my SO. BYE.

MONKEYGOD: Stay cool. Peace out.

RUSHTNME: Who the f*ck says "peace out" anymore?

LISAMAXX: This concludes tonight's Featured Forum.

RUSHTNME: What, no goodnight kiss?

LISAMAXX: To everyone except RU—thank you, and good night. BFN

RUSHTNME: Call me!

JOHNDOE99: Hey, RU, Bogie, I gotta go. My kid's crying. But it was a kick. Next time. CU

CARLOTEX: You guys are a-holes. XIT

RUSHTNME: Yeah, I'm an a-hole. I'm an a-hole who rules this f*ckin' planet. Bow down before my mighty swingin' mojo, mofos! I AM THE GOD OF H*LLFIRE. HEAR ME ROAR. CUL8R

LADYGWHIZ: LOL. Bye, RU. Bogie, are you still here?

BOGART27: Y

LADYGWHIZ: Oh, good! I've been trying to send you an IM, but no luck. Can you come over to AOL so we can talk privately?

BOGART27: AOL?

LADYGWHIZ: Yes. Can you come?

BOGART27: IMNSHO & FYI AOL SUX

LADYGWHIZ: Oh, well then, FU. BYE

TOEBUNNY: Mr. Clayton, I know you're offline, but I'm going to leave this here in case you come back and read it when the forum's posted to the Web site.

I could make you happy. And I know you could make me happy, too. The thought of you makes my toes tingle. So whenever you can't stop thinking about those poor people who were killed, or whenever you miss your little girl, or whenever you're just feeling sad, please remember there's a woman out here IRL who would like to tickle you all over with her pretty painted toes.

VBARBARINO: :-& -->

TOEBUNNY: And then you can sing this song, Mr. Clayton, and maybe it'll help you feel a little better than you did before.

> This little piggy went to market—
> This little piggy stayed home—
> This little piggy had roast beef—
> And this little piggy had none—

BOGART27: ATLPWWWWATWH

Episode Three: Odd Squad!

THE KNIFE HAD RIPPED DOWN the length of Danny's left sleeve, but it had left only a three-inch wound on his forearm. The wound had been bloody, but not deep. So Danny had wanted to carry his own luggage when he'd moved into the DeWitts' New York townhouse two days after the slashing. Everything he now owned fit into one suitcase and a gym bag.

But the Racist Ranger had carried the suitcase and bag up to Danny's room anyway.

"Dat arm dah still numb," the Ranger had said. "You jus' take kyer of 'er an' let ol' Rob do de hebby liftin'."

Now, five days later, Danny's itching wound was keeping him awake. So he sat up, turned on the nightstand lamp, and thought of oatmeal.

He wasn't hungry. But he had found that if he concentrated on things that were dull or bland, he could sometimes keep his laughter under control. He had tried concentrating on funny things too, since only sad or awful things made him laugh . . . but funny things depressed him. And that in turn made him think of sad or awful things—specifically, South Riverside Park—which could set off another laughing attack. So blandness was his best bet.

Plain oatmeal had done well today, but Phillips screwdrivers, dental floss, and Number Two pencils had all proven useful since he'd come to New York. So Danny was now on a constant quest for anything dull. The alternative was to take the DeWitts' drugs, and he hated doing that. The injections had stopped at his request—but now there were pills in rattling paper nut cups at mealtimes. He stashed most of them in his pockets until he could transfer them to his shaving kit.

But he kept three or four with him at all times. There were moments when a couple of peanut-M&M-sized blue nuggets were the only things that could keep him from howling.

Mainly, though, he was trying to rely on self-induced boredom. The problem with this was that any one dull thing worked for only a limited time. Oatmeal, for example, was now starting to fail because it was similar to Cream of Wheat, and he had just remembered burning the roof of his mouth with Cream of Wheat as a child. The memory made him chortle, so he had to switch to yellow legal pads. But then yellow legal pads reminded him of O.J. Simpson. So it was on to weatherstripping, which had only now occurred to him.

He had started carrying a gray spiral notepad of Dull Things to refer to whenever he became too laugh-racked to think straight. The notepad was on the nightstand now, so he picked it up, unclipped the pen from its cover, and flipped it open to the third page. So far, this page said:

okra
wooden (not rubber!) doorstops
indoor-outdoor carpet
gray spiral notepads
lanolin
the metric system
dry twigs
earned income credit
60-watt light bulbs

To this list he added:
weatherstripping
plastic ballpoint pens
hampers (not wicker)
Portland cement

A knock at the door stopped him. And that made him unhappy, which made him chuckle.

"Mr. Clayton?" a feminine voice called. "Are you awake? Or do you laugh in your sleep, too?"

Danny was nonplussed. The voice belonged to Porno Girl. But it was almost midnight, and Porno Girl always retired at nine-thirty. Besides, she hadn't said more than four words to him in the week since they'd met at the Stan Symmons debacle.

He had wanted her to, though. He had wanted that a lot. But now that it was happening, he was terrified. So to keep from falling over and roaring, he thought of spackle.

Then he put down his notepad, got out of bed, and picked up his robe from the floor. The robe was thick, soft, and white, and it said "Radisson" in blue thread on the left breast. The DeWitts had given it to him. He wondered if they had paid for it, or if rich radio shrinks were capable of petty theft from hotels.

"Mr. Clayton?" Porno Girl called again. Her voice was softer now. "I have something for you."

Danny went to the door but didn't open it. He was afraid that if he did, he would make a fool of himself. He was afraid that he would see how much Porno Girl's buttermilk complexion looked like Karen's. And he knew what that could lead to. Uncontrollable hilarity.

"Ms. Larkin?" he asked. "What can I do for you?"

"Let me in," Porno Girl said. She sounded tense. "I don't want to be overheard. Dr. Ralph and Dr. Carla went out, but they might come back. And the Ranger's still around somewhere."

"Milk of magnesia," Danny said, and then he opened the door far enough to reveal Porno Girl's pale oval face and enormous eyes. She was sweetly pretty, like a choirgirl. Yet she had probably just watched a videotape involving copious quantities of bodily fluids.

"What's up?" he asked, gritting his teeth to keep from giggling.

Porno Girl's forehead creased. "The DeWitts are confiscating our mail. I mean, I almost understand why they won't let us have Web access or e-mail—me, especially—but now they're keeping snail-mail from us too. And I don't think it's right."

Danny steeled himself with a thought of soil pH, then opened the door all the way and let her in. She was wearing a baggy sweatshirt and jeans and was carrying a stack of envelopes of various sizes and colors. And she smelled like peaches.

"Isn't it just hate mail?" Danny asked, trying to focus on the envelopes. "I don't care if they keep that."

Porno Girl sat on the edge of the bed. "No. This is stuff they should have given us. Lock the door."

Danny did as she said, then stood there awkwardly. His room didn't have any furniture other than the bed, the nightstand, and a desk with a plain black telephone that never rang. There was supposed to be a chair for the desk, but Dr. Ralph had told him that the room's previous occupant had thrown it out the window. So there was nowhere to sit except the bed. And Danny didn't think that sitting on the bed with Porno Girl would be a good idea for either of them.

Porno Girl began flipping through the envelopes and tossing some onto the bed beside her. "Yours," she said. "Yours. Mine. They've all been opened, by the way." She gave Danny a dark look. "Apparently, the good doctors see us not as patients, but inmates. I'm beginning to wonder if we could leave if we wanted to, or if big iron bars would drop as we approached the front door. Mine. Yours, yours. Mine. That's it. At least, that's all I found."

Danny took a step toward the bed, his eyes fixed on the six envelopes that Porno Girl had sorted for him. Maybe there was something from Lindy. She was only five, but she had written a letter to Santa Claus when she was three. "Where did you find these?"

"Dr. Ralph's study," Porno Girl said. "I was playing an old Traci Lords video down in the rec room this afternoon, and he confiscated it. He said that if a visitor saw it, we might all be busted for kiddie porn. So since he and Dr. Carla are out tonight, I went looking for it. But when I pried open his desk drawer, I found these instead." She gave a thin smile. "I broke the lock. There might be hell to pay for that, but I don't think I'll stick around for it. I think I'll leave."

Danny felt a twinge. "And do what?" He knew that Porno Girl had been fired from a Dallas law firm because of her compulsion, and that no other firm was likely to hire her. Furthermore, her family had made it clear, as recently as yesterday's *Oprah*, that she wouldn't be welcome at home until she was cured. They were all staunch Baptists.

Porno Girl looked toward the curtained window. "I can start my own practice. I'm famous enough that clients will beat a path to my door. They won't mind my . . . problem."

"You think?" Danny asked. He was dubious.

"Or I could accept one of my many other offers." Porno Girl held up an envelope. "See this? An adult film producer in Los Angeles says he'll pay me two hundred thousand dollars to lose my virginity in a gang bang featuring the twelve most well-hung studs in the business."

She was beginning to sound manic. Her cheeks were flushed, and her lips trembled.

"I don't think you're capable of that," Danny said.

Porno Girl stood and glared at him. "Why not? Why shouldn't I let a dozen hairy, sweaty . . ." She closed her eyes and covered her face with her envelopes. "Shit. I'd *feel* it, wouldn't I?"

Danny's gut tightened. He was about to laugh.

So he stepped closer. He had to let her know, before it happened, that he really did sympathize.

He touched her shoulder, and she jumped away as if he'd jabbed her with a soldering iron. Her envelopes went flying, and she backed up against the wall beside the nightstand with her hands held up like claws.

Danny guffawed.

"I'm sorry," he said, gasping.

Porno Girl lowered her hands. She was breathing hard. "Never touch me," she said. "Especially when I'm not looking. I might have torn out your eyes. So never, okay?"

Danny sat down hard on the bed. He was miserable. All he'd wanted to do was make Porno Girl feel a little better, and all he'd done was make her feel attacked. "Okay. Heeheehawhee. I won't. Hwahahah. Portland cement."

Porno Girl stared. "What?"

Danny pressed his fingers to his temples. "Portland cement. I'm thinking about dull things so I can stop—hoohoohoo—laughing."

"Oh." Porno Girl stepped away from the wall and began picking up her envelopes. "But why Portland cement? Why not concrete? Or stucco?"

The thought of concrete made Danny giggle. "Because people are always crashing into concrete highway barriers, and kids are always skinning their knees on concrete sidewalks. And stucco is just funny enough to depress me. It sounds as if it ought to be a Marx Brother. So I have to stick to something smooth and featureless, like Portland cement. Portland cement." The giggling subsided.

Porno Girl picked up her last envelope and sat down on the bed again, cramming herself up against the headboard. Danny took that as a hint, picking up his own envelopes and moving down to the foot of the bed.

They regarded each other across the expanse, and Porno Girl seemed to relax a little. "Thanks, L.B.," she said.

Danny winced. The New York *Post* had referred to him as "L.B." in yesterday's edition. "Call me Danny, please."

Porno Girl's eyebrows rose. "Well, then. Do you think of me as Amanda, or as Porno Girl?"

She had him there. He was ashamed, and chuckled.

"I guess we've never been properly introduced," he said. "I don't think the Stan Symmons show counts."

"Certainly not."

Danny put down his envelopes and extended his right hand. "Hi. I'm Danny Clayton."

Porno Girl looked wary, but set aside her own envelopes and reached toward him. "Amanda Larkin," she said.

Danny managed to grasp her fingertips for a few seconds before she pulled them away. They were warm and dry.

"Pleased to meet you," Danny said. He looked down at his envelopes. The red one on top was addressed to him in Karen's handwriting, but the name on the return address was Miss Linda Clayton. It was postmarked May 27. That was the day after he'd been slashed. "Thank you for bringing my mail, Amanda. Dr. Carla told me there were letters from wackos, but that there was no reason for me to see them. And I said that was fine." He picked up the red envelope. "But I didn't think they'd keep letters from my daughter. I'll speak to them about this. Okra."

Amanda looked down at her own mail. "I don't think speaking to them about it will do any good, Danny. We're nothing but guinea pigs to them."

Danny wasn't sure about that, but he was sure that he wanted to open the red envelope. He couldn't let himself do that, though, until he could make himself want it less. He had to wait until he could make it seem as ordinary as okra.

"Okra," he said. "Okra. I don't know. The DeWitts are publicity hounds, so I'm skeptical of them too. But in this case, maybe they're just trying to protect us from anything they think might exacerbate our problems, and they've gone a little too far. Okra, okra."

Amanda opened one of her envelopes and pulled out a Polaroid photo. "Oh, look," she said. "Here's a picture from my eighth-grade social studies teacher, of all people. But I don't know these men with her. Want to see it?"

"No, thank you. Okra, okra, okra."

"Do you really find okra bland?" Amanda asked, turning the photo this way and that. "I always found it rather exotic. But I grew up in Ohio, and Southern cuisine wasn't popular in the Buckeye State."

"I grew up in Kansas," Danny said, "and we had plenty of okra. Kansas is the Midwest, not the South."

Amanda shook her head. "No, Ohio is the Midwest. I don't know what Kansas is. Over the rainbow or something. Oh, here's another photo. My goodness, Mrs. Kincher! That can't be the same Basset hound you always talked about. He'd be dead by now, wouldn't he?"

At that, Danny allowed himself to open the flap on the red envelope. "Cleveland," he said. "Cleveland."

"Hey, I've been to Cleveland," Amanda said. "It's not all that boring, really. They've got the Rock and Roll Hall of Fame."

"Doesn't matter. It's working. Cleveland. Cleveland. Cleveland."

He pulled a piece of blue construction paper from the red envelope. It had been folded in half and cut into the shape of a lopsided heart. He could almost see the round-tipped scissors that Lindy would have used to make it.

I LOVE YoU DaDDY, the front of the card said. It was written in orange crayon.

Danny opened the heart, and there was more crayon inside.

The left side said I HOPE YoUR ARM GEtS BEtER.

The right side said LINDY, and it was surrounded by five-pointed stars.

Danny roared and fell off the bed. The laughter had hit him like the fat end of a baseball bat, and okra and Cleveland had been powerless to stop it. He couldn't see straight, and his breath came in shuddering gulps. A red-and-black checkerboard began to blot out what he could see of the floor.

Lindy appeared on the checkerboard, and she smiled at him before bursting into a red mist.

Danny tried to scream, but all that came out was more laughter.

Then a thin, high voice pierced through the howl.

"Lanolin!" it cried. "Lanolin! Lanolin!" There was a crisp *whick* of notepad paper whipping around, and the voice cried, "Baked potato! *Baked potato!*"

Danny saw a potato sitting on the checkerboard, and it split open to reveal that it was dry and overcooked. It was the plainest thing he had ever seen.

The red mist evaporated and the checkerboard faded, but the potato remained for a few moments before crumbling to dust. Then the dust faded away, and the roar of laughter faded with it.

Danny caught his breath and stared at the hardwood floor slats for a moment before rolling onto his back and looking up at Amanda. She was kneeling on the edge of the bed, holding his notepad at arm's length as if it were holy scripture.

"Earned income credit!" she yelled.

He gave her what he hoped looked like a grateful smile. "I'm okay now," he said. "Thanks."

Amanda closed the notepad. She looked relieved. "No problem. Maybe you can do something for me someday."

Danny thought of several things, but knew they were impossible for Amanda except as something to be observed. He put them out of his mind and thought of another potato just as someone began pounding on his door.

"Dan'l!" It was the Racist Ranger. "Is you all right in dah? Or does I need to bust dis heah do' all to flinders?"

Danny looked toward the door, and then at Amanda. "Was there mail for the Ranger in Dr. Ralph's desk too?"

Amanda frowned. "No. In fact, I think he might be in cahoots with the DeWitts. So I'm leaving just as soon as I can figure out where to go and what to do for money."

Danny realized then that Amanda didn't know the Ranger was still working for the FBI, and that the DeWitts were too. She didn't know there was more going on here than radio-shrink therapy.

But there was. So maybe there was more to the DeWitts' mail confiscation as well.

"Dan'l! Miz Lawkin!" The Racist Ranger rattled the doorknob. "I heah you bof in dah! I swah, you don' come en open de do' in de nex' ten seckens, en I'se a-gwyne to be a-barellin' thoo 'er lak a lokermoteev, dad fetch it."

Amanda lay back on the bed and covered her face with Danny's notebook. "Christ, he can do it, too. I thought he was going to take that guy in Chicago and rip him apart like a wishbone. Better open the door."

Danny got to his feet, wincing at the knots in his belly, and went to the door. He turned the button in the knob, and then he was knocked backward as the door flew open. He landed on the floor with the Racist Ranger on his chest, so his laughter was cut off before it could start.

"Whoo!" the Racist Ranger said. "Sorry 'bout dat."

The Ranger rolled off and stood up. He was naked except for a shoulder holster and Donald Duck boxer shorts. He offered a hand to help Danny up, but Danny scooted out of reach and stood up on his own, gulping air. He backed away until he was standing against the bed.

"I heerd a commotion," the Ranger said. "I heerd hollerin' 'bout baked potaters en lanolin en other sech truck en nonsense. En I wuz a-skyeered dat you wuz mebbe in a sitcherashun."

"We're fine," Danny said. "I just had a laughing attack, that's all. Amanda helped me."

The Racist Ranger looked from Danny to the supine Amanda. "I see dat. I see dat she done hep'd you." He stooped down and picked up a Polaroid from the floor. "Lawd! Is dat one er dem Basset houn's? Dog my cats ef it ain't de limberest one I ever did see."

Amanda sat up and snatched the photo away. "That's mine," she said.

"I done figgered *dat* much," the Ranger said.

Danny began to feel annoyed, and it made him grin. "That photo was part of the mail that's been kept from us, Agent Royce." He picked up his envelopes from the bed. "Now, I understand that you people have to watch for anything that might come from the terrorists, but there's a limit. My mother and daughter don't send letter bombs. And why intercept Amanda's mail at all? She isn't connected to the Massacre."

The Racist Ranger rubbed his chin. "Now, dat's perculyar. I ain't looked thoo yo' mail my ownse'f, but I reckon Sepeshial Agent Armstrong er one o' his mens been doin' it. Dey gots to, like you says. And Miz Lawkin *is* kerneckted now, kase she been seen wid you on de TeeBee—en dey might be folks mailin' her letter bombs ennyhow, kase dey doan' like pre-verts. But my ol' fren Mars Armstrong goan be passin' dat mail on thoo de DeWitts onest he done wid it. So ef you ain't been gettin' it, it's de doctahs keepin' it. Doan' be takin' it up wid nobody but dem."

Danny was surprised. He hadn't seen Special Agent Armstrong since Wichita, but apparently he was still around. "I'll do that," Danny said. "But if going through our mail is someone else's job, what's *your* job?"

Now the Ranger looked irritated. "Lawd," he said. "'Sides de fack dat I really is in therapy heah, I is keepin' an eye out fo' possible suspecks what might want to blow yo' head clean off. In shoat, I is yo' Fed'ral bodyguard. I doan' be wearin' dis Glock en shouldah holstah kase I enjoys de chafin'."

Amanda gasped. Danny looked at her and saw that her eyes seemed even larger than usual.

"Wait a minute," she said. "You're still a Fed? And you're our *bodyguard*?"

"I'm sho' nuff Dan'l's, ennyhow," the Ranger said. "What you think, dat man wid the knife 'uz a fluke? You think I be snappin' his spine out de goodness o' my heart?"

Amanda crushed her letters in her fists and stared at the window again. "I'm an idiot. I've been so preoccupied with my own sickness that I didn't even notice the sickness around me. I just looked at dirty pictures." She shook her head as if driving away a hallucination. "I have to get out of here."

Danny sat on the edge of the bed. "I don't think you should. If you leave now, people like that film producer will try to take advantage of you."

He was amazed that he didn't start laughing, because he hated himself for his duplicity. The truth was that he didn't want Amanda to leave because—aside from his other feelings for her—she was the closest thing to a friend that he had.

Amanda stood, clutching her mail. "I'll think about it." She started toward the door. "I'm not sure where I'd go, at that. But wherever it was, I doubt that I'd need to worry about terrorists."

"Mebbe not," the Ranger said. "But you wouldn' be safe, neither. You got some habits what kin git a young woman into a pickle er two."

Amanda paused at the door. "I'm *already* in a pickle or two. Even more so than I realized before coming up here." She gave Danny a weak smile. "For the moment, though, I think I've figured out how to unblock the naked channel on the cable box. So I'm going to go watch that since I can't find my Traci Lords tape. See you later, okay?"

The impulse to laugh surged up Danny's throat, but he slapped it down with drywall.

"Sure," he said. He ran his fingertips over Lindy's construction-paper heart. "Thanks again for finding our mail. I'll talk to Dr. Ralph about it tomorrow."

Amanda nodded. "Good luck," she said, and went out, closing the door behind her.

The Ranger looked at the door and adjusted his shoulder holster. "Dat girl's pow'ful messed up," he said. "She sholy gwine to do somepin dumb."

"She's smarter than you and me put together," Danny said. But he was glad that the Ranger was still there. A man in Donald Duck boxer shorts and a shoulder holster was ridiculous enough that Danny might be able to look through the rest of his mail without laughing.

He flipped through the envelopes. Besides the one from Lindy, there was an oversized envelope from CBS Television, two letters from his mother, and two more from Karen. He tossed the CBS envelope aside. It was the letters from his family that mattered. Until now, he'd thought they'd been shunning him. He had tried to call them several times, but all he'd gotten was constant ringing at both numbers.

"I doan' mean as whut Miz Lawkin ain't pooty smart," the Ranger said. "But pooty smart people kin do pooty dumb thin's. En I gots me a pow'ful sense dat she's a-gwineter do jus' dat. I kin see de signs."

"So what do you want to do about it?" Danny opened the letters from his mother first and found that they were both content-free except for references to the saving grace of Jesus. But at least they let him know that his parents hadn't been burned out of their home yet.

Then he opened the letters from Karen. They were dated just a few days apart, but one was from before the Stan Symmons show, and the other from after. Both were about the fact that he was now behind in his child-support payments. But in the letter written after his slashing, Karen assured him that she understood his situation . . . and that she would get by until he could do his share again.

"I cain't do nuffin 'bout Miz Lawkin if she decide to go," the Ranger said. "I gots to stay wif you. You is my one en on'y albatross until de Bureau be sayin' diff'ent."

Thank God for the Ranger, Danny thought. Otherwise, Karen's

letters would have had him on the floor again. If she was even *mentioning* finances, it meant that things were getting tight already.

Maybe, he thought, she could sell the sordid story of her former sex life with Laughin' Boy to the tabloids. But that wasn't the sort of thing she would do. At least, he didn't think so. Not that there was much of a story there anyway.

He refolded the letters. "Crap," he said. "I miss her."

"Who dat?" the Ranger asked. "Yo' li'l girl-chile?"

Danny didn't answer. Instead, he set aside Karen's letters and opened the one from CBS.

It was an offer for him to become a cast member of *Lanford's On Late!*, the late-night talk show hosted by comedian Larry Lanford. Danny wouldn't have to do much, the letter explained—merely laugh at any jokes that bombed. And since laughing at things that weren't funny had become his natural impulse, the job would be a piece of cake. For his services, he would receive three thousand dollars a night, five nights a week, for a minimum of four weeks.

The letter went on to say that the show might have something for Porno Girl and the Racist Ranger to do as well, but only if Laughin' Boy was part of the package. Specifically, the show's producers had a recurring sketch called "Odd Squad!" in mind. Each of the squad members would receive two thousand dollars for a three-minute sketch, with a guarantee of ten sketches.

Danny was stunned. The offer was sleazy and stupid, but sixty thousand dollars—plus twenty thousand in sketch money, if Amanda and the Ranger joined him—would solve his child-support problems.

"All righty, den, doan' answer ol' Rob," the Ranger said. He sounded indignant. "It ain't 'zif I gots troubles wid my own fambly ner nuffin. It ain't 'zif I even *gets* mail fer de doctahs to cornfiscate. So I'll jus' be goin'."

Danny looked up and saw the Ranger heading for the door. The Donald Duck boxers were riding low, and that made it possible for

Danny to speak without laughing.

"How'd you like to earn some extra cash?" he asked.

The Ranger stopped and turned. "How's I gwine to do dat?"

Danny read the letter aloud, and when he had finished, the Ranger crossed his arms and scowled.

"I doan' like dis," the Ranger said. "Nossuh, not one lil' bit. Dis heah soun' like jus' one mo' chanst fer de terr'ists to take a stab at killin' you. Dat's why I ain't let you do no mo' telebishion since Chicago. On'y dem radio interviews en de Internet chat."

"But I thought the whole idea was to use me as bait," Danny said. "And there's nothing better for that than being on TV. Besides, we don't know that the guy who attacked me in Chicago was associated with the terrorists. Wasn't he just a random nut?"

The Ranger looked at Danny without blinking. "Ain't no way to know now, honey, kase he dead. He done got up from de hospital bed en hung hisself wid de sheets dis moanin'. Leas' ways, dat's how it 'uz set up to look. De guards in de hall say nobody come in ner out, but it sholy do look funny—seein' as how he had hisself a spinal fracture, wuz unconshus, en 'uz tied down to de bed to boot." He clucked his tongue. "Nossuh, I b'lieve he 'uz a terr'ist flunky, en he 'uz kilt so's to keep 'im quiet 'bout it."

"Wallpaper paste," Danny said. "Navy beans."

"I beg yo' pardon?"

"Grout," Danny said. "Never mind. I get your point."

"Not all of 'er, you doesn't." The Ranger patted his pistol. "De p'int is, I expeck to hafter use disyear sidearm sooner er later, kase sooner er later someone's a-gwineter come arter you fer stealin' dey thunder. But I wants 'em to do it *hyear*. Dis townhouse is under surveylance, so dey cain't plant no bomb widdout us knowin'. En if dey tries to come in, dey gots to get pas' yo's truly. But down to de teebee studios, we could lose de advantage. It's blamed hard to watch ever'body what go in en out er a big ol' cor'prate buildin' like dat. So it doan' make no sense from de risk-assessment standp'int."

Danny stood and tried to look the Ranger in the eye without whooping. "Well, I can risk my life, or I can risk losing my daughter. I need money."

The Ranger pointed a finger at Danny. "You ain't a-gwine to lose dat chile even if you doan' never send her another plug nickel, kase you is her daddy. 'Cept iffen you gets yo'sef kilt, en den you ain't nuffin to nobody."

Danny was about to say that he wasn't anything to anyone *now*, but then the telephone on the desk rang and made him burst into a peal of laughter.

The Ranger gave the telephone a narrow glance as it rang again. "You 'spectin' a call?"

Danny bent over and hugged his belly, trying to crush the convulsions. "Shirt cardboard," he gasped. "Pea gravel. No. Nobody's ever called. And my parents and Karen are the only ones I gave the number."

"Den it mus' be one o' dem," the Ranger said. "You best pick 'er up fo' she ring offen de hook."

Danny didn't want to. He couldn't let himself laugh at anyone in his family. Especially not Lindy. He wished he had taken some of the blue pills this evening.

"You get it," he said.

The Ranger shrugged, then went to the desk and picked up the receiver. "Hello dah," he said. "Who dis on de line?" He listened for a moment, then frowned and covered the mouthpiece. "It's Sepeshial Agent Armstrong. But he doan' want to speak wid me kase he hates de soun' o' my voice. It 'bout breaks dis ol' heart, it sholy do." He held out the receiver. "Feel free to laugh inter his punkin haid."

Danny giggled, but he managed to take the receiver from the Ranger and put it to his ear. He was terrified that something had happened to Lindy, Karen, or his parents, and that Armstrong was calling to tell him.

Instead, Armstrong said, "Take the CBS job."

Danny was baffled. "What?"

"Take the CBS job," Armstrong said again. "The Lanford show isn't taped in their usual studios. It's in the Jackie Gleason Theater here in Manhattan, and we can make the building reasonably secure. You'll be safe enough, and your appearances could help draw out some suspects."

Armstrong's voice was cold. Danny didn't think Armstrong liked him any better than the Ranger.

"All right," he said between giggles. "I was planning to take the job anyway. But what about Agent Royce?"

Armstrong's voice grew colder still. "What about him?"

"Can he do the sketches? I'll make more money if he does. And get that much more exposure to lure suspects, too."

There was a pause, and Danny heard Armstrong take a long, slow breath.

"All right," Armstrong said then. "He can do it if he wants. But he can't accept payment."

"I'll give him the phone so you can tell him that," Danny said.

"He already knows. Any other questions?"

Danny chortled. "Yes. Since you've been opening my mail, I already figured that you'd read the CBS letter. But since you've called me just as I happened to be *talking* about it, I'm assuming you've also bugged my room. Am I right?"

The line was silent.

"Okay, then, here's the deal," Danny said. He was scared of Armstrong, so he had to fight hard to keep his laughter at a moderate level. "Hee-hee-hee. Number Two pencils. If you'll stop bugging my room and reading my mail, I'll promise to tell you or Royce if I receive anything that could be of any use to you."

"What could be of use to us is for us to decide," Armstrong said. "Besides, I should think you'd appreciate the fact that we check your mail for explosives."

"Whooop! Weatherstripping!"

"What?"

Danny spoke through gritted teeth, swallowing each laugh as it burbled up. "Let's compromise. Plaster of Paris. No bugs in my room, but you can open my mail."

There was another pause, and then Armstrong said, "I'll see what I can do. And I'll speak with the DeWitts, because I didn't know they were keeping mail I'd cleared. In the meantime, take the job." The line clicked and went dead.

Danny's urge to laugh subsided again as he put down the receiver and looked over at the scowling Racist Ranger.

"If you were going to put a listening device in this room," he asked, "where would it be?"

"Well, honey," the Ranger said, "de one I done *already* put in is stuck to de back er de headbo'ad. But dey may be others."

Danny grimaced. "Some friend you are."

"I ain't said I'se yo' fren'," the Ranger growled.

"All right, then. Co-star. We're going to be on television again, but as a comedy team."

The Ranger's scowl darkened. "Dat's de beatenes' notion in de worl'," he said. "But if you's gwine to do 'er, I gots no choice."

The door opened then, and Porno Girl stepped inside again. She was holding an empty water glass and rubbing her ear.

"Count me in too," she said. "I can use the 'Odd Squad' money to replace my Traci Lords tape, and then to get the hell away from the DeWitts."

Danny was glad she was back. She was weird and scary, and she made him feel things he didn't want to feel, but at least she was a woman who would talk to him. At least she was here. And at least she needed him . . . if only as a way out.

The Racist Ranger shook his head and rubbed the back of his neck. "Dad fetch it, Dan'l, I *tole* you dat girl 'uz gwine to do somepin dumb, en heah she *is!* Signs is *signs*, mine I tell you, en I knowed it jis' 's well as I'se a stannin' heah dis minute!"

Sound Bites (5)

It's Friday, June 2nd of the Year 2000 . . . I'm Ron Bartlett . . . and this is *Extra Hard Edition*!

(startling synthesized minor chord)

She's the beautiful ex-wife of the man who is either the world's most notorious sinner or most misunderstood saint—Daniel Clayton, the notorious "Laughin' Boy" of the Wichita Massacre. But except for one quick ambush-style interview, she's been completely out of the public eye, hiding herself and her child away from the media onslaught. So we've only been able to speculate as to her relationship with, and her reaction to the behavior of, the extra-hilarity of her hilarious ex.

Until now. Now, for the first time, Karen Clayton has broken her silence. And she's broken it by speaking with *Extra Hard Edition*'s own Julie Martini.

(Music In: "Somewhere, Over the Rainbow")

Thanks, Ron. I'm here in Wichita, Kansas, the site of the infamous Wichita Massacre, talking with Ms. Karen Clayton, the former spouse of Laughin' Boy.

Ms. Clayton, we'd like to start by thanking you for giving this exclusive interview to *Extra Hard Edition*. We realize that it's been a traumatic two weeks for you, and we're grateful that you've put your trust in us for your first voluntary interview.

First of all, Ms. Clayton—Why now? Why, after two weeks of seclusion and silence, have you decided to speak out at this time?

I promised to be totally honest, so here goes. I'm afraid the reason I'm talking to you now is because I need the money. You're not the first news organization to offer payment, you understand—Oprah was another—but you've offered the most. Now, Barbara Walters promised all sorts of things about lighting and tone and lines of questioning, but wouldn't pay me anything because of something about journalistic ethics. And I know it sounds mercenary or unethical for me to let money influence me—but I have my daughter to think of.

You're referring, of course, to your beautiful little five-year-old girl, Linda. I understand that you call her "Lindy," by the way. Why is that?

"Lindy" was—I mean, is—her father's nickname for her. When she was just a baby, he could get her to laugh by dancing around with her, and he claimed he was doing the Lindy. I don't think he was, but that didn't really matter.

So would you characterize Laughin' Boy as a good father?

He tries to be. But I'm not sure you can characterize someone as a good father just because he tries . . . just because he dances around with her or takes her trick-or-treating. On the other hand, that's certainly being a better father than someone who doesn't do those things.

You seem ambivalent about him. Why is that?

First of all, there's the whole horrible Laughin' Boy thing. And I'm far from alone in feeling ambivalent about that. It really was impossible to understand how he could do such a thing . . . and then the DeWitts came along and said that he's suffering from some sort of illness, and that his "battle" with it is heroic. So it's hard for anyone to have a clear notion of just who or what Danny is these days. And even leaving all that aside—For me, personally, he's a man I loved but had to divorce. And who wouldn't feel somewhat ambivalent about that?

I also can't help but wonder whether your ambivalence has something to do with your answer to my first question. You said that you're doing this interview because you're having financial problems and must think of the welfare of your daughter. Does that mean that Laughin' Boy has failed to provide child support?

Not exactly, but . . . You see, Danny's a teacher at a community college—or he was, up until two weeks ago—and he's never made a lot of money. But ever since we divorced last August, he's always paid his monthly child support. It wasn't a lot, but since I worked too—I was a teller at a credit union—we got by.

You say you *were* a teller. What happened?

Well, the Massacre happened. "Laughin' Boy" happened. The whole horrific mess happened. I couldn't go back to work after that. There would have been reporters and cameras in the lobby and the drive-through—not to mention the people who would have taken out their hatred of Danny on me. And I couldn't leave Linda at day care anymore for the same reason. She wouldn't have been safe.

Certainly not. In fact, we understand that you and she have both received death threats. How many, exactly?

I have no idea. The FBI intercepts all our mail now, and we have police cars at the house twenty-four hours a day. We have groceries delivered. We never leave. It's like being in prison.

I can attest to that. I, my cameraman, and my producer were practically strip-searched before being let inside—and *Extra Hard Edition* isn't exactly wanted for terrorism!

No, I suppose not.

But back to the question of Laughin' Boy's child support. Haven't you received anything at all from your ex-husband since May 20th?

No, we haven't. But he's lost his job too, so I understand—and yet I still need to pay my bills. The timing of this has been awful. Not that there's ever a good time for anything like the Massacre, you understand. But just for me and my daughter, personally, it's been bad. Among other things, I had to have my car worked on in May, and . . . this sounds so petty.

Not at all. A working mother needs a car. Please continue.

It's like this. Toward the end of each month, Danny would give me the next month's support check when he dropped off Lindy from one of his weekend visits with her. That way, I'd have the child-support money right away to help out with all those first-of-the-month bills. Linda's day care, for example, was due in advance each month.

But Laughin' Boy didn't come through this time?

No. But he couldn't. The weekend of May 20th normally would have been one of Danny's weekends with Linda, and he probably would have given me the check on the 21st. But because my mother was visiting, I called Danny to ask if we could switch his time to the next weekend. And he agreed.

It was a good thing he did, wasn't it?

Yes. Otherwise, he might have had her at the park with him, and . . . I don't even want to think about it.

That's all right. Take a moment.

I felt awful when I heard Danny's voice on the phone that morning. He was so disappointed he couldn't see her, and I remember thinking that I was the Wicked Witch of the West or something. But if I hadn't been, if I hadn't—

You did the right thing. You saved her.

But I didn't know that. How could I?

A mother's instinct. Or a premonition?

I don't know. He might not have even gone to the River Fest if I'd let him have Linda. Maybe instead of saving her, I doomed him to becoming Laughin' Boy.

Still, that doesn't change the fact that you lost your job and didn't receive your child support payment.

That's true. And I won't receive any for quite a while, because Danny won't have new income any time soon.

On the contrary, Ms. Clayton. We have some news for you on that front.

What do you mean?

We mean that Laughin' Boy is being offered a lucrative position. That doesn't necessarily mean he'll be paying you any child support, of course. The jury's still out on just what kind of man we're dealing with here. However, we thought you should know that he's about to have a source of potentially substantial income.

How can that be? The other news shows are saying that he can barely function—that he can't string two sentences together without laughing, and that the DeWitts have him drugged all the time. So how could he have a job?

Our sources at CBS tell us that Laughin' Boy is about to become a cast member of *Lanford's on Late!* —and that he'll do so in the company of his fellow DeWitt patient-celebrities, Porno Girl and the Racist Ranger. The word is, in fact, that they'll appear in comedy sketches together, making light of their psychological disorders and of the violent events that have occurred around them.

I can't believe that.

And I can't believe that Laughin' Boy hasn't informed you of this change in his fortunes.

Well, to be fair, he might be having trouble getting in touch. I had to have my telephone number changed because of all the hate calls. My mother paid for the change.

Didn't you tell Laughin' Boy your new number?

I tried to. I tried to find the DeWitts' office or home number in New York, but all I could get was the 800 number for their radio show. Which I guess is on hiatus for the summer, but the phone's still being answered. So I called and left my new number. But I'm wondering now whether Danny ever got it.

Even if he did, can you be sure he would call to tell you his news? Can you be sure he'd be willing to share the wealth that results from his newfound fame?

Yes. He has his faults—if he didn't, we'd still be married—but he's never been cheap, and he's always been conscientious about looking out for our daughter. If he ever did otherwise, he wouldn't be the Danny Clayton I know.

With all due respect, would the Danny Clayton you know ever laugh at bloodshed and misery?

No. No, he wouldn't. I see your point.

So it's possible that he's <u>not</u> the man you used to know.

I suppose it is. But the DeWitts—

And speaking of the DeWitts: What do you think of psychiatrists who would allow a patient with a serious emotional disorder to take a role on a late-night comedy show—a role that will capitalize on that very disorder?

I don't know what I think of any of this.

Setting that aside, then, let me ask you this: Why did you retain your ex-husband's surname after your divorce? Most women today would prefer to reassert their own identities after leaving men who weren't right for them.

I'm afraid that question is a little too personal for my taste.

Our contract states that "personal" questions are not out of bounds, Ms. Clayton.

That's true. But it doesn't say I have to answer them.

I'll just have my producer call one of our lawyers to find out about that.

Never mind. I'll answer the question.

That's up to you.

Thank you. I retained my married name because I prefer it to my maiden name.

Which was?

Carpenter. My name was Karen Carpenter.

Oh. I see.

No, I don't think you do. But to make things clearer, I'll tell you that Danny Clayton was the first boyfriend I ever had who didn't call me up and sing "Close to You." And I was so grateful, I married him.

So your marriage, then, was based on something other than love.

I didn't say that.

And how was your sex life with him? I know that's another personal question, but . . .

Our sex life was fine. He was a normal person.

Did he ever laugh in bed?

Really, now . . .

Inappropriately or excessively, I mean.

Not to my recollection.

Did your sex life change appreciably after giving birth?

For the love of—

What I'm trying to ascertain is whether Laughin' Boy might have any resentment toward his daughter. If your physical relations deteriorated after her birth, that might explain his current reluctance to pay child support—and might even have something to do with his psychological disorder, which manifests itself in behavior that could be considered childish.

I don't think so. As I said before, that part of our life was normal. And besides, as I've also said before, Danny has never denied Lindy, I mean Linda, anything. He's tried hard to be a good father.

Until two weeks ago, when that changed.

A lot of things changed two weeks ago. For a lot of people. Some of them far worse off than I am.

And it looks as if more big changes are in the works. For example, the rumor mill has it that Laughin' Boy may have gotten over you—

I would hope so.

—and that he's romantically involved with disgraced attorney Amanda Larkin, better known as Porno Girl.

I doubt that.

Do you know why she's called Porno Girl?

I know that she's declared her intention to remain celibate.

Do you think that would stop Laughin' Boy from becoming involved with her?

It would stop anyone, wouldn't it?

But if it didn't, what would you say to taking your revenge with the Racist Ranger?

What on earth are you talking about?

I'm just asking whether you find the Racist Ranger attractive.

The DeWitts say he's not really a racist, you know.

You seem to be avoiding the—

Assuming he's not a racist, and assuming that I'd never actually heard him speak, and assuming that I was fourteen, I'd have to say he's gorgeous.

I'm with you, Ms. Carpenter-Clayton.

Just Clayton.

Of course. And finally—We were hoping we could have a glimpse of your lovely daughter.

No, I'm afraid not. She and my mother are watching a video in the bedroom, and I don't want to disturb them.

A few moments ago you called her "Lindy," which is Laughin' Boy's nickname for her—but then you quickly changed it to "Linda."

Do you have a question?

We just wanted to note the poignancy and pain inherent in this tragic situation, and to conclude by wishing you and your lovely daughter all the very best of luck.

Thank you.

And we hope your financial situation turns around soon.

Thank you.

And we hope that none of the anger and rage that has resulted from the Wichita Massacre is misdirected at you or at Linda-slash-Lindy.

Thank you.

And we hope that nothing like what happened to the victims of the Wichita Massacre ever happens to you or to her, or to anyone, ever again.

Thank you.

And we hope you find love.

Uhh . . . thank you.

And thank you, Ms. Carpenter-Clayton.

So while the world may still be uncertain as to the exact nature of the enigma known as Laughin' Boy, one thing is certain: His ex-wife is one spunky single mom fighting the good fight in an uphill battle against violence, hatred, poverty, and adversity.

Clearly, a certain buffed-out former FBI agent could do a whole lot worse!

For *Extra Hard Edition*, I'm Julie Martini.

Back to you, Ron.

(Music Out: "Close to You")

Therapy Transcript (6)

[*Laughter Deleted*]

I'm ashamed.

You want to know how I feel, well, that's how I feel.

Not about what I did at the Massacre. I can't be ashamed of something out of my control. Don't get me wrong; I can be horrified and appalled along with everyone else. But I can't be ashamed.

What I'm ashamed of is that I've taken advantage of it.

Not that I'm alone in that. It's what everyone does. People fall all over themselves to get on TV, no matter the reason, because they can turn around and parlay that fame, however brief or ludicrous, into still more fame. And money. And then more TV, and more fame, and more money. Over and over, round and round, until finally the viewing public tires of them and the ratings implode. It doesn't matter whether they're on a talk show confessing to incest or on a game show swimming in pudding. They do it because people watch. They do it because it works.

And doctors, that's what the two of you have done as well. But at least you've never made any bones about who you are or what you do. Your obvious goal has always been to increase your audience, your fame, and your wealth. And maybe you've even helped a few people in the process, which puts you on moral ground at least a little higher than the average wife-beater on *Cops*. But maybe a little lower than this week's winner on *Jeopardy*, since that guy neither asked nor answered any questions about sleeping with his mother.

As for me, I'm currently down there in the muck with the gap-toothed, hairy-pitted, tube-top-overflowing, subject-and-verb-disagreeing swine on *Jerry Springer*. Because while I didn't choose to be part of a tragedy, it's now become my source of income.

They drop me down on a swing. They drop me down on a swing, get a quick shot of me hee-hawing over a bad joke about the President's bent penis, then haul me back up as soon as the audience starts hee-hawing along with me.

And the only reason it works is because everyone in that audience also saw me laughing over broken, bleeding bodies two and a half weeks ago.

Two and a half weeks ago they despised me. Now they laugh along. Why? Because their initial horror at my behavior has been warped by my growing fame. They've seen my image often enough now that I've become a celebrity—and celebrities, no matter how they got that way, are revered simply because they *are* celebrities. Even the critics who claim to despise celebrities actually love them, because *their* jobs depend on the celebrities' fame, too.

The paradox, for me personally, is that most of the public might still despise me even as they channel-surf in search of my image. But then, being despicable has never been an obstacle to fame and fortune. Not so long as there are cameras rolling and people who want to watch.

The next check I send to my daughter will be the result of the fact that I laughed when I saw people die. It will be the result of the fact that I laughed when I saw a little girl who was just about her age get shot to pieces.

[Eleven minutes pass.]

Not that I can see any alternative. TV has not only made me what I am, but has also taken away any opportunity I might have had to be anything else. Larry Lanford will hire Laughin' Boy, but he's not interested in hiring a former technical-writing instructor named Danny Clayton. And why would he be? Why would anyone, at this point?

I suppose I should just stop whining and deal with it. At least it pays.

Which is no doubt what the latest white-trash truck-stop hooker pregnant with her brother's triplets told herself as she cashed her check from *Ricki Lake*.

On the other hand, if I put myself in that category, then I have to put Amanda there too. And I can't do that. She has to do whatever she can to get back on her feet. No offense, doctors, but she can't stay with you much longer. She can't keep on being your little Porno Girl to trot out with the rest of the sideshow geeks whenever it suits you.

I believe that you're sincerely trying to help her. But let's look at the reality of the situation. She's been your patient for a lot longer than I have—almost a year, I'm told—and how much has she improved? How long has it been since you found a stack of hardcore sex magazines from Germany stuffed under her mattress? Just after lunch this afternoon, wasn't it?

She's not getting any better. And now she's reduced to wearing pink tights and looking like an idiot alongside the likes of me and Rob Royce.

Did you know she was a National Merit scholar? Did you know she made Law Review? Did you know she used to sing at every wedding held in her church? Did you know that she volunteered at animal shelters on Saturdays, and that she did pro bono work for the homeless?

Of course you did. But what does the rest of the world know about her? Well, thanks to you, they know that she can't get enough smut . . . and thanks to me, they know that she runs around in a leotard on late-night TV. Oh, and they also know that she's a virgin, which means that every psychotic stroke-book addict on earth now fantasizes about deflowering her. And the violent ones are probably making plans to do so.

No, I don't have the slightest idea what to do for her. If I did, I'd do it for myself too. All I know is that what's being done for her right now hasn't helped, and may have made her a target for rapists.

She deserves better. A whole lot better.

Shit, while I'm at it, I'll admit that I even feel a little sorry for the Ranger. I still don't like him, but from what I can tell, all he really wants to do is be a good cop. Or whatever the Feds call themselves instead of cops. But now that he's a member of the Odd Squad, what he's getting to be instead is Shemp to my Moe. And that's a fate I wouldn't wish on my worst enemy.

Speaking of my worst enemy—

Is there any evidence at all that the terrorists who committed the Massacre even care that I'm getting more and more famous? Is there any evidence at all that they even watch *Lanford's on Late*?

I mean, if there was a definite chance that something good might come from all this, I could feel better about it.

At least I know Lindy won't see me in that blue-and-silver getup. She's in bed hours before the show comes on. Karen would never let her watch it on tape, either. I can be grateful for that, at least.

You see, whatever else Karen might be, she's a great mother. That's one thing she was always determined to be, no matter what. She had strong ideas about raising kids from the moment I met her. In fact, I think I know why she chose me over all the other men she could have had: Because she wanted a father for her children who wouldn't get in her way. And for obvious reasons, she didn't think I'd be any trouble.

Guess I fooled her, huh?

I wish I felt as flip as that sounded. But the truth is that I'm scared. I'm so scared that it's all I can do not to laugh until my lungs bleed.

What if the bad guys *do* watch *Lanford's on Late*? What if they *do* resent me for taking the fame that they feel should have been theirs? And what if they can't punish me for it here in New York because the Racist Ranger and his buddies are in the way?

What if they decide to take it out on my family instead?

Video Clip (4)
Deus Ex Laughina

Fellow Righteous Caucasians!

Brothers and Sisters of the White Warriors for Jesus, Deceased!

Welcome to this week's encrypted video conference. My thanks to Brother Richard for implementing this technology and for thus helping me to feel closer to you than ever before.

Let us begin by thanking Sister Suellen for her stirring blessing. I declare, she has become one of the finest soldiers in the WWJD, having risen above the limitations of her gender through obedience and prayer. Why, if we could strike at GOG and MAGOG with words alone, Sister Suellen's tongue would be a grenade launcher. Let me hear you say *Amen!*

At ease. Those of you gathered together, please holster your weapons and be seated. As your Pastor, I have something to show you all.

I recorded this from network television last night. Watch, if you can, its deceitful images while hearing my words.

I'm sure you're familiar with this show, a MAGOG-inspired atrocity called *Lanford's On Late!* This is the opening segment, which features degenerate non-Caucasian music from the band and mindless applause from the brainwashed audience as Lanford walks onstage like a bowlegged chicken. But take heart, for there aren't as many people in the audience as it seems. It's either stock footage or a camera trick.

Lanford grins out at us like a gap-toothed race traitor. And sadly, that is *not* a camera trick.

Now the applause and the band fade away, and Lanford launches into his monologue.

He starts with a joke about the vice president, and the audience laughs. I have to admit I chuckled a bit myself, which only goes to show how insidious our enemies can be.

Several one-liners about a sportscaster's sex life follow, along with a joke about the pope's funny hat. I'll fast forward through these. As White Warriors, we already know what sportscasting and the pope are all about.

Here now is the crucial moment, and the reason I'm showing you this tape: Lanford is trying to tie previous jokes together by telling one about the pope's sex life. But it falls flat. Some of the audience groans, but most of them merely stare at him. He should have known better—after all, you can tell by looking at them that they're mostly Catholic.

So Lanford goes into his usual whoops-I-told-a-joke-that-bombed routine. There are the exaggerated grimace, the tie-straightening, the gulp, and the mock-pleading glance toward the band. But this time the drummer doesn't do his usual rim shot, so the audience doesn't break into its usual pity chuckle.

This is because Lanford has something else in mind.

He looks up at the ceiling, raises his hands as if in supplication, and cries out, blasphemously, "Great God Almighty, deliver me from that dud!"

The camera pulls back, and—there! Dropping down on a playground swing from the rafters, behind and above Larry Lanford, is the media terrorist named Daniel Clayton, the media terrorist that the GOG and MAGOG-controlled news networks and Web sites call Laughin' Boy!

He is howling like a madman. That's his alleged sickness, of course. He laughs at what isn't funny. And Lanford's pope joke wasn't funny. Note that he's clutching the chains of the swing so that he doesn't laugh himself off his perch. A convincing touch.

I have to hand it to the sound engineer. You couldn't hear the bastard's laughter until he dropped into view. So it's a nice surprise for both the studio audience and the home viewer.

Yes, Brother Wendell. I'm being sarcastic.

As you can tell from the roar of the studio audience, this hilarity-from-above stunt has had the desired effect. Laughin' Boy's sudden appearance has startled the sheep into suggestibility, so his laughter spreads through the crowd like an outbreak of ebola. (That's a disease, Brothers and Sisters, one of many concocted in the foreign laboratories of the Multicultural Allies of the Godless Occupation Government.) The band launches into a show tune, and Larry Lanford gives Laughin' Boy a bug-eyed stare.

The audience's laughter goes on and on, as does Daniel Clayton's as he rises up out of sight again.

Lanford looks upward, raises his hands again, and shouts, "Thanks, Big Dude!"

The audience goes wild, and the network cuts to a commercial featuring beer and sluttish young women, although it is unclear which is being sold.

I'll pause the tape here to let what we've just seen sink in.

If you're having trouble making sense of it, consider this:

Just a few short weeks ago, we of the WWJD carried out our first overt military strike in order to alert the Righteous Caucasians of the world to our holy cause so that they might join us in battle against GOG and MAGOG. In the course of this action, we had no choice but to take lives—and some small number of those lives may themselves have been among our potential Brothers and Sisters. But collateral damage is a reality of war, and is acceptable so long as the cause is just and ground is gained.

Verily, our cause is just. However, our attack, as well-conceived and bold as it was, has gained us no ground. We have not succeeded in alerting the RCs of the world, because the extended media attention that should have been ours has been usurped by this terrorist, this Daniel Clayton, this Laughin' Boy. Even our written communique taking credit for the attack and declaring war on GOG and MAGOG has been all but ignored by the major media, and has appeared in its entirety in only the *Village Voice* and the *Drudge Report*.

In short, Laughin' Boy, with the active support of GOG and MAGOG, has dissipated the impact of our action and claimed the attention of the world for himself—thus defeating us without ever facing us.

Furthermore, he has seen to it that those RCs who may have been felled by our friendly fire in Wichita have died in vain. Their blood is on his hands.

And that blood, Brothers and Sisters, must not go unavenged.

We must strike back and strike hard, lest GOG and MAGOG defeat the White Warriors for Jesus, Deceased, before we have even begun.

However, we must strike wisely, for GOG's chosen terrorist is crafty. Laughin' Boy has defeated us once by means of guile, and we must take care that he does not do so again. We must also keep in mind that he is not just one man, but has wily and powerful allies—agents of GOG—supporting him.

To wit, observe the next segment of *Lanford's On Late!*:

Larry Lanford, wearing a wig and women's clothes, is being held hostage, tied to a chair in what appears to be a rural shack, by five hooded figures wearing camouflage fatigues.

I know, Brothers and Sisters. This image alone is insulting. Rest assured that Mr. Lanford will be among the first traitors to be executed on Day One of the New Era of Righteousness.

Speaking in a falsetto, Lanford laments that his captors intend to violate him, and one of the captors replies that they're only holding him for ransom. So Lanford mugs exaggerated disappointment, and the audience belly-laughs. At least, the soundtrack would have us *believe* that the audience belly-laughs. Note that we don't see them.

Then Lanford cries out: "This is a job for—the Odd Squad!"

The camera pulls back, and as the laughter from the audience continues, the wall of the shack disintegrates in an explosion of paper and styrofoam. There's a puff of stage smoke, and then they're inside the shack: Laughin' Boy, Porno Girl, and the Racist Ranger, all wearing trench coats that they now throw off to reveal ludicrous superhero tights.

Laughin' Boy, in blue and silver, is giggling—an indication, if we are to believe his GOG-pawn celebrity psychiatrists, that the sketch isn't funny.

Porno Girl seems uncomfortable in her pink tights, but be aware that her air of innocence is an act. Her notorious consumption of pornography is meant by GOG and MAGOG to tempt young persons to do likewise, with the ultimate goal of moral decay and miscegenation—and note that the black briefcase she's carrying looks very much like something an agent of the Godless Occupation Government would carry. Remember, GOG operatives always reveal themselves to those who can spot the signs!

Finally, there's the falsely named Racist Ranger, robotic and cold in his black-and-white tights and Ray-Ban sunglasses. Brothers and Sisters, this man is supposedly a former GOG agent who was dismissed for lack of devotion to the multicultural agenda. But if that were the case, he would be an asset to our cause instead of an impediment to our triumph. And he would have allowed our late Brother Bobby to assassinate Laughin' Boy during the Stan Symmons broadcast in Chicago.

Do not misunderstand me. I was sorely vexed with Brother Bobby for acting without orders from his Pastor, because his rash behavior almost resulted in an interrogation that could have placed his Brothers and Sisters in jeopardy.

Nevertheless, his act was the result of a Righteous impulse, and none of us should condemn his soul. Bear in mind that our court-martial and its resulting sentence of death had nothing to do with our love for Brother Bobby, nor for our respect for his motivations. Rather, it was merely an affirmation of the necessity of maintaining our chain of command.

Our thanks, by the way, to Brother Wendell and Sister Suellen for their bravery, stealth, and efficiency in carrying out the court-martial's sentence.

Back to the videotape, on which it is seen that the Lanford sketch ends with the "Odd Squad" victorious:

Porno Girl has mesmerized one of the kidnappers by producing a glossy magazine from her briefcase and opening it so that a glaring light from its pages hits him in the eyes. He proceeds to mutter and drool, and then he collapses with his back to the camera. From his spasms, we are no doubt meant to assume he is masturbating. As if weakness of the flesh were amusing.

The Racist Ranger disables two more kidnappers by confusing them with his rendition of "De Camptown Races," then clobbers them with a watermelon. Each falls to the floor with half a watermelon jammed over his head. This might even be amusing if the sketch's hidden agenda were not so evil.

The remaining two villains attempt to attack Laughin' Boy with knives, just as our misguided Brother did. But Laughin' Boy simply guffaws in their faces—and his attackers, apparently blinded by the superhuman force or stench of his breath, wind up stabbing each other.

Porno Girl and the Racist Ranger free Lanford from the chair, and he rushes toward Laughin' Boy with open arms, squealing, "My hero! Take me, I'm yours!"

This repugnant sight isn't at all funny, so Laughin' Boy laughs yet again. At this, Lanford stops short, turns toward the audience, and mugs the same exaggerated disappointment as before.

"I *never* get a break!" he complains.

At this point, the APPLAUSE lights apparently come on, because the audience roars, and the picture dissolves to a commercial featuring multicultural whelps sucking on lumps of coagulated pudding. Therefore, as the sight of this MAGOG-produced nightmare induces nausea in your Pastor, I am shutting off the tape.

Now, then, Brothers and Sisters. The conclusions we must draw from what I have just shown you are obvious.

One: The impact of our strike in Wichita has been nullified by the appearance of and subsequent media attention lavished on Daniel Clayton, aka Laughin' Boy.

Two: Laughin' Boy clearly has the support and protection of GOG.

Three: Not content with merely waging war against the White Warriors, GOG and MAGOG also intend to further corrupt the RCs of the world by making media icons of Laughin' Boy, the Racist Ranger, and Porno Girl.

In short, the "Odd Squad" members are weapons of GOG and MAGOG aimed against the WWJD and those we are trying to redeem. And only when GOG and MAGOG are destroyed will our Jew-murdered Savior finally rise again.

Therefore, the "Odd Squad" must be deleted. They must have their bandwidth reduced to zero.

So let it be e-mailed. So let it be done.

Pastor Turner P. Williams has spoken, and the White Warriors for Jesus, Deceased, have their orders.

Let me hear you say *Amen!*

Episode Four
A *Laughin' Boy* Miniseries:
The City So Nice, They Named It Vice

Part 1

It was cold in the theater, and Danny was shivering despite the trench coat he was wearing over his costume. And the cut on his left arm was itching again even though the stitches were gone. But he was only vaguely aware of those discomforts because he was in a semi-stupor as a result of Dr. Ralph's post-sketch injection.

Another effect of the injection was that it was making the Racist Ranger's voice sound as if it were emanating from a thick wall of Jell-O. Lime Jell-O, Danny decided as he looked up at the Ranger, because he could see green waves rippling from the G-man's mouth. Or maybe that was just because Danny was sitting on a couch in the *Lanford's On Late!* Green Room in the Jackie Gleason Theater. The room wasn't green, but Dr. Ralph's injections sometimes made the figurative seem literal.

Danny hadn't wanted to start taking the shots again, but doing the Lanford show would have been impossible without them. He had his notepad of Dull Things in a coat pocket along with a baggie of blue pills, but they weren't enough. This was because the Lanford show contained great yawning chunks that not only weren't funny, but that were borderline horrific—and there was only so much laughter he could take. This was just his third night, but he knew he'd be dead already if he had stuck to his vow to rely only on Dull Things, pills, and willpower.

"Dan'l, has you seed Miz Lawkin?" the Ranger asked. He opened his trench coat far enough to reveal his black-and-white outfit. "I ax kase de wardrobe lady say we kin take off de costumes on account er de las' sketch is cut. De show's over in less den fo' minutes, in fack, so dey ain't a-gwine to need you on de swing agin neither. We done fer de day, but Miz Lawkin ain't nowhere to be foun'. En her reg'lar clothes is still in her dressin' room. So de DeWitts is runnin' roun' lookin' fer her like dey's headless chickens er sumpin." He stroked his chin and frowned. "I got me a pow'ful bad feelin' 'bout it."

Danny tried not to focus on the hypnotic green ripples, but on what the Ranger was saying. He was saying that Amanda was missing. He was saying that she had probably left the theater. And he was saying that she was still wearing her pink Porno Girl suit.

"I haven't seen her since the sketch," Danny said, trying not to slur his words. "So where will you start?"

The Ranger looked puzzled. "Start wid what?"

Danny rubbed his eyes. "You're going to go find her, right? You're the federal agent here, aren't you?"

The Ranger put a finger to his lips. "Shhh! In de fus' place, findin' Miz Lawkin ain't my job—en in the secken place, ain't nobody in dis room 'cept me en you s'posed to know what my aktual job is nohow."

Danny glanced across the room at the three blue-jacketed twentysomethings who were clustered around the monitor beside the backstage door. "There's nobody else here but interns, and they're not listening to us. They're wrapped up in the end of the show."

"Cain't say as I blame 'em," the Ranger said. "Dat Demi Mo' look like she kin crack Brazil nuts wid 'er butt cheeks."

Danny struggled to get up from the couch, wincing as his costume cut into him. The blue spandex was tight, but it was the stiff silver sections on the sides, chest, and crotch that were painful. He had complained to the wardrobe lady yesterday, but he'd been laughing at the time. So she hadn't taken him seriously.

"Royce," he said as he finally managed to stand, "I think I know where Amanda is."

The Ranger looked skeptical. "I is all ears."

Danny hesitated. "Well, I don't know the exact location. But I know the *kind* of location."

The Ranger's eyes widened. "Oh, Lawdy, you's right! We's in New York, en despite what de Mayor say, de city ain't been cleaned up *dat* much!"

Danny nodded, and it made him pitch forward. But the Ranger caught him.

"Let's ask Armstrong," Danny said, pushing away. "Maybe he'll authorize you to go after her."

The Ranger scowled. "He ain't a-gwineter do dat, Dan'l. Miz Lawkin is a patient er de DeWitts, but she doan' mean squat to de Bureau."

Danny turned toward the door that led to the theater's office wing. "We'll see," he said. He was trying to sound tough, but he was woozy and giggling, so he just sounded drunk. The Ranger came with him anyway.

Special Agent Armstrong and his crew were using an office opposite the Green Room as their command post. A young male agent dressed as a Lanford intern moved to block the door as Danny and the Ranger came across the hall, but he stepped aside at a scowl from the Ranger. The Ranger opened the door and gestured for Danny to go in first.

Inside, Armstrong and two of his subordinates were seated at a bank of video monitors. Danny caught glimpses of the Green Room, the backstage area, the stage, the audience, and other places inside and outside the theater before Armstrong swiveled toward him, glaring.

"Is there a problem, Mr. Clayton?" Armstrong asked. He was using the same tone of voice, Danny thought, that Marine Corps drill sergeants used in the movies.

"Amanda's missing," Danny said, bracing himself on the back of the nearest chair so he wouldn't fall over. "You have to find her."

Armstrong's glare narrowed. "Not so. She isn't under arrest, so she can go wherever she likes."

The Racist Ranger cleared his throat. "Now, Allan, honey, you knows as well as we does dat she's a sick young woman what ain't got no bidniss runnin' roun' dis city all by her lonesome, nossuh."

Armstrong ignored the Ranger. "Mr. Clayton, I suggest you discuss this with the DeWitts. And as luck would have it, here's Dr. Ralph now."

Danny looked back and saw Dr. Ralph standing in the doorway.

Dr. Ralph's round face was gloomy. "I'm afraid I don't know what to tell you, Daniel. Dr. Carla is still searching for some clue as to where Amanda might have gone. In retrospect, I suppose we shouldn't have allowed her to take part in this Larry Lanford business, but we assumed that with the theater in the hands of the FBI, there would be nothing to worry about."

"Once again, Doctor," Armstrong said, "I have to remind you that—"

Dr. Ralph raised a hand. "I know, I know. Her safety isn't your concern. Nevertheless, you have cameras and agents covering every nook and cranny of this building—and since the show is just now ending, there was no departing crowd to hide her. She was alone, and even with a trench coat over her costume, her identity would have been obvious. So surely one of your agents saw her leave, and surely you can tell me if that's the case."

Danny thought it was a good argument, and he turned to see Armstrong's reaction.

But Armstrong had swiveled his chair to face the monitors again. "Maybe," he said. "Wait in the hall and I'll let you know."

The Racist Ranger put one hand on Danny's shoulder and the other on Dr. Ralph's. "Come on, now, chillun," he said. "Bes' do what de man say."

Danny didn't argue, but he took another look at Armstrong's monitors before he let the Ranger steer him back into the hallway.

The agent-dressed-as-an-intern closed the door behind them and stood in front of it. He and the Racist Ranger exchanged unfriendly looks, and then the Ranger turned to Dr. Ralph.

"Doctah," the Ranger said, "ah cain't say ef dis hyear'll hep, but Dan'l thinks as what Miz Lawkin done run off to fine hersef somepin por-no-graphical."

Dr. Ralph looked at the Ranger as if at a simple child. "That much is obvious," he said. "And in that vein, I'll point out that New York is a big city. We have to know where to start looking."

"Maybe she-he-he," Danny began, and then choked down the giggles. "Maybe she just went back to your townhouse."

Dr. Ralph gave Danny the same look he had given the Ranger. "Given her compulsion," he said, "that seems unlikely."

The agent-intern coughed and pressed a finger to his ear. "I'm instructed to tell Dr. DeWitt that he might want to speak with Agent Enfield on the roof. Roof access for both DeWitts is approved for the next fifteen minutes." The agent-intern paused. "But it is not approved for Mr. Clayton or for Special Agent Royce. Agent Royce is instructed to concentrate on his assignment."

Danny knew what that meant: Babysit Laughin' Boy.

"Thank you," Dr. Ralph said. "I'll page Dr. Carla." He took a cell phone from his pocket and pressed a button, then spoke to the Ranger. "If you'll take Daniel into the Green Room, Dr. Carla or I will meet you there when we're ready to return to the townhouse."

Then he spun away and hurried down the hall, speaking into the cell phone as he went. By the time he reached the elevator at the end of the hall, Dr. Carla had joined him from a side passage. They entered the elevator and were gone.

Neither Danny nor the Ranger spoke as they reentered the Green Room. They had the place to themselves now, because the interns had left to attend to their end-of-show duties. The credits were rolling on the monitors, and the band was squealing its last squeal. The final celebrity guest had gone out to her limousine, and Larry Lanford and the band would bypass the Green Room on their way to their top-floor dressing rooms. So Danny and the Ranger would be alone in the Green Room until someone came in to clear away the deli tray. At least twenty minutes.

"Might's well git comf'tible," the Ranger said, sitting down on the couch. He looked unhappy.

Danny thought he knew why. The Ranger had been something of a hero for most of his career . . . but now, thanks to a psychological glitch that had turned him into a reprehensible freak, he was condemned to the lowly task of watching over yet another reprehensible freak. It was a far cry from the glory of running down serial killers or busting up the Klan.

But Danny couldn't let himself give a damn about that. For one thing, the Ranger's situation wasn't his fault. And for another, Danny already had too much to give a damn about as it was: His daughter. His parents. His ex-wife. Not to mention all those people who had been at South Riverside Park with him, and all their families and friends who thought he had been entertained by their deaths.

And then there was Amanda, whose own particular freakishness made her seem both pure and debased, both vulnerable and untouchable. The combination and contradiction of it were irresistible.

So it was too much already, and there was no room at the inn for the Racist Ranger. And if Danny tried to make room, he would laugh himself into a coma.

The monitors went dark as the video feed from the stage shut off, and Danny heard the muffled rumble of the audience getting up to leave.

It gave him an idea, and he thought he might actually be able to act on it. The drugs were making him brave. But he wasn't seeing any green ripples right now, and he wasn't giggling. So he felt almost competent, and he didn't want to waste it.

What he wanted was to do what the Feds wouldn't and the DeWitts couldn't. He wanted to go out and search every X-rated movie theater and adult bookstore in the five boroughs until he found Amanda and made sure she was safe. It would be a hopeless task, and he wanted to do it anyway.

So he began to try to think of how he could slip away from Royce.

"I want to go downstairs and change," he said. He and the Ranger had been assigned a closet-sized dressing room in the basement, and to get to the stairwell that went down to it they would have to leave the Green Room through the backstage door. That might open up some possibilities.

The Ranger's eyes narrowed. "Dr. Ralph say to stay heah."

Danny forced himself to look the Ranger in the eye. "Since when do you work for Dr. Ralph?"

The Ranger stood up. He towered over Danny, and the muscles in his jaw rippled. "De Bureau puttin' dey faith in de DeWitts when it come to you," he said, "so I got to foller dey lead. You know dat, so why you messin' wid me?"

Danny took a step back. "I just thought it would save time to get into our street clothes now." Then he paused, trying to gauge how the Ranger would react to what he said next. "Besides, don't you feel stupid in these costumes?"

The Ranger crossed his arms. "'Course I does! But if part er mah job is to dress up lak a blamed comical-book joke, den dat's what I'se gwineter do."

Then he paused too. "But I s'pose it ain't a-gwyne to take us long to change." He waved at the backstage door. "Well, den, arter you, Dan'l."

Danny turned toward the door, trying to hide his dismay. He had wanted the Ranger to leave the Green Room and start down the stairwell first. That way, he might have been able to take advantage of what he had seen in the command post: The closed-circuit camera covering the backstage area was askew, and several square yards between the stairwell and the exit onto 53rd Street weren't covered. Plus, only the left third of the exit door itself, the side with the hinges, was visible. Someone who kept to the right might be able to squeeze out without being spotted.

It would have been risky. Still, it would have been a chance, however slim, to find Amanda. And it would have been a chance to gain a sliver of control over his own life.

Not that his lack of control was the Racist Ranger's fault. Or even the FBI's. Even before the Massacre, he hadn't exactly been a take-charge guy, now, had he? He had taught technical writing at Butler JuCo as a way of avoiding anything scarier, such as actually writing. And he had let Karen dictate the terms of both their marriage and divorce, as well as of their custody arrangement for Lindy.

He had even let her determine where he had been on the 20th of May. "Would it be all right if I kept Lindy this weekend?" she had asked on the phone that morning. "My mother's here, and I already promised we'd do something with her. Maybe you could go down to the River Festival with some friends or something instead? The music would be too loud for Lindy anyway, wouldn't it? And you can have her next weekend, if you want."

So he had gone down to the Festival by himself. And he knew he should thank God for that, because it had meant that Lindy hadn't been anywhere near the Massacre . . . although he and Lindy would have spent their time at the games and rides, and skipped the concert. Because it *would* have been too loud, and he would have kept Lindy away from the stage. He was almost sure of it.

And all of the people killed had been near the stage, hadn't they?

No. No, that wasn't quite true.

All of the people killed had been near *him*.

Karen had been right to keep Lindy away from him that day. In fact, Karen had been right about everything.

She had stated the problem directly on the day that she had asked him to leave: "It's not that you've done anything wrong. It's that you don't really *do* anything at all. So things just happen *around* you."

Things like the Massacre. It was clear now. He had no will of his own, so the universe had filled the void around him with chaos. In other words, as far as the universe was concerned, he was a joke.

He began to chuckle.

The Ranger tapped his shoulder.

"Dan'l?" the Ranger asked. "Is we gwyne to go change dese hyer costumes, or is we?"

Danny clenched his teeth, fighting to swallow the laughter.

"Yes," he said. "Yes, we are."

He went to the backstage door and pushed it open. The area beyond was empty. So all he had to do was dash around the railing surrounding the stairwell, and he would have a clear path to the exit. If he stayed to the right. And maybe the Ranger would be startled enough that he could actually make it outside.

But the Ranger was quick. He had proven that in Chicago. Besides, even if Danny made it outside, where would he go first? Where were all the porn shops now that Giuliani had cleaned up Times Square?

First things first. Get outside, get lost—and then ask around. Porno houses couldn't be that hard to find.

Four steps to the stairwell. And at the third he leaped forward and began to sprint.

Then his head snapped back, his feet flew out, and he landed on his ass. He could feel Royce's fist clamped on his coat collar.

Danny guffawed, then coughed because he was starting to choke. He looked up at the Racist Ranger in a silent plea for mercy.

The Ranger eased the pressure, but didn't let go.

"Jus' what 'uz you gwineter do, honey?" he asked. "Lemme guess. Fust you 'uz gwyne to run 'way from me as if I 'uz lame en a punkinhaid to boot, en den you 'uz gwyne to run 'way from de agent who's a-stannin' right outside dat exit. En arter dat you 'uz gwyne to run roun' de streets o' Manhattan wid no money, en wearin' yo' Laughin' Bo' costume under yo' coat wid de silver boots a-showin'. En ef all dat's so, I mus' ax you, jus' who is de punkinhaid hyear?"

Danny coughed again. "That would be me," he said.

The Ranger let go of Danny's collar. "I sholy lay it would, at dat." He frowned at the stairwell, then at the door to the street, and then at the stairwell again. "I does wisht we could change out er de costumes fust—'cept ole Mars Armstrong got a man down in de basement, too, en we's apt to raise his surpishyuns. 'Sides which, we cain't waste no mo' time ef we's a-gwyne to blend in wid de audience crowdin' out onto de sidewalks. So I s'pose we kin git by long's we keep wearin' de trench coats. En I gots cash en credit cards hyer in my pocket on 'count o' I 'uz a Boy Scout, en I is allus prepared."

Danny grasped the stairwell railing, pulled himself to his feet, and stared at the Ranger. "You'll—heeheehee—go with me to find Amanda?"

The Ranger nodded. He had an expression of bemused resignation. "I sholy will. Sepeshial Agent Armstrong tol' me I 'uz to stick close to you, but he ain't said nothin' 'bout keepin' you in de theater. 'Course, it 'uz implied—but it weren't *said*, en I lay as how I ain't de fust gov'mint agent what decided to stretch de boundaries o' de job at han' bekase o' what was er weren't *said*."

Danny glanced at the exit, then up at the spot on the shadowed ceiling where he thought the surveillance camera ought to be. He couldn't see it, but it was there somewhere. "We'll have to stay to the right so we don't—haw—show up on Armstrong's monitor. It only covers the left side of the door."

The Ranger gave a wry smile. "We cain't count on dat." He turned back toward the Green Room. "Backtrack wid me jus' a secken, en stick close."

Danny followed, but he was dubious. "Why? I thought you were going to help me look for Amanda."

"Shush yo'sef en trus' ol' Rob jus' dis oncet."

At the door to the Green Room, the Ranger squinted up at the ceiling. "Stan' right 'side me, Dan'l. Now looky, ef Mars Armstrong er one er his posse has been watchin' us, dey's gwyne to *stop* watchin' now en move to 'nother mon'ter, kase we out er de picture. We back in de Green Room, far as dey know, kase de camrer in dah don't pick up 'till almos' de couch. So all we gots to do—"

The Ranger reached up over the door, grasped a thin black cable, and gave it a few sharp tugs.

"Won't they notice if a monitor goes dark?" Danny asked.

"I ain't a-yankin' 'er out. I'm jus' twitchin' 'er to de lef' so we gots a clean shot to de do'. Dah, dat oughter do 'er." The Ranger turned and started toward the exit. "You hang back, en I'll git de do' guard to look east'erd. Den you run *west*'erd down to Eighth Av'nue en wait fer me roun' de coahnuh." He stopped at the exit door. "Enny questions?"

Danny took a deep breath and tried to quell his trembling muscles along with his impulse to laugh. "Whee-whee-which way should I turn at Eighth?"

"South, 'cross 53rd. Ef Miz Lawkin's still in Manhattan, we's likely to fine her down to'ards de Po'at Autho'tee. Dat's whah de po'no dat's still aroun' hyear is mos'ly located." He gave Danny a narrow look. "Now, ef you tries to run off, er ef you does sumfn else you ought not, I'll a-drag you back hyear by yo' ears. You got dat?"

Danny nodded. He was still struggling not to laugh, and he knew he stood a better chance of making it out the door and down the street if he just stayed quiet.

"All righty, den," the Ranger said. He put a hand on the door's crash bar. "Le's go."

Danny stood against the wall as the Ranger shoved open the door, stepped into the dusk, and spoke to someone Danny couldn't see. "Agent Goahdon, Mars Armstrong say dey's a whole stack o' water-moccasins off to de Broadway side!"

Then, almost immediately, the Ranger leaned back inside and waved for Danny to run.

Danny pushed off from the wall, grabbed the doorjamb, and yanked himself out to the sidewalk. He instantly collided with three people in the throng that was streaming past, and he almost fell. But he caught himself against the brick wall, and then he was running westward, dodging as many people as he could.

He was amazed at how most of them ignored him. Here was a guy in silver boots and a trench coat running through them as if this were a pinball game, and almost no one seemed to notice. Each of them had seen Laughin' Boy on their televisions or PCs more times than they could count—yet now he was among them, and he might as well have been as invisible as New Jersey was from here.

For a moment, Danny wondered whether the crowd's obliviousness to him, a symbol of death and pain, meant that they also would have been oblivious to death or pain itself. Had they been in Wichita on May 20th, would they have ignored the carnage in South Riverside Park the way they might ignore a mugging on the IRT?

But that thought started him giggling, so he forced himself to think of dried Elmer's Glue instead.

He reached the corner just as the light changed to stop traffic on 53rd, so he dodged a few more pedestrians and leaped into the intersection, bouncing off the fender of a taxi as it squealed to a halt. Then he lurched the rest of the way across the street as the taxi driver screamed behind him. Danny didn't know the language, but he knew that he was being cursed. Too late, he thought.

He stumbled onto the curb, collided with another pedestrian (big, fragrant, hairy), and then staggered southward far enough to be out of sight of the Gleason. He slumped against a cornice, breathing hard and sweating . . . but not laughing. And that amazed him. Maybe, he thought with a small thrill of hope, he was cured.

Then he felt a hand on his shoulder, looked around, saw the movie-star-handsome face of the Racist Ranger, and sank to his knees from the force of the guffaws.

"Dat's enuff o' dat," the Ranger said. "It's gittin' ole, dad fetch it. 'Sides, we got to be movin' 'long, kase ole Mars Armstrong, he gwyne to notice dat we gone soon. So git up offen yo' knees befo' somebody git de idear dat you's mah boyfren er sumpin."

Danny reached into his trench coat pocket and closed his fist around the baggie of blue pills. *Drywall nails*, he thought. *Curbside recycling. Mutual funds.*

It did the trick, barely, and his laughter subsided despite the fact that the Ranger grabbed his coat collar and hauled him up to his feet.

"Les' head on down-river," the Ranger said. "Ef Miz Lawkin done set out wid a mine to fine hersef a po'no palace dat's bot' sleazy as all get-out en mo' er less close to de theater, den we kin start lookin' 'bout ten er 'lebben blocks south o' hyear. Hump yo'sef!"

They took off at a run.

Part 2

Danny didn't know New York, so he took the Ranger's word on where the nearest sleaze pits were located. They ran south for eleven blocks, Danny struggling to keep up in his clunky silver boots—and he discovered that the more he ran, the more his urge to laugh diminished. Yet he was becoming more and more anxious about Amanda, so he knew that he should have been howling.

Royce crossed Eighth on the south side of 42nd Street, waving for Danny to follow, and a few moments later they were in front of the hulking Port Authority bus terminal. The Ranger stopped beside a set of glass-and-steel doors, and he pulled Danny up against the wall. People were streaming in and out of the Port Authority and cramming the sidewalk, and if the Ranger hadn't pulled Danny out of the way he would have been trampled.

Danny was breathing hard, but he wasn't laughing. And because he wasn't laughing, he was sharply aware of everything else: the hammering of thousands of footsteps, the rumble and screech of countless tires, the angry bleats of horns, the darkening sky, the dazzling colors of the lights that were coming on everywhere, and the mingled stinks of rubber, exhaust, perfume, mustard, sauerkraut, and sweat. And some of the stink was his. His costume was clinging to him like plastic wrap to pudding.

"Now den," Royce said without breathing hard at all. "We jus' passed some dirty book sto's dah on de noath side o' Foaty-Secken, dis side o' Eighth—"

He pointed across the street, and Danny saw a flashing sign that read ADULT PLAYGROUND MAGAZINES VIDEO PEEPS XXX.

"—but I figger Miz Lawkin done seed plenty o' de kind o' truck dey gots dah," the Ranger continued. "So dis time, she's a-gwyne to be arter moah ex-treme doin's."

Now he pointed south. Danny tried to look that way, but so many people were going in and out of the Port Authority that he couldn't see much. All he got was a vague impression of mingled light and darkness.

"Now, down dat way a couple blocks," Royce said, "dey's things you ain't never gwyne to see back in de merry ol' land o' Oz. En dat's whah she'll be, ef she's still in Manhattan." He looked down at Danny with a grim expression. "It could git kind o' rough. Kin you deal wid it? En does you trus' me to call de shots?"

Danny nodded. He was still breathing hard, and his legs were like jelly, but he wanted to get moving again. Otherwise his laughter might return at any second, and then he'd be no good to Amanda at all.

The Ranger took off again, pushing through the throng of bodies at the Port Authority doors and clearing a path for Danny. But once they reached 40th Street, pedestrian traffic began to dwindle, since most of those coming out of the Port Authority had headed north.

They crossed 40th, 39th, and 38th, passing rundown bodegas, empty storefronts, narrow doorways with lounging boys, a dark alley that emitted a hissing sound, and two more dirty bookstores. The Ranger shook his head at the first of these, then stepped inside the second for a moment before coming out with the comment that it was "too tame fo' Miz Lawkin." Danny didn't know how Royce could tell, but he had promised to trust him, so he said nothing.

Then, between 37th and 36th, on a stretch of sidewalk where the only pedestrians were a few men with downcast eyes and hunched shoulders, they encountered a young, scrawny barker standing beneath a yellowed sign that displayed three red letters: XXX. The sign was lit from within by a low, ominous light that made Danny think of a burning building seen from a distance.

"Yo yo yo," the scrawny kid said in a monotone as they approached. "Check it out, check it out." He was white, pimply, and dressed in grungy clothes that were baggy enough to hold two of him. His hands darted in and out of a canvas pouch at his waist, and he made gestures as if handing out flyers. But there were no flyers. The pouch was empty.

"What you got in dah?" the Ranger asked, looming over the kid with practiced FBI-agent intimidation.

The kid didn't seem to see him, but kept on offering invisible flyers to an invisible throng. Danny hung back, watching the kid's eyes, and decided that he wasn't faking it. He was crazy.

"Yo yo yo," the kid repeated, and then began yammering a steady stream of calm words that promised depravity. "Check it out, check it out. Live girls and boys, live boys and girls, live girls and girls, live boys and boys. All ages, all sizes, all colors, all legal in their countries of origin. Check it out, check it out. Live anything, live everything. Heather, Megan, Regan, Tiffany, Brittany, Rin Tin Tin. Three shows for one price, two always in progress, plus a Tijuana surprise every hour on the hour, plus peeps, plus chat booths, plus holes of glory the use of which is entirely your business, plus ladies skilled in both worldly conversation and Oriental massage. Yo yo yo. As seen on the World Wide Web until our temporary legal difficulties ensued, please sign our petition. Twenty-five-dollar cover, satisfaction guaranteed, cash only, no credit cards, no refunds, drinks and other amenities extra. Gratuities encouraged but not required. Check it out, check it out. Couples welcome, babysitting available. Representatives of the NYPD and ASPCA are required to sign statements to the effect that they have no affiliation with either organization. Live girls, shaved Sallies, shower shows, you know what I'm sayin', all tastes represented, check it out, check it out. Hot bodies, hot action, hot oil, hot dipsticks, hot pretzels, hot melted cheese. Girls with pretty shoes, girls with pretty feet, girls with no shoes, girls with no feet. Yo yo yo."

The Ranger looked at Danny. "Ef Miz Lawkin come down dis hyear street," he said, "she sholy went in *dah*." He pointed past the yammering kid to a set of concrete steps that led to a rust-stained door in a brick facade with blacked-out windows.

Danny nodded. He still wasn't laughing, but he was dizzy from running, from worry, and from the stink of the city. "All right, then. Let's go."

"You got fifty dollahs?"

Danny started for the door. "You know I don't."

Royce fell in beside him, and they went up the steps together. "You is gwyne to pay me back, den, en don' think you ain't. I on'y gets a gov'mint paycheck, jus' like ol' folks on fixed incomes."

Behind them, the kid was still yammering. "Yo yo yo. Check it out, check it out. The portal to paradise awaits, the holy of holies, the alpha and omega, the wettest slap and tickle in town, check it out, check it out."

At the door, Danny glanced back and saw that the kid was still handing out the invisible flyers, too.

The door didn't have a handle, but when the Ranger knocked, it swung inward, revealing a long hallway lit by blacklight tubes. The place smelled of mildew and hand lotion, and muffled shrieks and bass thumps emanated from behind a series of doors on both sides of the hall. Danny once again began to feel an urge to giggle.

"C'mon in," a voice with a thick Brooklyn accent said. A head the size and shape of a cinder block appeared around the edge of the door, and its slick hair glowed like algae in the blacklight.

The Ranger nudged Danny, and they both stepped inside.

The block-headed man closed the door and jerked his thumb at a dirty Plexiglas window in the wall. "Youse guys pay the lady," he said, and then he grinned. His teeth glowed green.

Danny didn't know what was more ominous—those teeth, or the fact that Block-Head had actually spoken the words "youse guys" without irony.

And then he couldn't help it: He gave a series of short, staccato hiccups of laughter.

Block-Head glowered. "Somethin' funny?"

Danny shook his head. "N-n--yipe!--no, sir."

The Racist Ranger cleared his throat. "Nevvuh you mind dis boah," he said. "De po' lil' fella ain't seed no big-city humpin' befo', en his coan-hole Kansas ass is a mite jittery. 'Sides, he's kinder simple, know whut I mean?"

Block-Head grinned again. He seemed to like the Ranger's dialect. "Sure, I get it. Just pay the lady, and have a good time."

Danny choked back his laughter, and he and Royce stepped around Block-Head to the Plexiglas window. Danny could just see the outline of someone who might be a woman behind it.

A metal drawer slid out below the window. "Fifty dollars for two one-visit memberships," a metallic voice said from a grille beside the drawer. "No exit and reentry without repayment. By paying the membership fee, you are agreeing to abide by the rules of the New York Pleasure Club, and you are affirming that you have no affiliation with any law enforcement agency of any kind."

The Ranger reached into a coat pocket, brought out a wallet, and tossed three twenties into the drawer. "What's de rules?"

The drawer closed. "Membership in the NYPC provides access to all rooms, but does not cover tips or personal arrangements. Also, additional charges may apply for special services or hygienic materials. No firearms, knives brought from home, or nonconsensual violence are allowed. Membership can be revoked at any time at the discretion of management, but refusal by male guests to comply with a weapons check will always result in immediate expulsion."

"Why jis' *male* guests?" the Ranger asked.

Block-Head stepped up behind him. "Broads never bring in nothin' they shouldn't. But men do. So youse guys stay cool for a minute." He put his hands on Royce's waist.

Danny was sure that this would result in trouble—but the Ranger remained stock-still as Block-Head's hands moved up and down his body and in and out of his trench coat.

"Okay, now you," Block-Head said, and moved behind Danny.

It only lasted a few seconds, but Danny had to hold his breath to avoid giggling like a maniac.

Then Block-Head stepped back to his post beside the door, grinning his greenish grin again. No doubt he was amused to have discovered that his friskees were wearing spandex leotards.

"Welcome, gentlemen," the voice from the grille said. "As you proceed down the hall, the three doors on the right will lead you to our live-show amphitheaters. Those on the left will lead to chat booths and video peeps. Enjoy."

"You owe me ten dollahs," Royce said.

The grille remained silent.

"You owe me ten dollahs," Royce repeated.

Block-Head made a warning noise in his throat.

Danny grasped the Ranger's sleeve. "Come on," he said, and was relieved when Royce came with him down the hall.

"I'll be gittin' dat ten dollahs back," Royce murmured. "You wait en see."

Danny was annoyed. "I'll pay you back the whole sixty if we find Amanda. That's why we're here, after all. Or had you forgotten?"

"I ain't fo'got. But princ'ples is princ'ples. You don't give a man his change, you ain't professyunnel."

"If you say so." Danny lowered his voice to a whisper as they reached the first door on the right. "And speaking of being professional, since when don't you carry your, uh, professional tools?"

"Since I been wearin' black-en-white pajamas en actin' like a dancin' bear. How's I gwyne to carry a Glock in dem circumstances? Now, is you a-gwineter open de do'?"

The door had a handle with a thumb latch. Danny tried to reach for it, but then he began laughing.

"What ain't funny now?" the Ranger asked.

Danny struggled to control himself. "A lot of—hee hee—things aren't funny," he said. He reached for the door handle again, and this time he was able to make his fingers close on the greasy metal. "Such as the fact that you just led these people to believe you aren't a member of a law enforcement agency, and if that lie winds up getting Amanda hurt—"

"Hush yo' mouf'!" the Ranger hissed. "I didn' sign nuffn, en dese punkinhaids ought to know dey ain't no proteckshun 'gainst bein' lied to by a G-man les' you gits him to sign sumfn—en even den you bes' git it notarized. Now, is we gwyne to git in dah en look fer her er ain't we? Open de dad-blame do'!"

So Danny pushed down on the latch and pulled the door open, and he was hit with a red wash of light and noise along with an intensification of the mildew-and-hand-lotion odor mingled with the smell of a high-school locker room. Four tiers of red-velvet theater seats were set in circles around a low pit, and Danny couldn't see what was down there at first. The pit was too low, and too many chair backs and heads were in the way. There were about eighty seats in the room, and almost half of them were occupied.

In the top row, to the left of the door, an unshaven man with runny eyes turned in his seat and glared.

"Shut the door!" he snapped. His voice was barely audible over the bass-and-drums noise thumping through the room. "You're distracting them!"

Danny and the Ranger stepped inside, and the door swung shut behind them.

Now, standing at the top of an aisle, Danny could see into the pit. He didn't want to stare, but he had to look long enough to be sure that none of the tangled bodies on the black wrestling mats was Amanda, being used against her will—and at first he couldn't even be sure how many there were or how many were black or white or Cuban because there was a man wearing nothing but a Fidel hat and a fake beard with a smoldering cigar, and then he was buried under cream and coffee flesh, and somebody was doing something with a thing that looked like a peach-colored softball bat, and three of them began moving faster as a woman screamed something about diesel fuel and a man bellowed that it was suppertime—and then Danny was reeling spinning *laughing* and was sure he was going to be sick right on the bald crown of the man with the runny eyes.

"Dan'l!" The Ranger was shaking him. "Dan'l, she ain't in hyear! Git up, en le's move on."

Danny realized then that he was sitting on the wine-colored carpet at the top of the aisle. The aisle, lit by circles of red light, ran down to a pit where four naked men and three naked women were going through the motions of spectacular group coitus. But they were sneaking glances up at Danny. And the thirty or forty men seated around the pit were all staring at him.

Amanda wasn't here. So the Ranger was right. They should move on.

Except that Danny couldn't move. The music was still thumping, and the naked people were still humping, but all eyes were on him. They transfixed him, pinning him to the floor. He was the show now.

And then, with an effort, he looked down at himself and saw why. His trench coat had fallen open. He was sitting in the center of a red circle, but even in that light his costume was unmistakable. His silver briefs and boots shone with a painful brilliance.

The Racist Ranger hauled him to his feet.

"Nex' room," the Ranger said. "Nex' room, *now*."

But it was too late. Across the pit in the first row, a white-bearded, big-bellied man stood up and pointed. He was about sixty, and if his clothes hadn't been black, he would have looked like Santa Claus.

"God damn!" the perverted Santa cried, his voice piercing through the music. "It's that son of a bitch who thinks it's funny when kids get killed! It's *Laughin' Boy!*"

Now the naked people in the pit stopped what they were doing and sat up. The one with the peach-colored softball bat smacked it into his palm.

"I thought the country had changed its mind about me," Danny said, chuckling as Royce pulled him out of the room. "But some of those people seem pissed."

"Well, den," Royce said as they emerged into the hall and the door slammed shut behind them. "I reck'n dat some folks still got dey sense o' moral outrage arter all." He released Danny and headed for the next door. "But don't worry none. Dey'll soon fo'get dat you here, what wid de nekkid folks en all."

Danny was doubtful, but he couldn't run away now. Not until he found Amanda, if she was here. So he thought of kitchen sponges to suppress his chuckling, then stepped in front of the Ranger and opened the second door.

The second room was constructed and illuminated like the first, but here the music was only a low, pulsating hum. The audience was smaller. And in the center of the pit stood a thick wooden post with iron rings.

A pale, nude woman was chained to one side of the post, facing outward, with her arms over her head. A nude man was chained to the other side, facing the post. Stalking around them, growling, were two people dressed in squeaking black leather who were carrying short whips. Danny couldn't tell whether they were male or female, or one of each. They were wearing masks and hoods and were walking hunched over. Every now and then one of them would lunge toward the post, sometimes striking, sometimes not, but always eliciting a shriek from the victim.

Danny tried to concentrate on searching the audience for Amanda. Unlike the first room, there were a few women here, all watching the action in the pit with the same rapt expressions as the men.

One woman across the room in the third row was wearing a trench coat, but the spotty lighting left her face in shadow. So Danny started around the room, walking between the top row of seats and the wall, to get a better look. But then the woman leaned forward, and the trench coat fell open to reveal that she was naked underneath, and that she had a tattoo of the Virgin Mary between her breasts. She also had bright orange hair cut into a flattop that was shaved down to stubble over her ears. She was not Amanda.

Danny glanced back down at the pit and saw why the woman had leaned forward. The Leather Guys had closed in and were violating their victims with the whip handles. Danny's stomach lurched, and he gave a short giggle. But the chained man and woman had begun to scream, so no one heard him.

He started back the way he had come, and the loose belt of his trench coat brushed the gray hair of a man seated below him. The man looked up, his wide eyes magnified by thick glasses, and then he stood and stared at Danny. He was short, ruddy, and wore an olive-drab army jacket over a gray T-shirt and grubby jeans. He gazed at Danny's costume for a moment, and then he looked up into Danny's eyes.

"Ten-hut!" he said, and then he snapped to attention and saluted.

Danny heard the "Ten-hut!" because the screaming in the pit had stopped. So he looked down and saw that both the torturers and the victims were now staring up at him just as the performers in the first pit had.

"I pledge my allegiance to you, Laughin' Boy," Army Man said in a clear, earnest voice. "I pledge my allegiance to you and to the joy you take in pain."

Trying to keep from giggling, Danny turned away from Army Man and saw the Racist Ranger waiting for him at the door. It was time to continue to the third room.

Danny started toward him, but then the door was yanked open and the black-clad Santa Claus from the first room charged in, leading a group of ten others. The Ranger disappeared among them.

Santa spotted Danny and bellowed. "I got family near Wichita! If they'd'a been there, you'd'a laughed at *them*!"

Then he charged.

Danny whirled and tried to run, but Army Man grabbed his trench coat.

"Stay and fight!" Army Man cried. "They're no match for your powers!"

Danny struggled to pull himself out of the trench coat, and he had almost made it when Santa knocked him to the gritty strip of carpet that ran along the wall.

"Laugh at *this*, asshole!" Santa snarled, then grabbed Danny's hair and began thumping his forehead against the floor. "Laugh-at-*this*! Laugh-at-*this*! Laugh-at-*this*!"

The floor made booming sounds that matched the drumbeat bleeding in from the first room.

Danny began to shudder with laughter just as some of the men who had followed Santa started kicking him. There wasn't much room for them to work since Santa was still trying to crack Danny's skull, but they managed.

"No!" a voice cried. "He's the Messiah! He came to tell us the truth!"

At that, Danny managed to twist around enough to see Army Man clamber over the chairs, wrap an arm around Santa's throat, and yank him backward. They collided with the men who had been kicking Danny, and Danny got to his hands and knees and scrambled away, laughing.

"He came to teach us that life is pain!" Army Man shrieked behind him. "And that pain is *good!*"

Still laughing, Danny managed to stand up and look back. The men who had been kicking him were now in hand-to-hand combat with some of this room's audience, and the rest of the audience had rushed to the aisle and were trying to get out. Danny couldn't see the Ranger anywhere.

Meanwhile, Santa had turned the tables on Army Man and was beating his head against the floor as he had Danny's.

"Die, pervert!" Santa roared.

Danny didn't think the head-beating had done him much harm, but it made him angry to see Santa do the same thing to the much smaller Army Man. So he reached into his coat pocket, fished a blue pill from the baggie, and jumped back toward Santa.

As he did, everything went into slow motion, and his laughter stopped. He saw everything—Santa, Army Man, the blue pill—with crystal clarity, and he even noticed a dark spot on the blue Spandex of his left sleeve. His knife wound had torn open, but it didn't hurt. So he didn't have to laugh.

He skidded to a stop on his knees and threw the pill into Santa's open mouth. Then he grabbed Santa's hair in one hand and his beard in the other and slammed the old man's mouth shut.

Startled, Santa let go of Army Man and grabbed Danny's left arm at the bloodstain. But Danny still didn't feel a thing. He held Santa's mouth closed until he saw his Adam's apple bob.

"Smile," Danny said. "Laugh, even. Because you're alive—a dirty old man like you is *alive*—and there's no reason why you or anyone else should be. Which is pretty goddamn funny."

Then he released Santa's hair and beard, pulled away from the old man's grip, and stood.

Santa and Army Man both looked up at him, and for that moment, none of the tumult in the room existed.

Army Man was smiling. "Thank you, Laughin' Boy," he said.

Santa had a silly grin. And then he began laughing out loud, and Army Man joined him.

Just as when he had been running, though, Danny didn't need to laugh at all. His heart was pumping hard, his breath was coming fast, and he felt as if he could take the whole place apart with his bare hands.

And if that was what it took to find Porno Girl, that was what he would do. But he would try another way first.

He climbed down over the rows of chairs until he was standing in the pit next to the post. The Leather Guys backed away, and the Whipping Boy and Girl whimpered.

At the top of the aisle, a dozen men were still punching and wrestling with each other. The women in the audience had vanished. And the Racist Ranger was still nowhere to be seen.

Danny took off his trench coat and waved it over his head. He had a plan. He didn't know why he or Royce hadn't thought of it in the first place.

"Hey!" he yelled. "Heyyyyyy!"

The fighting continued. So he turned to the Whipping Boy and Girl.

"Help me get their attention," he ordered.

The Whipping Boy peered at him around the post. "Uh, how?"

"Scream or something."

The Whipping Girl shrugged, rattling her chains. "We can do that."

Danny glanced at the Leather Guys, who were now huddling together near the edge of the pit.

"You guys too," he said, and then he began yelling at the crowd again. "Hey! Hey! Heyyyyyy!"

The Leather Guys and the Whipping Boy and Girl added their voices to his, and by their third and loudest scream, the men above had stopped what they were doing and were glaring down at them. But Danny noticed that Santa Claus and Army Man were gone.

He looked back at the Leather Guys and the Whipping Boy and Girl and made a slashing motion across his throat. They fell silent, and he turned back toward the mob and pointed up at them with what he hoped was authority.

"Good citizens of New York!" he cried, although even as he said it he knew that he should have left out the "good." "My name is Daniel Clayton, although you may know me as Laughin' Boy. I'm looking for a friend of mine. Her name is Amanda Larkin, and she was last seen wearing a pink Spandex leotard and a trench coat like this one." He held up the coat and then tied its sleeves around his neck so it hung behind him like a cape. "You may know her as Porno Girl. I'm worried that she might be in trouble, and so I ask you, regardless of what you may think of me, to help me find her. Have any of you seen her here this evening?"

The men above mumbled and shook their heads. Three of them turned and left the room in a hurry.

"Excuse me," a voice said behind Danny. It was quiet, but still audible over the low hum of the music that was still playing.

Danny looked back and saw that the voice belonged to the Whipping Girl.

"The guys who come in here won't be much help," she said. "In fact, I'm amazed they snapped out of it long enough to get into a fight. Most of the time they don't even see *us*, since they mainly just watch the shows in their heads. So I doubt that any of them would have noticed Porno Girl unless she was doing a show, or a booth. And even then, maybe not."

Danny tried to imagine Amanda working at the NYPC, and couldn't. "She wouldn't participate. Not unless someone forced her."

The Whipping Boy shook his head, and his chains rattled. "I wouldn't put it past management, but the performers look out for each other. We'd know if someone was a slave, and we wouldn't put up with it. You'd have to go to Staten Island to find something like that."

"And I'd recognize Porno Girl if I saw her in the break room," the Whipping Girl said. "I haven't."

Danny turned away, afraid that he was starting to stare at the stripes on the Whipping Girl's belly. "Thank you," he said. "If you do see her, please call Drs. Ralph and Carla DeWitt at 1-800-SHRINKS."

He moved toward the aisle, but a gloved hand on his left arm stopped him. The hand closed over his wound, and he winced as a jolt of pain throbbed up to his shoulder.

A black-hooded head appeared before him then, with only pale blue eyes and purple lips showing to prove that it was human.

"I just wanted to say that I'm a big fan," the purple lips said in an androgynous voice. Then the eyes looked down at Danny's arm, and the gloved hand released its grip. "You're hurt. We have a first-aid kit in the break room."

"Thank you," Danny said, starting up the aisle, "but I'm all right."

"We also have coffee. And Pop-Tarts."

Danny didn't want to be impolite, but he thought it best not to reply again. He didn't have time for Pop-Tarts.

There were still nine men clustered around the door, watching him approach, and the Ranger was not among them. Maybe, Danny thought, Royce had been dragged out of the room during the melee. But given Royce's skills, that didn't seem likely. So maybe he had abandoned Danny and had left to continue looking for Amanda without him.

Whatever the reason, the Ranger was gone, and the door was blocked by glaring men—some of whom might be allies, but some of whom weren't. Danny would have to get through them somehow . . . and the ugliness of the solution that came to him made him start chuckling again.

Raising his left arm, Danny peeled back his sleeve to reveal the bleeding knife wound.

"Step aside," he said, chortling, "or I'll give you my *disease*."

They all scrambled to get out of his way, and Danny strode toward the door with his arm held high. He was reaching for the crash bar when the door opened and Block-Head stepped into the room.

Block-Head glared down at Danny with red-rimmed eyes, and Danny could smell the scorched funk of dope on his breath. Block-Head had been getting stoned, and he was not pleased that he had been interrupted.

"I heard something," Block-Head growled. "Somebody need to be thrown out?"

Danny brandished his bloody arm. "It's all right now," he said with a giggle. "Some of these men tried to attack me, but I've kept them at bay with the threat of infection."

Block-Head looked at the men cowering against the wall. Then he turned back to Danny. His upper lip curled.

"That's low," he said. "And most of these guys are regulars. You're not. So you're the one I'm tossing."

Danny jumped back as Block-Head reached for him. He couldn't be thrown out. He hadn't found Amanda, and now Royce was missing too. He couldn't leave without them. They were the only people who knew him now.

The crack of a whip cut the air like a rifle shot.

"Dwight, Laughin' Boy's telling the truth!" the androgynous voice cried from the pit. "Those naughty boys at the door started it!"

"Shut up, Butch!" Block-Head yelled as he came toward Danny. "You're just a slave to the media, you know that?"

Danny couldn't tell whether that comment was directed at him or at Butch, but he didn't have time to ask for a clarification because Block-Head was almost upon him. He jumped back again, then raised his bloody arm in defense.

Block-Head sneered. "I'm already HIV-positive, dipshit. Bring it on."

Danny was stunned. He hadn't meant to imply that he was threatening to infect his attackers with HIV. He had meant to imply that he was threating to infect them with laughing disease.

But he didn't have time to explain that, because Block-Head lunged. And he would have had Danny by the throat if Santa Claus and Army Man hadn't leaped up from either side of the aisle. Santa hit Block-Head high, and Army Man hit him low, and all three hit the floor.

Danny stared at them. Santa and Army Man were wearing surgical masks and latex gloves. And they were having a hard time holding Block-Head down.

"Well, go on, L.B.!" Santa bellowed. A round, wet circle appeared on his surgical mask. "Get out of here!"

Danny gave a yelp of laughter and jumped over Block-Head to the door. He slammed into the crash bar, and then he was out in the blacklit hallway. The door hissed shut behind him. No one followed him, and those who had already fled the Whipping Room had vanished. He was alone.

Part 3

Danny didn't think Santa Claus and Army Man would be able to hold Block-Head for long. So he went to the third door, opened it, and stepped inside.

This room was set up like the first two, but it was darker. The only light was a golden beam that shone down on the pit, where a brass bed seemed to float in a shifting, shuddering pool of smoke.

The golden light illuminated a nude man and woman on the bed. They were having sex—slowly, silkily, as if in imitation of the smoke that rose up around them. Their soft moans mingled with orchestral background music.

Danny couldn't help watching them. They were mesmerizing. But then they rolled over, and he saw the woman's face. She reminded him of Karen, so he was able to look away.

He had to walk around the room behind the top row of seats in order to see the dark shapes of the people in the audience. The seats were split into four sections by aisles that led down to the pit, so Danny performed the search quarter by quarter, moving counterclockwise.

The first quarter contained three shapes, one of which he thought might be Amanda. But when he went down the next aisle for a closer look, he saw that it was the same woman he had seen in the second room, the woman with the orange flattop and the Virgin Mary tattoo. She was watching the brass bed with rapt attention, so he backed up the aisle and continued around the circle. He didn't think he had disturbed her.

The second quarter contained two shapes, seated together in the fourth row. Danny couldn't tell whether they were male or female, but he was sure that neither was Amanda. They seemed to be trying to imitate the couple on the bed, insofar as they could do so while remaining in their seats.

The third quarter contained only one large, bulky shape rocking back and forth. Danny moved on.

The fourth quarter, which brought Danny back almost to the door, contained two dark shapes seated far apart from each other. The one in the top row seemed to be asleep, but the one in the middle seat of the second row was watching the lovers intently. And this shape was small enough and had a slender enough neck that it might be Amanda.

Danny made his way down the main aisle to the second row. Here he was close enough to the pit that wisps of stage smoke curled around his ankles, and the smoke shifted from white to black as reflected light from the lovers' bodies shone first in one direction and then another.

One of those reflections revealed that the person he had spotted in the second row was indeed Amanda.

Danny was so relieved that he had found her and that she seemed to be all right that he almost shouted her name. But she was engrossed in the show, and it would be a bad idea to startle her. So instead, he shuffled sideways into the row and sat down next to her.

She didn't react, but he resisted the impulse to put his hand on hers to let her know he was there. He remembered what had happened the last time he had touched her.

But he had to do something. Without the Ranger, they would both be in big trouble if Block-Head or any of the Laughin'-Boy haters came in here.

"Amanda," he whispered.

She didn't take her eyes off the pit. But she flinched and her trench coat fell open, revealing her shiny pink tights in the next flash of reflected light. And for the first time since coming into the New York Pleasure Club, Danny began to feel a stirring of sexual arousal.

It was bizarre and sad, so he couldn't help letting out a short guffaw.

"Shhh," Amanda whispered. "You'll disturb them."

Danny glanced at the man and woman on the bed. He didn't think machine guns would have disturbed them.

That turned out to be a bad thought to have, because it reminded him of South Riverside Park, of the little blonde girl, and of all the others. He began to laugh louder.

Amanda turned to glare at him. "Stop it!" she hissed.

Danny tried, but nothing seemed to work. All the Dull Things he could think of—dirt, dead grass, khaki—only evoked more images of May 20. Even the man and woman in the pit reminded him of the people in the park. They were gasping, moaning, and writhing.

Amanda gripped his left arm and squeezed, which was amazing to Danny because he knew how much she hated physical contact. And it hurt so much that he laughed even louder.

"I mean it," Amanda said, furious. "Stop it or leave!" Then she released his arm and saw that her hand was smeared with blood. She stared at it in horror.

Danny, still laughing, pulled his sleeve down over his wound and then fumbled for his coat pocket. It was hard to get to since the coat was hanging behind him. But he finally managed to retrieve a blue pill, and he swallowed it dry. Then he clamped his hand over his mouth until his lips began to feel numb and his laughter diminished. It didn't take long. The blue pills worked fast.

Amanda was still staring at her hand, so Danny took a chance and held it while wiping it clean with his coat.

"I hate body fluids," she whispered, pulling her hand away. Then she resumed watching the action in the pit.

In a distant part of his brain, Danny knew he ought to be getting them out of there—but the blue pill was making everything seem much less urgent than it had seemed a few minutes ago. So he thought it might be all right to take his time and try to coax Amanda rather than force her.

"If you hate body fluids," he said, keeping his voice low, "then you'd better stop watching."

The corner of Amanda's mouth twitched. "You haven't been paying attention," she said. "My watching things like this has nothing to do with what I like or don't like."

"I know," Danny said. "But you ought to stick with magazines and videos. A place like this can be dangerous."

"Nonsense." She leaned forward as the couple on the brass bed changed positions. "In fact, this may be what cures me. I'm gaining insight."

Danny looked at the bed, then away, and the movement set off a sound like ocean waves in his skull. The blue pill was getting down to serious work.

"Okay, so tell me," he said, slurring his words. "What insight have you gained tonight, Porno Girl?"

Amanda didn't react to the name. Instead she raised her hand and pointed, punctuating each of her next words with a tilt of her index finger.

"I'm just trying to figure out," she said, "why they do it."

As Amanda said "do it," the waves in Danny's head began to pulse outward and become visible, mingling with the rising stage smoke and turning Amanda's face into an image seen as if through blue water. It was even more pronounced than the lime Jell-O effect he had experienced at the Gleason.

"I can answer that," Danny said, and wasn't surprised to hear that he sounded as if he were gargling. "People in this business do what they do for the same reason that anybody does what they do.

To earn a living. There, mystery solved." He was beginning to worry that if they didn't leave soon, they would have to swim.

Amanda shook her head. "I'm not talking about those two people, specifically. I'm talking about anybody."

A bubble containing the word "anybody" emerged from Amanda's mouth and floated upward.

"You're looking for reasons," Danny said, watching to see if any of his own words emerged in bubbles. "But there aren't any. What there is, is an urge. I think that's why people do *anything*: Because they have an urge."

The word "urge" floated up after "anybody."

Amanda sighed, and it came out as a long stream of bubbles. "The only urge I've ever had," she said, "is to try to understand why other people have urges."

Danny wanted to smile, but he didn't know how. "Well, if you're doomed to just one urge, at least it's powerful."

Amanda did smile. "I'll say."

Now, Danny thought. Maybe if I ask her to leave with me now, she might.

And he was just about to ask when he felt a touch on his right shoulder.

"I have a powerful urge, too," a soft voice whispered. "And I knew you'd come to Porno Girl. I only wish your nigger-loving henchman was here too."

Danny turned toward the whisper and saw the woman with the orange flattop, the woman who was wearing a trench coat that was open far enough to reveal a tattoo of the Virgin Mary between her breasts.

She was right beside him. And when he looked down at the tattoo, he saw that the pupils of the Madonna's eyes were tiny swastikas. And the infant she held in her arms, its pudgy right hand raised in Teutonic salute, was a cherubic Adolf Hitler.

The woman grasped the coat-sleeve knot at Danny's throat with her left hand and reached into her own coat with her right.

"Laugh at this," she said, pulling out a stainless-steel semiautomatic.

And despite the blue pill and the liquid air, Danny began laughing as soon as he saw the gun. By the time its muzzle brushed his lips, he was howling.

The Virgin Mary stuck the barrel into his mouth.

So he laughed even harder, and he began to gurgle and drown. The water around him tasted like cold, oily metal.

He was glad Lindy was too young to be embarrassed or ashamed because her father had been killed at a live sex show while wearing a leotard. Karen would be appalled, and his parents would be mortified. But maybe the Racist Ranger would explain to them that Laughin' Boy had only been there to rescue Porno Girl, and that would make the humiliation bearable.

Porno Girl. Amanda.

The Virgin Mary wouldn't stop with him. After she sent his brains squirting into the smoky ocean, she would turn her pistol toward Amanda.

He didn't think he could stop that. But maybe he could delay it. And then maybe Amanda would stop watching people screw long enough to get away.

It was a thin hope, but it was all he had.

So, laughing wildly, he pushed himself up from his seat, driving the gun barrel deeper into his mouth, and pounced on the Virgin Mary, knocking her into the aisle. They fell together through the liquid haze, and the Virgin Mary landed on her back.

As Danny collapsed onto her, he saw tiny white chips and scarlet threads float down toward her violet eyes, and he realized that his teeth had broken on the pistol barrel.

Not that it would matter in a moment. The Virgin Mary's eyes were inches from his, and he could see the intent that burned inside them. He could see the butt of the gun reflected in her infinite black pupils, and he could see her slender finger curling around its trigger. Somewhere in the watery distance, he could hear her screaming a curse. Something about God hating him. No, broken teeth and lacerated gums wouldn't matter at all.

He was only vaguely aware that he was still laughing as Porno Girl's bright pink boot kicked the pistol from his mouth, twisting his head to the left and sending more bits of white and scarlet flying toward the pit.

The man and woman on the bed were looking toward him in shock. And he wanted to shout to them, Please, don't mind me, go on with what you were doing. But he didn't have time to try, because at that moment a tall, black-and-white figure rose up from the smoke that swirled around the bed.

It was the Racist Ranger. He had shed his trench coat, and as he stood there in his tights wielding an enormous black Glock, he looked like a panel from one of the comic books Danny had loved as a teenager.

The Ranger started forward, but he didn't fire. And as Danny turned back to his right he knew why. There was no clear shot at the Virgin Mary. He was still on top of her, and Porno Girl, off balance, was falling into the aisle beside them.

And the Virgin Mary was turning her pistol toward Danny's face again.

So he did the only thing he could. He pressed his mouth over her purple lips and laughed into her throat.

He saw his face in her eyes, saw the muzzle of the pistol brush the hair over his left ear, and kissed her as he waited to finally stop laughing.

But then there was a loud snapping sound, and he was pulled away from the Virgin Mary just as she bit down, nipping the tip of his tongue. He tumbled over Porno Girl and fell hard in the aisle behind her. The impact knocked the laughter out of him, and he rolled onto his back gasping.

Standing over him were Santa Claus and Army Man. Both were holding Glocks.

"Stay down," Santa Claus ordered.

"FBI," Army Man said. He gave Santa a wry look. "If you don't tell them that, they don't stay down."

Santa grimaced. "Here, Clayton," he said, taking something from his pants pocket and dropping it. "You look like you need it more than I do."

It was the blue pill Danny had popped into Santa's mouth. It floated down like a piece of confetti, bounced off Danny's nose, and tumbled away through the ocean.

Danny tried to see where it went but lost it as it flew past Porno Girl, who was lying next to him as if they had bedded down together. She tried to sit up, but Santa put a foot on her shoulder and stopped her.

Beyond Amanda, the Virgin Mary had risen to her knees, her trench coat open far enough now to expose not only her Madonna-and-Child tattoo but her breasts as well. LOVE was tattooed above her right nipple, and HATE above her left.

The Racist Ranger was standing over her, twisting her wrist with one hand while tearing away her pistol with the other. His Glock had disappeared.

Past the Virgin Mary and the Ranger, down in the smoke-shrouded pit, the man on the bed was screaming while the woman clamped her hands on his thigh. She was doing her best, but blood was coming up between her fingers anyway. Danny knew then that the Ranger had grabbed the Virgin Mary's wrist in time to keep her from shooting him in the head—but her pistol had still fired, and the bullet had struck the man in the pit.

Somehow, watching the nude woman try to stanch the flow of blood from the man's leg seemed even more voyeuristic than watching them have sex. So Danny looked back at the Virgin Mary, whose face was contorted in hatred and pain.

Yet she still managed to reach into a coat pocket with her left hand.

"Death to GOG and MAGOG!" she cried.

She brought out another stainless-steel pistol, and the Ranger dropped the first one to lunge for it. But his hand closed on air as she put the muzzle into her own blood-smeared mouth and fired.

Danny howled as LOVE and HATE fell away, taking the Madonna and Child with them.

Part 4

The doors opened, bright lights came on, and the smoke machine stopped. And as the fog began to clear, so did Danny's head. The blue pill was wearing off from the onslaught of adrenaline, and things began sounding and looking as if they might not be at the bottom of the ocean after all.

The Virgin Mary was covered with a gray blanket, but dark-suited Feds kept lifting it, thus exposing her tattooed torso and burst skull over and over again.

"Guess she's holey now," one of the agents said. "Get it?"

The performer with the thigh wound had been hustled away by ambulance attendants who had arrived with remarkable speed. His partner was now wearing a robe and sitting on the edge of the bed answering questions from Army Man. The Whipping Girl and one of the Leather Guys had come in and were sitting with their arms around her shoulders.

Meanwhile, Santa Claus was questioning some of the NYPC patrons up by the door—and the Racist Ranger was, once again, nowhere to be seen. He had vanished as soon as the more traditionally attired agents had shown up.

Danny and Amanda were seated in the top row near the door, where Santa Claus and Army Man had told them to wait. Amanda had expressed doubt that either Santa or Army Man had the authority to tell her to do anything, but then Santa had shown her his badge and his Glock. So she, like Danny, had done as she was told.

Danny was dabbing at his lacerated gums and chipped teeth with a gauze pad that one of the ambulance attendants had given him. To his surprise, he didn't seem to be too badly damaged. Only three teeth had chipped, and they didn't hurt. His scraped gums and nipped tongue did hurt, but they had almost stopped bleeding. He didn't think they were any worse than if he'd made a slip with a fork or eaten soup that was too hot.

Once again, Laughin' Boy had emerged from the midst of violent death virtually unscathed. But this time, he was able to keep his laughter down to a low, steady chuckle.

In the seat beside him, Amanda was grumpy. "I don't know why we have to stay," she said. "There's a dead body on the floor. There's no sex. And we didn't see anything that the FBI people didn't see too. So what's the point of keeping us here?"

Danny lowered the gauze pad. "It's probably for our protection," he said, trying to ignore the stinging sensation as he spoke. "The Virgin Mary—I mean, the woman who tried to shoot us—might not have been alone."

Amanda looked around at the strutting FBI agents and cowed performers. "Well, if she was with anyone, they've run off. So there's no reason I can't go check out the video peeps. The Ranger's flyer said the New York Pleasure Club has the raunchiest loops in the U.S.A., and that's a pretty bold claim."

An alarm went off in Danny's head. It sounded like Woody Woodpecker laughing.

"The Ranger had a flyer?" he asked. "When was this?"

Amanda gave him a sidelong look. "Earlier this evening, back at the theater. Why?"

Danny chortled. He was beginning to feel sick. "Did he give it to you?"

Amanda shook her head. "Not exactly. I was downstairs in the ladies' room after our sketch, and when I came out, he passed by and said we were done for the day. Then he said he was going up to the Green Room, and he put a piece of paper into the trash can at the bottom of the stairs. But it got stuck in the flapper. So when I started upstairs myself, I saw what it advertised, and I . . . got the urge. I left the building quicker than Elvis."

Danny guffawed, reached into his coat pocket for another blue pill, and stopped himself. He didn't want to be doped up now, didn't want to be immersed in green Jell-O or trapped at the bottom of the ocean. He wanted to be sure of what he was thinking.

"Portland cement," he said. "Kitchen sponges. Where was the Ranger when you left the theater?"

"I don't know. By the time I read his flyer, he was upstairs. In the Green Room, I guess."

"Did you use the door out to 53rd Street? The one by the backstage stairwell?"

"Sure. I didn't want to go out front with the riffraff."

"Heeheehee. Lawn fertilizer. So if the Ranger had been watching the door from the Green Room, he would have seen you."

Amanda was scowling now. "I suppose so. What's your point?"

A hand closed on Danny's shoulder, and he jumped.

"Yes, Dan'l," the Racist Ranger's voice said behind him. "Jis' what *is* you sayin'?"

Danny pulled away from Royce's grip and almost let out a peal of laughter. But he was able to stop it. What he had just realized was grim and ugly, and wanted to give it the response it deserved.

"Oatmeal!" he cried, and then he shot up from his seat, spun, and threw a punch at the Ranger's nose.

Royce didn't move. He didn't even blink. But Special Agent Armstrong, stepping in from the side, caught Danny's fist in one hand as if it were a tennis ball.

Royce gave Armstrong a surprised look, but Armstrong ignored him and glared at Danny.

"Sit down, Mr. Clayton," Armstrong said. "I'll tell you when we're ready to escort you back uptown."

Danny looked past Armstrong at the Ranger. "You sent her down here on purpose," he said. His voice didn't contain even a hint of a giggle.

"I said sit down, Mr. Clayton," Armstrong growled.

But Danny remained standing, and he stayed focused on the Ranger. As soon as Armstrong released his hand, he would try to hit the son of a bitch again.

"You did a great job faking me out," Danny said. "Jerking the camera away from the door and all that. And then acting as if you had to figure out where Amanda might have gone—when you knew *precisely*."

The Ranger still hadn't blinked. "Looky heah," he said, his voice low. "I is swoahn to mah duty, en dat's what I'se done. But I wouldn' expeck you to grasp dat, kase it ain't like you ever tried to unnastand ol' Rob's sitchyashun ner give a good God damn 'bout him, now, is it? So I don't s'pose I need no judgin' from de likes o' you."

"You knew the terrorists were watching the theater," Danny said. "You knew they'd follow if one of us left without an agent. You were *hoping* some of them would go after Amanda, and you knew what would happen here if they did."

A muscle under the Ranger's left eye twitched. "I tol' you b'fo', Dan'l. You is bait. En you cain't ack ez ef you didn' know dat."

Danny stared at the Ranger for a long moment before speaking again. When he did, his voice was low. "That's fine for me, Royce. But Amanda didn't sign up to be shot."

"She wouldn't a been."

"She almost *was*."

Armstrong squeezed Danny's fist hard enough to make the knuckles crack. "That's enough. Agent Royce, back up and cool off. And Mr. Clayton, once again, sit down."

Danny yanked his fist away, then turned just enough to glare into Armstrong's eyes.

"Fuck you," he said.

The words were clear, sharp, and laughter-free.

Danny realized then that his rage was doing the same thing for him that hard running had done earlier. He wanted to throttle the Racist Ranger, kick Special Agent Armstrong in the balls, and then beat their heads together until he couldn't tell which was black and which was white. And as a result, he had no urge to laugh at all.

"Excuse me?" Agent Armstrong said. His eyes were narrow.

"I said *fuck you!*" Danny yelled. "You and your Nigger Jim there, too! Aftah all, you is jis' two gummint slaves, ain't you? You is bof jis' workin' fo' de same Unka Sam—or is dat Unka Tom? Yassuh, you is jis' a couple o' i-dentical nigger *twins!*"

Beside him, Porno Girl gasped.

He looked down at her then and realized that he was furious with her for falling for the Ranger's trick, for giving in to her compulsion at the expense of her safety—and most of all, for having made him fall in love with her so he would run after her just as the Ranger had known he would.

"And fuck you twice, you cheap little pervert," he said.

Then he turned away from her, stepped into the aisle, and shoved past Special Agent Armstrong. The Racist Ranger reached for him—but Danny spat a bloody gob at him, and the Ranger stopped as if he'd been shot.

Danny was out of the room, down the hall, and out of the New York Pleasure Club in seconds. And as he went down the steps to the sidewalk, he saw the Virgin Mary's shrouded body being wheeled toward an idling ambulance. It had to have been taken right past him during his confrontation with Royce and Armstrong, but he hadn't even noticed.

The scrawny young barker was walking alongside the gurney, trying to hand one of his invisible flyers to the body.

"Yo yo yo," the kid said. "Check it out, check it out."

Danny turned away.

He was worse than any of them. Worse than Armstrong and his cool federal self-righteousness. Worse than the DeWitts and their self-aggrandizing "therapy." Worse than Stan Symmons, Larry Lanford, and their cheesy show-biz exploitation. Worse than the Racist Ranger and his anything-for-duty duplicity. Worse than Porno Girl and her contradictory naivete.

He was worse because he should have become enraged in the first place.

He should have become enraged at South Riverside Park. Instead of letting himself be struck down by the horror of what he had seen there, he should have gone berserk. He should have run screaming at the camouflaged cowards.

But rage hadn't even shown up for the fight. Horror had knocked him to his knees and had come so close to crushing the life from him that his only defense had been to laugh.

After all, that was what his mother and father had told him to do when he was in fifth grade. *When those bullies come after you, Danny, just laugh it off. They won't know how to handle it, because they'll be expecting you to cry. But if you laugh, you'll show them they can't hurt you.*

So he had shown them, all right. And instead of being hurt, he had come away with the constant memory of all those murdered people to make him laugh . . . and especially of that little blonde girl who could have been Lindy. That little blonde girl who *had* been *someone's* Lindy.

And as if that weren't already too much, now there was this. There was another human being he had watched die from a gunshot.

Okay, so maybe the Virgin Mary had been one of the bad guys. It didn't matter. Maybe some of the people who had been killed in Wichita had been bad guys too. How would he know?

That wasn't the point. The point was that because he had let the universe treat him like a joke and fill the void around him with chaos, he was now cursed to see more and more people blown apart.

Unless he found a way to get the universe to take him seriously. Unless he found a way to redeem himself.

He began running back north along Eighth Avenue, his trench-coat cape flapping behind him. He had no idea of how to redeem himself. But as he ran, he made a mental list of the things that he was sure wouldn't be of any use.

Blue pills wouldn't. Spackle wouldn't. Dr. Ralph and Dr. Carla wouldn't. *Lanford's on Late* wouldn't. Being a good little piece of bait for the FBI wouldn't.

Even falling in love with Porno Girl wouldn't.

Loving his daughter wouldn't hurt, he supposed, but he wasn't sure that it would help, either. It hadn't so far.

And laughter was no good at all.

Beyond that, all he was sure of was that whenever or however a chance for redemption presented itself, he would have to be ready to recognize it and take advantage of it. And no horror, fear, sadness, or other bait-like reactions could be allowed at that moment.

Only rage. Only rage had proven its worth.

Danny stopped in front of the big glass-and-steel doors of the Port Authority and faced the people coming out. He knotted his fists and thrust out his blue-and-silver chest.

"Fuck you three times!" he screamed.

Most of the people averted their eyes and walked around him. But one person, a small, wizened man wearing a yarmulke, had a response.

"Same to you, fairy," he said.

At that, Danny's rage was penetrated by a twinge of despair.

And he giggled.

Then he looked back south and saw that at least five TV camera crews were following him. And he convulsed, laughing wildly.

His plan for redemption was not getting off to a good start.

Video Clip (5)
Public Service Annulment

Selected segments from the late-night celebrity roundtable, *Publicly Indecent*, taped and broadcast from Los Angeles on Thursday, June 8, 2000:

As the lights come up, the MODERATOR, thin and nattily attired in a silk suit, bounds onto a set constructed to resemble the interior of a medieval castle. A Round Table with six high-backed chairs sits before him, and a faux tapestry depicting the ride of Lady Godiva hangs behind him.

MODERATOR: Good evening, lords and ladies, and welcome to another nakedly ambitious edition of *Publicly Indecent*!

AUDIENCE: [Applauds.]

MODERATOR: Thank you for that applause-sign triggered welcome. I'm your host and moderator Phil Moore, and if I seem more relaxed than our always noxious topics would seem to warrant, it's only because I commit an act of self-abuse before each and every show. Thank you, thank you so much.

AUDIENCE: [Applauds again.]

MODERATOR: I know you're all anxious to hear what this evening's Knights of the Round Table have to say about the latest development in the ongoing saga of Laughin' Boy, so let's get right to it. Our first Knight is the best-selling author of such novels as *Releasing the Ducks*, *The Two-Point-Takedown Motel*, and *The Princess of Pawtucket*—as well as the Oscar-winning screenplay for the motion picture *Pawtucket Princess*. Lords and ladies, here's the glamour boy of American letters, Irwin James!

The AUDIENCE applauds, and IRWIN JAMES steps out grinning, his teeth a brilliant white against his butterscotch tan. He is tall, broad-shouldered, and strapping in crisp jeans, a white linen shirt, and a suit-tailored brown leather jacket. His thick hair is shot through with gray, but his fifty-six-year-old face is still handsome in a small-eyed, jowly sort of way. He shakes hands with the MODERATOR, whispers something to him, and then takes a seat at the Round Table as the applause fades.

MODERATOR: Yikes! Believe it or not, folks, he just asked me what I'm doing after the show. Careful, Irwin—you'll jeopardize your he-man wrassler image.

AUDIENCE: [Uncertain laughter.]

IRWIN JAMES (in a deep, upper-crust-New-England accent): I just thought we could go out for a beer!

MODERATOR (winking): Sure you did. But alas, I have plans for after the show. I'll be abusing myself again.

AUDIENCE: [Groans.]

MODERATOR: Oh good, a judgmental crowd. Our next Knight will fit right in. She's the young activist who lived with miniature porcupines in a London shrubbery for two and a half years to prevent its being torn out to make room for yet another wing of the British Museum. That's right, let's welcome the protector of habitat for all things small and spiky—Emily "Hedgehog" Dale!

EMILY "HEDGEHOG" DALE, somewhat small and spiky herself, wearing a loose hemp blouse and trousers, comes out to applause and snickers. She shoots a glare toward one section of the AUDIENCE and a smile toward another, then kisses the MODERATOR on the cheek and takes a seat across the Round Table from IRWIN JAMES.

MODERATOR (rubbing cheek): Emily, your hairdo nearly put my eye out. But as for the kiss itself—wow! I may never wash again. Tell me, what's that like?

AUDIENCE: Haw!

EMILY "HEDGEHOG" DALE: Go bugger yourself, Phil.

MODERATOR: Later. But for the time being, I'll just bring out our third Knight. He's the founder and former president of the Christian Action Committee of Kentucky, or CACK, and he currently makes his living as a political consultant, conservative lobbyist, and public relations specialist. We're going to put him across the table from Emily, because if the two of them ever came into contact, the universe would evaporate in a blinding flash. Here he is, a man who believes that if Jesus were alive today, He'd own a logging company, a cigarette factory, a nuclear power plant, and carry a concealed Uzi—Brian Baines!

BRIAN BAINES, a thirtyish man in a blue business suit, strides out to a mingled reaction from the AUDIENCE. Some clap politely; some cheer and yell "Bruuuuuuuce!"; and some boo, hiss, and yell "You stink!"

BRIAN BAINES nods to the MODERATOR and goes directly to his seat next to IRWIN JAMES.

MODERATOR: There they are, Baines and James. Say, didn't you guys used to sell wine coolers?

The AUDIENCE titters weakly, and IRWIN JAMES and BRIAN BAINES give insincere smiles.

MODERATOR: Ouch! I'd run for the exit, but then I'd miss our final Knight. Now, you may have noticed that there are *three* chairs remaining. The chair facing the center camera is mine, of course—but why are there two chairs beside the funkalicious Ms. Dale? And why does one of those chairs contain this year's edition of the Greater Los Angeles Yellow Pages? Well, it's because our fourth Knight needs a translator, and he also needs a booster seat. He's the six-year-old Cuban refugee and/or kidnap victim who had America's undivided attention until Laughin' Boy came along—so everyone please welcome young Jorge Luis Martinez and his third-cousin-twice-removed, Esmerelda Juanita Martinez MacMurray!

Little JORGE LUIS is led onstage by ESMERELDA, a young woman of perhaps twenty. JORGE LUIS is wearing a Mickey Mouse

T-shirt, blue shorts, and sneakers with flashing lights in the heels. He is staring at the television cameras and the AUDIENCE, hanging back in obvious apprehension. ESMERELDA, wearing a lime-green pantsuit with a low neckline, has to tug on JORGE LUIS's hand to get him to come along.

The MODERATOR escorts them to their seats and helps ESMERELDA settle JORGE LUIS onto the phone-book-boosted chair next to EMILY "HEDGEHOG" DALE. Then he bows to kiss ESMERELDA's hand before going to his own chair.

MODERATOR (sitting down): Sorry to have behaved like a gentleman, folks . . . but it was the only way I could lean over and look down while standing in front of Esmerelda.

AUDIENCE: [Groans again.]

MODERATOR: Double yikes. I will now deftly escape by jumping into our topic. As you all know, what appears to have been a botched sting operation by the FBI took place yesterday evening in New York City at, of all places, a live-sex-show theater called the New York Pleasure Club.

AUDIENCE: [Various gasps and murmurs.]

MODERATOR: Okay, maybe you all *didn't* know. Details are still sketchy—but it's clear that Laughin' Boy, Porno Girl, and the Racist Ranger were all involved, because television crews caught them on tape. In fact, the first TV crew went to the NYPC because of a call from a club employee who recognized the "Odd Squad" as they went inside. And by the time the crew arrived, shots had been fired. One unidentified woman was killed, but a spokesman for the Justice Department claims that she was, quote, "a terrorist who recently took part in the murder of innocent Americans." The implication seems to be that she was involved in the Wichita Massacre. So, Knights, what's going on? A cover-up, a conspiracy, or just the usual federal incompetence?

BRIAN BAINES: Those choices aren't mutually exclusive, Phil. What happened yesterday was yet another chapter in the current administration's campaign to place a jackboot on the necks of the American people. The mindset that led to the debacles at Ruby Ridge and Waco was alive and well last night in New York City.

IRWIN JAMES: Goodness! Can it be that the founder of the Christian Action Committee is actually upset because the FBI shot up a *porno theater?*

AUDIENCE: [Laughs.]

BRIAN BAINES: They shot up the right place, but they did it for the wrong reasons. A daycare center or a church would have been fine with them, too—which is why it's imperative that we elect a Republican president in November.

IRWIN JAMES: Because, as we know, no federal agents have ever misbehaved in a Republican administration.

AUDIENCE: [Laughs again, but not as heartily.]

EMILY "HEDGEHOG" DALE: Excuse me, but the news so far suggests that no one from your FBI "shot up" anything at all. According to the *New York Times*, only two shots were fired, both of them by the woman who died. The first wounded a sex worker, and the second was an act of suicide.

BRIAN BAINES: Even as a foreigner, Miss Hedgehog, you ought to know better than to call prostitutes "sex workers" or to trust anything printed in the *New York Times*.

EMILY "HEDGEHOG" DALE: It was reported on CNN as well.

BRIAN BAINES (rolling his eyes): Well, then, it *must* be true!

MODERATOR: Look, maybe the FBI shot up the place, and maybe they didn't. What's more interesting, I think, is what the presence of the Odd Squad implies. Does this mean that they're federal agents themselves, and that their whole personality-disorder melodrama has been a cover?

IRWIN JAMES: Not necessarily. The employee who tipped off the TV crews said that Porno Girl was watching a sex show for quite some time before Laughin' Boy and the Racist Ranger arrived. Now, I am not a fan of these people—in fact, I'm appalled at how fascinated the nation has become with a trio so jejune—but objectively, it seems that the two men merely followed Ms. Larkin, and that the FBI agents followed *them*.

BRIAN BAINES: What about the woman who was killed? Do you believe for a second that she was really a "terrorist"? If so, why was she alone? And just whom did *she* follow?

IRWIN JAMES: I have no idea. So far, there isn't enough information about her for me to form an opinion.

MODERATOR: And that's my cue, lords and ladies. My producer showed me a fascinating video just before the show, one that various news organizations and networks have been receiving today via UPS and the Internet. Knights, please watch our studio monitors—and everyone at home, take a gander at Lady Godiva.

JORGE LUIS (in Spanish, to ESMERELDA): *Can we go get Happy Meals now?*

MODERATOR: Hold it, don't roll tape yet. Esmerelda, does Jorge Luis have a comment?

ESMERELDA: He asks if the show is over already, and if it is he is concerned because he has not heard anyone condemn Castro.

MODERATOR: In that case, Jorge Luis, let me just say that *Castro sucks!*

JORGE LUIS (in Spanish): *Why is he yelling at me?*

ESMERELDA (in Spanish): *He's joking. We're going to watch TV now, like when I show you Barney, all right?*

JORGE LUIS (confused): Que?

MODERATOR: 'kay! So let's roll tape.

The image of the MODERATOR dissolves to the faux tapestry of Lady Godiva, which in turn dissolves to an image of a man (we assume) dressed in black and wearing a hood with eyeholes. He is standing on a rocky promontory with blue sky and white clouds as a backdrop—but the rocks, sky, and clouds have the unreal crispness of computer-generated graphics.

The view zooms in tight on the man's head, and now we see that he has the white square of a clerical collar at his throat.

"Let all who have ears hear," a deep, stentorian voice says. (We assume it comes from inside the hood.) "And let all Righteous Caucasians take heed."

JORGE LUIS (v.o., in Spanish): *That's not Barney.*

ESMERELDA (v.o.): Shhhhhh.

MODERATOR (v.o.): What's wrong?

ESMERELDA (v.o.): Jorge Luis is afraid this hooded man might be Castro.

"I am the Pastor of the White Warriors for Jesus, Deceased," the hooded man says, "and I know my sheep."

MODERATOR (v.o.): Just sheep? How about hedgehogs?

EMILY "HEDGEHOG" DALE (v.o.): Very funny.

The AUDIENCE laughs over the hooded man's next few words. It's difficult to fill in the blanks because we can't read his lips.

When we hear him again, he's saying, "—the murder of our Sister by a deceitful agent of the Godless Occupation Government and its Multicultural Allies. Hear then my decree: Any Righteous person or persons of non-miscegenistic Caucasian descent who shall carry out the sentence of death on one Daniel Clayton, known as Laughin' Boy, shall be rewarded with seven hundred and fifty pounds of gold bullion and a place of honor among my Apostles when GOG and MAGOG have fallen.

"Surely, the new world comes quickly.

"Death to GOG and MAGOG.

"Death to Laughin' Boy.

"Stop aborting white babies.

"Amen."

The hooded figure dissolves to Lady Godiva again before the picture cuts to the MODERATOR.

MODERATOR: That was an edited version. There's more, but it's mostly babble about GOG and MAGOG, racial purity, Jewish conspiracies, fluoridation, and things along those lines. Now it's our turn, Knights. Your reactions?

EMILY "HEDGEHOG" DALE: I'm appalled, of course.

IRWIN JAMES: As am I. Who wouldn't be? [He shoots a pointed look at BRIAN BAINES.]

BRIAN BAINES: What was that for, Mr. James? Do you suppose that I have anything in common with that criminal? If so, let me note that I'm even more appalled than you and Miss Hedgehog.

MODERATOR: All right, so we're all appalled. Except perhaps for Jorge Luis, who has pulled up his shirt and found something of great interest in his belly button.

JORGE LUIS (looking up): Que?

MODERATOR (to Esmerelda): Ask him what he thought of the guy we just saw.

ESMERELDA (in Spanish): *Jorge, did that man on TV frighten you like Castro?*

JORGE LUIS (in Spanish): *He was in a suit that covered his head like Barney, but he didn't sing any songs. He didn't laugh like the man who wears the blue and silver suit, either.*

ESMERELDA: Jorge Luis says that the man in black frightened the music and laughter from his heart, much as Castro does.

MODERATOR: So our shortest Knight thinks the Pastor is a Commie. But what do we do about him? Do we even take him seriously? Or do we follow the same procedure we've followed with, say, Castro, and just wait for the crazy son of a bitch to die?

EMILY "HEDGEHOG" DALE: Well, first of all, I must say that this Pastor's rhetoric smacks of racism and Nazism, and racists and Nazis tend to be anti-Communist.

BRIAN BAINES: Just a minute. *I'm* anti-Communist. So that makes me a Nazi?

EMILY "HEDGEHOG" DALE: I didn't say that, Mr. Baines. If you had listened—

IRWIN JAMES: But Mr. Baines isn't capable of listening to you, Ms. Dale, because he's classified you as an Enemy—which gives him something in common with this terrorist organization. In fact, although the so-called "Pastor" was using rhetoric that pegs him as crazy, some of his positions jibe with those of Mr. Baines. For example, they share the same rabid, unreasoning opposition to abortion.

BRIAN BAINES: Opposition to abortion is neither rabid nor unreasoning. It's reverence for life. And that's something that the writer of that appalling *Princess* movie wouldn't understand. And neither would Laughin' Boy, given his glee at the murder of innocent children. You and he seem to have *that* in common with each other—and, for that matter, with both that hooded terrorist and Fidel Castro.

EMILY "HEDGEHOG" DALE: Mr. Baines, it has been established that Laughin' Boy didn't really take pleasure in watching people die, but that he suffers from a mental disorder. Furthermore, I must point out that it's ludicrous to equate terrorism with reproductive rights.

BRIAN BAINES: They're precisely the same thing, but I wouldn't expect someone who prefers hedgehogs to human beings to understand that.

EMILY "HEDGEHOG" DALE: It's true that I've never known hedgehogs to attack each other with automatic weapons.

IRWIN JAMES: Once again, Ms. Dale, I have to warn you that you're wasting your breath. Mr. Baines calls himself "pro-life," and yet he's served as a lobbyist for both the firearm and tobacco industries. So one suspects that the only reason he opposes abortion is because his clients require more fodder for their deadly products.

EMILY "HEDGEHOG" DALE (frostily): And one suspects that the only reason you *support* abortion, Mr. James, is because you fear that too many underclass children will force an increase in your property taxes.

IRWIN JAMES (taken aback): Excuse me?

EMILY "HEDGEHOG" DALE: While Mr. Baines's two-faced politics are well-known, your own hypocrisy, Mr. James, is comparatively well-shrouded. But the publicists you've hired to present you as liberal, wise, and sexy haven't been able to hide it completely.

IRWIN JAMES (to MODERATOR): I didn't realize this would be a session of *ad hominem* attacks. I thought we were here to talk about Laughin' Boy and domestic terrorism.

MODERATOR (eyes gleaming): Don't worry, we'll get to that stuff after the commercial break. In the meantime—Miss Dale, you have ninety seconds to explain what you meant by that intriguing assault on one of America's leading literary lights and humanitarian voices.

EMILY "HEDGEHOG" DALE: If Mr. James is what passes for either a literary light or a humanitarian voice in the U.S., then I thank God I'm British. At least someone of Mr. Baines's ilk doesn't attempt to hide the fact that he's a fascist arse, while someone of Laughin' Boy's ilk is demonstrably ill. But despite his reputation, Mr. James might be both ill *and* an arse. After all, he's become rich by writing stories full of sympathy for the downtrodden—and yet he's campaigned against educating poor children.

IRWIN JAMES: That's a lie!

MODERATOR: Sixty seconds, Miss Dale.

EMILY "HEDGEHOG" DALE (speaking rapidly): Mr. James lives in a wealthy school district, so his children have attended a fine school, while children in poorer districts have attended poor schools. Recently, though, his state legislature decided to spread the money around so every child received an equal share—and Mr. James threw a fit because he didn't want his taxes to buy books for, as he put it, "trailer trash." He also implied that persons of low economic status had no right to reproduce in the first place because it placed a burden on rich people, whom he claimed were an oppressed minority.

BRIAN BAINES: I'd like to interject that I'm stunned to find myself in agreement with Mr. James about something.

IRWIN JAMES (pointing across at EMILY "HEDGEHOG" DALE): I wasn't against educating poor kids! I was against taking resources away from *my* kids to do it!

EMILY "HEDGEHOG" DALE: Because the fruit of *your* loins is what's most important in this world, I suppose? And your legislators should recognize the superiority of your genes?

IRWIN JAMES (sitting back, steepling his fingers, his voice chilling): Spare me. You don't know the first thing about me or my children—or, for that matter, about trailer trash. But I'll enlighten you to this extent: Even trailer-trash genes are superior to those of *hedgehogs*.

EMILY "HEDGEHOG" DALE (eyes flashing): Leave the hedgehogs out of this!

MODERATOR: Yikes! I hate to cut this off, but I will anyway. We'll be back after these messages, most of which are aimed at neither trailer trash nor Academy Award winners . . . but at the sort of people who despise both!

JORGE LUIS: Que?

MODERATOR: You bet it is!

FADE OUT TO:

Commercials for lite beer, steak tenderizer, Microsoft (Bill Gates in a lumpy sweater, looking like Mr. Rogers packing heat), five-cents-a-minute long-distance telephone service, frozen toaster sandwiches, feminine hygiene spray, and a George Clooney movie. There's also an anti-heroin spot featuring a girl who uses a cast-iron skillet to bust up a kitchen with a manic fury that can only be the result of methamphetamines.

FADE IN TO:

A wide shot of the entire Round Table. IRWIN JAMES, BRIAN BAINES, and EMILY "HEDGEHOG" DALE are engaged in a three-way glaring contest. ESMERELDA is whispering to JORGE LUIS, who has been given crayons and paper and is happily drawing while humming and swinging his legs. The MODERATOR is looking at JORGE LUIS with an amused expression.

MODERATOR: And we're back at the Round Table on *Publicly Indecent*. Our adult guests were offered Valium during the break, but they preferred to nurture their rancor much as a Zen master nurtures his rock garden. Young Jorge Luis, on the other hand, seems to be having a fine time. And unless I'm mistaken, he's humming the "Internationale."

ESMERELDA: No, he's humming a song from a McDonald's commercial!

MODERATOR: Whoops, my bad. What's he drawing?

ESMERELDA (to JORGE LUIS, in Spanish): *Show the man your picture.*

JORGE LUIS, still humming and swinging his legs, holds up his drawing toward the MODERATOR.

MODERATOR: Yikes! That's one scary dude you've got there, Jorge Luis. Esmerelda, see if you can get him to turn it toward a camera so the folks at home can see.

ESMERELDA nudges JORGE LUIS toward the nearest camera, and our view cuts to what appears to be a blue-and-silver monster surrounded by green squiggles, brown stick figures, and blobs of red.

ESMERELDA (v.o.): As you can see, Jorge Luis is terrified of being sent back to Cuba. The big monster is Castro, and the bodies surrounding him are the freedom-loving Cubans he has tortured and killed.

Our view cuts back to a wide shot of the Round Table.

MODERATOR (in Spanish): *Jorge Luis, could you tell me what your picture is about?*

JORGE LUIS (in Spanish): *It's the man who laughs all the time. See, these orange things are his laughs. And these are all the dead people making him laugh. They're telling him elephant jokes.*

MODERATOR: *Gracias.* Lords and ladies, Jorge Luis has just informed me that his drawing is actually of Laughin' Boy—which gives me a perfect segue to a discussion of the recent events surrounding the notorious Mr. Clayton. That is, if our Knights can get past their own agendas for two minutes.

ESMERELDA (flustered): You speak Spanish!

MODERATOR: Now that I think of it, I guess I might have picked up a word or two during that semester in Costa Rica. For example, I can usually recognize the name *Castro*, and so far I haven't heard it from Jorge Luis.

ESMERELDA: He's too afraid to say it out loud!

MODERATOR (to Jorge Luis, in Spanish): *I'll get you a Happy Meal. You can eat it right here at the Round Table.*

JORGE LUIS (in Spanish): *Can I have the one with McNuggets?*

MODERATOR (turning to shout to someone offstage): Hey, let's get this kid a McNuggets Happy Meal, *pronto!* (To JORGE LUIS, in Spanish): *It's on the way, partner.*

JORGE LUIS (smiling, drawing on a fresh sheet of paper): *Gracias.*

ESMERELDA: Well, then, I'll have a Big Mac.

MODERATOR: *No comprende*. All right, Knights, from this point on Jorge Luis is the only one here allowed to behave like a six-year-old. *Si?*

BRIAN BAINES: You're one to talk, Mr. Self-Abuse.

MODERATOR: I don't do that like a six-year-old. Trust me. Now, to recap: Yesterday, the Odd Squad turns up at a porno house, and a female member of something called the White Warriors for Jesus, Deceased, is killed. Today, the so-called Pastor of that group puts a price on Laughin' Boy's head. So as usual, I'm looking for uninformed knee-jerk opinions. Knights?

EMILY "HEDGEHOG" DALE: My suggestion would be for Laughin' Boy to leave the U.S. You have any number of gun-happy maniacs here who would have loved to shoot him even before this video, and now they have the incentive of a reward from a neo-Nazi. Time to bloody go.

BRIAN BAINES: Sure. Things get tough, so cut and run. But what Miss Dale doesn't understand is that the vast majority of gun owners in this country are law-abiding citizens who would have no interest in shooting even a monster like Danny Clayton, reward or no. Furthermore, even those who *would* bother to shoot him won't be any more inclined to do so after the Pastor's video, because the reward is contingent upon the WWJD taking over the country. And that won't be too likely after we give the White House back to a conservative.

IRWIN JAMES: Mr. Baines's questionable logic aside, I must say that I find myself less inclined to disagree with him than with Ms. Dale. Laughin' Boy shouldn't run away. For one thing, he'd be abandoning his child.

MODERATOR: But what good will he be to his child if he's whacked?

IRWIN JAMES: In that case, she'll grow up knowing her father loved her enough to take that risk. A good father will do anything for his children.

EMILY "HEDGEHOG" DALE: Then perhaps Mr. Clayton should not only leave the U.S., but take his daughter, his ex-wife, and his parents with him. After all, aren't they in danger as well? If the terrorists are thwarted in their attempts to get to him, won't they try to harm his loved ones?

BRIAN BAINES: Well, they will *now*.

IRWIN JAMES: Yes. Good job, Ms. Dale.

MODERATOR: Guys, I'm sure the terrorists could have thought of that one on their own.

EMILY "HEDGEHOG" DALE: Quite. You Americans pride yourselves on your ingenuity.

BRIAN BAINES: And that ingenuity will eventually result in the capture of this Pastor wacko and the destruction of his organization. It'll take a while because the FBI is currently corrupt—but again, that will change when a new President takes office.

EMILY "HEDGEHOG" DALE: So you're saying that the situation will only get worse for the next six months.

BRIAN BAINES: Yes. But it's a historical truism that things have to get really bad before the public will elect real leaders.

IRWIN JAMES: In other words, it's all right for the WWJD to commit whatever horrors they please if it leads to the election of your brand of right-wing demagogue.

BRIAN BAINES: Give me a right-wing demagogue over a left-wing demagogue any day of the week. Or would you prefer that our country be saddled with a Castro?

ESMERELDA (interjecting): Thank you!

BRIAN BAINES: Perhaps you would, since both you and he are in favor of baby-killing.

IRWIN JAMES (rising from his chair): You want to wrestle, Baines?

BRIAN BAINES (recoiling): Have you lost your mind?

IRWIN JAMES (sitting back down): I'm using wrestling as a metaphor, Mr. Baines. Can't you grasp a metaphor?

BRIAN BAINES: I can when it makes sense.

EMILY "HEDGEHOG" DALE: I didn't quite grasp it either, but since it has something to do with a pastime of wealthy Americans—the insane upper-class killer John DuPont was a wrestler, wasn't he? —it's no wonder it slipped by the likes of me.

MODERATOR (jumping in before IRWIN JAMES can respond): Well, since we've also slipped by the likes of our topic yet again, the least we can do is give our youngest Knight his fair share of air time. So, does anyone have a question for Jorge Luis?

EMILY "HEDGEHOG" DALE: I can oblige. Jorge Luis, did you know that a child born to rich Western parents will use two hundred times more of the Earth's resources than a child born to poor Third-World parents? Did you know that the elite, even as they argue for rugged individualism, are passing laws to ensure that their children will inherit still more money and resources that those children have done nothing to earn? Did you know that such unchecked consumption will result in the destruction of innocent creatures such as hedgehogs? And finally, how does all that make a poor Third-World child such as yourself feel?

IRWIN JAMES: Oh, brother.

BRIAN BAINES: I'll say.

MODERATOR: Congratulations, Emily! You've managed to broker a peace between our left-wing author and our right-wing lobbyist. Have you considered a trip to the West Bank? Or perhaps you could arrange a joint speaking tour for the Pastor and Laughin' Boy. In the meantime, though—Esmerelda, would you like to take a crack at translating Emily's questions? And I promise that I won't hassle you if you condense, paraphrase, or mention Castro.

ESMERELDA (frowning for a moment, then speaking to JORGE LUIS in Spanish): *Jorge Luis, would you like to be rich even if it meant the death of funny-looking animals?*

JORGE LUIS (standing up on the phone book and clapping his hands): McNuggets!

A STAGEHAND places a Happy Meal box on the Round Table in front of JORGE LUIS, who sits down again, opens the box, and begins to eat.

ESMERELDA: What, no drink?

STAGEHAND: Uh, it came with a Coke, but somebody backstage snagged it.

ESMERELDA: Never mind, then. I give him a Coke, he's up all night playing Sega.

The STAGEHAND leaves, and there are a few seconds of dead air while everyone at the Round Table watches JORGE LUIS eating his McNuggets.

MODERATOR (clearing his throat): Well, we seem to have lost Jorge Luis.

BRIAN BAINES: But I have a question for him too.

MODERATOR: Take your best shot.

BRIAN BAINES: Jorge Luis, should we laugh when people are hurt?

ESMERELDA (in Spanish): *Jorge Luis, is it funny when people are injured?*

JORGE LUIS (concentrating on his Happy Meal): I don't know.

MODERATOR: Hey! The kid speaks English!

ESMERELDA: Not really. That's the only phrase he knows, and he uses it when he doesn't want to be bothered.

MODERATOR: No kidding? Me too!

EMILY "HEDGEHOG" DALE (looking ill): Excuse me, but I can't sit here while the flesh of helpless creatures is being consumed.

BRIAN BAINES: What, *chickens?*

EMILY "HEDGEHOG" DALE: If I were to leave now, would I still receive payment for my appearance?

MODERATOR (smirking): I don't know.

BRIAN BAINES: Well, it seems that our activist isn't really too interested in the problems of others—in Laughin' Boy, in the woman the FBI killed last night, or even in her precious hedgehogs. At the end of the day, she just wants her money.

EMILY "HEDGEHOG" DALE (weakly, slipping down in her chair): I need it for a hedgehog preserve . . .

MODERATOR: "Hedgehog Preserves"? I'll stick to strawberry, thanks.

EMILY "HEDGEHOG" DALE (more weakly still): At least I've maintained my beliefs, while you Americans shift like smoke in a hurricane. Your national reaction to Laughin' Boy is a case in point—first you hate him, then you pity him, then you make him a comedic hero, and then you hate him again, all depending on what you've seen on the telly most recently. It makes me queasy.

MODERATOR: I thought that was the McNuggets.

EMILY "HEDGEHOG" DALE: It's also the realization that more than eighty people were murdered in the center of your nation not three weeks ago, and already you speak of the incident as if it were nothing more than a playing card in a political poker game. You don't seem to be grieved at all, except in the vaguest lip-service sort of way.

BRIAN BAINES: Look here, Miss Hedgehog. The world is a complex place, and most Americans recognize that. The Wichita Massacre was a tragedy, and it won't be forgotten. But even so, the Earth went on spinning, didn't it?

EMILY "HEDGEHOG" DALE (whispering): Not for those who died. Not for their families. And not for Laughin' Boy.

BRIAN BAINES (angrily): Don't you dare put that monster in the same class as the people he found so amusing!

IRWIN JAMES: Ms. Dale, I believe that the point Mr. Baines was trying to make before his pushbutton rage overwhelmed him was that those of us who live in the real world cannot afford to concentrate all our attention on any one event, no matter how tragic. We must continue living our lives, or the terrorists will have won. Yes, we will remember the victims of the Massacre, and yes, we will do whatever we can to bring their killers to justice. But the most effective way to accomplish that is to keep on doing what we do best. I, for example, cannot track down the White Warriors because I am not a detective . . . but I can and will use my skills as a writer to condemn all that they stand for.

BRIAN BAINES (snorts): In the words of today's young people—How *lame!*

IRWIN JAMES (turning toward BRIAN BAINES): And just what, sir, are *you* doing in response to the Massacre?

BRIAN BAINES: I'm praying, of course. I'm also keeping my weapons loaded and ready. And that's *not* a metaphor. If the Pastor, his Warriors, Laughin' Boy, or anyone else shows up at my door uninvited, they'll wish they hadn't.

MODERATOR: So let that be a warning to all you Jehovah's Witnesses, teenage Mormon Elders, and census takers who might be thinking of going door-to-door in Mr. Baines's neighborhood. Oh, and you Girl Scouts—Peddle your damn cookies somewhere else!

AUDIENCE: [Laughs.]

BRIAN BAINES: Actually, that's good advice.

EMILY "HEDGEHOG" DALE (still weak and slumping): That's right. If there's a problem, just shoot it dead with one of your ubiquitous firearms. And then this Pastor bloke really will have won, because you'll be his disciples. You'll have a Massacre in a different city every weekend, and each state will have its own official Laughin' Boy for just such occasions.

BRIAN BAINES: I'd like to point out that you English didn't mind our ubiquitous American firearms when we saved your asses from the Germans.

EMILY "HEDGEHOG" DALE (perking up a bit): Good God, how much longer will you be falling back on that one? My *parents* weren't even born 'till the mid-1950s—so not only did your firearms not save *my* arse, they didn't even save the eye that held the twinkle that would *become* my arse.

MODERATOR: Don't you just love the way the Brits say "arse"? It sounds so much more dignified than a plain old "ass." Like it's wearing a powdered wig or something.

IRWIN JAMES: Dignified derrieres or not, Ms. Dale does have a point about guns in America. There are too many people with too many weapons and too little sense. Therefore, we ought to institute stringent registration and testing requirements to ensure that mental defectives such as the Pastor and his followers have a much harder time getting their hands on instruments of death.

EMILY "HEDGEHOG" DALE: Just out of curiosity, Mr. James, would you be able to fulfill the requirements you have in mind? Would your children?

IRWIN JAMES: I imagine so. I've taught my boys gun safety.

EMILY "HEDGEHOG" DALE: I see. So the America you envision wouldn't be gun-free—it's just that all of the guns would belong to the elite. That way, when the "trailer trash" expect you to help pay for decent schools, you can shoot them without fear that they'll shoot back.

IRWIN JAMES (rising): Do *you* want to wrestle?

EMILY "HEDGEHOG" DALE (clearly feeling better): I'm quite sure that *you wish*.

BRIAN BAINES: I just want to point out that every American has the right to bear arms. But the productive people who earn the most money can afford *better* arms—so the kind of qualifying test Mr. James proposes is already in place. As for Miss Dale's implication that guns are a detriment to a free society, let's just ask Jorge Luis whether citizens are allowed to bear arms in a repressive regime like Cuba.

ESMERELDA (in Spanish): *Jorge Luis, can people in Cuba own pistols and rifles?*

JORGE LUIS (munching fries): I don't know.

AUDIENCE: [Scattered chuckles; murmurs of "Isn't he cute?"]

MODERATOR: And now, lords and ladies, we're coming up on our final break, and my producer tells me there won't be time after that for more than a quick see-ya-later-buy-the-home-version. So I'm throwing out one last question, and each Knight will have thirty seconds to answer.

EMILY "HEDGEHOG" DALE: Lovely. You Yanks always examine every issue in such depth.

MODERATOR: Well, y'know, Emily, we don't all have two and a half years to hang out with the hedgehogs. Some of us are trying to make a living.

EMILY "HEDGEHOG" DALE: And such hardworking blokes you are, at that.

IRWIN JAMES: I know *I* am.

BRIAN BAINES: Ditto.

EMILY "HEDGEHOG" DALE: Come now, Mr. James. You're a *writer*, which with the possible exception of "tenured professor" is without a doubt the laziest profession on the planet. And Mr. Baines, you're in *politics*, which is all about getting people to spend money *on* you and do your work *for* you. And Mr. Moore, well, you do this *television* thing, which isn't exactly life in the gulag, now, is it? So I'm quite confident in saying that even a slumbrous hedgehog works harder for his supper than any of *you*.

BRIAN BAINES: Miss Hedgehog, if you don't think political courage is a full-time job—

IRWIN JAMES (half-rising): And any time you want to hit the mat and try to write a *Princess of Pawtucket*, Ms. Dale—

MODERATOR (interrupting): Chill out, Knights. Mr. Baines, Emily's a naive girl from a distant land who doesn't understand the grueling lot of the American lobbyist. And Mr. James, we've already established that she doesn't want to wrestle. But if you have your heart set on a match, I'll give you a list of L.A.-area nightclubs where any number of young men will be happy to oblige.

JORGE LUIS: Happy Meal?

MODERATOR: You've already had yours, kid. Now, everybody stop flinging your feces long enough to answer this question, inspired by Ms. Dale: First he seemed a villain, then a semi-heroic victim. But given his bizarre TV appearances with the Odd Squad, the even more bizarre shootout at a porno house last night, and the even *more* bizarre death threat from a terrorist group called the White Warriors for Jesus, Deceased—just what the hell *is* Laughin' Boy, really? Mr. James, you may answer first. And if you threaten to wrestle anyone, I'll tell the world that your screenplay for *Pawtucket Princess* was ghostwritten by Joe Eszterhas.

IRWIN JAMES (rising): That's a *damned* lie!

MODERATOR: Just answer the question, Irwin.

IRWIN JAMES (sitting back down, but glaring): My answer is that Laughin' Boy, while he may have begun his life as a flesh-and-blood man, has now dissolved into metaphor. He no longer has any existence except as an idea in the vast marketing mind of the mass media. He is an ephemeral image created to sell a nonexistent product, and therefore he cannot be killed by anyone, terrorist or no, until he has ceased to be profitable for his creators.

MODERATOR (shaking his head like a stunned cartoon character): Wow! With a line of b.s. like that, Mr. James, it's no wonder that Ivy League panties fall like autumn leaves whenever you guest-lecture.

AUDIENCE: [Laugh as if they don't quite get it.]

MODERATOR: And now, Mr. Baines, the conservative view?

BRIAN BAINES: Mr. James is partially correct. Our view of Laughin' Boy *has* been warped by the liberal media. But when you look past the hype, it's plain that he is both a coward and a crass opportunist. Why else would he laugh at the pain of others, slink to the FBI for protection, and then appear with a racist thug and a pornography addict in comedy sketches on a so-called "entertainment" show known for its attacks on family values? Now, I'm not suggesting violence, or support for the WWJD, or anything of the sort—but I *am* suggesting that our children will be better off once Laughin' Boy has been wiped from our national consciousness once and for all.

MODERATOR: Yikes. I'm gonna go out on a limb here, Brian, and guess that there aren't quite so many autumn leaves falling after your own guest lectures at Bob Jones University.

BRIAN BAINES: I beg your pardon?

MODERATOR: That's nice of you, but I have to move on to sweet, spiky Emily, who seems to have recovered from her McNugget-induced ennui.

EMILY "HEDGEHOG" DALE: Yes, thank you. I do feel much better now that they've been consumed and I don't have to look at them.

MODERATOR: He's still working on the fries. Think of the poor doomed tubers.

EMILY "HEDGEHOG" DALE: I'd rather not. As for Laughin' Boy, however, I shall reemphasize that he is a mere human being suffering from an illness—and so I pity him. But inasmuch as he is also a creation of the media, I fear for him. For whether he deserves it or not, he is now a hero, a villain, an icon . . . and a target. Thus I have no doubt that the WWJD will try to carry out their death threat. After all, despite the fact that *they* took so many innocent lives, it is *Laughin' Boy* who has received the lion's share of the media's attention in the days since. And because that attention is what they crave—hence today's video—they will do whatever they can to take it away from its usurper.

AUDIENCE: [Dead silence.]

MODERATOR: Damn. No autumn leaves falling from your tree, eh, Emily?

EMILY "HEDGEHOG" DALE: None of which you shall ever be aware.

MODERATOR: No matter; I'm currently in a committed relationship with myself. So to hasten my next date, let's conclude with our Knight of the Crayon, Jorge Luis. Esmerelda, if you will?

ESMERELDA (in Spanish): *Jorge Luis, what do you think of the laughing man in your picture? Is he good or bad?*

JORGE LUIS (in Spanish): *He does funny things on TV in his pajamas. Can we have ice cream now?*

ESMERELDA: Jorge Luis says—

MODERATOR: Allow me. Jorge Luis says: "Laughin' Boy looks ridiculous in Spandex—just like Castro!"

AUDIENCE: [Laughs.]

MODERATOR: And that's it for tonight's edition of *Publicly Indecent*! We'll be back tomorrow with more semi-famous folks who enjoy insulting each other.

EMILY "HEDGEHOG" DALE: I can't say that I enjoyed it.

MODERATOR: Which reminds me, Emily—you might want to check your messages once we're off the air. The voice in my ear tells me that a certain London shrubbery has just been torn out in its protector's absence.

EMILY "HEDGEHOG" DALE (leaping up, eyes wide): *No!*

MODERATOR: Hedgehogs were flying through the air like wiffle balls!

IRWIN JAMES: I'm not sure they have wiffle balls in the UK.

JORGE LUIS: Que?

MODERATOR (standing): You better believe it is! And by the way, lords and ladies, our bookers are working to see if we can get the Odd Squad themselves here next week!

BRIAN BAINES: If so, your bookers ought to be ashamed of themselves.

MODERATOR: That was covered when they booked *tonight's* lineup. Good night, lords and ladies! Remember, we might have Laughin' Boy himself at the Round Table very soon—but you'll never know unless you keep coming back for more public indecency on *Publicly Indecent*!

The theme music comes up, the camera pulls back so we can see Lady Godiva, the AUDIENCE applauds, and the credits roll. EMILY "HEDGEHOG" DALE runs offstage; IRWIN JAMES stands and offers BRIAN BAINES a handshake; BRIAN BAINES pretends he doesn't see the proffered hand. The MODERATOR goes to ESMERELDA and JORGE LUIS, eyes ESMERELDA's cleavage, then whispers in JORGE LUIS's ear.

JORGE LUIS listens intently. Then he stands up on the phone book, faces the AUDIENCE, and laughs. And laughs. And laughs, and laughs, and laughs.

MODERATOR (v.o., shouting to someone offstage): Hey, let's get this kid some ice cream, *pronto!*

JORGE LUIS points at the AUDIENCE and continues laughing as we FADE OUT to commercial.

Therapy Transcript (7)

Session Not Held (see below)

Thursday Evening, June 8, 2000

Dear Dr. Ralph and Dr. Carla:

You might not worry when I don't come downstairs for breakfast tomorrow, but you'll investigate when I don't show up in Dr. Ralph's study for our usual 10:00 AM session. In my imagination, I think of you trying to break down my locked door, fearing that I've committed suicide.

But I'm sure you've kept a key.

I haven't killed myself, by the way. This isn't a suicide note. Not that I wouldn't be tempted—except that I have Lindy to think of. It's bad enough that she'll be saddled with the memory of a father who became Laughin' Boy. I won't also saddle her with the memory of a father who killed himself. Besides, I can't ask for her forgiveness if I'm dead.

So, like Jesus and His tomb, I am not here. And I haven't flown the coop only to die on the streets of NYC, either. Although you might prefer it if I did. After all, if I were to drop dead today—somewhere other than your townhouse, so you couldn't be blamed—you'd be able to write your book about me and be fairly certain that it would be the final (or at least bestselling) word on the Laughin' Boy phenomenon.

Instead, you'll now have to live in fear that I'll publish my *own* book. Because it would really cut into your sales, wouldn't it?

I might do it for no other reason than that.

Sorry if I sound bitter. But it seems clear that my "cure" is far down on your list of priorities. In fact, I'm not sure it's on the list at all.

So I'm terminating our therapist-patient relationship. And it might interest you to know that I'm terminating my player-pawn relationship with the FBI, too.

Your motives, doctors, should have been clear to me from the outset. But I was too wracked with laughter to see straight. After almost three weeks, however, I've become angry enough that my vision has cleared somewhat. And now I can see that you aren't in this for me—or for any of your other patients, either.

You aren't even in this to help out the FBI, although your interests overlap whenever the cameras come on.

You're in this for the ratings. You're in this for the PR. You're in this for the book deal. You're in this for that big jump from radio to television. It wouldn't surprise me if you were contemplating feature films and computer games.

As for the Feds—

Their motives may be pure. They may sincerely hope to nab the bad guys. More likely, though, they just want to preserve their jobs. And that means that if they don't have a workable plan of action, they'll settle for any plan at all. Anything to look as if they're doing something.

I don't blame Special Agent Armstrong. I think he wants to lock up the terrorists who committed the Wichita Massacre for a thousand years. But I also think he's at the mercy of higher-ups who have forced him into using me as mass-media-dangled bait—a course of action which now seems not only dangerous, but hopeless as well.

I suspect that you, doctors, are well acquainted with those higher-ups. I also suspect that using me in this manner was your idea. After all, what better way to market your new franchise—the "treatment" of ultra-freaks—than to enlist the free assistance of the federal government?

Perhaps you'll now say that in addition to my other problems, I've become paranoid. Well, go right ahead. I won't be around to listen.

If I'm paranoid, it's justified. Despite the fact that the Racist Ranger saved my life in Chicago, his behavior has proven that I can no longer trust him. And since he works for the FBI, I can no longer trust them either.

I'm not the only one who should be paranoid, either. The Ranger deliberately lured Amanda Larkin to the New York Pleasure Club. (Not that he had to try too hard. Amanda seems all too willing to let her compulsion get her killed.)

And that's another reason I have to leave. The Feds know that I'm Amanda's friend, so as long as I'm here, they'll use her in order to better use me. But if I'm gone, maybe they'll leave her alone.

I suggest that you do the same. If you do, I promise that I won't write my own book.

I wonder how much you really knew on Wednesday evening. I wonder, Dr. Ralph, whether your apparent friction with Special Agent Armstrong was real or staged. I wonder whether you and Dr. Carla really were searching the theater for Porno Girl, or whether you just needed to disappear long enough for the Racist Ranger to get me outside.

The Ranger's good. He even made me think that going after Amanda was my idea. Maybe he learned that particular trick from you. You're the headshrinkers, aren't you?

Maybe you made him think it was *his* idea, too.

Hell, maybe you're making me think that my leaving *now* is my idea, too. Maybe this is just a new wrinkle in the plan: Get me off on my own so the bad guys can have a clear shot at me. And then you can still have your own clear shot at the bestseller lists. And a syndicated TV show.

Enjoy. But as for me, I'm out of here.

And the only reason I'm writing this note before I go is so you'll know there's no chance that I haven't just run off on impulse, in a panic. So you'll know that you'll never get me back here. So you'll know that if you try some legal maneuver to do so, I'll tell the news media that you have kiddie porn hidden somewhere in the townhouse.

Remember Amanda's Traci Lords tape? That counts. So even if you've destroyed it, you'll have a hard time denying the allegation. Because it *was* here, wasn't it?

And no one will blame Amanda. After all, she's *sick*. But you, on the other hand, are respected psycho-celebrities who know the difference between right and wrong. And who were supposed to be monitoring poor Porno Girl so she didn't do anything wrong.

The fact that you're not child pornographers will be lost in the ensuing electronic noise . . . and while you're struggling to explain yourselves, your book-and-TV deals-in-the-making will be lost as well.

Oh, the people in charge will know you're blameless. But that won't matter.

Welcome to my world.

Now leave me and my daughter alone. And you might want to do your best to convince everyone else to do the same.

I haven't seen Amanda since the Pleasure Club debacle. So maybe she's taken off as well. I hope so.

But if not . . .

Say goodbye to Porno Girl for me.

Web Surfing [Graphics Disabled] (3)

<click> *Connecting to HTTP Server . . .*

It is June 8 of the Year 2000, and you have reached the World Wide Web site of THE AMERICAN COALITION FOR FAMILY VALUES (ACFV).

The ACFV is a nationwide coalition of families, churches, and businesses dedicated to the proposition that a strong moral foundation must be restored to both the government and population of the United States of America. Otherwise, we are a nation damned to perdition.

For our positions on the various problems facing our nation, as well as for their solutions, please click on any of the following links:

Fornication
Masturbation
Hollywood's Cultural War Against Our Children
Interracial Marriage
Wicca, Witchcraft, and Satanism
Bilingual Education
NAFTA and the Threat from Mexico
Federal Corruption and Coercion
Canada: Subversion from the North
The Danger of Catholicism and Other False Religions
Mormons in the FBI
Multiculturalism

<click> *Connecting to HTTP server . . .*

MULTICULTURALISM is a code word for the dilution and destruction of fundamental, born-again Western Christianity via the pollution of our core values under the guise of "tolerance."

In the United States today, Federally-funded public schools are teaching our children that all cultures and beliefs are valid and must not only be tolerated, but respected and integrated into our own American culture. And while that sounds quite sweet on the surface, the horrifying truth is that this government-sponsored brainwashing leads our children to accept the tenets of Hinduism, Judaism, Islam, Wicca, Buddhism, Animism, Paganism, Scientology, Druidism, Unitarianism, and other anti-Christian doctrines as fine and dandy. Should we be surprised, then, when our children turn away from the teachings of the Scriptures and engage in drug use, sexual promiscuity, the worship of rock musicians, sorcery, syrup-drinking, gambling, bestiality, abortion, blasphemy, and eco-terrorism?

Clearly, a fundamental change is necessary at the Federal level if we are to reverse this trend and assure that our children are raised not in a confusing and corrupting stew of negative influences, but in the wholesome and truthful Bread of Life.

We do not have the space here to fully explain all of the dangers of MULTICULTURALISM and how it affects you and your family. More information, however, can be found at the links below:

Pat Buchanan for President
Eagle Forum Online
Parents for English Only (Pueblo, Colorado)
The Thin Brown Line: Tales of the Border Patrol
Ritual Abuse of Children in "Mainstream" Religions
Buddha, Mohammed, and Jesus—NOT Three of a Kind
The Christian Minority's Battle for Survival
The Case for Segregation
Heritage Under Siege

Fluoridation, Busing, and Gangs

Compassionate Conservatism and Bible-Based Education

The Persecution of the Western European

Abortion: Dr. Satan vs. the Christ Child

Integration and Miscegeny

School Vouchers: Regaining What Was Lost

WWJD

<click> *Connecting to HTTP server . . .*

Welcome to the unofficial Internet Home of the **White Warriors for Jesus, Deceased.**

In order to proceed, click I AGREE after the following statement:

I affirm that I am not a member of any governmental law enforcement agency, whether local, county, state, or Federal. I further affirm that I will not utilize any of the material contained herein in any manner that would result in investigation, prosecution, inconvenience, or harm to any person or persons connected with this Web site in any way whatsoever. <I AGREE>

<click>

We, the Non-Combatant Political Auxiliary of the White Warriors for Jesus, Deceased, invite you to learn more about our Righteous Cause by reading the answers to the following—

Frequently Asked Questions:

Why is this site "unofficial"? The WWJD is under siege by the current puppet government of the United States of America. Thus any "official" Web site—that is, any site actually maintained by White Warriors—would expose the active Brothers and Sisters in the WWJD to the demonic wrath of Federal "law-enforcement" agents. Therefore, this site is being maintained by RC (Righteous Caucasian) sympathizers whose function is to fight GOG and MAGOG with words alone. This does not mean, however, that there is no danger in what we do, and we are well aware that by maintaining this site we are putting ourselves at risk. While we have set up firewalls and have otherwise attempted to preserve our anonymity, we realize that our identities may well be discovered by agents of GOG. As a result, we have no direct contact with any active White Warrior lest we expose our Brothers and Sisters to additional risk, and although we occasionally receive communiques regarding the Pastor's doctrine and policies, we have no way of tracing these to their source(s).

Who are the White Warriors for Jesus, Deceased? The WWJD is a courageous group of Righteous Caucasian Brothers and Sisters who have banded together to take direct military action against GOG and MAGOG. By so doing, they hope to hasten the climax of the Last Days and thus help to bring about Christ's Thousand-Year Reign, during which the Unrighteous and the Seed of Cain shall be purged from the Earth.

Why "Deceased"? Jesus Christ came back to life three days after His Crucifixion, but GOG and MAGOG have corrupted the masses into behaving as if He were dead. So the WWJD fights not for Christ's literal Resurrection, but for a resurrection of White Christian values. Until our victory, then, we refer to Jesus as "Deceased" to remind ourselves that although His literal Resurrection has been accomplished, His Resurrection in the hearts and minds of His children has yet to be fully realized.

Who is the Leader of the WWJD? The Commander-in-Chief of the WWJD is the Lord God Almighty—while His Son, Jesus Christ, can be thought of as the Secretary of Defense. Their Field Marshal on Earth is Pastor Turner P. Williams.

Who is Turner P. Williams? Pastor Turner P. Williams is a Righteous Caucasian who has heard the Voice of God and accepted the burden of Holy Christian Resistance to GOG and MAGOG. He has devoted the past thirty years of his life to this struggle, first as an author and spiritual leader, and then as chief strategist for the WWJD's military operations. For a visionary and entertaining explication of Pastor Williams's story, the reader is referred to his autobiography, *My White Christian War*, as well as to his stunning novel of the Last Days, *The Robertson Journals*. Both are available from RC Publications, P.O. Box 777, Bushville TX 78877. (Please contact RC Publications directly for price and shipping information.) We hope to be able to offer both of these volumes for sale on this Web site soon, but must first ascertain to what extent such an offer would expose us to an immediate attack from GOG and MAGOG.

What are GOG and MAGOG? There is no simple answer to this question, and for complete details we must refer you to your Bibles. However, this question does provide the opportunity for us to offer a quick Glossary of Terms for those whose sight of the Truth has been all but obscured by the Enemy:

GOG. GOG is an acronym for Godless Occupation Government, and it refers to the current illegitimate overlords of the United States of America. This is the same GOG referred to in the Holy Bible as one of the Enemy Nations in the Last Days.

MAGOG. MAGOG is an acronym for Multicultural Allies of the Godless Occupation Government, and it refers to the many non-Christian, non-Caucasian, non-American mercenaries utilized by GOG in its war against the Righteous. One need only look at the employees of the current Federal government to see that Jews, Muslims, Negroes, Mexicans, Mormons, Catholic French Canadians, and other enemies of Righteous Caucasians abound therein.

Righteous Caucasian. A Righteous Caucasian is any Bible-believing Christian of Western European descent who recognizes that Judaism, Catholicism, Islam, anti-Fundamentalism, and Multiculturalism are weapons arrayed against the Lord God and His Followers in these the Last Days.

Seed of Cain. Prior to the Creation of Earth, a Great Battle was fought in Heaven between those Angels loyal to the Lord God and those Angels loyal to the rebellious Lucifer. At the end of that Battle, Lucifer and his Angels were cast into Hell, where they became Demons and where they suffer torments to this day. Meanwhile, those Angels loyal to the Lord God became exalted, and many of their souls would later come to earth as Righteous Caucasians, descendents of the fair-skinned children of Adam and Eve. However, there was a third class of Angels as well—those who, while not aligned with Lucifer, did not defend the Lord God as Righteously as was their duty. These Angels have had their souls come to Earth as descendants of Cain, the murderer whose sin turned his skin the color of coal. The Seed of Cain therefore cannot partake of the blessings bestowed upon the Righteous, but must suffer punishments and tribulations during the Last Days and during the Thousand Year Reign to atone for their lack of fervor during the Great Battle in Heaven. And since many of the Seed of Cain resent this punishment and continually plot to avoid it, all of their ilk must be viewed as the enemies of the Righteous.

The White Warriors for Jesus, Deceased. As already explained, the WWJD is a group of Righteous Caucasians who have pledged to undertake military action against GOG and MAGOG at the behest of their Pastor in the Last Days. (*W*hat *W*ould *J*esus *D*o? He told us the answer Himself: "Think not that I am come to send peace on earth: I came not to send peace, but a sword." *Matthew* 10:34.)

Brothers and Sisters. Broadly, "Brother" and "Sister" are terms that can refer to any Righteous Caucasian of the appropriate gender. In the context of this discussion, however, "Brother" (or "Sister") refers specifically to a White Warrior. (An exception is Turner P. Williams, who is referred to not as "a Brother," but as "the Pastor.")

The Last Days. We are living in the Last Days, and it is the goal of the WWJD to help bring them to their Divine Conclusion.

Did the WWJD carry out the act popularly known as "The Wichita Massacre"? The WWJD has issued a communique stating that several of their Brothers and Sisters undertook a military operation in Wichita, Kansas, a sinful city where many unborn Caucasian babies have been murdered, on 20 May 2000 A.D. They did so upon orders from their Pastor, who issued said orders after receiving a Divine Revelation from the Lord God Almighty. Unfortunately, Satan and GOG sent a demon to distort the intent and the result of this military operation—and thanks to the MAGOG-controlled mass media, this demon has so far been largely successful in deceiving the public. However, the Lord God will not allow His people to be deceived for long. It will therefore soon become clear that the term "Wichita Massacre" is a misnomer—for the fact is that the vast majority of "victims" in the operation were not of the Righteous, but of the Seed of Cain and other anti-Christian, pro-Satan groups. It will also soon become clear that the demon known as "Laughin' Boy" is guilty of deceit and other crimes against the Lord God Almighty, and so he shall be punished as an example to all those who follow GOG and MAGOG.

How will Laughin' Boy be punished? Details of any plans of the WWJD must be kept confidential for reasons of security. However, the Pastor has condemned Daniel Clayton of Wichita, also known as Laughin' Boy, to the sentence of death for his treasonous actions. As of today, 8 June 2000 A.D., a reward has been offered to any Righteous Caucasian who carries out the sentence. For details about the reward, <Click Here>.

What will happen at the climax of the Last Days? Again, this is a question for which there is no simple answer. All we can say for certain is that the Bible tells us this climax is coming soon, and that the Pastor has seen through Divine Revelation that the White Warriors will play a major role in bringing it to fruition. It also seems likely that Laughin' Boy is the Beast referred to in Scripture (for he was born on the 6th day of the year 1966), and thus it is all the more probable that Armageddon is imminent.

For further illumination of this topic, we suggest that you read *The Robertson Journals*, an excerpt from which may be found <here>.

<click>

And then Robertson dismounted his motorcycle—his good, American-made Harley-Davidson, not one of those crappy Jap kiddie bikes or clunky Italian grease-burners, although a well-engineered German BMW might have been all right if one had been available—and gazed up at the body of the pretty white woman hanging from the corner lamppost that burned with pure blue mercury-vapor fire, so much purer than the sickly yellow of sodium, that sickly yellow like a crafty gook's complexion, and he wondered what such a lovely Aryan girl could have done to deserve such treatment, and he even began to feel a bit annoyed at the obvious waste of a perfectly good child-bearer, when he saw the crisp white placard hanging from her bent and bruised neck, a crisp white like newfallen snow with bold black lettering as striking and honest as a sturdy swastika, and then, sadly but with a firm masculine jaw and no weakness or regrets, he understood. DATED AN EPISCOPALIAN, the placard said, and so Robertson, shaking his head not with dismay at the woman's fate but with honest bafflement at her deliberate flaunting of all that was necessary for the preservation of the Righteous of the Earth, remounted his magnificent two-wheeled instrument of muscular salvation and continued up the street, his pump-action Remington shotgun cradled in one arm, at the ready for any further attack from the Seed of Cain, and soon he noted that from every lamppost hung yet another white woman displaying yet another placard announcing her perfidy and betrayal of the Lord God Almighty and of freedom-loving Righteous Caucasians the world over. MARRIED A CONGRESSMAN FROM NEW YORK, said one placard. DONATED TO THE UNITED NEGRO COLLEGE FUND, said another. SHOOK HANDS WITH JESSE JACKSON, said a third.

RENEGED ON A PLEDGE TO THE 700 CLUB, said a fourth. And on and on it went, up the street, into the night, until Robertson began to fear that no strong-hipped white women would be left with whom he could repopulate the Earth, until finally, when the long street ended in an unexpected and strikingly clean cul-de-sac, a beautful blonde girl of perhaps eighteen stepped out from behind the neatest and straightest white picket fence Robertson had ever seen, a Mac-10 automatic pistol slung over her perfect milky shoulder, and gave Robertson a strong, true, and utterly heartfelt Aryan salute as he brought his sturdy machine to a halt beside her. And then, at last, he knew that God's plan could not be foiled. He was in love.

<click> *Logging Off . . .*

Episode Five
Laugh Track at 20,000 Feet

THE BLUE VINYL CHAIR HAD a ragged split down the middle, but that was okay with Danny. He was seated behind the check-in counter for Gate D7 at LaGuardia, facing the windows, with the whole row to himself. The chairs under the windows were empty, too.

No one seemed to have recognized him so far, and he thought it was because he had disguised himself with clothes he'd bought from a stagehand on the Lanford show—scuffed white running shoes, faded jeans, a black T-shirt, a gray windbreaker, and Ray-Ban aviator sunglasses. And he had slicked down his hair with some gel he'd found at the DeWitts'. But the gel smelled like overripe bananas, so there was a price to pay for his anonymity.

He picked at the polyester stuffing that was trying to escape from the split in his chair, thinking that he might add "blue vinyl" and "polyester stuffing" to his notebook of Dull Things. He still needed his Dull Things. Rage was difficult to sustain, and it had proven to be an imperfect solution to his problem.

Unfortunately, the Dull Things notebook was crammed deep inside his gym bag, and trying to get it out would result in fifteen minutes of repacking. But it was already 7:15 AM, and his 7:30 flight would be boarding any second. In fact, it should have boarded already, and he was worried that there might be something wrong with the airplane. It was an MD-80. He could see it through the windows, and he had watched the crew board half an hour ago.

He looked back down at the copy of *The New Yorker* he had bought at a concourse newsstand. It was folded open to "The Talk of the Town," and he was drumming it on his knee. Trying to read the jumping words helped distract him from the human noise and soft-pretzel smell of the terminal. Not to mention the stench of bananas. So far, he had managed not to twitch and howl like a gutshot dog.

"You read 'The Talk of the Town' yet?" a deep voice asked. "It says Britney Spears had recorded a cover of 'Satisfaction'. Now, Junior Wells recorded one before he died, and I can see that—but Britney damn Spears? That's got to be the sixth sign of the Apocalypse."

Danny looked up and giggled. Seated across from him, under the windows, was Special Agent Allan Armstrong.

"Isn't it hard to read when you bounce it around like that?" Armstrong asked.

Danny thought hateful thoughts and rolled up the magazine as if making a weapon.

Armstrong stood, stepped across, and sat down beside Danny. "Look at that, someone took a knife to your chair," he said, shaking his head. "And there are cigarette burns on this one. People are pigs."

"So are federal cops." Danny wanted to get up and walk away, but there was no point. If Armstrong was here, then his minions were nearby. All he had to do was crook his finger, and they'd put Danny in a hammerlock.

"Oh, now I'm a pig," Armstrong said, lacing his fingers together. "Guess I've stepped up a notch. Night before last, you called me a nigger."

Danny felt a twinge of shame, but he wasn't about to let Armstrong know it. "I might do it again, too."

"Don't." Armstrong's eyes became hard. "It's bad enough I have to hear an Amos 'n' Andy routine from one of my own colleagues, much less a trite slur from a hick like you."

Danny tried to make his eyes look hard too, but then realized that Armstrong couldn't see them through the Ray-Bans.

"Why couldn't you just let me go?" he asked, looking out toward the MD-80. "Why'd you have to track me down?"

"What 'tracking down'?" Armstrong leaned closer. "See, one of the first things they teach us at special-agent school is that if the fugitive loses you at JFK but hasn't picked up a boarding pass, check LaGuardia." He leaned away again. "Besides, I knew you were ready to bolt when you didn't go on the air last night. So I asked Larry Lanford point-blank, and he told me his company had bought you an unrestricted coach ticket. You should've worked a hush-money kickback into your contract. Or simply told me what you were planning to do."

Danny twisted the *New Yorker*, imagining it was Armstrong's neck. "You didn't tell me what *you* were doing Wednesday night when you were playing with my life and Amanda's. Besides, I'm not under any legal obligation to you, or even to the DeWitts. The only company I've signed a contract with is Lanford's. And now that it says I can work from my hometown, I'm going."

Armstrong frowned. "In other words, you're still going to do *Lanford's on Late* segments as Laughin' Boy, but you're going to do them from Wichita."

"That's right. We have videotape and satellite hookups in Hicksville now."

Armstrong reached into his suit coat and pulled out the baggie of blue pills that Danny had left in his room at the townhouse. "Think you'll be able to make use of all that technology without these?"

"I'm done being Dr. Ralph's experiment. I'll manage without that stuff."

Armstrong tucked the pills back into his coat. "In Wichita. Where your neighbors were gunned down. And where you laughed at them."

Danny stiffened. "The whole country knows that wasn't my fault."

"Really? Now, if my wife or kid had been shot, and I had seen you whooping it up over the body . . . well, I might not give a rat's ass what they thought in Peoria."

"American Airlines Flight 1610, service to Dallas and Los Angeles, will now begin preboarding," the loudspeaker said. *"Passengers traveling with small children or needing special assistance may board at this time through Gate D7. First Class passengers may board at any time."*

"Finally," Danny said, glancing at his watch. It was twenty-five after. He leaned over and unzipped his bag just far enough to stuff his magazine inside. "I change planes in Dallas, by the way. In case you have someone following me."

"You don't fall into any of the categories the lady just announced, do you?" Armstrong asked.

"Not unless they'll count me as handicapped." Danny struggled to close the zipper over the *New Yorker* and couldn't quite do it.

"You reek of spoiled fruit," Armstrong said, "but that won't count. Here, let me." He leaned down and brushed Danny away from the gym bag. "Just sit back and let me keep trying to scare you out of going."

Danny sat up and gave a derisive snort. "You've already implied that the entire city of Wichita wants to kill me. So if I'm not already scared, you're out of luck."

In fact, he *was* already scared. But he had been scared for three weeks now, and he was getting used to it.

Armstrong closed the zipper on the gym bag. "Your fellow Wichitans may be the least of your worries," he said, sitting up. "What about the WWJD?"

Danny was confused. "'What would Jesus do?' Are you saying the Son of God wants me dead too?"

Armstrong looked at him as if he were the stupidest man on earth. "I'm referring to the organization that the tattooed redhead belonged to. It stands for 'White Warriors for Jesus, Deceased.' Haven't you seen their video? Or a newspaper?"

"I've been busy," Danny said. It was true. Since running from the New York Pleasure Club on Wednesday, he had spent every waking minute planning his return home. He hadn't watched TV, and until picking up the *New Yorker*, he hadn't seen any magazines or newspapers.

Instead, he had been at the Jackie Gleason Theater negotiating his new contract and trying to make phone calls to his parents and Karen. He had reached his parents, but Karen had changed her number for the second time. She had called his mother with the new number, but his mother had already misplaced it. Still, at least he knew that Karen and Lindy were all right.

Then, late Thursday, the Lanford show had bought him an electronic airline ticket under the name on his Kansas driver's license: Daniel M. Clayton. So he had returned to the DeWitts' long enough to grab a few hours of sleep, write a stern note, and pack the gym bag. He had slipped out before dawn, taken a cab to JFK—and then taken another to LaGuardia, hoping to confuse anyone tailing him. Once at LaGuardia, he'd checked in with a sleepy counter attendant who hadn't even looked at the name on his driver's license.

But then, most people didn't know him by his real name anyway.

Armstrong reached into his coat again and handed Danny a folded sheet of paper. And Danny, automatically, took it and unfolded it.

It was a printout from the CNN web site. A photo depicted a hooded figure standing on a digital rock, and the surrounding text was a transcript of the figure's words. He was saying that he was the Pastor of the White Warriors for Jesus, and that he would give a fortune in gold to anyone who killed Laughin' Boy.

Danny's stomach lurched. But the photo was just ridiculous enough that he didn't laugh. "This is somebody's sick idea of a fairy tale," he said.

Armstrong tapped the photo. "Unfortunately, under that hood is a real-life sack of crap named Turner P. Williams. He's fifty-eight, Caucasian, and as reasonable as a rabid bat. I'd call him a violent anti-government racist, but that'd be like saying Jeffrey Dahmer had a mild eating disorder. Among other things, Mr. Williams is a big fan of Adolf Hitler—and the rumor is that he and several male followers have each had a testicle removed in homage to Der Fuhrer's legendary one-nuttedness. We can't confirm that, however, because Mr. Williams has been in hiding for eight years. He could've had his butt cheeks transplanted to his forehead for all we know. I suppose that would explain the hood."

"American Airlines Flight 1610, service to Dallas and Los Angeles, will now begin general boarding. Rows 20 and higher only, please."

Danny handed the printout back to Armstrong. "I'm in Row 17," he said, looking toward the gate door. About twenty people were waiting in line. "And this doesn't look like a full flight, so they'll be calling me soon. But before I go, I want to thank you for approaching me yourself instead of sending Royce." He spoke the name as if it tasted vile.

Armstrong tucked the printout back into his jacket. "Well, I thought I'd have a better chance of talking some sense into you."

Danny leaned over to pick up the gym bag with his left hand. The bandage on his forearm tugged at his skin as he propped the bag on his knees.

"You were wrong," he said. "The Ranger betrayed my trust, but I didn't have any trust in *you* to begin with."

Armstrong glowered. "I didn't make up that WWJD story, Mr. Clayton. They've put a price on your head—and they're getting better organized all the time, thanks to the Internet. That's how the Pastor has eluded capture for so long. See, they've got what amounts to a Web-based underground railroad for white supremacists. And what do you want to bet they don't see the irony?"

Danny eyed the queue at the gate door. It wasn't moving fast enough. "Can't you trace their e-mails?"

"Dead ends. We think they have software that lets them use innocent people's Web sites as encrypted mail drops." Armstrong lowered his voice as a man and a woman walked past. "But however they communicate, they do it quickly. So you can bet that your Uncle Sam isn't the only one who knows you're about to fly home. Sunglasses and a windbreaker aren't an effective disguise."

"They are as long as I'm not having a laughing attack. No one's recognized me except you."

"No one who wanted you to know it. But they'll be waiting for you in Wichita. They might even come after you when you change planes at DFW."

"I don't think so," Danny said, making no effort to lower his voice even though more people were walking past. "An airport hit would be tricky."

"'An airport hit?' Since when do you talk like a goombah?"

Danny looked at Armstrong's grim expression and couldn't suppress a chuckle. "Since I started hanging out with the FBI. You guys are a mob unto yourselves."

Armstrong shrugged. "I suppose it depends on your perspective. See, when I think of a 'mob,' I think of those gunmen at South Riverside Park, and of their friend the tattooed redhead—who, by the way, was seen at Chicago O'Hare on June 2nd, just a few hours after your knife assailant supposedly hung himself in his hospital room. And then she showed up at that sex show on June 7 with two shiny Colt semiautos."

Danny wished they'd call his row. "What's your point?"

"Just that these people are organized. And if we're going to catch them, we have to be better organized than they are. That's why

I urge you to stay in New York. Here, we have our operation in place, and sooner or later it'll bear fruit. And I can promise you a reasonable degree of protection. But I'm not sure I can do that in Wichita—at least, not quickly enough. You'll be vulnerable immediately because there, you might be attacked by *anyone*. Here, though, your potential assailants are more likely to be with the White Warriors. We proved that on Wednesday, and would have had a major break if not for a stroke of bad luck."

"You mean when the tattooed woman ate her own gun."

"Yes. Live suspects are generally preferable to dead ones. The interrogations tend to be more productive."

"American Airlines Flight 1610, service to Dallas and Los Angeles, now boarding rows 15 and higher at Gate D7."

Armstrong put a hand on Danny's left wrist. "Think of your parents, Mr. Clayton. Your little girl. Your ex-wife. Hasn't it occurred to you that someone trying to kill you might also harm *them* if you're nearby?"

Danny pulled away from Armstrong, winced as the bandage on his arm shifted, and stood up. "On the contrary," he said. "It seems to me that if I stay here, someone in Wichita might take out his frustration on my family. But if I go back, then whatever happens will happen to me alone—so long as I keep my distance. I'll never go to their homes, and I won't meet them anywhere without airtight security. Which I know may not be possible."

Armstrong stood too. "I see. You're thinking you'll throw yourself on the grenade that's been tossed into their midst."

"All I know is that they've been taking abuse that should've been mine. Last weekend, my parents' car was set on fire in their church parking lot. And Karen has had to keep Lindy indoors—when she ought to be out swimming, playing ball, or choosing her first kitten. But instead, she's been getting pictures of dead people in the mail along with notes that say, 'Your daddy thinks this is funny.'" Danny took a breath. "Good God, Armstrong, she's supposed to start kindergarten in the fall—"

He began giggling. For a moment, he had sounded just like his father.

"Your reasoning makes sense," Armstrong said. "The trouble is, your enemies don't."

"Polyester stuffing," Danny said, and turned toward the gate door. After a few steps, he glanced back.

Armstrong was already gone.

So Laughin' Boy continued to the jetway. He was bound for home, where he knew who his friends were.

There were none. But knowing that was more than he had known the entire time he'd been in New York City.

★

Each row in the coach cabin had two seats on the port side and three on the starboard. All five seats in Row 17 were empty when Danny came down the aisle.

He slid into Seat A, next to the port window, and stuffed his bag under the seat in front of him. Then he stared out the scratched oval Plexiglas and listened to the thumps in the baggage compartment below him. That way, he didn't have to look at or listen to his fellow passengers as they settled in around him. Most of them would be going to places that weren't Wichita . . . but he still didn't want to know whether any of them resembled the people he had seen killed. He was afraid he might start laughing.

The scratches on the window gleamed like silver filaments as they caught the morning sun. If Danny hadn't been wearing his Ray-Bans, he would have had to close his eyes against their brightness. They shone like the costume-jewelry tiara that Lindy had worn with her fairy princess costume last Halloween.

The fairy princess costume had been Karen's idea. He had countered by suggesting Bigfoot, but that had only been because Lindy had squealed in mock revulsion every time he'd mentioned it.

He and Karen had taken Lindy trick-or-treating together, and he had been grateful for that. It had been fun, too, considering that Danny had known he would have to go back to his tiny rental house when it was over. They had all eaten enough peanut butter cups and malted milk balls to make their stomachs hurt.

Karen had even hugged Danny after they'd put Lindy to bed. And the last thing Danny had seen before the door had closed had been the little silver tiara atop the TV set.

Silver. Like the Virgin Mary's pistols.

He didn't quite stop the giggle, but managed to squelch it so it came out as a hiccup.

"Blue vinyl," he murmured. "Old, cracked, blue vinyl."

His hands were cold, so he slid them into his windbreaker pockets . . . and found a business card in the left pocket. He took it out, and the side he saw first was blank except for a handwritten question:

What about Amanda?

He turned it over. The other side was printed with the words FEDERAL BUREAU OF INVESTIGATION—SPECIAL AGENT ALLAN L. ARMSTRONG. There were also two phone numbers, a fax number, and an e-mail address. And in cramped handwriting under those were the words *Phone in bag. Use if needed.*

Danny leaned down, tugged his bag from under the seat, and opened the zipper partway. Sure enough, a small black cell phone had been squeezed in atop his *New Yorker*.

He zipped up the bag and restuffed it under the seat, unimpressed with the gift. Sure, the phone might help the Feds, if he called them as the WWJD was about to kill him. Then Armstrong might show up in time to nab the bad guys, but not in time to do much for Danny. Which was probably the idea.

He started to crumple the business card, but was distracted by the welcome-aboard announcement over the intercom. A moment later a prim brunette flight attendant appeared in the aisle next to Row 17 and began performing a safety-procedure pantomime. The intercom said her name was Betty.

Danny had seen Betty's demonstration three times in the preceding three weeks, and Betty herself looked familiar. So he looked back down at the business card, which he had turned over again without realizing it.

What about Amanda?

Well, what about her? She had almost gotten him killed at a live-sex show. Or maybe he had almost gotten her killed. Either way, he hadn't seen her since.

So what if he was infatuated with her? Hadn't he felt something similar for that female FBI agent in Wichita?

Only one difference came to mind: In Amanda's case, the odds of sexual contact didn't merely approach zero, but *were* zero.

Danny finished crumpling the card and stuck it into the seat pocket in front of him. Then he pulled down the plastic window shade over the silver scratches and closed his eyes, hoping he could be asleep before takeoff.

Takeoffs were the worst. At least with landings, you could be sure that one way or another, you were going to wind up on the ground.

★

"Excuse me, sirs? You both need to buckle your safety belts. And sir, please place your seat in its full upright position."

Danny had leaned his seat back and begun to doze off, but now he opened his eyes and saw Betty looking down at him. He also saw the graying sideburn of a man sitting next to him in the aisle seat.

"Sorry," Danny said, pushing the button to raise his seat back.

Betty moved up the aisle, and Danny buckled his lap belt and turned toward the window again. The shade was down, but he pretended to look through it.

"Why, Dan'l," a deep voice said into his right ear. "Is you ignorin' yo' bes' fren'?"

Danny's spine stiffened, and then he turned to glare through his Ray-Bans at the Racist Ranger.

But instead of the Ranger he saw a lean, craggy-faced man of about fifty. The man's close-cropped hair was iron gray, his skin was the color of a pink rubber ball that had been left in the sun, and his pale blue eyes were unblinking behind wire-rimmed glasses. He was wearing a charcoal business suit with a white shirt and no necktie. The shirt was buttoned all the way up.

The man chuckled, and his Adam's apple bobbed above his tight collar. "I apologize," he said in a smooth voice. "But I recognized you despite your sunglasses. I've seen you and that Ranger fellow on television."

It's gonna be a long flight, Danny thought. But at least the rest of Row 17 was empty, and Row 16 was empty except for a woman in the starboard window seat. Glancing back, Danny saw that Row 18 also had only one occupant, a fat man in 18E who appeared to be asleep. So he didn't think anyone else had heard the iron-haired man identify him.

"Don't worry," Iron Hair continued. "I won't rat you out. I think it's terrible the way the media has been hounding you."

Danny had to say something, so he nodded and said, "Okay." Only a hint of a chuckle escaped.

Then a loud chirping noise made him jump, and he let out a sharp laugh as the noise repeated.

Iron Hair reached into his suit coat and brought out a chrome cell phone. It was the same color as the window scratches, Lindy's tiara, and the Virgin Mary's pistols. "I'm so sorry," Iron Hair said, and then he flipped open the phone and turned away.

The top of Iron Hair's boarding pass was protruding from his jacket pocket. The name on it was CUNNINGHAM, RICHARD. Danny thought it was funny that this grizzled businessman had the same name as a freckle-faced 1970s sitcom character, and that helped suppress his continuing urge to giggle.

Now Betty reappeared, frowning. "Sir, I'm sorry," she said to Cunningham, "but you'll have to turn off your phone. We're about to take off."

Cunningham raised an index finger. "Just a minute."

"I'm terribly sorry, sir," Betty said. Her voice was tight. "You'll have to turn it off *now*."

"All right," the man said, but then spoke into the phone. "That's good. No, just make her comfortable."

"Sir, if you don't turn off your phone," Betty said, "I'll have to tell the captain."

"We'll join you shortly." The man was still speaking into the phone. "Probably A33, but check the monitors."

Danny felt the airplane turning. They were entering the runway. He wished Cunningham would stop making trouble.

"*Sir*," Betty said, "I'm informing the—"

Cunningham snapped the cell phone shut just as Betty began to turn toward the cockpit, and he slipped it back into his jacket. "All done," he said.

At that moment the captain came on the intercom to announce that flight attendants should prepare for departure. Betty gave Cunningham a cold smile and headed back toward the tail. Danny wanted to go with her.

The airplane began its takeoff run with a loud whine. Danny clenched the armrests, stared straight ahead, and thought of home improvement warehouses. He could feel Cunningham looking at him as the plane lifted off the runway and the wheels folded in with loud thunks.

"Silly woman, eh?" Cunningham said. "After all, we've managed to get into the air despite my nasty old telephone call, haven't we?"

Danny wanted to ignore the question, but didn't want to piss off Cunningham. He didn't need any more trouble than he already had. "Yes," he said. "We did."

"Here's to a smooth flight, then." Cunningham leaned back in his seat and closed his eyes.

Danny hoped that meant he would be able to spend the three and a half hours to DFW in peace. But before turning back toward the window, he glanced at Cunningham's boarding pass again.

Cunningham's seat assignment was 22F.

"Tell me something," Cunningham said, opening his eyes.

Danny flinched, banged his head on the plastic-shaded window, and let out a whoop. But he managed to clap a hand over his mouth, and no one but Cunningham seemed to hear him. The airplane cabin was filled with a fuzzy whistling noise now that it was airborne, and Danny would have had to laugh long and loud for anyone else to notice.

Cunningham gave a thin smile. "You're flying to Dallas in pursuit of Porno Girl, aren't you?"

Danny uncovered his mouth. He was baffled. "I—no. What?"

Cunningham leaned toward him. "Porno Girl. I thought you and she were an item. All the tabloid shows and magazines say you've been living with her in the psychiatrists' house. And since she flew to Dallas yesterday evening, I assumed you were going to her."

The whistling in the cabin began to pulse in Danny's ears. "I don't know anything about her going to Dallas," he said. "And I don't know how you would, either."

Cunningham's eyebrows rose. "It was on TV last night. Some reporters spotted her at LaGuardia. They asked her why you weren't with her, but she wouldn't talk to them. She wouldn't even say why she was going, although the story this morning is that her law firm has called her back. Apparently a wealthy client is smitten with her and wants her to handle his legal matters. I'm surprised you didn't see any of this. Don't you watch TV, Mr. Clayton?"

"Not much."

"That's odd. How else are you to know where you stand in the world?"

Danny's jaws were tight. "Ever since May 20th," he said, "I don't want to know."

"I see." Cunningham leaned back again, then pulled the in-flight magazine from the seat pocket in front of him and began turning pages.

Danny pushed up the shade and looked out the window. The airplane was still climbing, but the highways below were already like strands of spiderweb. They were no wider than the scratches on the window.

He couldn't believe Amanda had left New York without telling him.

But then, he had just left without telling *her*, hadn't he?

He turned back toward Cunningham. "You're FBI, aren't you?"

Cunningham didn't look up from his magazine. "No."

Danny thought he could hear the lie, and it infuriated him. "Sure you are," he said. "The Bureau wouldn't let me go without sending a goon along. You even changed seats to sit with me. You're supposed to be in 22F."

Now Cunningham gave him a glance. "22F has a mysterious stain on the seat cushion. And although there might be federal agents aboard, I'm not one of them."

"Yet you knew who I was even though I'm in disguise."

"Again, Mr. Clayton, perhaps you've heard of television. You've been all over it for weeks. Not to mention radio, the Internet, the papers, and the odd dance revue. Wearing sunglasses and putting some sort of rancid mousse on your hair can't counteract all of that. Now, if you don't mind, I'll just read my magazine."

"I don't mind one goddamn bit," Danny said, trying to drive Cunningham off to some other seat.

But Cunningham only said, "Don't blaspheme," and returned to flipping magazine pages.

Danny stared out the window again. They were over a gray floor of clouds now, so there was nothing to see. He kept staring anyway. He was thinking about taking a walk.

He felt Cunningham's weight shift, and then something fell onto his lap. He looked down and saw a copy of *USA Today* on his knees. It was folded to a page with a photo of Amanda in an airport waiting area.

"In case you don't believe me," Cunningham said.

The article accompanying the photo repeated Cunningham's story about Amanda's Dallas job. It also said that she had obtained a release from her *Lanford's On Late!* contract. But nobody at the show had mentioned that while Danny had been renegotiating his own contract.

The article also mentioned the WWJD's death threat against Laughin' Boy and referred the reader to a Page One story. But Danny stayed with the one about Amanda, which closed by saying that since neither Ms. Larkin, the DeWitts, or Larry Lanford would speak with reporters about Ms. Larkin's departure, there was no information available regarding the future of the Odd Squad or of Porno Girl's rumored romance with Laughin' Boy.

Danny studied the photograph. Amanda hadn't tried to disguise herself. It was as if she hadn't realized that anyone might recognize her. She looked right at the camera as if it were something she didn't understand, but in which she was intensely interested. As if it were porn.

And there, in the grainy background, was someone who *had* tried to disguise himself with bushy sideburns and a black New York

Yankees jacket. The attempt had apparently fooled the reporters. But Danny recognized the posture of a man ready to attack. He also recognized the movie-star jawline. It was the Racist Ranger.

The airplane hit a bump of turbulence, and Danny began chuckling. But it was low, in his throat, and he didn't think even Cunningham could hear it.

He ran his tongue around inside his mouth, probing his chipped teeth and sore gums, thinking of what he had risked for Amanda the night before last. If she was going to fly off with someone, it ought to be him, not Robert Royce.

On the other hand, why would she fly off with *anyone* who didn't have a stash of Ginger Lynn videos?

Danny put the newspaper into the seat pocket so that the photo of Amanda still showed. But then he looked out at the floor of clouds again.

He had told his parents he was returning to Wichita, but he hadn't told them when. He'd hoped that if no one knew when to expect him, he might be able to sneak in and see Lindy before the media found out he was back. But now Cunningham would probably tell someone in Dallas that he'd been seated next to Laughin' Boy—and by the time Danny reached Mid-Continent Airport, it would be swarming with camera crews.

So since his chance to see Lindy was about to be ruined, why not stay in Dallas a few days? That way, he could find Amanda and say a proper goodbye. He didn't want her to think he hated her. After all, Wednesday hadn't been her fault. She couldn't help being at the mercy of her illness.

He really wanted to see her at least once more.

The Racist Ranger, though, was another story. If Royce was with Amanda, Danny would try not to spit on him unless it was necessary to keep from howling.

"Excuse me," Cunningham said. "Are you aware that you're laughing? It's not loud, but it's annoying."

Danny's anger flared, and his chuckling died. He turned on Cunningham.

"So move to another seat," he said. "You aren't supposed to be sitting here anyway."

Cunningham gave a thin smile. "As I explained earlier, 22F has a stain."

"There are plenty of others."

"Mostly middles. I like windows and aisles."

"All right, then. *I'll* go sit in 22F." Danny unbuckled his lap belt.

"No, Mr. Clayton." Cunningham's voice changed. It wasn't so smooth anymore. "Stay here so I can keep an eye on you."

It was almost funny. They were about six miles high. Where did Cunningham think Danny could go?

"I knew you were FBI," Danny said. "They must teach you guys to lie on your first day of G-man school."

Cunningham looked bemused. "Don't you know me yet? No, wait, I forgot—you don't watch TV. Or read the papers, apparently. Not even the one I just gave you. You're quite out of touch."

Danny eyed him. This guy seemed so self-important that if he wasn't FBI, he was probably a dot-com billionaire who thought his sudden wealth was the result of talent instead of dumb luck. Or maybe he was a state senator. Either way, he was someone who had no idea what Danny had seen—or worse, he was someone who knew but didn't care, someone who thought of violence and death in terms of *Entertainment Weekly* reviews. I'll give that decapitation a C-, that disemboweled child a B, and that gun-in-the-mouth suicide an A+, because she made me believe it.

"Let me guess," Danny said. "You're the Pope."

Cunningham gave him that thin smile again. "Not even close. Here, I'll show you." He glanced around, then turned to face Danny and began to unbutton his shirt.

Danny pressed back against the window. He thought about reaching up to hit the call button, but he didn't know what Betty could do about this. He giggled.

Cunningham stopped when he reached his belt buckle, then pulled open his shirt.

A blue tattoo of a crucifix began at the hollow of his throat and ended at his navel. The ends of the crosspiece touched his nipples. A patch of gray hair in the center of his chest served as a loincloth for the Christ figure, whose hands and feet were pierced by red nails.

But while Christ's body was the traditional stretched, anguished figure, his face was that of Adolf Hitler. Instead of a crown of thorns, he wore an SS death's-head cap. And above that, instead of a rough sign that read "INRI," there was a crisp black swastika.

Danny clamped both hands over his mouth to hold in the guffaws.

*

Cunningham had just finished rebuttoning his shirt when Betty came by with a notepad and asked if he would like something to drink.

"Virgin Mary, please," Cunningham said.

Then Betty looked over at Danny and saw that he was pressed up against the window with his hands clamped over his mouth.

"Sir, are you ill?" she asked. "Do you need anything?"

Danny almost uncovered his mouth, almost shouted through his laughter that what he needed was for any federal agents on board to get to Row 17 immediately. But then he saw Cunningham giving him a sidelong look, and he knew that if he did that, something awful would happen.

So he did his best to concentrate on his newborn hatred for Cunningham, and he was just able to stop laughing and uncover his mouth.

"I'm okay," he told Betty. "I just got a little queasy from the turbulence. But I'm over it now."

Betty didn't look convinced. "Well, there's an airsickness bag in your seat pocket. Just ring for me if you use it, and I'll take it away. In the meantime, would you like something to drink?"

"Sparkling water might calm your stomach," Cunningham said. Mr. Helpful Guy.

Danny nodded. "That sounds fine."

Betty jotted it down. "I'll be back in a few minutes." She moved up to the next row.

Cunningham eyed Danny. "If you sit like that all the way to Dallas, you'll be so stiff you won't be able to move."

Danny stayed up against the window. "Aren't you going to kill me right here?"

"A little louder, Mr. Clayton. I don't think they heard you in the cockpit. And no, I'm not going to kill you here. You and I are going to walk off this plane together at Dallas-Fort Worth International Airport, where the White Warriors for Jesus, Deceased, will reacquire what you've stolen."

So Armstrong had been right. The terrorists weren't even going to let him reach Wichita.

All right, then. So hate them. Hate them all, but especially hate Cunningham. That's the only possible way through this. Hate him the way he hates everyone else.

Danny lowered himself into his seat and leaned over so he was almost nose-to-nose with Cunningham. Cunningham smelled of onions and Old Spice.

"What *I've* stolen from *you*?" Danny snarled. "You demolished my life. And I was the *lucky* one that day."

Cunningham didn't blink. "Those of the Righteous who died by our hand did so for a cause. But then you robbed their deaths of meaning and took their glory for yourself. However, we'll set that right in a few hours."

"I don't think I can wait that long. How about if I just stand up and yell for the Feds?"

"Bad idea," Cunningham said. "If you and I don't step into the terminal at DFW together, and I don't give a sign to indicate that all's well, Miss Larkin will be executed. You see, she's in the custody of the White Warriors. In fact, the client who insisted on her return to Dallas is a Brother. And another Brother in New York made sure that your ticket would bring you through Dallas as well. In fact, our hope was that you and Miss Larkin would take the same flight."

"Sorry to disappoint you."

"Not at all. This will be fine. When Miss Larkin arrived last night, she was met at the gate by a Sister who claimed to work for her law firm. But they never left the airport, and a television crew waiting outside the terminal noted that fact. So the media are wandering around the concourse this morning, trying to solve the mystery."

Danny saw where this was going. "So there'll be cameras on hand for your next bloodbath."

"'Bloodbath' implies a large number of casualties," Cunningham said. "But if the TV crews record the event as it happens, we can keep the body count low and still make our point. Dallas is a major media market, you know. Not like Wichita . . . which, quite frankly, is Hicksville."

Danny couldn't help giggling now. "And just what is your point—Pastor Williams, is it?"

Cunningham giggled too, mocking Danny. It was a dry, rattling noise. "Oh, I'm merely a humble Brother. And our point is simple: The Lord's Anointed must accept their destiny, and the seed of Cain must resume their penance. All Righteous Caucasians must rise up and throw off the shackles of the Godless Occupation Government and its Multicultural Allies."

"Wow," Danny said, still giggling. "That's a mouthful."

"We usually just say 'Death to GOG and MAGOG.'"

Danny didn't understand Cunningham's jargon, but he assumed it meant he was screwed. So he was terrified, but he was also angry enough to stave off a laughing fit. "Speaking of Wichita," he said, "I'm not going to make it back, am I?"

"No. You and I will proceed from our arrival gate to a rendezvous with Brothers and Sisters who are waiting in a prearranged location at DFW. And then the WWJD will make a public example of you."

"You mean of me and Amanda."

Cunningham frowned. "No, Miss Larkin is your motivation to do as I say. If you and I arrive together and I give the sign, she'll be released."

Danny was dubious. "Aren't you forgetting about the FBI? Won't they follow us?"

Cunningham smiled, and this time his teeth showed. They were perfect white squares.

"I'm counting on it," he said. "I'm assuming, as a matter of fact, that the Negro I saw you with at LaGuardia was a GOG agent, and that he wasn't alone. One way or another, though, we'll make sure that GOG sends plenty of its minions to DFW soon enough. I only pray that one of them will be Robert Royce. He's responsible for the loss of Brother Bobby in Chicago and Sister Suellen in New York, and it's time he knew the wrath of the Lord."

Danny glanced at the newspaper in the seat pocket. He was sure that the man in the background of the photo was the Racist Ranger. But if Royce had gone to Dallas with Amanda, why hadn't he prevented her kidnapping?

Maybe this was all another evil FBI mousetrap operation like the Pleasure Club debacle. Maybe Royce had known the White Warriors would take Amanda, and he had just stood back and watched.

Or maybe Cunningham only *thought* his Brothers and Sisters had Amanda. Maybe the cell-phone call had been made by a Brother with the Ranger's Glock at his head.

"You know," Danny said, "I think it's about fifty-fifty that you have Porno Girl at all. So if I start screaming for J. Edgar Hoover, it's fifty-fifty that she'll be fine and you won't."

Cunningham's eyes narrowed. "If we hadn't taken Miss Larkin, we'd have returned to Wichita and taken your daughter. But the Lord revealed that Miss Larkin would be more suitable in terms of positive media attention. However, if anything should derail us at DFW, we'll acquire young Linda next."

Danny stopped giggling. Now he wasn't just angry. Now he wanted to rip off Cunningham's head and shit down his neck.

"I can read your mind," Cunningham said. "So I think you should know that a Brother who happens to be a maintenance worker for this airline left something on board for me." He opened the right side of his jacket far enough to reveal a nylon-web shoulder holster with a silver pistol identical to the ones the Virgin Mary had used. "An in-flight gun battle with federal agents would probably culminate in a crash, and the media would describe how one of the Lord's soldiers and a planeload of passengers gave their lives to rid the world of Laughin' Boy. Then my Brothers in Dallas would carry out their part of the mission, in which several dozen more people, Porno Girl included, would necessarily perish."

Danny closed his eyes. Everything had gone to hell. Again.

"Lawn clippings," he murmured. "Lard. Linoleum."

"Ah, there was something about this on *Hard Copy*," Cunningham said, his voice piercing into Danny's skull. "You've been overheard muttering the names of inanimate objects during moments of stress. Why is that?"

Danny opened his eyes and glared at Cunningham. But then he realized that Cunningham couldn't see through the Ray-Bans any better than Special Agent Armstrong had.

"Thinking of dull things helps keep the laughter down," Danny said. "So does getting angry."

The corners of Cunningham's mouth twitched. "Oh dear," he said. "Should I be afraid?"

"I doubt that a guy with a tattoo of a crucified Hitler is afraid of much." Danny tilted his head so he could look over the tops of the Ray-Bans. He wanted Cunningham to see his eyes now. "Then again, I wouldn't think that a woman with a tattoo of the Blessed Virgin cradling an infant Fuhrer would be afraid of much either. But I guess she was, since she wound up feeding herself a bullet."

Cunningham's face darkened. "Sister Suellen feared only the wrath of God. And what I do today, I do in her memory, and in the service of our Lord."

Danny thought of the Virgin Mary lying with her head in a black puddle, of the sex-show man on the bed bleeding and shrieking, of the little blonde girl in South Riverside Park, and of all the others. Some Lord.

"I understand," Danny said. "Snow tires. Oven mitts."

Cunningham smiled so that his teeth showed again. "I suggest you relax for now. There's nothing more to be done until we reach DFW."

So Danny reclined his seat and tried to imagine what a real superhero would do in his situation. And the answer was obvious: A real superhero would use his or her special powers in a way that would lead to the defeat of the bad guys.

That's it, Danny thought bitterly. *I'll giggle them into submission.*

Heck, it had worked on TV.

*

Ten minutes after Betty brought their drinks, Danny had to take a piss. He held it for a while, then gave up and turned to Cunningham. "I don't suppose I'm allowed to use the lavatory."

Cunningham was still sipping his Virgin Mary. "Go right ahead," he said, licking tomato juice from his lip. He folded up his tray table to clear the way to the aisle.

Danny was suspicious, and he chuckled as he thought of Cunningham shooting him in the back. "You're just going to let me go?"

Cunningham finished his drink. "As much as you deserve to be in discomfort," he said then, "I don't want you urinating in the seat right next to me. So you can go this one time. But I'll be watching you. Any untoward behavior will result in the midair disaster we've already discussed."

So Danny stood, squeezed past Cunningham, and almost fell once he reached the aisle. He grabbed the top of Cunningham's seat to steady himself, thinking that the plane had lurched—but when the wobbly sensation persisted, he realized it was because his legs were trembling. And then he felt the laughter trying to bubble up in his chest.

"Go," Cunningham said.

Danny began stumbling down the aisle toward the tail of the airplane, hoping he could get into a lavatory in time to have a laughing fit in private. If it hit him out here, a Fed—if there were any on board—might approach him. And everything would be over.

Not that everything wouldn't be over soon anyway. But if there was any chance that Cunningham was telling the truth, any chance that following his orders would keep Amanda and Lindy safe, Danny had to take it.

There were two lavatories at the rear of the plane, one on each side. Betty came out of the starboard lavatory as Danny approached, and she stepped into the galley area in front of it to give him room to get by.

She looked at him with concern. "Are you feeling ill again, sir?"

He glanced back, peering over his Ray-Bans. Cunningham's right hand was visible on his armrest, holding a pocket watch with the lid flipped up. Inside the lid was a mirror.

Danny looked back at Betty and shook his head.

"Well, if you're sure," Betty said.

Then, as he stepped past her, she covered her mouth as if about to cough. And he heard her say, "Use the one on your left."

Danny stumbled, but had enough presence of mind not to pause or look at Betty again. Instead, he went to the starboard lavatory—the one on his left—and found that the slide-lock in the door was pushed over to the little red sign that said OCCUPIED.

But as he stopped, the lock slid over to the green sign that said UNOCCUPIED. And Danny wanted to take a few seconds to think about it before going in, but he knew that he couldn't with Cunningham watching. So he reached for the steel handle, turned it, and opened the door. It swung out to the left, blocking the aisle and Cunningham's view.

Inside the lavatory, seated on the toilet lid, was the Racist Ranger. He was wearing fake sideburns and a black Yankees jacket, but the disguise was ruined by a wire that trailed down from his right ear.

Danny stared, rage and relief fighting it out in his gut, until Royce stood up and made a get-in-here-you-idiot gesture. So then he stepped inside, belly-to-belly with the Ranger, and pulled the door shut behind him. The Ranger reached around and locked it, knocking Danny's Ray-Bans askew in the process.

"It's jis' as tight en blimblammin' loud in hyear as if we 'uz in a barrel bein' beat wid sticks, ain't it?" the Ranger said. "De noise is kase one er de engines is right t'other side o' dis hyear wall. But it mean yo' travelin' companion ain't a-gwyne to hear us jawin' even ef he come back dis way. As fer de tightness, well, dey ain't nothin' to be done fer it. I swah, I ain't never b'lieved dat trash 'bout de Mile-

High Club. How's two peoples s'posed to do de deed effen neither one er dem gots room to shuck dey drawers? You answer me dat, now."

Danny adjusted his sunglasses and tried to step back so that he wasn't in actual contact with the Ranger. But there was nowhere to go.

"Maybe if you sat down again," he growled. "Or if you stood on the toilet."

"En bash my haid on de ceilin'? As fer sittin' down, well, le's turn roun' en *you* sit down. I been a-sittin' on dat lid fer too long as it is, en I'll be a-sittin' dah fer a few hours mo' befo' we gets to Dallas."

So they shuffled around until Danny could sit on the toilet lid, a process that was complicated by sudden turbulence. But Danny was finally able to collapse onto the toilet, and he stared up at the Racist Ranger in the white glare of the light over the tiny stainless-steel sink. He was glad for the Ray-Bans.

"I take it you know about the terrorist sitting next to me," he said. He was thinking about straightening a leg and kicking Royce in the crotch. "Otherwise you wouldn't be on the plane, would you?"

The Ranger frowned. "Not eggzackly. I 'uz gwyne to be on de plane anyhow, since stickin' wid you is my job. Mars Armstrong didn' know jis' what de sitcherashun'd be, but he tol' me I had to wear a dis-gize <u>and</u> hide out back hyear, jis' in case. He said it 'uz kase you hate me so, en kase I'd need de el'ment o' sur-prize if de White Warriors put someone on de plane—but I is of de opinion dat ol' Mars Armstrong jis' liked de idear o' makin' me put on fake whiskers en spendin' fo' hours in dis flyin' outhouse."

Danny shifted on the toilet seat as the plane hit another bump. He remembered now why he had come back here, but he guessed he would just have to hold it.

"The Warriors did send someone," Danny said. "The name on his boarding pass is Richard Cunningham, and he's sitting right next to me. He's been telling me all about the Lord's Heavenly plan for me. And for Amanda."

The Ranger held up a hand. "I knows. He figgered dat kase o' de airplane noise, no 'un else'd hear. But while he 'uz braggin' to you, he 'uz braggin' to de Bureau, too. Now, dey's a chanst he knowed dat, so mebbe he didn' tell you de whole truth. Er mebbe he figgers de Pastor's plan is a-gwyne to work whether we knows it er not. He prob'ly figgers dat since dey already gots Po'no Girl, dat now he gots us by de sho'at hairs." The Ranger gave a grim smile. "But he ain't entirely kerrect."

"How could you hear him?" Danny asked. "It was hard for *me* to hear him sometimes."

The Ranger eyed Danny as if afraid of how he might react. "Dat cell phone Mars Armstrong done give you is a listenin' dee-vice, en a pooty good 'un. Even in yo' bag, en even wid de noise, it's been a-pickin' up yo' chattuh well enuff fer us to make it out."

Danny was only surprised for a second. "I should have known. Is that thing in your ear the receiver?"

"Nope. Dis jis' keeps me in touch wid t'other two agents on bo'ad. One is in de cockpit wid de bug receiver, so you ain't seed him. But I figgered you'd reckernize t'other'un, kase you seemed taken wid her in Wichita. 'Co'ase, dis time she's wearin' a wig, pushin' a drink cart what also contains a sawed-off shotgun, en callin' hersef Betty. En I 'spec you *have* been sorter preoccupied, what wid a psycho killuh beside you en all."

No wonder Betty had looked familiar.

"En I s'pose I kin tell you," the Ranger continued, "dat ole Mars Cunningham's pistol is loaded wid a clip o' blanks. Dat's kase Betty en I searched de plane be'fo you en t'other passengers got on bo'ad. We 'uz surspicious kase one o' de maint'nance boys had hisself a swastika tattoo. En sho' nuff, we foun' de pistol—jus' a common ol' Colt Defender. But we didn' want whoever 'uz s'posed to find it to wonduh whah it got off to, so we decided ter put it back whah we foun' it. But dat meant we had ter call Mars Armstrong fer de blanks fust, en dat's why de plane 'uz late bo'adin'. It took a pow'ful long time to git de clip delivered."

So Cunningham's gun didn't have real bullets. That was good news. But somehow it didn't make Danny feel any better. "Anything else I should know?"

"Jis' dat de way he's wearin' de gun on his right side means he's prob'ly lef-han'ned," the Ranger said. "Effen you needs to fight 'im, dat could be good to know."

"*Fight* him? Why would I have to—"

"En by de way, his name prob'ly ain't Richie Cunningham."

"Thanks a lot. I already guessed that much."

"Dat's kase you is smarter den de average Laughin' Boy. Now, I'se gwyne to tell you one mo' thing: Thanks to de cell-phone bug, we gots agents lookin' fer Miz Lawkin at DFW. But de bad news is dat de place is 'bout de size o' Rhode Islan', en dey's lots o' places whah de terr'ists kin hole up, 'specially ef dey gots frens on de inside. So ef our boys don't git lucky, dey's still a-gwyne to be lookin' when we lands. En if dat's de case—"

Danny chuckled. It was Wednesday all over again, courtesy of Robert Royce and the FBI. Assholes. "Then I have to go along with Cunningham. I have to let him take me to her so you can follow."

The Ranger looked at the floor.

"Nossuh," he said. "Ef we does dat, dey's too much kin go right fer dem en wrong fer us, same's it did at de Pleasure Club. Kase no mattuh what Richie done tole you, I lay dat his fren's ain't a-gwyne to let Miz Lawkin go. Dey's gwyne to shoot her on de teebee same as you. En dey ain't a-gwyne to be usin' blanks, neither. So ef dey gits you to whah dey has Miz Lawkin, all dey gots to do is git a telebishion camera in de vicinity, den bring de two o' you out en commence de carnage." He looked up. "Nossuh. Ef de agents at DFW doan' locate en rescue our sweet lil' Amanda by de time we lan', den we gots to go to either Plan B . . . or, if I have my druthers, Plan C."

"Plan C." Danny didn't like the sound of it.

"Yassuh. 'Bout twenny minutes ago I had me an idear I done tole to Betty, en she done relayed it to Mars Armstrong. En he say okay. So when you headed back hyear, I axed Betty to pint you to dis lav'try. Kase I wants to let you know what's a-gwineter go down when de manure commences to flyin'."

Danny took off his Ray-Bans and stood up, chest to chest with the Ranger again. "Like you did Wednesday?"

Royce's face was like rock. "Nope," he said. "Dat Pleasure Club bidniss 'uz Mars Armstrong's plan—but I went 'long, kase I'se a Bureau man, en you en Miz Lawkin 'uz jis' a means to an en'. But I been ponderin' fo' two days now 'bout how dat bidniss went to de dickens, en I figger dat God 'uz tellin' me somepin."

"Great. So now you're taking orders from God like Cunningham and his Pastor."

"I ain't as crazy as dey is, Dan'l. But I'se as crazy as *you* is, en dat's what God's been a-sayin'."

The Ranger sounded so solemn that Danny giggled.

"Right dah," the Ranger said. "Dat's what I'se talkin' 'bout. Y'see, whatever else I is, I is also a dern *freak*—jis' like you. Sho', I'se gwyne to do my duty, but I ain't a-gwyne to betray 'nother *freak* to do 'er. Not no mo'. You see what I'se sayin'?"

"Yeah, sure." Danny was still giggling. He thought he might be sick to his stomach. "You want us to be friends."

The Ranger shook his index finger, whapping Danny's nose. "*Nossuh!* You kin choose yo' friends, but ain't nobody ever choose to be no freak. Yet here we is, you en me en Miz Lawkin. En ain't nobody else a-gwineter look out fer us, so we gots to look out fer each other. Unnerstan'?"

Danny closed his eyes and thought of Elmer's glue, axle grease, and naval jelly. His giggling stopped.

"Yeah," he said, putting his Ray-Bans back on before opening his eyes. "We're like family."

"Dat's it right dah. So I'se gwyne to tell you bof Plan B en Plan C so's you kin do yo' part wid full knowledge. En so we kin git Miz Lawkin 'way from dem danged ol' neo-Nazis, you en me." He gave Danny a searching look. "Is you willin' to do dat?"

Danny thought about it, and he crammed down the laughter. "It depends."

"Depen's on what?"

"On why you were at LaGuardia last night."

The Ranger looked startled. "Dad fetch it," he said. "I ain't a-gwyne to ask how you knowed dat, kase it don't mattuh. What does mattuh is dat you think I knowed Miz Lawkin 'uz headed fo' trouble. You mebbe even think I 'ranged it."

Danny let the rage boil up. "You've done it before. You gave her that flyer and sent her down Eighth Avenue. So all this talk of freaks looking out for each other doesn't mean dick if you've done it again."

Royce shook his head. "I hain't, Dan'l. I jis' took 'er to de airpo'at kase she axed me to. En I didn' tell Mars Armstrong ner de DeWitts dat I 'uz doin' it, kase dey'd a-bolluxed 'er up. Ding-bust it, I figgered she'd be *safer* out o' New Yoak aftuh de po'no club shootin'. I didn' figger de WWJD would go aftuh her ef she 'uz away from you en me."

Danny's rage warped into jealousy and guilt. Amanda had called on the Ranger, not him. She'd thought Royce was the only one who cared what happened to her.

The Ranger put his hand to his ear. "En now I gots to tell you Plans B en C real quick-like, Dan'l. Betty say Cunningham's a-turnin' roun' in his seat en lookin' back hyear like he's wonderin' why you's a-takin' so long."

Danny took a deep breath and gave a brief chuckle. "All right. But could you turn around first?"

"Now why's I gwyne to—"

"Because I really have to take a leak."

So the Ranger turned toward the door and then told Danny what would happen once they landed. Danny had a violent attack of laughter and almost made a mess.

"Yassuh," the Ranger said as they faced each other again. "It's a-gwineter be int'restrin'. But it's yo' call. Think 'er ovuh fer a few minutes." He pressed a finger to his earpiece. "Betty say Cunningham's lookin' fo'ard agin. Go."

Danny thought of window caulk and wastewater treatment as he reached for the lock. "Great. Two more hours sitting next to one of the rat bastards who made me what I am."

The Ranger flipped down the toilet lid and sat. "Look at de bright side: You might could make 'im naus'yated en dizzy wid dat 'nanner-smellin' hair o' yourn. En at least you ain't stuck in de shitter."

"Says you." Danny opened the door, went out, and glimpsed the Ranger giving him a thumbs-up sign as he closed the door again. It was pretty damn funny, so it helped Danny keep from laughing.

★

Cunningham shifted his knees toward the aisle to let Danny in. "You were back there eight minutes," he said as Danny settled into 17A. "That's a long time for urination."

"Sorry," Danny said, "but it turned out that I had to do more."

"So I scared it out of you."

Cunningham sounded pleased, and Danny thought of what the Ranger had said when Danny had laughed like a maniac because of the disaster potential of Plan C.

"Lookee hyear," the Ranger had said. "Why you think Cunningham sit down by you en tell you all 'bout what he's a-gwyne to do? Why you think he didn' jis' sit back in Row 22 en den walk off de plane wid you aftah we lan'?"

Danny had thought for a few seconds. "Because he wants to see me squirm."

The Ranger had nodded. "Dat's right, but dey's one mo' reason. It's a charac'tristic he has in common wid ever' other hateful murd'rer dey's ever been: Deep down in his soul, he's jis' as dumb as a mothafuckin' stump."

Danny had wondered then whether the Racist Ranger's affliction was really what Royce had always said it was. He was pretty sure that Jim in *Huckleberry Finn* had never said *mothafuckin'*. Or *shitter,* for that matter.

But now Danny saw the raw, stupid joy that Cunningham took from believing he had frightened another human being into a bowel movement. And Danny knew that whatever else the Ranger was, he was was right about the depths of Cunningham's soul.

Betty came by with a basket. "Would either of you gentlemen care for peanuts or pretzels?"

"I'll have one of each," Cunningham said.

"I'm sorry, sir. I'm not supposed to—"

"It's all right," Danny said. "He can have mine. I don't want any."

So Betty gave Cunningham a package of peanuts and another of pretzels and moved on. Cunningham tore open the peanuts with his teeth and grinned at Danny.

"I take it you're not hungry," he said.

Danny looked out the window. "No."

"Your choice. But just so you know, there's no last meal for you in the Pastor's plan."

Danny stayed quiet, letting Cunningham think he was scared. Which he was.

There was no last meal in Plan A. In Plan A, Cunningham would take Danny to the place at DFW where the White Warriors for Jesus, Deceased, were holding Amanda. Then the WWJD would alert the media and give them a gate number where Laughin' Boy and Porno

Girl had been spotted. The camera crews would come running. Laughin' Boy and Porno Girl would be thrust before them . . . and carnage would ensue. Anyone present who didn't belong to either the White Warriors or a major media outlet would be sacrificed for the Holy Cause.

In Plan B, on the other hand, the federal agents on the airplane would separate Danny and Cunningham. Then they would try to force Cunningham to reveal Amanda's location so that the agents at DFW could attempt a rescue—which, if Cunningham failed to cooperate or if something on the ground went wrong, would only get Amanda killed. And Cunningham would almost certainly fail to cooperate.

Then there was Plan C.

Under Plan C, the WWJD would still get what they wanted.

Only a whole lot sooner than they expected.

When Betty had asked "peanuts or pretzels?" she had been asking whether Danny wanted the Feds to separate him from Cunningham either immediately or upon landing. But by turning down both snacks, Danny had activated Plan C. So whatever happened now would be because of him.

Danny looked out at the solid floor of clouds. He laughed softly.

"What's so funny?" Cunningham asked around a mouthful of peanuts.

Danny pointed at the window. "These scratches," he said. "They're the same color as a tiara I bought for my daughter last Halloween."

He looked back at Cunningham, who seemed puzzled.

"That's not funny, Mr. Clayton," Cunningham said.

Danny turned back toward the window.

"Of course not," he said. "Haven't you been paying attention?"

Notes on an Airsickness Bag

The psychopath beside me is dozing. So this is my chance to write a few last words.

By the way, "psychopath" is a judgment call on my part. I really don't know much about him except that he thinks God wants him to kill people. And historically speaking, that doesn't make him a psychopath. After all, God has always insisted on a certain amount of murder and warfare.

Or maybe God is just whatever we need Him to be in order to justify whatever we'd be doing anyway.

But enough about homicidal maniacs.

There's a tradition of doomed airline passengers writing their last words on airsickness bags. But that's usually when the whole plane is going down. This time, I hope it's just me. And that hope is all that's keeping me from screaming. If I raise a ruckus, you see, the psychopath has promised that we'll all fall from the sky. And there are about ninety-five people on board. That's a light load for an MD-80—but it's still more than died in the Wichita Massacre. Which was too many. And you remember what I did then.

I may be about to die, but I'm determined not to die laughing.

So maybe if I go along with Cunningham (the psychopath's alias), this White Warrior for Jesus, maybe I'll be the only one he shoots.

Or maybe—

Forget it. The odds are too long.

This, then, is the probable end of my mostly dull and innocent, but recently shocking and guilty life. My death will no doubt make me even more infamous than I already am. For a little while. Say fourteen and a half minutes. But at least I won't be around for it.

(Over)

I'll have to write smaller. Only one side of the bag left. Goodbyes, then.

To Mom and Dad: I've always treated you as if you were creatures from another dimension . . . but recent events have shown me that you seemed that way only because you built a home that was a safe haven from this razor blade of a world. It must have been a more difficult task than I ever realized, and I'm sorry to have screwed it up. But thank you for trying. You were wonderful. I love you.

To Karen Carpenter Clayton: You said I was too apologetic, too quick to take blame. So now I want you to know that I'm not sorry for anything in my life that had to do with you. I'm not sorry for our marriage, or even for the fact that it ended. I'm not sorry that I wasn't a man you'd want to stay with. And I'm especially not sorry for knocking you up. It's the best thing I ever did.

Take care of yourself and our child. I insisted that the Lanford show write a death-benefit clause into my new contract, and although it's only a hundred and fifty grand (the most they'd go for; they knew the odds), it's all for the two of you. There's also the life-insurance policy I bought when Lindy was born, but that one might not pay up since I missed the premium that was due on June 1.

If I could, I would help you make a place for Lindy that was even safer than the one my parents made for me. But I know you'll do great. You always do.

To Robert Royce, the "Racist Ranger": If I don't live through this and you do, you'd better hope there are no such things as ghosts. (Jim in Huckleberry Finn believed in ghosts, didn't he?)

I'll make you a deal. Keep my family—and Amanda—safe, and I won't haunt you. Promise.

I trust you to do your best. I'll do mine, too.

To Amanda Larkin: I wasn't fair to you after the incident at the New York Pleasure Club. I was angry that you had succumbed to your disease to the extent that it put your life in danger . . . but that was hypocritical of me. As I write this, your life is in danger again, and it's because of me and my disease.

I'm trying to rectify that situation. Still, I doubt that I'll ever see you again. So I want you to know that I consider myself fortunate to have known you for even a few weeks.

I'd elaborate, but there's too little room on the bag. Just know that I hold you in the highest regard, and that anything cruel I ever said to you was the result of the fact that I'm an idiot and an asshole. But at least I feel bad about it.

To my daughter Lindy: When you're old enough to read this, I hope you'll realize that your daddy loved you very much. And I hope that when you see the tape of me laughing when I shouldn't have laughed, you'll know that it wasn't really me. I hope instead that you'll remember the time we went to the zoo and the elephant sprayed me with water from his trunk. When I laughed then, that was really me.

More than anything, I wish I could watch you grow up.

End of the bag. And the crazy Jesus soldier beside me is stirring.

Goodbye.

Episode Six/Video Clip (6)
The Great Texas Terror Telecast and Table Dance

THE FASTEN-SEAT-BELT LIGHTS went out, and Betty's voice over the intercom said, "Welcome to Dallas-Fort Worth International Airport." Then anything else she said was lost as passengers lunged into the aisle and grabbed their luggage from the overhead bins.

Cunningham remained in his seat and looked at Danny. "We'll exit last," he said, "so I can keep an eye on you."

Danny was thinking of primer coats and lug nuts. He had to believe that the Ranger knew what he was doing. He had to believe that Amanda would be all right. He had to believe that he would see Lindy again. But he didn't believe any of it. That's why he needed the Dull Things.

"I won't try to get away," he said. "I know you'd hurt Porno Girl if I did."

Cunningham smiled like a cobra. "Yes. But sometimes the Unrighteous forget about the welfare of others. As you did in Wichita."

The Dull Things failed then.

Danny laughed so hard that it hurt, so hard that the passengers waiting in the aisle looked at him. But they only looked for a moment, and Danny was able to choke back the laughter by thinking of how much he wanted to hurt Cunningham . . . and by trying to imagine the expression that would appear on Cunningham's face when they stepped into the terminal.

At the moment, though, Cunningham's expression was grim. "Control yourself, Mr. Clayton," he said in a low voice. "We don't want you drawing attention until it's time. Then you may laugh to your heart's content."

Danny stifled one last chuckle and then leaned toward Cunningham. "I'll try to do better, Your Reverence. Oh, and by the way—" He leaned in even closer. "Up yours."

Cunningham smiled again. "We'll see."

The people in the aisle began moving. When the last of them was ahead of Row 17, Cunningham stood, moved into the aisle, and stepped back so that Danny would have to walk in front of him.

"Remove your sunglasses and put them in the seat pocket," Cunningham said. "Your face needs to be seen. But take your bag. And stay no more than a step ahead of me."

Danny took off his Ray-Bans and stood. "Why take the bag? It's not like I'm going to need it."

"It'll look strange if you leave it. And I'd prefer it if your hands weren't entirely free."

So Danny picked up his bag, stepped into the aisle, and started walking. The man ahead of him was already in the First Class section, almost to the exit.

Cunningham was right behind Danny, the toes of his shoes brushing Danny's heels.

"Nice and easy pace," Cunningham said. "You're not in a hurry, but you're not dawdling. That's right."

Danny stepped past the bulkheads into the First Class section. Four steps later, he turned left to exit. Betty was standing across the aisle from the open cabin door, her back against the drink cart in the forward galley.

"'Bye, now," she said, smiling.

The door to the cockpit was open a crack. And as Danny turned, he thought he caught a glimpse of a man who looked like Special Agent Allan Armstrong.

So maybe the Feds had it together. Maybe it would all turn out the way the Ranger had said. Maybe monkeys would fly out of Danny's ass.

He stepped out to the stuffy, hot air of the Gate A33 jetway, then walked up the carpeted slope toward the terminal. The floor vibrated with the footsteps of the people ahead of him, and that prompted Danny to slow his pace. He didn't want to be anywhere near those people. He wanted to give them a chance to get away.

"Keep moving," Cunningham said, his breath thick and wet on Danny's ear. "There's no point in trying to delay the inevitable. The Lord's will must be done."

"I know," Danny said.

Then he emerged into the cold air of the terminal, and men and women rose from the waiting-area seats and pulled video cameras from their coats and bags. Simultaneously, crews swarmed in from the concourse with hot lights and shoulder-cams and microphones, cutting Danny and Cunningham off from everyone else who had just deplaned, cutting them off from everyone on the concourse, cutting them off from everything on earth but the glass eyes and the watching world.

And Danny could feel it as they sucked up his image, multiplied it a billion times, and shot it to mobile studios and satellites and Web servers and every television set and video terminal on the planet.

It felt as if a giant electronic straw had been jabbed into his heart, and Danny could only hope that Cunningham felt it too.

Laughin' Boy steps into Terminal A from the Gate 33 doorway. He is twenty feet behind the passenger who stepped in ahead of him. But the man behind him—tall, vulture-like, gray-haired, wearing a charcoal suit—is so close that he is almost stepping on Laughin' Boy's heels.

So we surround them both. There are too many of us to count—too many cameras, too many lights, too many Talents thrusting microphones like rapiers. We can show you thirty, forty, fifty different angles as Laughin' Boy and Vulture Man enter. If you have enough bandwidth, you can see them all at once.

From dead-on ahead: Laughin' Boy reacts to us, begins to giggle.

From the left: Laughin' Boy begins to double over. Vulture Man is wide-eyed, grimacing, his nostrils flaring.

From the right: Vulture Man turns toward us and raises his right hand. The picture shakes as someone collides with us.

From farther back on the right: We see a man and a woman, a young couple in white shirts and charcoal jackets, pushing past a camera. They are trying to get away. But why would they do this? The other non-media civilians remaining in the A33 waiting area seem bemused, surprised, or thrilled—not panicked. Who, after all, would want to escape a Media Event?

From the left again: Vulture Man stops, grasping Laughin' Boy's shoulder with his right hand and stopping him, too.

From above (damn, we're good): Vulture Man reaches into his suit coat with his left hand, crosswise across his chest, as if reaching for his wallet.

Meanwhile, still more TV cameras, camcorders, and microphones are pouring into the Gate A33 area from the concourse, surging, surrounding, clamoring. Laughin' Boy and Vulture Man are engulfed.

"Laughin' Boy! Are you here to marry Porno Girl?"

"Mr. Clayton! Is this man your bodyguard?"

"Laughin' Boy! How do you plan to respond to the death threat from the WWJD?"

"Is it true that you've offered your own reward for the capture of the WWJD's Pastor, dead or alive?"

"What about the rumors that you'll be starring in your own sitcom on CBS in the fall?"

"What was your reaction when you heard about the firebombing of your parents' car last weekend?"

"Will you ever return to Wichita? And if so, how do you plan to make amends to your hometown?"

"Any truth to the rumor that you're dating Monica Lewinsky?"

"When is your interview with Barbara Walters scheduled, and how much will you be paid?"

"There are over six hundred Web sites claiming to represent you and your views! Which of these do you actually endorse?"

"Laughin' Boy! If you were a tree, what kind of tree would you be?"

"How do you plan to respond to the victims' lawsuit against you?"

"Larry Lanford says you're the funniest guy he's ever worked with! Do you feel the same way about him?"

"Is Porno Girl really still a virgin?"

"Are you ashamed to be so closely linked to the Racist Ranger? If not, what is your response to the Reverend Sharpton's recent comments?"

"Will you accept the Senate's invitation to speak at hearings on new gun-control legislation?"'

"Why DID you laugh when all those people were shot?"

These and dozens of other questions pile up one upon the other until they become a continuous cacophonic rumble. Every few seconds we can make out a word or two, and we can also hear hints of someone at the periphery screaming curses—but for the most part, we are listening to Niagara Falls.

All that is left for us to make sense of, then, are the pictures.

With rapid cuts, now, from every angle:

The man and woman who were trying to get away realize that there is no escape. So now they turn back toward Laughin' Boy and Vulture Man. The man reaches into his jacket, and the woman reaches into her purse. But then the media mob surges, and the two stumble, fall, and vanish.

An electric cart on the slick tiled curve of the concourse tries to plow through the crush with its cargo of elderly men and women in red felt cowboy hats. It goes nowhere.

A woman stands atop the Gate A33 check-in counter. We can see her lips forming the words "Laughin' Boy! Laughin' Boy!" over and over again. And then she pulls up her shirt and shakes her breasts—at which point she is joined by a man who drops his pants and shakes his buttocks.

Vulture Man pulls a stainless-steel pistol from his suit coat. He points it at the closest cameraman and fires. A blue flame leaps from its muzzle, and a sharp crack cuts through the cacophony. The cameraman falls.

The shouted questions become panicked screams, and the mob reverses direction. They have been closing on Laughin' Boy and Vulture Man like water on a drain, but now the camerapersons, Talents, and hangers-on fall over each other trying to escape.

From above, we see the mob surge away and leave Laughin' Boy and Vulture Man in an empty space like the eye of a hurricane. The cameraman who has been shot is dragged away by the rest of his crew.

From eye level, we see jumbled, jagged images of microphones, earlobes, fingernails, flying spit, and a bank of arrival/departure monitors. We hear more cries and curses and another pistol shot.

The man and woman on the counter jump down behind it, their clothing in disarray.

The electric cart on the concourse is flipped on its side, and its passengers tumble like toothpicks. Camerapersons and Talents dive behind it and then extend their lenses and microphones over and around the edges.

From one of those shaky lenses we see Vulture Man wrap his right arm around Laughin' Boy's head and force him into the concourse. Vulture Man is pointing his pistol first one way and then another.

And now we hear Laughin' Boy. We hear him loud and clear, even through the echoing roar of the screams and shouts and running feet. Trapped in a headlock, being dragged by a murderous gunman, Danny Clayton is laughing as if seeing Buster Keaton for the first time.

He is laughing as if he's an eight-year-old on a water slide. He is laughing as if being tickled by the Playmate of the Month. He is laughing as if he's having the most fun he's ever had in his life. And he hasn't even let go of his gym bag, which is bumping against his knees with every step.

Vulture Man pulls Laughin' Boy up the concourse, waving his pistol and shouting garbled warnings that we can't quite make out. Most of the camerapersons and Talents have stopped at a distance and are now recording events as best they can from behind chairs, counters, pillars, cappuccino kiosks, and the overturned electric cart. The elderly passengers from the cart are crawling and hobbling away, clinging to their red felt hats, but Vulture Man ignores them.

Now, as Laughin' Boy and Vulture Man come abreast of the cart, we can finally decipher Vulture Man's shouts even through the peals of Laughin' Boy's laughter.

"Stay right here!" Vulture Man shrieks. "Don't go anywhere, dupes of GOG and MAGOG! We'll be back! *The Lord will triumph!*"

He hauls Laughin' Boy past the cart, past airline ticket counters, and past Gate A34. The two of them remain in a bubble of empty space defined by invisible lines that sweep from the swinging pistol. Our cameras creep after them at a distance, at crotch level.

"Where are the police?" one of the Talents whispers into his microphone, his voice a fuzzy hiss. "Where are the security guards?"

No answer is forthcoming. Vulture Man is free to do as he will.

And what he does, when he comes abreast of Gate A35, is lunge across to the convex wall on the landside of the concourse. He yanks Laughin' Boy by the throat, and Laughin' Boy's laughter is choked to a gurgle that we may only imagine we hear.

Vulture Man pounds on a windowless door with his elbow. One of our cameras zooms in to the small sign beside the door, and we see that this is the Ambassadors' Lounge, an exclusive club for business travelers.

The door opens inward—and as it does, a man dressed in a black jacket with a white New York Yankees logo bursts from the creeping circle of media and runs up to Laughin' Boy and Vulture Man. Yankee Man has a camcorder pressed to his face, so we have no idea who this brave, idiotic newshound may be.

But whoever he is, Vulture Man shoots him in the chest, and he falls to the floor as his camcorder tumbles into the Ambassadors' Lounge. Incredibly, he crawls after it, getting most of the way through the doorway before Vulture Man tramples him and drags Laughin' Boy inside. The door slams on Yankee Man's ankles, then reopens just enough for his feet to disappear inside.

The door slams shut, and now the only thing our camera eyes can see is a blank slab of wood, beyond which God only knows what horrors are about to take place.

Maybe Yankee Man's camcorder is still running. We hope so. We'd hate to miss anything.

Cunningham flung Danny to the carpet. Danny landed on his side howling, and his bag went flying.

He did his best to concentrate on pine mulch, and it worked well enough to cut his laughter down to a chuckle. And then he found himself looking at the top of the Racist Ranger's head.

The Ranger was lying face-down on the floor, and he didn't seem to be breathing. But Danny knew better. At least, he hoped he did.

He looked up at Cunningham, who was glaring into the Ambassadors' Lounge.

"Who alerted the media?" Cunningham barked. "The Pastor's plan required you to wait for me!"

"We did, Brother Richie," a male voice answered. "I don't know what happened." Other voices chimed in.

As Cunningham's comrades proclaimed their innocence, Danny looked down again and saw that the Ranger's camcorder was lying just in front of Cunningham's toes. It was also just inches from Danny's face. So, still chuckling, he scooted a few feet away and stood up.

Now he saw that he was in a dark-paneled, windowless room with blue carpeting, and that six people—four women and two men—were lying on the floor against the far wall. They were blindfolded and gagged with blue linen napkins, and they were bound at the wrists and ankles with plastic strips like garbage-bag ties.

To the left of them, closer to Danny, were four more men and a woman. But these were all standing, and all were dressed in charcoal suits and white shirts without neckties, like Cunningham. Each held a stainless-steel pistol, and two of the men also carried short black assault guns on shoulder straps.

Seated on a chair in their midst was Amanda. Her hands were bound behind her back, but she wasn't bound at the ankles. Nor was she blindfolded or gagged. She was, however, dressed in an ill-fitting pink costume that Danny assumed was meant to look like her Porno Girl outfit.

Her eyes widened when she saw him. "I didn't expect to run into *you* again," she said. Her voice quavered at first, but then became bitter. "Last I heard, you thought I was a 'cheap little pervert.'"

Danny winced and giggled. "Are you okay?"

"Do I *look* okay?" Amanda bit her lip. "You wouldn't happen to have a dirty magazine on you, would you?"

Danny was about to offer his *New Yorker*, because it was all he had. But then Cunningham hit him over the ear, knocking him to the floor again. He fell on his side with his neck twisted so he was looking upward.

"Stay down until I tell you to get up!" Cunningham snarled. Then he tucked his pistol into his belt and began to berate his fellow

WWJD soldiers, waving his hands like a tent preacher threatening brimstone. One of them had committed a sin. One of them had called the news crews too soon. One of them had endangered the Pastor's plan, and thus had endangered the salvation of the Righteous as well.

Danny untwisted his neck and found himself nose-to-nose with the Racist Ranger. The Ranger's eyes were staring, and blood was dripping from his mouth. But a piece of gelatin was visible on his teeth, and the sight of it helped Danny stop laughing long enough to hear Royce's whisper.

"How many mo' is dey?"

Danny managed to blink five times.

"How many sivvilyuns?" the Ranger breathed.

Danny blinked six times, then a seventh to count Amanda.

Now the Ranger spoke aloud. "Bes' close yo' eyes en cover yo' ears," he said.

Danny closed his eyes, buried his face in the carpet, and clapped his hands over his ears just as he heard Cunningham say "What?" And then the flash bomb in the camcorder went off, and the insides of Danny's eyelids glowed bright red.

He felt the Ranger leap up. And even with his ears covered, he heard the gunshots and screams that followed.

It set off another laughing attack, and he couldn't stay face-down any longer without suffocating. So he rose to a crouch and lunged for the door. He hit the Ranger's shins.

The Ranger toppled, and Danny collapsed under him.

There was another gunshot. And then the Ranger rolled away, and Danny was able to get up to his hands and knees.

Something hot burned against the back of his neck.

"Stand up," Cunningham said, and Danny knew then that the thing at his neck was the muzzle of a pistol.

As he stood, he saw the Racist Ranger lying face-down on the floor with a hole in the right shoulder of his Yankees jacket. The

Ranger wasn't moving. His Glock was on the floor a yard away.

And then, once Danny was standing, Cunningham took the pistol away from his neck and shot the Ranger square in the back. Another hole appeared in the Yankees jacket, and bits of white fluff flew up. The Ranger still didn't move.

But Danny didn't laugh. It didn't seem possible that the Ranger could be dead. Royce was as strong as a bull. Aside from River Raft Syndrome, that was what defined him.

But he sure was awfully still now.

Cunningham put the pistol against Danny's neck again. "Do only what I say. And don't try to pick up a weapon. If you bend toward the floor, I'll finish it here, cameras or no. Understand?"

"Okey dokey," Danny said. It was what his mother had always said whenever it was time to do an onerous chore.

"Good. Turn this way."

The hot metal went away, and Danny turned to see Cunningham pointing two pistols at him.

Behind Cunningham, his five comrades were lying on the floor. One of the men was moaning, but the others were silent, their bodies twisted and bent where they had fallen. The woman had blood at her throat, and dark stains were soaking the carpet under two of the men.

The Ranger had done a job on them. But apparently Cunningham had managed to duck down and grab one of their pistols. And then he had shot the Ranger twice with that gun before taking his own from his belt again.

Now the room had a sharp metallic odor that cut at Danny's lungs with every breath. It smelled like Wichita, and that made him giggle. But the giggle didn't become a guffaw, because Amanda was still seated on her chair and seemed to be unhurt. She was trembling, but Danny couldn't see any wounds. And the hostages against the wall seemed to be all right too. They were screaming into their gags, but they weren't bleeding. The Ranger had taken pains not to hit any of them. And that was probably how Cunningham had gained his advantage—by putting himself in a spot where Royce couldn't shoot him without shooting a "sivvilyun" too.

So now the Ranger was down, and Cunningham had two pistols. One of them—the one in his left hand, most likely, since he had tucked it into his belt with his left and would have taken it out the same way—had to contain the clip of blanks. But the other one was the real deal.

"Go help Miss Larkin stand up and bring her here," Cunningham said, edging around Danny toward the door. "We're going out to face the media now. The Pastor's plan remains in effect."

Danny went to Amanda, who was blinking furiously as tears streaked her face. "I have to touch you," he said.

"Don't." She didn't sound as if she was crying. She sounded angry. "My hands are tied, but not to the chair. I can stand up on my own."

So Danny let her. She got to her feet, but looked wobbly. And she kept on blinking, and the tears kept coming.

"I can't see anything but a big white spot blooming over and over again," she said.

Danny glanced back at Cunningham, who had his ear pressed against the wall beside the door. He was still watching Danny, but he was listening to whatever was happening out on the concourse.

"The Ranger had a flash grenade," Danny whispered to Amanda. "That's why you can't see. It didn't seem to affect Richie Cunningham, though."

"Who?"

"The guy who brought me in."

"Oh. He was looking toward me when it went off," Amanda said. "His back was to it." Then she gasped. "Oh God, what if I never see again? I need *visual* pornography. The telephone stuff is too fake. I'll go out of my mind."

Over by the door, Cunningham made a throat-clearing noise. "Don't worry about the future, Miss Larkin."

Danny spun to face him. "The deal was that if I did what you said, she'd be okay!"

Cunningham pointed a pistol at the Racist Ranger's motionless body. "Is that Robert Royce?"

Danny hesitated, then said, "How should I know?"

Cunningham smiled his cobra smile again. "You cheated. Our agreement is void. And my only regret is that we don't have time to find the Laughin' Boy costume my Brothers were supposed to bring for you. If we wait any longer, agents of GOG will arrive and make the camera crews disperse. But at least Miss Larkin is dressed like the Whore of Babylon."

"Lead me to him, Danny," Amanda said. "If he's going to shoot me anyway, I want to kick him in the balls first."

Danny almost told her that Cunningham probably had only one ball anyway—but then he noticed his gym bag on the floor beside the Ranger's feet.

"I have my Laughin' Boy costume from the Lanford show in my bag," he said. "All except the boots."

It was the truth. The Lanford people had told him to take it to Wichita. But he had left the boots because they were too big for the bag.

Cunningham's eyes narrowed. "What else do you have in your bag, Mr. Clayton?"

"Clothes. A cell phone. A magazine. It's not like *I* could have smuggled a gun onto the plane."

Cunningham seemed to consider for a second, then stepped up to Danny and jabbed him in the chest with both pistols. "Strip first. No underwear, no nothing. No place to hide a weapon. Then open your bag, get your costume, and put it on. But do it *fast*. If you're not finished in one minute, I'll push you out and kill you naked. Think of your mother watching that."

Danny looked at Amanda. "Uh -- "

"I still can't see," she said. "So don't worry about unfavorable comparisons."

"Fifty-five seconds," Cunningham said, stepping back and leveling the pistols at Danny's face.

So Danny stripped as fast as he could, then jumped to his bag and opened it. The cell phone that Special Agent Armstrong had given him was still on top.

"I guess you're twice as tough now that you've picked up a second gun," Danny said as he took the cell phone from the bag and set it on the floor. He hoped it was still working. He hoped Armstrong was still listening.

"Thirty seconds," Cunningham said.

Danny threw his copy of *The New Yorker* aside and then frantically pulled out clothes. He had packed the Laughin' Boy suit first, so it was at the bottom.

"Fifteen seconds," Cunningham said.

Danny pulled on the suit legs, slipped his arms into the sleeves, and then threw back his shoulders to snug up the silver-and-blue chest and shoulder sections. He turned his back to Cunningham.

"Zip me?" he asked.

"Miss Larkin can do it," Cunningham said.

"My hands are tied behind my back and I'm blind," Amanda said. "Otherwise I'd be glad to."

Danny heard the pistols click together, then felt Cunningham pull up the costume's zipper. It made him queasy enough to chuckle.

"Let's go," Cunningham said. "Take Miss Larkin's elbow and walk her out. I'll hold the door."

Danny went to Amanda. "I'm sorry," he said, "but I really do have to touch you now. Just on your elbow."

He put his right hand on her left elbow, and she took a sharp breath.

"Now we'll walk forward," he said.

But Amanda didn't budge. "This is ludicrous," she said, her voice rising. "They kidnap me, they tie me up with plastic handcuffs, and now I'm supposed to walk out like a sheep so Opie can have an audience when he shoots me? I don't think so." She began yelling. "You hear me, Dobie Gillis? If you're going to do it, you're going to have to do it here!"

"All right," Cunningham said. He took a step toward Danny and Amanda. "Sister Wanda was supposed to bring a video camera. It must be in her purse. The networks can show the tape later."

Danny held up his free hand. "No!" he yelped, and then gave a high-pitched laugh. "No, no! We'll do as you say!"

"Why?" Amanda shouted. "Why should we?"

Danny wanted to tell her. He wanted to tell her that the cell phone was transmitting, and that Special Agent Armstrong was listening. He wanted to tell her that if they stepped out to the concourse, Armstrong or one of his agents would blow off Cunningham's right hand in the first ten seconds, because they would know that his right hand held the pistol he had taken from his comrade. He wanted to tell her that the pistol in Cunningham's left hand held only blank cartridges. He wanted to tell her that if they stayed in here, either Cunningham would shoot them on purpose or the FBI would shoot them accidentally. And he wanted to tell her that he thought he was in love with her—although it might only be because they were both freaks.

But he couldn't tell her any of that. So instead, he told her the one other thing that he knew was true and that she might believe.

"Because if we go out there," Danny said, "we'll live one more minute. And anything can happen in one minute."

After all, one minute in Wichita had changed everything for him. It had cost him his job and his daughter, and had made him an object of alternating hatred, adulation, and amusement the world over.

He laughed. "I should—*ahuhahuhahuh*—know."

Amanda turned her face toward him and blinked again, and he thought that she might be able to see him now. Maybe he was an amorphous blob of blue and silver. Maybe he looked better to her than he ever had before.

"Okay, then," she said. "When you put it that way." She even gave him a brave smile. "Sure. I'll take one more minute, Laughin' Boy."

She was beautiful, sad, and wonderful, so Danny convulsed and howled.

"Perfect," Cunningham said. He tucked his left-hand pistol into his belt, then grasped the doorknob and waved at Danny and Amanda with his right-hand pistol. "For the glory of the Lord God Almighty, and in honor of the Righteous Caucasians who have been sacrificed in His name. Let's go."

Danny, yipping like a hyena, staggered forward on bare feet past the still form of Rob Royce. His hand stayed on Amanda's elbow, and she staggered forward with him.

Cunningham yanked open the door. The breeze from that motion caught in Danny's throat and eyes, and he laughed so hard he wept. But he kept moving, and so did Amanda. Cunningham fell in behind them.

Together, Laughin' Boy and Porno Girl stepped out to the glare of lights and lenses. Before them were the hungry eyes of a waiting world. Behind them were the hands of a vengeful God. They were moments from death, and it was all Laughin' Boy could do not to fall to his knees whooping.

"This sucks," Porno Girl said.

Danny convulsed, and then the gun went off.

The door swings inward, and Laughin' Boy and Porno Girl come out to the empty floorspace we've left for them as we cower behind counters, waiting-area seats, and the overturned electric cart. Where are the police? we whisper into our microphones again. Where are the SWAT cops in black body armor? Nowhere. Only we are here. Only the eyes and ears of a grateful world. And so we will show you the horrible scene about to unfold, and we will show it from every angle and with every combination of wide and tight shots. Those of you watching on the Web may choose from the dozens of views available. Those of you watching on television may choose from the dramatic edits your various networks will provide with real-time speed. And before the signal reaches you, our sound engineers will add punch and echo to every gunshot, every scream.

Because you deserve it, then, here is the bloody climax of three weeks of a global media phenomenon:

Laughin' Boy and Porno Girl emerge. Right behind them is Vulture Man, he of the white shirt, dark jacket, and gray hair. He has a gleaming pistol in his right hand, and as he rises from a crouch we can see another stuck in his belt.

Laughin' Boy is in his silver-and-blue costume, but he is barefoot. Porno Girl is in her pink tights, but they're looser and less flattering than they were in her "Odd Squad" appearances. Perhaps she's lost weight. If so, it was rapid and remarkable. And if she is killed today, we may never know the secret of the Porno Girl Diet.

Laughin' Boy is laughing as if he's the happiest man on earth. Porno Girl's hands are tied behind her back (kinky!), and Laughin' Boy seems to be guiding her with a hand on her elbow. She is blinking her eyes as furiously as Laughin' Boy is laughing, and her face looks dirty or scorched.

Prodded by Vulture Man's pistol, they step out to the center of the concourse. We see Porno Girl's lips form these words:

"This sucks."

Laughin' Boy releases her elbow and doubles over, shrieking like a howler monkey.

Vulture Man places the muzzle of his pistol against Porno Girl's head, and we all zoom in. Vulture Man opens his mouth as if about to shout a proclamation.

But then an arm in a black sleeve stabs into frame from behind Vulture Man's head, grabs his wrist, and twists it so the pistol points at the ceiling. The pistol fires, and we zoom back out again to see Yankee Man crushing Vulture Man's wrist.

Now, finally, we have a good view of Yankee Man's face, and we know that he is Robert Royce, the Racist Ranger. He is doing what he does best—inflicting damage on a criminal—except that he is doing it with just his left arm. His right arm is hanging as if by a rubber band. And as he and Vulture Man spin away from Laughin' Boy and Porno Girl, we see two holes in the back of his jacket. The hole in the right shoulder is wet.

They spin to face us again. There is no hole in the front of the jacket. But we saw him shot there. We know we did.

Now Vulture Man begins to crumple, and the pistol in his right hand falls to the floor. The Ranger kicks it away.

It looks as if this is almost over, and that the Odd Squad will emerge victorious once again. Laughin' Boy has dropped to his hands and knees and is slapping the floor. Porno Girl is swaying on her feet with a dazed expression on her face. And the Racist Ranger is about to crush his second terrorist assassin in as many weeks.

But then Vulture Man turns in the Ranger's grip and faces him. He grasps the Ranger's right arm with his left hand and yanks downward.

The Racist Ranger's mouth opens wide, but we hear nothing over Laughin' Boy. And then the Ranger's eyes roll up, his head flops back, and he collapses.

Vulture Man pulls his right wrist from the unconscious Ranger's grip, then uses his left hand to take his second pistol from his belt. He steps over to Porno Girl and puts the muzzle of the pistol against her head again. And once more, he opens his mouth as if to shout a proclamation.

But instead we hear voices close to our microphones, close enough to be heard over Laughin' Boy: "Porno Girl! Over here!"

Our cameras swivel toward the cries—and we see the man and woman who earlier exposed portions of their bodies while atop the Gate A33 counter. But now they're atop the Gate A35 counter, and they're both nude. The man is lying on his back with the woman straddling him, and many of us have to cut away because we aren't allowed to broadcast that sort of thing (although those of you with certain satellite channels or Internet accounts may be in luck).

Cut back to Porno Girl:

She stops blinking. Her eyes widen. It is as if she has been blind, but now she sees. It is as if she is filled with a golden light.

And with a sudden, Herculean wrench, Porno Girl bursts free of the plastic strip binding her wrists behind her back. Her arms fly up, and one of her elbows knocks Vulture Man's gun hand away from her head. Her other elbow catches him under the chin. His head snaps back, his pistol points upward, and another round is fired at the ceiling.

Porno Girl sprints out of frame in the direction of the naked people.

Meanwhile, Vulture Man stumbles backward and trips over Laughin' Boy, who is still on his hands and knees howling. Vulture Man crashes to the floor—but then rises to his knees. And so does Laughin' Boy.

They face each other.

Vulture Man has his pistol in his left hand, and its muzzle is two inches from the tip of Laughin' Boy's nose.

As if a switch has been thrown, Laughin' Boy falls silent.

"In the name of the White Warriors for Jesus, Deceased," Vulture Man cries, "I declare Holy War on the demons of GOG and—"

He stops because Laughin' Boy has stuck his finger in the muzzle of the pistol.

Vulture Man jerks the pistol away, then puts the muzzle against Laughin' Boy's forehead.

"In the name of the White Warriors and their Most Righteous Pastor," he begins again, "I hereby—"

And he stops once more. Then he looks into Laughin' Boy's eyes and says something else. Something quieter.

We can barely hear him over the moans of the people having sex on the Gate A35 counter.

"Why aren't you laughing?" he asks. And then again, louder: "Why aren't you laughing?"

Laughin' Boy, the pistol against his forehead, shrugs.

Vulture Man's voice grows louder and louder. "You're supposed to be laughing!" he cries. "If you're not laughing, they won't know you're Laughin' Boy! They won't understand that you're their enemy! They won't understand that you're a demon of GOG, and that I'm a Righteous Angel of the Lord! They won't understand—WHY AREN'T YOU LAUGHING?"

And when Vulture Man pauses to take a shuddering breath, Laughin' Boy answers.

"I only laugh at what horrifies me," he says. "And a pistol loaded with blanks doesn't."

Vulture Man looks as if he has been hit across the face with a skillet.

"You're lying," he says. But we can hear the doubt in his voice.

Laughin' Boy shrugs again, then reaches up and snatches the pistol away from Vulture Man's grasp.

Vulture Man's expression turns to one of shock. He hasn't expected this. Neither have we.

Neither has Laughin' Boy. He looks amazed.

"Wow," he says. "This is just like TV."

Then Laughin' Boy points the pistol at Vulture Man's forehead and pulls the trigger.

Vulture Man's head explodes like a dropped watermelon.

We see it from every angle. From the front. From the side. From far, from near. From above (damn, we're good.)

Stay tuned for slow-motion replays.

Vulture Man flops backward, his legs bent beneath him, and he doesn't move again.

The Talents and camera crews are shouting, screaming, and cheering.

The people having sex decide to stop, and Porno Girl pouts. The Racist Ranger regains consciousness and sits up.

And at this moment, the young man and woman who earlier tried to flee now emerge from the throng and rush forward. Each is carrying a pistol. Each is screaming something about a Pastor. They approach the Racist Ranger from behind and point their weapons at him.

But then a tall African-American man in a dark suit dives into the picture and hits the young man at waist level, knocking him into the woman and forcing them both to the floor. One of the pistols skitters across the tiles, and the other is ripped away by swarming men and women in blue windbreakers that say FBI in big yellow letters.

As the young couple is handcuffed, the Racist Ranger looks up at the African-American man who has just saved his life. The African-American man looks back.

And then they both turn to look at Laughin' Boy.

Laughin' Boy is still on his knees. His lips are parted. He is staring at the spectacular mess that used to be a Righteous Caucasian of the White Warriors for Jesus, Deceased.

He doesn't laugh.

Newsgroup Posts (6)

Subject: Holy S@&%!
From: johndoe99@bullmoose.net (Nathan Lawrence)
Date: 2000/06/09
Message-ID:
<johndoe99-558735)FM4.348NT6@bullmoose.net>
Newsgroups:soc.us.violence.terroralt.fan.laughin-boy

Jeez Louise, anybody reading LB posts right now at about 11:42 AM EDT go turn on your TVs or surf over to CNN or something because Laughin' Boy, that's right Mr. Clayton himself, has just SHOT THE TOP OF A GUY'S HEAD OFF in the Dallas airport. It happened live on the g*ddamn air a few minutes ago, and swear to Jesus, it looked like a war or something was going on right there next to the Chock Full o' Nuts or whatever at DFW, and then LB just takes this old dude's gun right from his hand and POW, and that was it, man. And he's not even cracking a smile, much less laughing. So it looks like all you guys (RU, you out there?) who've been saying that the whole LB thing was a cover were right. Turns out he's some kinda government assassin. He didn't flinch, just POW, like I said. Made even the RR look like a candyass by comparison. RR, by the way, is down and looks hurt, maybe shot, although it's not clear who did it. Anyhow, turn on the tube. Peter Jennings is saying the guy LB shot was a terrorist, but I dunno, he looked like my Uncle Mike. Porno Girl's there too, but near as I can tell she hasn't KILLED anyone. Christ on a CRUTCH!

Subject: Re: Holy S@&%!
From: toebunny@aol.com (Anonymous)
Date: 2000/06/09
Message-ID:
<toebunny-9632LLB41.LSMFT@aol.com>
Newsgroups: alt.fan.laughin-boy

JohnDoe, I'm watching the same thing you are at the same time, but I'm not seeing the same thing at all. Mr. Clayton did NOT act all cold and assassiny (is that a word?). When there was a close-up you could see in his face that he had no idea what had just happened. He didn't mean to, you could tell. Watch the replays, you'll see. He is a kind and decent man who has been caught up in forces he can't deal with or understand, and the WWJD has used him horribly. I think our own government has too. But all I know for sure is that he didn't mean to laugh at the Wichita Massacre, and he didn't mean to kill your Uncle Mike. And Mr. Clayton, if you ever read this, the offer I have made here many times still stands. I believe you are a good person and I would like the chance to prove it to you. I know you must be hurting even though you don't seem to be laughing now. Or maybe you're hurting _because_ you're not laughing now. OK, so I don't understand—but I want to. I want to very very much, and if you ever want to laugh again I think I can help you do it. And don't worry about shooting that man in the head. I'm sure it was an accident.

Episode Six Coda
Required Romantic Epilogue

DANNY KNEW SPECIAL AGENT Armstrong was standing next to him. He even knew Armstrong was speaking. But he couldn't make out the words. All he could hear was the reverberation of the shot. All he could see were Cunningham's body and blood on the slick floor.

Armstrong took the pistol from him and helped him to his feet, and then Danny was able to look away from the body. He saw Armstrong offer to help Royce up as well, and saw Royce accept.

The Ranger's right arm dangled as he stood. "No 'fense, Allan honey," he said. "I 'preciate what you jis' done. But whah in de dingbusted fuck has you been? Fer a minute dah I 'uz afeared you 'uz a-gwyneto let dat Richie Cunningham shoot de whole lot o' us."

Danny looked at Armstrong's face and thought he saw the black stone crack a little.

"The cell-phone bug indicated that the suspect still possessed our altered weapon," Armstrong said. "So when you relieved him of the weapon in his right hand, I assumed the one he retained was harmless. I therefore decided to hang back in the hope that he might reveal something useful while he still believed he was in control."

Danny felt as if he were seeing and hearing everything from inside a Plexiglas box. Or as if it were playing on a distant TV set. "I'm sorry," he said. "I'm so sorry. I just wanted to scare him the way he'd scared everyone else. I thought it was the one with the blanks."

"I know you did, Mr. Clayton," Armstrong said.

The Ranger coughed and began to look as if he might collapse again. "Well, dad fetch it, so did I."

Betty appeared beside Armstrong then, but she looked different than she had on the plane. She was wearing a navy windbreaker that said FBI on the front, and she was cradling a shotgun in one arm. She also had her hair tied back, which revealed a black wire trailing from her right ear.

"We've evacuated the hostages," she said. "But except for the two that you apprehended, Agent Armstrong, all of our suspects are deceased." She looked at Royce. "And it turns out that the weapon you took from Cunningham contained the dummy clip. He must have swapped weapons from one hand to the other at some point."

Now Danny realized when it had happened. It had been when Cunningham had zipped up the Laughin' Boy costume. He decided not to mention it.

The Ranger began to sway. "I thought mebbe he'd picked up *two* new'uns when I jumped up arter bein' shot in de ches'." His voice weakened. "But I reckon 'stead o' guessin' 'bout de blanks, he figgered I 'uz wearin' a vest. Which I is. Ain't dat ironic? Dat'd 'splain why he shot me in de shouldah—kase de armor don't kivver it all de way. But den he shot me squah in de back, so mebbe he didn' know nuffin. My back sho' nuff hurts, though . . . "

He crumpled, and Armstrong caught him. Two paramedics ran up with a gurney, and Armstrong lowered the Ranger to it.

"Another thing, sir," Betty said. "Items found on the suspects indicate that 'Cunningham' was Turner P. Williams. It seems he wanted to play a major part in his own plan."

"You heah dat, Dan'l?" the Ranger said. "You done shot de Pastor. En he 'uz de one behind dat mess in Wichita. So don' you feel bad 'bout killin' him, now." His head tilted. "But mebbe you *doesn't*, kase you ain't a-laughin' no mo'."

It was true. A rivulet of the Pastor's blood was about to touch Danny's bare feet, and Laughin' Boy wasn't even chuckling.

"Maybe I'm cured," he said.

The Ranger gave a weak grin. "Well, den, I sholy do wisht you'd'a let *me* blow de sumbitch's haid off. Den mebbe *I'd* be de one what 'uz cured."

"Wouldn't that have been nice," Armstrong said drily.

"Yassuh," Royce said. "But since you's jis' saved my mis'ble life, Mars Allan, we is even fer dat time I done de same fer you. So you don' have to be grateful no mo'. You kin relieve me o' duty fer real now effen you wants."

Armstrong scowled. "You're not weaseling out from under my command. But I think we'd both better learn sign language." He looked at Betty. "Once you've finished here, please take Mr. Clayton and Miss Larkin to the Marriott. We'll debrief later. Right now, I'm going to the hospital."

Betty nodded, but then frowned and pressed a finger against her ear. "Just a minute, sir. Command post reports a private jet has arrived from New York. It's the DeWitts."

"Damn," the Ranger said. "Dat 'uz fast."

Armstrong shrugged. "Not really. They probably took off for Wichita as soon as they realized Laughin' Boy had split. Then they diverted to Dallas when the media began reporting on our situation." He looked at Danny. "Perhaps you could use their counsel now, Mr. Clayton. After all, you've just killed a man."

Danny tried to imagine dealing with the DeWitts again, and couldn't. "No. I'm done with them. Whether I'm cured or not, being a doped-up dancing bear for Dr. Ralph and Dr. Carla's media circus won't help. I don't want to see them."

"Fine," Armstrong said. "So don't."

"That's all right with you?" Danny asked.

The Ranger coughed. "Dan'l, honey, de terr'ists done took de bait en paid de price, so de DeWitts ain't no use to de Bureau no mo'. Er to me neither, since I couldn' never take dey med'cine, en dey other methods didn' do a blimblammin' thing. So ain't nobody give a rat's rump whether you ditches 'em too."

"But for the time being, they still have their Bureau IDs," Betty said. "Which means that they've been allowed into the terminal where their plane arrived, at Gate 8. They'll be here shortly."

Armstrong put a hand on the Ranger's gurney. "Well, Agent Royce needs medical attention, so he and I aren't sticking around for the reunion. You'll have to avoid or deal with the DeWitts on your own, Mr. Clayton."

Danny didn't like that idea. "Can't Betty get rid of them?"

"She has more important things to do, such as take fingerprints from dead suspects. Besides, your relationship with the DeWitts is no longer the Bureau's business. As far as I'm personally concerned, though, you can feel free to shoot them." Armstrong pointed at the paramedics. "You have thirty seconds to get this gurney into an ambulance."

"'Bye, y'dern freak," the Ranger said to Danny. He extended his uninjured arm as the gurney began to roll.

Danny hesitated, then reached down and grasped the Ranger's hand before it was pulled away. "Same to you," he said. Then he glanced at Armstrong. "And to you."

"I grasp your implication," Armstrong said. "But I'll let it go because I'm too busy to kill you."

Danny watched as Armstrong and the paramedics wheeled the Ranger away and disappeared behind a line of men and women wearing navy windbreakers like Betty's. He wished he were being wheeled away too.

Beyond the line of windbreakers, various media types jockeyed for position. There were a lot of them, but not as many as before. Some of the earlier ones, Danny saw, were now among those wearing windbreakers. So were all of the agents from the Gleason Theater detail, and so were Santa Claus and Army Man from the New York Pleasure Club. Or maybe they were all just projections on the surface of Danny's Plexiglas box.

Then Amanda stepped through the line of windbreakers, and the Plexiglas box disintegrated. Everything became sharp and clear now that he could see her again.

But Amanda stopped when she caught sight of the Pastor's body. So Danny went to her, and they met halfway between the pool of blood and the press.

"I can see again," Amanda said. She sounded almost happy. "But the naked people who performed the miracle have vanished." Her forehead creased. "I think they were Feds. I mean, I've seen a lot of people having sex, and those two were doing it as if they'd have to file a report afterward."

Danny resisted the urge to put his arms around her. "I don't care who they were. I'm just glad you're all right."

"Me too." She glanced over her shoulder as a reporter shouted her name, and then she turned back to Danny. "You wouldn't believe what I just heard out there among the newshounds. The cameramen were arguing over who had the best angle when Potsie's skull blew up, and the reporters were betting on whose version of events will win the most awards." She shuddered. "And they say *I'm* perverted scum."

Danny tried to smile. "Well, you're a lawyer."

"Oh, very nice." Amanda reached out so that her fingertips brushed the back of his hand. "But thank you for suggesting that my porno compulsion might not be the worst thing in the world."

Danny was amazed that she had been able to touch him. "You're welcome. But speaking of the worst thing in the world, Dr. Ralph and Dr. Carla are in the terminal. And I don't want to see them."

"Neither do I, unless they're returning my Traci Lords tape," Amanda said. Then her eyes widened. "Hey, wait a minute. This is all pretty horrible. How come you're not laughing?"

Danny shook his head. "Beats me. I just blew open a man's head, and I'm surrounded by corpses and cameras. On top of that, the DeWitts are coming with another syringe of rope-a-dope and a bottle of blue dum-dums. And if there are any more White Warriors for Jesus out there in the wilds of America, they no doubt still want to kill me. Which means that I still can't see my daughter any time soon. So I should be whooping it up. I should be rolling on the floor. I should be in stitches."

"It's all pretty rib-tickling, all right," Amanda said. "Or would be for Laughin' Boy. So maybe that's not who you are anymore."

"That'd be a silver lining, at least." He looked past the windbreakers at a commotion in the midst of the camera crews. "And now I think our shrinks have arrived."

Amanda followed his gaze. "Yeah, I can see the glare from Dr. Ralph's head. But maybe the Feds will keep them over there with the media. Or maybe they'll just be happy there without us. After all, that's their natural habitat."

"But they need people like us to keep them there," Danny said. "If there's one thing I've learned, it's that winning the ratings war is all about maintaining a higher freak factor than the other guy in your time slot."

And then he knew what to do.

"Amanda," he said, "I know it's a lot to ask, but . . . could I hold your hand?"

Amanda's eyes narrowed. "Why?"

"Because I just thought of a way to pre-empt the DeWitts."

Amanda still looked dubious. "Are you sure we have to touch?"

"I think it would help," Danny said. He looked over at the commotion again. Now he could see both Dr. Ralph and Dr. Carla in all their gray-suited glory because they had stepped through the line of windbreakers and were heading toward him and Amanda. And they were bringing the media with them.

Amanda looked at them too, then closed her eyes for a moment before turning back to Danny. She gave him a brave smile and held out her hand.

Danny took her hand in both of his just as the media and the DeWitts surrounded them. Her hand was warm and smooth. He wanted to hold it forever.

"Daniel," Dr. Ralph said. "Amanda. Dr. Carla and I came as soon as we could."

"We're sorry you had to go through this alone," Dr. Carla said. "But we're here for you now."

Danny ignored them and got down on one knee. And at that moment, as he had known they would, all of the cameras turned away from the DeWitts and focused on him and Amanda. He was glad they were both wearing their costumes.

From the corner of his eye, Danny saw that Dr. Ralph was opening his mouth to speak again. So there was no time to waste.

"Porno Girl," Laughin' Boy said, "will you marry me?"

And to Danny's surprise, Amanda answered immediately.

"Now, *that's* funny," she said.

After that, all he could hear was noise.

Radio Talk (2)

. . . and no members of the "Odd Squad" have been seen or heard from in the three days since the shootout. This, when considered in combination with Porno Girl's apparent superhuman strength, the Racist Ranger's derring-do, and Laughin' Boy's deadly aim, has led to speculation that all three are government agents who lured the White Warriors into the open. This in turn has led to severe criticism of the FBI, with citizens' watchdog groups infuriated that innocent civilians at DFW were deliberately placed in harm's way. A spokesperson for the FBI, however, points out that all of the casualties at DFW, save one, were WWJD members. The other casualty was the former FBI agent Robert Royce, whose wounds were serious but no—

Hold it, Miss Candi. Some nut has climbed a flagpole at the Ballpark in Arlington, and he's threatening to fling himself to his death—or possibly urinate on those below if the cops try to bring him down.

That's terrible, Jimmy Joe Bob.

Says you. The guy has a cell phone, and we've got him on Line One! Hello, Carl in Arlington, you're on the air with Jimmy Joe Bob and Miss Candi.

Hi, Jimmy Joe Bob. How are you this morning?

Well, I don't have a flagpole stuck up my butt. How about you?

I'm in a secured harness, Jimmy Joe Bob. So I want to point out that if a police sharpshooter kills me, I'll just hang here and rot.

You sound like a Cubs fan, Carl. So why are you pulling this stunt in an American League park?

I'm a Rangers fan, Jimmy Joe Bob, but I'm not a fan of this stadium. And now that Laughin' Boy is on his way to being old news,

I'm taking this opportunity to tell the world how the citizens of Arlington have been screwed.

Go right ahead, Carl.

Uh, Jimmy Joe Bob, I think I know where this is going.

Hush, Miss Candi. We've got a lunatic on a flagpole here, for crying out loud. We're talking big ratings, not to mention the possibility of an audible splat. So Carl, please continue. You're upset about the Ballpark because—

Because the state stole the land for it, and it was paid for with public money that we were told would be paid back. But it was all a big lie told by thieves. And the smirking s.o.b. behind it was the man the rest of y'all made Governor, the man who wants to be the next PresSQUEEEALLLL

Well, folks, we seem to have lost Carl's feed. But that's okay because he's insane, and I'd like to urge those police sharpshooters he mentioned to go ahead and do that voodoo that you do so well. I'd also like to emphasize that Crazy Carl's comments do not reflect the opinions of this station, nor of myself or Miss Candi. So there's no need for any prominent Texas family to sic their attorneys on us.

I told you, Jimmy Joe Bob.

Yeah, well, you're always telling me something, Miss Candi. How am I to know when it stems from a legitimate concern rather than from your usual hormonal tsunamis?

Rather than rise to that bait, I'll continue with the news. The Friday gun battle at DFW resulted in—

You know something, Miss Candi? So far, nothing you've said about that shootout has touched on the real tragedy of the event—that is, how it affected me personally.

Forgive me, Jimmy Joe Bob. I don't know what I was thinking.

A hot babe like you wasn't put on this Earth to think.

So what's your excuse?

Ouch! And thank you. I've really missed the way you hurt me, Miss Candi—because, as our listeners know, we were on vacation last week.

Mark the Mongoloid Producer ran some Classic Jimmy Joe Bob shows instead, although he ignored the list I gave him. But I was off partying in the Garden State, so I didn't know or care. Which reminds me, Miss Candi—where'd you go?

I visited my mother in Omaha, Jimmy Joe Bob.

You're such a virgin. As for me, I hit Atlantic City, baby, and I came back with some of that peckerhead Donald Trump's money. And yes, folks, I can say "peckerhead." It's not on the list.

Did you bring me anything from your trip, Jimmy Joe Bob?

Why yes I did, Miss Candi, gift-wrapped in my Levi's. Now as I was saying, I was in Atlantic City all week, and I came home to Dallas guess when? That's right, gang—on FRIDAY! My freakin' luck, I came home on FRIDAY, and my flight taxied up to Terminal A at DFW just half an hour after Laughin' Boy blew a hole in Pastor Williams's noggin! Speaking of which, Miss Candi, have you noticed that people's heads have a tendency to explode whenever Mr. Clayton's around?

That does seem to be the trend.

And as if that weren't bad enough, do you know what it meant for me personally last Friday?

I'm guessing it meant you were delayed.

You're damn right I was delayed! The whole effing plane was delayed! In fact, every effing flight in or out of DFW was delayed! And since DFW is the largest and busiest effing airport in the world—

Actually, Jimmy Joe Bob, that's not quite—

I SAID, since DFW is the LARGEST and BUSIEST effing airport in the WORLD, that meant that the whole effing WORLD was delayed because the effing Feds and effing Laughin' Boy decided to turn Terminal A into an effing Branch Davidian compound. I mean, I'm sittin' out there on the effing tarmac, I can see the gate is free, and we're not MOVING.

That must have been frustrating.

And you should know from frustrating, you perpetual tease. So we sit there for, I don't know, forty-five minutes, and the effing First Class galley has run out of effing Chivas, and they won't even tell us WHY we're just sitting there. Now, the rest of y'all had watched Laughin' Boy plug the Pastor fifteen or twenty times by then, but the only news that we poor schmoes on the tarmac were getting was "There's a problem with the jetway." Which was an effing LIE! The REAL problem was that the U.S. Government created a Frankenstein's monster and then let him loose in an airport with an effing Colt .45!

Now, Jimmy Joe Bob, it seems likely that the WWJD terrorists were the aggressors, and that Laughin' Boy and the rest of the Odd Squad acted in self-defense. So I'm surprised at your attitude, because you usually approve of people defending themselves with firearms.

Not when it's inconvenient for ME. Anyway, after about an hour—

You said it was forty-five minutes.

—after about an hour and a half, they decide to move the plane to Terminal C and unload us there. But of course my girlfriend was trying to pick me up at Terminal A, and no one would let her in or even tell her that my plane had been shuffled to C. And I can't tell her myself, because the goofy broad let the battery in her cell phone go dead! So I have to call the apartment and leave a message, hoping she'll check the machine. But of course she DOESN'T—

Wait a minute, Jimmy Joe Bob. You went to Atlantic City for a week and didn't take your girlfriend along?

Well, I wanted to take her. But she refused to go because she had a premonition that the White Warriors would perpetrate an Atlantic City Massacre.

Really?

Nah. I just didn't want her cramping my style. See, she's twenty-two and has a rack that'd give Russ Meyer a coronary, but hoo boy, what a ditz. That's why I wanted to take YOU, Miss Candi. You've got it all.

And I intend to keep it. But please finish your DFW story so we can get back to the news.

Okay, the upshot is that I eventually had to lug my bags over to Terminal A and find my chick bawling in my Lexus in a traffic jam. Thirty minutes and some curb-hopping after that, and we're finally on our way back to the condo, where I turn on the big-screen and see a hunk of the Pastor's temporal lobe doing lazy cartwheels through the misty red air thanks to Mr. Clayton of Kansas.

That must have put a damper on your reunion with your beloved.

Actually, it sorta got the ol' testosterone flowin', if you know what I mean. Damn it, where'd the cart for my BOIIINNGGG sound effect go? I swear, Mark, one more screwup and you're out the effing door. As for you, Miss Candi, please continue with your newscast while I go offmike and chew Mark's ass.

Thank you, Jimmy Joe Bob. In Wichita today, reaction to Friday's events was mixed. Mayor Tom Dilworthy said he was still suspicious of any man who would laugh at a tragedy, but Police Chief Martha Hartounian suggested that Laughin' Boy did the world a favor by killing the terrorist behind the Wichita Massacre. Meanwhile, however, most Massacre victims' relatives seemed to feel that the Pastor's death won't bring back their loved ones . . . but that Danny Clayton's laughter will haunt their nightmares for years.

In other news, President Clinton has announced that—

No one cares what that fat, horny bastard has to say.

You just described yourself to a tee, Jimmy Joe Bob.

Yes, Miss Candi, but MY radio show actually has listeners. And speaking of which, here's one on the line now. Dr. Carla DeWitt, are you there?

Yes, Jimmy Joe Bob. But I'm not one of your listeners, because I live in New York.

If you call that living. Is Dr. Ralph joining us too?

I'm afraid not. Dr. Ralph is currently in discussions with agents of the Federal Bureau of Investigation.

Oh-oh! Is the good doctor in trouble?

Not at all. He is informing the FBI of the potentially dire consequences should they continue to prevent us from seeing three of our patients, sometimes referred to as the "Odd Squad." We've been kept from them all weekend.

And what "dire consequences" might result from this?

Permanent psychological damage. You see, the government claims that Mr. Clayton, Mr. Royce, and Ms. Larkin have chosen to terminate their courses of treatment of their own free wills. However, the emotional states of those three patients are so precarious that we feel there is a strong chance they've made their choice under duress from the FBI—or at least without understanding the consequences. Mr. Clayton's ludicrous 'proposal' to Ms. Larkin in the midst of the carnage in Dallas is evidence that he's either suffered a psychotic break or is on the verge of one.

Excuse me, Dr. Carla, but I have to jump in here. First of all, I thought Laughin' Boy's proposal to Porno Girl was a healthy, life-affirming reaction to the violence and death around them. So perhaps you object to it because their new bond with each other means that they no longer need therapy at all—or because at that moment, the TV cameras turned away from YOU.

Second of all, why on earth would the FBI care whether the Odd Squad continues being treated for their disorders?

Because the federal government is evil, Miss Candi!

Sadly, that's not too far off the mark. Dr. Ralph and I fear that the FBI intends to keep these three patients psychologically off-balance in order to continue to use them as weapons, as they did last Friday. Under proper care, you see, a fundamentally gentle soul like Danny Clayton could never behave like the cold-blooded killer who shot the WWJD Pastor.

So you're saying that Laughin' Boy is like the Wichitawian Candidate or something? Don't tell me that bitch Angela Lansbury is at it again!

I know it sounds bizarre, but I assure you that it's more than possible. And we've all seen the proof.

Personally, I'm not sure that we saw "proof" of anything other than that violence begets violence—and perhaps that, despite what the White Warriors claimed, God doesn't take sides after all.

Why must you always play Scully to my Mulder, Miss Candi? If the Shrinks to the Damned say that Laughin' Boy is implanted with a space-alien kill chip, then that's good enough for me.

It's not space aliens and it's not a chip, Jimmy Joe Bob, but you have the basic concept. And Dr. Ralph and I will be exploring that concept in greater detail when we bring our own radio show back to the air in a few weeks. We're ending our hiatus early because of the importance and danger of what we see happening.

Oh, now I get it. You're relaunching as an "anti-government-conspiracy" show, and you're trying to use MY show as free advertising. So let me explain something, Dr. Carla: If you want a plug on MY time, you can shell out the bucks and/or give me oral pleasure just like everyone else. In the meantime, though, you can go peddle your tinfoil helmets somewhere else!

No, Jimmy Joe Bob, you don't underCLICK.

Dang, we seem to have lost Dr. Carla. How'd that happen?

Good for you, Jimmy Joe Bob!

Thanks, Miss Candi. And good for you too, because your comment about God not taking sides has provoked a response. Elijah from Palestine, you're on the air.

You don't remember me, do you?

I only just now met you, bubba. Say something interesting and then ask me again.

I called you three weeks ago after the so-called Wichita Massacre. I tried to tell you what that event was really all about, and you accused me of being a homosexual.

Oh, I remember this guy, Jimmy Joe Bob. He's a WWJD sympathizer.

Yikes! Well, Ebeneezer, I'm sorry to hear that. You must've had a rough weekend, what with your spiritual leader's brains doing cartwheels and all.

The Pastor and the Brothers and Sisters who gave their lives will be replaced. It may take weeks, or it may take decades. But the

Righteous Caucasians of the world will reclaim what is theirs, and the Lord God Almighty will be with them. Miss Candi is mistaken if she thinks otherwise.

Well, now, Sneezy—

Elijah. How did you get Sneezy from that?

Guess I'm allergic, Ellie Mae. But what I was about to tell you was that since Miss Candi is a lady with a lovely mocha complexion, she's naturally going to doubt that the Lord God Almighty is strictly on the side of you Righteous Caucasians.

I might also point out that I doubt the Lord God Almighty is on the side of you UNRighteous Caucasians either, Jimmy Joe Bob.

I could've told you that myself, sweetheart.

I didn't realize that Miss Candi was born of the Seed of Cain. But now that I do, I have to say that the Lord will punish you, Jimmy Joe Bob, for attempting to defile the purity of your race by having congress with a Negress.

Oh, come on! The Lord can't blame a guy for trying!

Hmmm. You're starting to look a little better to me, Jimmy Joe Bob.

Don't torment me, Miss Candi!

I will pray for your destruction, Jimmy Joe Bob. And when I am in Heaven, I will spit down upon you as you languish in Hell with Miss Candi. Even as Laughin' Boy mocks me and mine now, so shall I mock you then. And so shall I mock Porno Girl, and the falsely named Racist Ranger. And Laughin' Boy, too. For I am Man, beloved of the Lord God Almighty, created in His image.

"Man," eh? Oh, Ellie, you silly girl. Settle down for a soak in the cee-ment pond and listen to what Satan, while visiting Earth, wrote about "Man" in a letter back home to the incredulous angels in Heaven:

"He believes the Creator is proud of him; he even believes the Creator loves him; has a passion for him; sits up nights to admire him; yes, and watch over him and keep him out of trouble. He prays to Him, and thinks He listens. Isn't it a quaint idea?"

Don't blaspheme, Jimmy Joe Bob.

Hush, Ellie Mae, there's more:

"He prays for help, and favor, and protection, every day; and does it with hopefulness and confidence, too, although no prayer of his has ever been answered. The daily affront, the daily defeat, do not discourage him, he goes on praying just the same. There is something almost fine about this perseverance. I must put one more strain upon you: he thinks he is going to Heaven!"

You made all that up. You don't know what Satan would write. You aren't a demon. Not like Laughin' Boy, Porno Girl, or the Racist Ranger.

In that case, I must inform you that Satan's letter was transcribed by Samuel L. Clemens, who also created the character whom the "demon" Robert Royce admires to the point of pathology. So there might be a chance that he knew a few things you and I don't.

Um, Jimmy Joe Bob . . .

Yes, Miss Candi?

Didn't Clemens, still quoting Satan, also write that "the human being, like the immortals, naturally places sexual intercourse far and away above all other joys—yet he has left it out of his Heaven!"

Why yes, Miss Candi, I believe he did.

I don't understand you, Jimmy Joe Bob. Sometimes you can be going along and more or less making sense, and then all of a sudden you start blaspheming and quoting dead people that the rest of us never heard of. You do it all the time, and it's starting to get—

Yeah, yeah, whatever, Ellie. Just be quiet for a minute, will you? Miss Candi and I are having a moment here. Aren't we, Miss Candi?

That depends. You don't really have a girlfriend, do you? You just made her up for the DFW story, right?

I'll tell you off the air.

I look forward to that, Jimmy Joe Bob.

You're both going to Hell.

Probably so, Ellie Mae. But I don't mind too much, because they have things in Hell that you ain't gonna get in Heaven. Things like rock and roll, Jack Daniel's, dancing, fart jokes, and that sexual intercourse thing Mr. Clemens mentioned. And if you ask me, I think THAT's why it's so darn hot. So when you try to "spit down upon" us, the heat'll just vaporize it. And then we'll look up at you—me, Miss Candi, and all three members of the Odd Squad, too—and you know what we'll do? Do you know what we'll do despite the horrors we've seen in our lives, despite our damnation for all Eternity?

You'll burn. *CLICK*

Well, in a manner of speaking, I suppose we will. But mainly, Ellie Mae—and I know you're still listening out there—we're just going to take a cue from Mr. Danny Clayton of Wichita, Kansas. We're going to laugh. We're going to laugh a lot. Am I right, Miss Candi?

Maybe just this once, Jimmy Joe Bob. Just this once, I think that maybe you are.

Newsgroup Posts (7)

Subject: Goodbye
From: SCREENNAME WITHHELD
Date: 2000/06/20
Message-ID: ID WITHHELD
Newsgroups: alt.fan.laughin-boy

I'm not sure I should do this, but it seems wrong to vanish without a last word to anyone . . . especially since some of you have been understanding and supportive. And this is better than appearing on TV again. TV and I do not have a healthy relationship.

My name is Danny Clayton. I am, for better or worse (mainly worse), known as "Laughin' Boy."

I believe that I'm now cured of whatever it was that made me laugh so inappropriately. In fact, I may be overcured. Ever since accidentally shooting Turner P. Williams (or whoever he was) at the Dallas airport, I haven't laughed at all. Not once. I don't feel bad, mind you, although I probably should. I'm just not laughing.

But I'll always be "Laughin' Boy" to most of you anyway, won't I?

It's not your fault. That's just the way things happen here at the cusp of the 21st Century. Even a hick like me knows that much.

So I'm famous, or infamous, and I will be so for some time to come. And I know there are people who would kill for that. Heck, I guess I _have_ killed for that. But the kind of fame or infamy that I have comes with lawsuits and death threats galore. It's no way to live.

The lawsuits are dwindling, because most judges are throwing them out. But the death threats keep coming, and not just from people like those in the White Warriors for Jesus, Deceased. I'm told that such threats will keep on coming as long as my name and face are in the public eye.

Therefore, I will no longer do any television, radio, or Internet interviews, and I've terminated my contract with the _Lanford's on Late!_ show. If I ever hope to lead anything like a normal life again, I must avoid all media attention from here on out. And I certainly can't be appearing on a variety show wearing silver-and-blue tights. (Besides, I doubt that Larry Lanford would still want me there now that I've stopped laughing.)

So I'm disappearing until no one remembers who "Laughin' Boy" was. And I'm not sure how I'll know when that happens. An event even worse than the Wichita Massacre would probably do the trick, but I sure don't want to wish for that. So maybe the termination of this newsgroup would be a step in the right direction. I urge you all to consider it.

By "disappearing," I mean that I am changing my identity—as are my friends Amanda "Porno Girl" Larkin and Robert "Racist Ranger" Royce—with the assistance of the federal government.

Furthermore, my daughter and my ex-wife are moving away from Wichita, but they will NOT be moving anywhere near me. (And since my ex-wife is thinking of remarrying, her name may change as well.) My parents, too, are leaving their longtime Wichita home—but they won't be relocating anywhere near me, either.

I'm sorry to spend your tax dollars like this. But I don't see any other way. Besides, I believe you'll get your money's worth. Ms. Larkin will be working for a certain federal agency as an attorney specializing in First Amendment issues. And if his recovery from gunshot wounds allows, Mr. Royce hopes to once again serve as a federal law-enforcement officer. Both still suffer from their well-known behavioral afflictions, but they are determined to excel at their jobs regardless.

Ms. Larkin, by the way, remains single. For now.

As for me—

I'll be writing copy for the Government Printing Office, which I can do from anywhere. So the next time you pick up a pamphlet on crop rotation, the Jefferson Memorial, or free cheese, think of me.

On second thought, please don't.

One last thing: A month ago today, 86 people were murdered in my hometown. I couldn't cry for them then.

But I did today.

P.S. to Toebunny: Thank you for the offer, but I can't accept. I doubt that I'm the man you have in mind anyway.

Nothing you see on television looks that way in real life. Trust me.

Video Clip (7)
Wichita PD Remote Surveillance Camera
Twentieth of May Memorial Site, South Riverside Park
Sunday, 5/20/2001. 11:14 P.M.

THE LAST NEWS VAN TO leave looks translucent against the gray trees on the far side of the lane. The lights atop the lampposts are fuzzy white spheres, and the van disappears into the glow of those in the distance.

The only vehicle remaining after the dedication ceremony is a police cruiser parked on the lane. Two officers inside the cruiser are drinking coffee and gazing out over the two-acre field. Their faces are unclear because of our grainy resolution. But we know what they're looking at.

Eighty-six small granite obelisks stand in a seemingly random pattern, each lit from below by lights embedded in the grass. In black-and-white, each three-foot obelisk is a pale finger pointing at the sky.

Another car approaches. As it draws near, we see that it's a black sedan. Its windows are black, too.

The sedan stops beside the police cruiser, and a tall African-American man in a dark suit emerges from the front passenger door. He steps to the cruiser and shows the officers a wallet. The cruiser moves fifty yards up the lane.

Now a large, square-jawed Caucasian man emerges from the sedan's driver's door, and he and the African-American man survey the area using bulky goggles. Then the African-American man gestures, and the sedan's rear doors open.

Two Caucasian women, a little girl, and another Caucasian man emerge. One of the women is tall and dark-haired and is wearing a dark dress. The other woman is shorter with lighter hair, and she's wearing a dark pantsuit. The girl, a child of six or seven, looks like a miniature blonde version of the tall woman. The man is wearing dark slacks and a short-sleeved, light-colored shirt. He is cradling a paper-wrapped bundle of flowers in his left arm. They might be yellow roses. Or perhaps white.

He extends his right hand, and the girl grasps his fingers. They walk down a gentle slope into the field of obelisks while the others remain behind.

The man leads the child to an obelisk near the center of the field. He leans down to her and speaks, and then they both kneel and bow their heads.

They remain there for thirty seconds. Then the man kisses the girl on the cheek and places the flowers on the ground at the base of the obelisk. Light shines up through the paper and petals, and a silver kaleidoscope pattern appears on the granite.

The man stands and picks up the girl, hugging her to his chest. And now we see a three-inch scar on his left forearm.

He carries the girl to the sedan, and when he puts her down, she claps her hands and somersaults back down the slope.

The other adults seem startled, but the man with the scar jumps down and scoops up the girl again. We can see the girl's face just well enough to know that she's laughing as the man tosses her into the air and catches her.

He takes her back up the slope and hands her to the tall woman, who reenters the sedan with her. Then the others begin to reenter the sedan as well. The man with the scar is last. He looks back over the field of obelisks for a moment, and then his gaze moves up to the spot where the little girl somersaulted.

We don't think he laughs.

But we're pretty sure he smiles.

Then he gets into the black sedan . . . and it turns around, glides past the police cruiser, and disappears into the light at the end of the lane.

★★★

About the Author

Born in Wichita, Kansas, in 1958 (and a resident of Austin, Texas, since 1988), Bradley Denton is the author of the novels WRACK & ROLL, BUDDY HOLLY IS ALIVE AND WELL ON GANYMEDE, BLACKBURN, and LUNATICS, and of the short-story collections ONE DAY CLOSER TO DEATH, A CONFLAGRATION ARTIST, and THE CALVIN COOLIDGE HOME FOR DEAD COMEDIANS. His short fiction has also appeared in *The Magazine of Fantasy & Science Fiction, Asimov's, Amazing, Pulphouse,* THE YEAR'S BEST FANTASY AND HORROR, and YEAR'S BEST SF.

Brad's work has been honored with the Theodore Sturgeon Memorial Award (for his novella "Sergeant Chip"), the John W. Campbell Memorial Award (for BUDDY HOLLY IS ALIVE AND WELL ON GANYMEDE), and the World Fantasy Award (for A CONFLAGRATION ARTIST and THE CALVIN COOLIDGE HOME FOR DEAD COMEDIANS).

LAUGHIN' BOY is Brad's fifth novel. It exists thanks to the continuing belief and support of Barbara Denton, for which Brad is (as ever) amazed and grateful.

Brad would also like to thank Caroline Spector for her invaluable comments, criticism, and friendship ... Howard Waldrop for his inspiration and encouragement ... Professor James E. Gunn for setting the standard ... the entire Saturday Morning Breakfast Bunch for continual grounding in Reality ... William K. Schafer of Subterranean Press for the first edition ... Darin Bradley for the stunning cover of this new edition ... Deborah Layne for its beautiful typesetting and interior design ... and Wheatland Press for bringing this definitive LAUGHIN' BOY into the world.

Bradley Denton is now at work on his sixth novel.

Wheatland Press

Wheatland Press was founded in Wilsonville, Oregon in 2002. Beginning with the critically acclaimed *Polyphony* anthology series, the Press has established a reputation for publishing cutting edge speculative fiction in high quality trade paperback editions.

For a full listing of titles, please send a self-addressed stamped envelope to:

Wheatland Press
Catalogue Request
P.O. Box 1818
Wilsonville, OR 97070

Or, visit the Wheatland Press website at:
http://www.wheatlandpress.com

www.ingramcontent.com/pod-product-compliance
Lightning Source LLC
LaVergne TN
LVHW050920080826
845145LV00001B/146

9780979405440